PENGUIN

A LANDSCAPE-PAINTER
AND OTHER TALES: 1864–1874

Henry James was born in 1843 in Washington Place, New York, of Scottish and Irish ancestry. His father was a prominent theologian and philosopher and his elder brother, William, was also famous as a philosopher. He attended schools in New York and later in London, Paris and Geneva, entering the Law School at Harvard in 1862. In 1864 he began to contribute reviews and short stories to American journals. In 1875, after two prior visits to Europe, he settled for a year in Paris, where he met Flaubert, Turgenev and other literary figures. However, the next year he moved to London, where he became so popular in society that in the winter of 1878–9 he confessed to accepting 107 invitations. In 1898 he left London and went to live at Lamb House, Rye, Sussex. Henry James became naturalized in 1915, was awarded the OM and died in 1916.

In addition to many short stories, plays, books of criticism, autobiography and travel, he wrote some twenty novels, the first published being *Roderick Hudson* (1875). They include *The Europeans*, *Washington Square*, *The Portrait of a Lady*, *The Bostonians*, *The Princess Casamassima*, *The Tragic Muse*, *The Spoils of Poynton*, *The Awkward Age*, *The Ambassadors* and *The Golden Bowl*.

•

Roger Gard was educated at Abbotsholme School, Derbyshire, in the Royal Artillery and at Corpus Christi College, Cambridge. He now lectures in English at Queen Mary College, University of London. Among his previous publications are books on Henry James, Jane Austen and the teaching of fiction in schools.

•

General Editor for the works of Henry James in the Penguin Classics: Geoffrey Moore.

HENRY JAMES

A Landscape-Painter
and Other Tales:
1864–1874

EDITED WITH AN INTRODUCTION
BY ROGER GARD

PENGUIN BOOKS

PENGUIN BOOKS

Published by the Penguin Group
27 Wrights Lane, London W8 5TZ, England
Viking Penguin Inc., 40 West 23rd Street, New York, New York 10010, USA
Penguin Books Australia Ltd, Ringwood, Victoria, Australia
Penguin Books Canada Ltd, 2801 John Street, Markham, Ontario, Canada L3R 1B4
Penguin Books (NZ) Ltd, 182–190 Wairau Road, Auckland 10, New Zealand

Penguin Books Ltd, Registered Offices: Harmondsworth, Middlesex, England

First published 1990
1 3 5 7 9 10 8 6 4 2

Made and printed in Great Britain by
Cox & Wyman Ltd, Reading
Filmset in Linotron 202 Plantin

Contents

List of Abbreviations

Life *The Life of Henry James* by Leon Edel, London, 1953–72. References are to the 'Definitive Edition', Harmondsworth, 1977.

HJL *Henry James, Letters*, selected and edited by Leon Edel, 4 vols, London and Cambridge, Mass., 1974–84.

CT *The Complete Tales of Henry James*, edited and introduced by Leon Edel, 12 vols, London, 1962–4.

Introduction

I

Henry James's early tales are, considering their charm and merit, surprisingly little known. They need to be more current. It is the object in this selection of eight out of the twenty-six he published between 1864 and 1874 to re-advertise, as it were, the strong first decade of a young genius. The reader will quickly appreciate the quality and range of the work – from the straight masculine directness of 'The Story of a Year' to the fine oblique and witty style of 'A Light Man' or 'Madame de Mauves'. The tales, although some of them were revised in the late 1870s and early 1880s, may not quite have the seamless refinement of art sought later by James or for that matter the almost flawless bravura of Jane Austen, but that does not prevent their being extremely striking. So the first question is: why are they not better known?

Perhaps it is because James's first big acknowledged novel, *Roderick Hudson* (the actual first, *Watch and Ward* of 1871, dropped so far from sight that it scarcely seems to count), did not appear until 1875, when he was thirty-two, that it is generally rather easily and ignorantly agreed that he was a 'late developer'. Or agreed that only the few tales he himself picked out for refurbishment and republication in the years immediately afterwards are worthy the attention of anyone but an archivist or a scholar. The reprint by Leon Edel of *The Complete Tales of Henry James* in 1962–4 is the response of one of these to this situation; and a most valuable act. But the fact that critics, and by implication readers, have responded in so meagre a fashion to the treasures there offered, while commentaries on later posers such as 'The Figure in the Carpet', in 1896, and 'The Turn of the Screw', 1898 (and, of

7

course, that dull etiolated giant of a short story, beloved of theorists, *The Sacred Fount*, 1901), every year assume a bulk more massive and more formidable – almost a literature, of a sort, in itself – is an uninspiriting testimony to the flatness and conventionality of unbraced academic taste. Even in 1988 a quite lively critic can publish a book with the sub-title 'The Neglected Short Fictions of Henry James', and actually set about re-ordering 'the canon', without so much as mentioning a single work before 1875.[1] On the earliest tales only the fresh and acute (though necessarily brief, and occasionally brusque) remarks of S. Gorley Putt,[2] and the sensitive (though slightly meandering) commentary on 'A Landscape-Painter' by John Bayley[3] stand out from a ground of satisfied silence or merely routine mention. And the publishing history reflects this. With the exception of Edel's edition these stories have been hard to come by (see Note on Texts, pp. 322–4) – and three of them were untouched by James himself after their first appearance in magazines.

James himself: he indeed may be the key to our unadventurous taste. He seems to have suffered in acute form from an author's commonly observed desire to be finished with and put behind him, possibly with the benefit of a complimentary *envoi*, his finished work – especially if engaged, as James constantly was, with the forging of a new – for him the best possible – manner. The exclusions from the New York Edition of 1907–9 are a notorious example of this: no room for *The Bostonians* (1886), no room for that perfect small masterpiece *The Europeans* (1878), no room for anything before 1875 save 'A Passionate Pilgrim' (1871), 'The Madonna of the Future' (1873) and, reprinted here though not in the New York version, the *nouvelle* 'Madame de Mauves'. But – and this may account for the notion of late development – the keynote of his references to his first works was always that of a slightly embarrassed and surprising *diffidence*. Even allowing for the exigencies of letters to parents etc. it is curious when reading the early correspondence to find one often so sprightly being so regularly and for so long so shy: 'on the whole it is a failure, I think, tho' nobody will know this, perhaps, but myself. Do not expect anything: it is a simple story, simply told . . .' (of 'The Story of a Year' to T. S. Perry, March 1864); 'It is not much you'll see . . .' (of 'At Isella' to Grace Norton, July 1871); 'I'm sorry you didn't like my *Galaxy* tale, which I haven't seen . . . I hoped it was sufficiently pleasing. But one can't know . . .' (of 'The Sweetheart of M. Briseux' to William James, June 1873) – and so on. His most positive extant remark provides a precise confirmation of this trend. It is in the context of the plan (which bore fruit in 1875) 'to make a volume . . . of tales on the theme of American adventurers in Europe, leading off with the *Passionate Pilgrim* . . . They will all have been the work of the last three years and be much better and maturer than their predecessors' (to his mother, March 1873). Of the rest he says, decidedly: 'I value none of my early tales enough to bring them forth again, and if I did, should absolutely need to give them an amount of verbal retouching which it would be very difficult here [in Rome] to effect.' There, with the important exception of some of this retouching for a few tales in the early 1880s, the matter rested for James.

II

By now the reader may be reflecting that James himself, together with generations of his readers, is most likely after all to be right – and the present selection merely another squeezing of the last (or rather the first) oozings from the store of an important author, another resurrection of that which has been quite properly buried by the public, like *Edmund Ironside* or Charlotte Brontë's *Juvenilia*, or the first version of *La Tentation de Saint Antoine*. Only a reading of the stories themselves can really test and destroy such misgiving. And it would be boring to claim that they are little masterpieces, perfect; or that there are not very evident angularities and cases of failure to realize parts of the lively inspiration. Nevertheless I want to suggest some reasons why they are very much worth reviving, and why their zest grows on the reader instead of fading once the outcome in each case is known: and to suggest these, incidentally, without indulging in that editor's vice of giving away the plot(s) and thus hitting out the heart of our lovely basic desire to know what happens only when it happens – a vice which causes many readers rightly to skip introductions or to read them only with fearful half-closed eyes. So I shall leave the subjects to speak for themselves and confine my remarks to some reasons for their eloquence: to general considerations which point up the strength and creative intelligence of James's experiments in and evolution of *methods*. First in his marking out of the imaginative space in which a compressed action may fruitfully operate and be seen. Second in his very rewarding ways of handling narrative.

But before this a point so obvious that it can be as easily overlooked, as are most obvious things. When James started writing, short stories – as opposed to sketches or occasional or failed fictions such as Fielding's *Shamela* or Stendhal's *Le Rose et le Vert* – were rare. We are so familiar with a type created in the later nineteenth century and thoroughly exploited in the twentieth, that we take for granted the existence of a respectable short form in prose fiction. Definitions of 'the short story' tend, like most literary definitions other than the ostensive, to be leaky or frangible or both. And the market is notoriously unstable. But the modern reader is obviously confident of something substantial being there when he can recall by a mere flick of the mind the achievements of James himself, G. W. Cable, Joyce, D. H. Lawrence, Saki, Elizabeth Bowen, Hemingway, Katherine Mansfield – to make only an uncontentious list, and only of writers in English. In fact most of our contemporaries are at ease in switching from novels into shorter works.

In the 1860s things were different. What was there to look at? Quite a lot in a way, if the look was (somewhat implausibly) intent. Among other things: parables; dramatized moral episodes like those in the essays of Addison or Johnson; chivalric and courtly tales; animal fables; fairy tales whether irresponsible or deeply symbolic or both; the *Decameron* and Cervantes' *Exemplary Novels* which were imitated in English by, for example, Aphra Behn; and, of course, folk tales and plain anecdotes. Considering these things we get close to delivering some deep platitude about narrative being as old as time. But we do not get close to what we normally and automatically class as short stories. In the little relevant English literature James may well have been aware of Maria Edgeworth's shorter works (though it does not appear that he had read Jane Austen's *Lady Susan*, published in 1871) and he clearly responded directly to Hawthorne's stories in 'A Romance of

Certain Old Clothes' (1868) and 'The Last of Valerii' (1874).[4] In French, Balzac and Mérimée can be shown to be in the background; and the greatly admired Turgenev (in French too for him) emerges out of it to become an increasingly influential model. But this is about all. Even Wilkie Collins's nice *Little Novels* did not appear until 1887. Thus in producing realistic stories about contemporary life James was being much more unusual and innovatory a young writer than if he had embarked at once on the dominant prose form of the age, the three-volume novel.

What is primarily interesting about his experiments as experiments is that they tend so brilliantly to eschew the anecdotal. The obvious and natural thing to do with story material – which we all do all the time with our own experience – is to shape it into a neat narrative with a neat point, or even a twist, at the end. This is familiar in art from, for example, the lesser works of de Maupassant, and even more familiar from such experienced and wily descendants of his as W. Somerset Maugham (and so on downwards). Here the whole point lies simply in what happened – which is usually odd or surprising or pleasant to our sense of knowing the world. Everyone knows the kind of thing (i.e. the genre) – and so much so that life sometimes pays an inadvertent tribute to art when the neatly illustrative fiction becomes part of the general lore, and we hear it retold in bars or at meals or in common rooms as true as well as amusing. Such stories (I have in mind things like Somerset Maugham's 'Jane' or 'Episode') can be special and intriguing. But they leave an entirely different taste from the grander and more genuinely suggestive and creative article in which Henry James normally deals. Sometimes throughout his career, it is true, his tales degenerate into climaxes which are either melodramatic or too predictably a matter of shallow symmetrical shaping (here only 'Master Eustace' and 'Professor Fargo' seem to me open to these charges, and they could be defended). Perhaps these climaxes are a panicked response to the general stupid demand from his reviewers for something 'with a story'; perhaps a consequence of some obscure need of his own imagination. They cease at any rate at that point to be serious reading, as does a lot of other fiction. Which need not matter vastly, for the real value is often elsewhere, in the characters and their interrelations and their place and significance before the simplification of an ending. But usually in these stories the really fruitful dramatic effect derives from a fine tension between what we in our banal selves expect and continue to expect and the much more sensitive and live reality of what actually turns out to happen – or not happen. This is thus not a question of smart surprises or baffling reversals, but of the evocation of an imagined experience which is truer than any tight little plot would be.

Another, rather impressionistic, way of putting this is to say that from 'The Story of a Year' onwards the tales incline to be implied novels. They give out intimations of having, both before and after the action, a larger experiential context, so to speak. It is as though part of a continuum were sliced out and illuminated: beginning in the middle of things and capable of going on after the ending. The reader will see what I mean as soon as the introductory paragraphs of any story are over. We tend to feel the presence of what could exist outside the present episode, but actually need no other context than that which our imagination of there *being* one readily supplies. Yet of course the stories are at the same time perfectly self-sufficient. The actions are important in themselves – if they really were parts of novels they would be the climaxes. And this impressive economy leads to the very 'Jamesian' (i.e. charac- teristic of his later work, but by no means confined to it or to him) feature of a partial completion, satisfying enough but not a total closing up. The action comes to a point near to the end where certain resolutions, definite probabilities, are indicated at the expense of random resolutions.[5] An ending is chosen, sometimes, as I have said, melodramatically. But we do not feel the significance of that to be absolute: we are left just a little in the air, and therefore the imagination is kept engaged at the very moment when it is being satisfied:

'I forbid you to follow me!'
But for all that, he went in.

is an excellent example of this kind of ending.

The impression of some such indefiniteness imparts a certain richness to many of the tales. It asks us to reconsider the action in a way that very precise formal endings, especially good ones, do not. But I do not mean to imply that this kind of art is automatically superior to that of more enclosed forms. Nor that it is especially 'modern' in the way that later James is often claimed to be. Rather what such observations suggest is that these stories are more sophisticated and worked out and written than most critics, including James, have credited or allowed. Original artists are always stepping out vulnerably into what does not (yet) exist. Here we see James in his twenties creating, in a misleadingly seemly fashion, a type of fiction peculiarly his own and of which he was to become the first great master.

III

So James's relations with the anecdote are complicated and interesting – even complex. But this praise is bound to sound dry and abstract without backing from some experience of the stories. I shall try to recommend their excellence by more specific reference, yet again without revealing the plots and their various excitements. One of James's most famous, and in practice most fruitful, insistencies in criticism is on the importance of 'point of view' in fiction: on, in effect, examining the source and angle from which stories, and so ultimately realities, are seen and therefore related. This partly resembles an epistemological question: what is the nature of our knowledge?; partly a quasi-forensic one: who says what, and how far are they to be believed? Such considerations are pertinent to nearly all narratives, not just artistic ones. But they become especially amusing when applied to clever structures like these tales. If we ask the simple question, 'Who is the narrator?' and link it with the equally simple, 'Who is the most important and/or interesting consciousness?' the replies reveal surprisingly rich and various patterns.

For example, the narrator of 'The Story of a Year' establishes himself immediately as a story-teller in a traditional mould, even intrusively in control and privy to the secrets of his creatures, though critical of them. 'My story begins as a great many stories have begun . . .' he starts, and continues about 'a young couple I wot of' and about what he is or is not offering: 'Good reader, this narrative is averse to retrospect.' Such self-conscious and self-regarding narration has a certain angular resemblance to the cultivated manner of Thackeray or Trollope or even early George Eliot. It is so familiar a convention that when this voice steps in later with:

Many of us have sisters and daughters. Not a few of us, I hope, have female connections of another degree, yet no less dear. Others have looking glasses. I give you my word for it that Elizabeth made as pretty a show as it is possible to see.

it does not occur to us to object (should we know it) that the author is not a worldly-wise middle-aged clubman but a man of twenty-one or -two. Rather the point is that a specific type of narration has been chosen and that this involves the appropriate implied equipment of experience and easy wisdom. It is a medium we do not question as to events and which can adapt to a wide range of effects. It can go from psychological *aperçus* (delivered from above) such as the reference to Ford's 'sublime egotism of protection' (which makes him temporarily oblivious of Lizzie's response); to the pleasant deflation involved in the description of her good resolutions ('She would practice charity, humility, piety, – in fine, all the virtues: together with certain *morceaux* of Beethoven and Chopin'); to free indirect speech, of the kind evolved by Jane Austen, in presenting the drama of her consciousness; to fine, though sometimes over insistent, analyses of her charmingly un-deep and un-moral nature; to elaborate metaphors about her mental moods:

. . . I think Lizzie was hardly aware. She was like a reveller in a brilliantly lighted room, with a curtainless window, conscious, and yet heedless, of passers-by.

– and to many other things besides.

But naturally James does not rest with this particular mode, though he is quite prepared to return to it. To glance through the stories lightly: 'A Landscape-Painter' is a journal with all the immediacy and suspense and 'writing to the moment' (as Richardson called it) which that can involve, yet has a frame which – at first sight a flat and ordinary ground – assumes with every reading a more and more poignant significance. In 'A Day of Days' – which is an embodied denial of the anecdote – the narrator leaves the story after the first few, witty, paragraphs to the minds and, increasingly, the voices of the characters. 'A Light Man' *is* the admirable self-communing voice of its central character playing for and against the title. In 'Master Eustace' the frame is confined to the first sentence (with its description 'old-maidish' thrown out for us to consider) and then much of the subsequent interest resides in the self-revelation and self-creation of the narrator, governess and family friend. This early exploration of feminine sensibility is varied and refined in 'The Sweetheart of M. Briseux' where the demure yet wittily assertive heroine – 'I allowed myself to wonder, by way of harmless conjecture, how a woman might feel who should find herself married to an ineffective mediocrity' – follows on from the equally clever but very distinct male narrator with his own brand of urbane commentary on '. . . a few elegant landscapes exhibiting the last century view of nature, and half a dozen neat portraits of French gentlefolks of that period, in the act, as one may say, of taking the view in question'.

Appreciation of the variety of these experiments in narrative should prepare the reader for a full experience of the strength and subtlety of 'Madame de Mauves', James's masterpiece up to that date. The subtlety depends vastly on the reader's being critically conscious – but this is really very simple – of the provenance of the attitudes which the narration and the central figures seem at first glance to invite and endorse. For the tale is not, as many contemporary commentators and some modern ones have carelessly imagined, a relatively banal piece of easy indignation (with some incidental felicities about French scenery) pitting virtuous Americans against corrupt continentals. Quite clearly not – in the very process of the introduction to our hero, Longmore, we learn that besides being an amiable young New Englander he has 'made a languid attempt to investigate the records of the court of the exiled Stuarts'. No sensible reader can take this as much of a recommendation. Nor are we meant to. It is important to see that it is not James, nor his confidently humorous narrator (slipping in and out of the minds of the characters) who is a slightly embarrassing aesthete and a touch of a prig – it is Longmore being beautifully 'done' (as James might have said), and precisely by means of such remarks. The same applies to the lovely and almost equally sympathetic Euphemia, and *a fortiori* to judgements such as that about 'a sweet American girl who marries an unclean Frenchman'. The tale derives its distinction from a fine taking up and releasing of sympathies and antipathies between individuals and nationalities. And we miss a good part of what James later called (in the New York preface) 'a certain inexpert intensity of art' if we are not easily aware of the general point arising from a look at the narrative methods in the early tales: that there is a careful, though usually benign, distancing of the author from the narrator, or the narrator from the characters, or the reader from both, which has the result of liberating meaning and point (in the senses of both creating them and freeing them from restraint) in much the same way as James's airy endings do. It is a very considerable art; and clearly not to be ignored as merely apprentice work.

There are two further related impressions of 'Madame de Mauves' which may enhance a sense of its richness. The first is of the way in which it assimilates creatively the fructifying influence of James's favourite, Turgenev. He had been reading and writing on the Russian when composing the *nouvelle* (see HJL, I, 405). But there is no sense of a simple copy: rather what happens is that Turgenev's gift of 'finding an incident, a person, a situation *morally* interesting'[6] is so properly and deeply felt as to become James's own natural happy mode. In both writers there follows a development, seemingly casual and humorous, in which the characters of the tale become – by progressive revelation and not by authorial *diktat* – protagonists representative of a generation, a nationality, or a phase in a drama which has a general cogency without losing either its private and individual character or that knack of 'catching the very note and trick, the strange irregular rhythm of life' which James valued as one of the prime gifts of prose fiction.

My second impression is also related to other writing, and to a very different use of another's sensibility. It is that the element of the slightly ludicrous in Longmore's passion – it is only an element – is much clarified, though it is felt in any case, if we are familiar at first hand with the characteristic diction of that important cultural force of the last century later described by James as 'faint, pale, embarrassed exquisite Pater'. Pater is just the man for

Longmore to have read, or be reading, in 1873 when his *The Renaissance* was published. He is the great donnish theorist of the sensuous, and a tremendous influence on 'aesthetic' youth. Invocations such as:

While all melts under our feet, we may well grasp at any exquisite passion, or any contribution to knowledge that seems by a lifted horizon to set the spirit free for a moment, or any stirring of the senses, strange dyes, strange colours, and curious odours, or the work of the artist's hands, or the face of one's friend. Not to discriminate every moment some passionate attitude in those about us, and in the very brilliancy of their gifts some tragic dividing of forces on their ways, is, in this short day of frost and sun, to sleep before evening . . . For art comes to you proposing frankly to give nothing but the highest quality to your moments as they pass, and simply for those moments' sake. ('Conclusion' to *The Renaissance*)

– find echo after echo in later decades, and even now. So it is with the amusement of recognition that we find Longmore, his New England codes in disarray, and tempted by the idea of (high minded) abandon, feeling the crisis in just such haunting rhythms and phrases. The fecund fields of France:

. . . seemed to utter a message from plain ripe nature, to express the unperverted reality of things, to say that the common lot is not brilliantly amusing, and that the part of wisdom is to grasp frankly at experience, lest you miss it altogether . . . It is perhaps because, like many spirits of the same stock, he had in his composition a lurking principle of asceticism to whose authority he had ever paid an unquestioning respect, that he now felt all the vehemence of rebellion. To renounce – to renounce again – to renounce forever – was this all that youth and longing and resolve were meant for?

The similarity is striking. It makes one like Longmore all the better. But again the point is that it is not Henry James himself who is saturate with the plangent rhetoric of the aesthetic philosopher, but his respectable young protagonist.

IV

To move, finally, from methods to subjects. Looking only at the surface it is obvious that the range and implication of these stories is ample – more ample, some may think, than that of the later fiction – and that preoccupations overlap from story to story. There are several settings in the New England of James's youth. The first three are in a very strong sense 'about' that country and civilization at least as much as they are about their ostensible matter of love, the war, art and money. The description of the cloudscape at the beginning of 'The Story of a Year', the fine evocations of the coast by the protagonist of 'A Landscape-Painter', and the fresh September warmth of 'A Day of Days' give a feel of a particular place at a particular time which is valuable and moving in itself. Nevertheless they are not vivid only in this way. The lush breathtaking panoramas and suggestive immediacy of the cinema have made prose representations of nature seem redundant, antiquated, dodo-like nowadays – as they have almost certainly killed the enormous reputation of the novels of Sir Walter Scott. But James is typically both writing in an accredited manner and doing something additional with it. His American settings – including the luxurious interiors and fresh romantic views which counterpoint the glittering narrative of 'A Light Man' – have a clear and detailed appropriateness to the action and moral atmosphere of their respective tales which is sometimes almost explicit and does not need expounding. The same is true of the terrace, woods and cafés in 'Madame de Mauves' (the river scene is almost a prediction of a celebrated climactic episode in *The Ambassadors*). And a related pressure to express a great deal of matter in the short form is evident in the taking of very grand subjects (treachery, death etc.) into the tragi-comedies of domestic life in 'A Light Man' and 'Master Eustace'. 'The Sweetheart of M. Briseux' is explicitly a fable about the nature of artistic truth – a subject dear to James throughout his life, and better done here, I think, because of the brilliance and warmth of its characterization, than in the better known 'The Madonna of the Future'. And as we have seen already 'Madame de Mauves' is one of the first in a long line of 'international contrasts' for which James became (ultimately to his dismay at being, as it were, typecast) celebrated – while it also reflects like many others of his early fictions his response to his enraptured response to Europe. Finally 'Professor Fargo', though it rather lapses at the end, is a very funny and sad account, through the eyes of a commercial traveller and with its oddly attractive mountebank, of the raw, new, dismal, hick America, the critique of which is a strong constant in James – and often underemphasized by those who want him always to be the poet of high refinement. Someone who knows his work well may think of Mr Crawford the toothpick-chewing silver miner from Arizona in 'Guest's Confession' (1872), of Herman Longstraw in 'Lady Barberina' (1884), of the quack Selah Tarrant and his daughter in *The Bostonians* (1886); and, much later, some of the last tales, the brilliant travel book *The American Scene* (1907) and the unfinished novel *The Ivory Tower*.

Tolstoy remarks of moving house: 'as always happens . . . they found they were one room too short'. This luminous general truth is likely to be echoed by the selector of good literature even where the selection is large. Far from having to dress up the lifeless for re-presentation I have found these stories jostling for a place. Some out of the twenty-six published before 1874 are poor; but some are nearly as good as those I have been able to include. So perhaps the reader will go on from here.

ROGER GARD

NOTES

1 George Bishop, *When the Master Relents*, Ann Arbor, 1988.

2 *A Reader's Guide to Henry James*, London, 1966.

3 *The Short Story: Henry James to Elizabeth Bowen*, Brighton, 1988.

4 Neither of these is reprinted here, the former because it is not very successful in a mode which requires complete success to achieve any at all, the latter because it is – unusually – easily available elsewhere.

5 As Kenneth Graham says of 'Madame de Mauves' this 'is not the kind of open endedness which defeats significance'. *Henry James: The Drama of Fulfilment*, Oxford, 1975.

6 From James's review of *Spring Torrents* etc. in April 1874.

The Story of a Year[1]

I

My story begins as a great many stories have begun within the last three years, and indeed as a great many have ended; for, when the hero is despatched, does not the romance come to a stop?

In early May, two years ago, a young couple I wot of strolled homeward from an evening walk, a long ramble among the peaceful hills which inclosed their rustic home. Into these peaceful hills the young man had brought, not the rumor, (which was an old inhabitant,) but some of the reality of war, – a little whiff of gunpowder, the clanking of a sword; for, although Mr John Ford had his campaign still before him, he wore a certain comely air of camp-life which stamped him a very Hector to the steady-going villagers, and a very pretty fellow to Miss Elizabeth Crowe, his companion in this sentimental stroll. And was he not attired in the great brightness of blue and gold which befits a freshly made lieutenant? This was a strange sight for these happy Northern glades; for, although the first Revolution had boomed awhile in their midst, the honest yeomen who defended them were clad in sober homespun, and it is well known that His Majesty's troops wore red.

These young people, I say, had been roaming. It was plain that they had wandered into spots where the brambles were thick and the dews heavy, – nay, into swamps and puddles where the April rains were still undried. Ford's boots and trousers had imbibed a deep foretaste of the Virginia mud; his companion's skirts were fearfully bedraggled. What great enthusiasm had made our friends so unmindful of their steps? What blinding ardor had kindled these strange phenomena: a young lieutenant scornful of his first uniform, a well-bred young lady reckless of her stockings?

Good reader, this narrative is averse to retrospect.

Elizabeth (as I shall not scruple to call her outright) was leaning upon her companion's arm, half moving in concert with him, and half allowing herself to be led, with that instinctive acknowledgment of dependence natural to a young girl who has just received the assurance of lifelong protection. Ford was lounging along with that calm, swinging stride which often bespeaks, when you can read it aright, the answering consciousness of a sudden rush of manhood. A spectator might have thought him at this moment profoundly conceited. The young girl's blue veil was dangling from his pocket; he had shouldered her sun-umbrella after the fashion of a musket on a march: he might carry these trifles. Was there not a vague longing expressed in the strong expansion of his stalwart shoulders, in the fond accommodation of his pace to hers, – her pace so submissive and slow, that, when he tried to match it, they almost came to a delightful standstill, – a silent desire for the whole fair burden?

They made their way up a long swelling mound, whose top commanded the sunset. The dim landscape which had been brightening all day to the green of spring was now darkening to the gray of evening. The lesser hills, the farms, the brooks, the fields, orchards, and woods, made a dusky gulf before the great splendor of the west. As Ford looked at the clouds, it seemed to him that their imagery was all of war, their great uneven masses were marshalled into the semblance of a battle. There were columns charging and columns flying and standards floating, – tatters of the reflected purple; and great captains on colossal horses, and a rolling canopy of cannon-smoke and fire and blood. The background of the clouds, indeed, was like a land on fire, or a battle-ground illumined by another sunset, a country of blackened villages and crimsoned pastures. The tumult of the clouds increased; it was hard to believe them inanimate. You might have fancied them an army of gigantic souls playing at football with the sun. They seemed to sway in confused splendor; the opposing squadrons bore each other down; and then suddenly they scattered, bowling with equal velocity towards north and south, and

22

gradually fading into the pale evening sky. The purple pennons sailed away and sank out of sight, caught, doubtless, upon the brambles of the intervening plain. Day contracted itself into a fiery ball and vanished.

Ford and Elizabeth had quietly watched this great mystery of the heavens.

'That is an allegory,' said the young man, as the sun went under, looking into his companion's face, where a pink flush seemed still to linger: 'it means the end of war. The forces on both sides are withdrawn. The blood that has been shed gathers itself into a vast globule and drops into the ocean.'

'I'm afraid it means a shabby compromise,' said Elizabeth, 'Light disappears, too, and the land is in darkness.'

'Only for a season,' answered the other. 'We mourn our dead. Then light comes again, stronger and brighter than ever. Perhaps you'll be crying for me, Lizzie, at that distant day.'

'Oh, Jack, didn't you promise not to talk about that?' says Lizzie, threatening to anticipate the performance in question.

Jack took this rebuke in silence, gazing soberly at the empty sky. Soon the young girl's eyes stole up to his face. If he had been looking at anything in particular, I think she would have followed the direction of his glance; but as it seemed to be a very vacant one, she let her eyes rest.

'Jack,' said she, after a pause, 'I wonder how you'll look when you get back.'

Ford's soberness gave way to a laugh.

'Uglier than ever. I shall be all incrusted with mud and gore. And then I shall be magnificently sunburnt, and I shall have a beard.'

'Oh, you dreadful!' and Lizzie gave a little shout. 'Really, Jack, if you have a beard, you'll not look like a gentleman.'

'Shall I look like a lady, pray?' says Jack.

'Are you serious?' asked Lizzie.

'To be sure. I mean to alter my face as you do your misfitting garments, – take in on one side and let out on the other. Isn't that the process? I shall crop my head and cultivate my chin.'

'You've a very nice chin, my dear, and I think it's a shame to hide it.'

'Yes, I know my chin's handsome; but wait till you see my beard.'

'Oh, the vanity!' cried Lizzie, 'the vanity of men in their faces! Talk of women!' and the silly creature looked up at her lover with most inconsistent satisfaction.

'Oh, the pride of women in their husbands!' said Jack, who of course knew what she was about.

'You're not my husband, Sir. There's many a slip' – But the young girl stopped short.

'Twixt the cup and the lip,' said Jack. 'Go on. I can match your proverb with another. "There's many a true word," and so forth. No, my darling: I'm not your husband. Perhaps I never shall be. But if anything happens to me, you'll take comfort, won't you?'

'Never!' said Lizzie, tremulously.

'Oh, but you must; otherwise, Lizzie, I should think our engagement inexcusable. Stuff! who I am that you should cry for me?'

'You are the best and wisest of men. I don't care; you *are*.'

'Thank you for your great love, my dear. That's a delightful illusion. But I hope Time will kill it, in his own good way, before it hurts any one. I know so many men who are worth infinitely more than I – men wise, generous, and brave – that I shall not feel as if I were leaving you in an empty world.'

'Oh, my dear friend!' said Lizzie, after a pause, 'I wish you could advise me all my life.'

'Take care, take care,' laughed Jack; 'you don't know what you are bargaining for. But will you let me say a word now? If by chance I'm taken out of the world, I want you to beware of that tawdry sentiment which enjoins you to be "constant in my memory." My memory be hanged! Remember me at my best, – that is, fullest of the desire of humility. Don't inflict me on people. There are some widows and bereaved sweethearts who remind me of the peddler in that horrid murder-story, who carried a corpse in his pack. Really, it's their stock in trade. The only justification of a man's personality is his rights. What rights has a dead man? – Let's go down.'

They turned southward and went jolting down the hill.

'Do you mind this talk, Lizzie?' asked Ford.

'No,' said Lizzie, swallowing a sob, unnoticed by her companion in the sublime egotism of protection; 'I like it.'

'Very well,' said the young man, 'I want my memory to help you. When I am down in Virginia, I expect to get a vast deal of good from thinking of you, – to do my work better, and to keep straighter altogether. Like all lovers, I'm horribly selfish. I expect to see a vast deal of shabbiness and baseness and turmoil, and in the midst of it all I'm sure the inspiration of patriotism will sometimes fail. Then I'll think of you. I love you a thousand times better than my country, Liz. – Wicked? So much the worse. It's the truth. But if I find your memory makes a milksop of me, I shall thrust you out of the way, without ceremony, – I shall clap you into my box or between the leaves of my Bible, and only look at you on Sunday.'

'I shall be very glad, Sir, if that makes you open your Bible frequently,' says Elizabeth, rather demurely.

'I shall put one of your photographs against every page,' cried Ford; 'and then I think I shall not lack a text for my meditations. Don't you know Catholics keep little pictures of their adored Lady in their prayer-books?'

'Yes, indeed,' said Lizzie; 'I should think it would be a very soul-stirring picture, when you are marching to the front, the night before a battle, – a poor, stupid girl, knitting stupid socks, in a stupid Yankee village.'[2]

Oh, the craft of artless tongues! Jack strode along in silence a few moments, splashing straight through a puddle; then, ere he was quite clear of it, he stretched out his arm and gave his companion a long embrace.

'And pray what am I to do,' resumed Lizzie, wondering, rather proudly perhaps, at Jack's averted face, 'while you are marching and countermarching in Virginia?'

'Your duty, of course,' said Jack, in a steady voice, which belied a certain little conjecture of Lizzie's. 'I think you will find the sun will rise in the east, my dear, just as it did before you were engaged.'

'I'm sure I didn't suppose it wouldn't,' says Lizzie.

'By duty I don't mean anything disagreeable, Liz,' pursued the young man. 'I hope you'll take your pleasure, too. I wish you

25

might go to Boston, or even to Leatherborough, for a month of
two.'

'What for, pray?'

'What for? Why, for the fun of it: to "go out", as they say.'

'Jack, do you think me capable of going to parties while you are
in danger?'

'Why not? Why should I have all the fun?'

'Fun? I'm sure you're welcome to it all. As for me, I mean to
make a new beginning.'

'Of what?'

'Oh, of everything. In the first place, I shall begin to improve
my mind. But don't you think it's horrid for women to be
reasonable?'

'Hard, say you?'

'Horrid, – yes, and hard too. But I mean to become so. Oh,
girls are such fools, Jack! I mean to learn to like boiled mutton
and history and plain sewing, and all that. Yet, when a girl's
engaged, she's not expected to do anything in particular.'

Jack laughed, and said nothing; and Lizzie went on.

'I wonder what your mother will say to the news. I think I
know.'

'What?'

'She'll say you've been very unwise. No, she won't: she never
speaks so to you. She'll say I've been very dishonest or indelicate,
or something of that kind. No, she won't either: she doesn't say
such things, though I'm sure she thinks them. I don't know what
she'll say.'

'No, I think not, Lizzie, if you indulge in such conjectures. My
mother never speaks without thinking. Let us hope that she may
think favorably of our plan. Even if she doesn't' –

Jack did not finish his sentence, nor did Lizzie urge him. She
had a great respect for his hesitations. But in a moment he began
again.

'I was going to say this, Lizzie: I think for the present our
engagement had better be kept quiet.'

Lizzie's heart sank with a sudden disappointment. Imagine the
feelings of the damsel in the fairy-tale, whom the disguised
enchantress had just empowered to utter diamonds and pearls,

should the old beldame have straightway added that for the present mademoiselle had better hold her tongue. Yet the disappointment was brief. I think this enviable young lady would have tripped home talking very hard to herself, and have been not ill pleased to find her little mouth turning into a tightly clasped jewel-casket. Nay, would she not on this occasion have been thankful for a large mouth, – a mouth huge and unnatural, – stretching from ear to ear? Who wish to cast their pearls before swine? The young lady of the pearls was, after all, but a barnyard miss. Lizzie was too proud of Jack to be vain. It's well enough to wear our own hearts upon our sleeves; but for those of others, when intrusted to our keeping, I think we had better find a more secluded lodging.

'You see, I think secrecy would leave us much freer,' said Jack, – 'leave *you* much freer.'

'Oh, Jack, how can you?' cried Lizzie. 'Yes, of course; I shall be falling in love with someone else. Freer! Thank you, Sir!'

'Nay, Lizzie, what I'm saying is really kinder than it sounds. Perhaps you *will* thank me one of these days.'

'Doubtless! I've already taken a great fancy to George Mackenzie.'

'Will you let me enlarge on my suggestion?'

'Oh, certainly! You seem to have your mind quite made up.'

'I confess I like to take account of possibilities. Don't you know mathematics are my hobby? Did you ever study algebra? I always have an eye on the unknown quantity.'

'No, I never studied algebra. I agree with you, that we had better not speak of our engagement.'

'That's right, my dear. You're always right. But mind, I don't want to bind you to secrecy. Hang it, do as you please! Do what comes easiest to you, and you'll do the best thing. What made me speak is my dread of the horrible publicity which clings to all this business. Nowadays, when a girl's engaged, it's no longer, "Ask mamma," simply; but, "Ask Mrs Brown, and Mrs Jones, and my large circle of acquaintance, – Mrs Grundy, in short." I say nowadays, but I suppose it's always been so.'

'Very well, we'll keep it all nice and quiet,' said Lizzie, who would have been ready to celebrate her nuptials according to the rites of the Esquimaux, had Jack seen fit to suggest it.

'I know it doesn't look well for a lover to be so cautious,' pursued Jack; 'but you understand me, Lizzie, don't you?'

'I don't entirely understand you, but I quite trust you.'

'God bless you! My prudence, you see, is my best strength. Now, if ever, I need my strength. When a man's a-wooing, Lizzie, he is all feeling, or he ought to be; when he's accepted then he begins to think.'

'And to repent, I suppose you mean.'

'Nay, to devise means to keep his sweetheart from repenting. Let me be frank. Is it the greatest fools only that are the best lovers? There's no telling what may happen, Lizzie. I want you to marry me with your eyes open. I don't want you to feel tied down or taken in. You're very young, you know. You're responsible to yourself of a year hence. You're at an age when no girl can count safely from year's end to year's end.'

'And you, Sir!' cries Lizzie; 'one would think you were a grandfather.'

'Well, I'm on the way to it. I'm a pretty old boy. I mean what I say. I may not be entirely frank, but I think I'm sincere. It seems to me as if I'd been fibbing all my life before I told you that your affection was necessary to my happiness. I mean it out and out. I never loved anyone before, and I never will again. If you had refused me half an hour ago, I should have died a bachelor. I have no fear for myself. But I have for you. You said a few minutes ago that you wanted me to be your adviser. Now you know the function of an adviser is to perfect his victim in the art of walking with his eyes shut. I sha'n't be so cruel.'

Lizzie saw fit to view these remarks in a humorous light.

'How disinterested!' quoth she: 'how very self-sacrificing! Bachelor indeed! For my part, I think I shall become a Mormon!' – I verily believe the poor misinformed creature fancied that in Utah it is the ladies who are guilty of polygamy.

Before many minutes they drew near home. There stood Mrs Ford at the garden gate, looking up and down the road, with a letter in her hand.

'Something for you, John,' said his mother, as they approached.'It looks as if it came from camp. – Why, Elizabeth, look at your skirts!'

'I know it,' says Lizzie, giving the articles in question a shake. 'What is it, Jack?'

'Marching orders!' cried the young man. 'The regiment leaves day after to-morrow. I must leave by the early train in the morning. Hurray!' And he diverted a sudden gleeful kiss into a filial salute.

They went in. The two women were silent, after the manner of women who suffer. But Jack did little else than laugh and talk and circumnavigate the parlor, sitting first here and then there, – close beside Lizzie and on the opposite side of the room. After a while Miss Crowe joined in his laughter, but I think her mirth might have been resolved into articulate heartbeats. After tea she went to bed, to give Jack opportunity for his last filial *épanchements*.[3] How generous a man's intervention makes women! But Lizzie promised to see her lover off in the morning.

'Nonsense!' said Mrs Ford. 'You'll not be up. John will want to breakfast quietly.'

'I shall see you off, Jack,' repeated the young lady, from the threshold.

Elizabeth went upstairs buoyant with her young love. It had dawned upon her like a new life, – a life positively worth the living. Hereby she would subsist and cost nobody anything. In it she was boundlessly rich. She would make it the hidden spring of a hundred praiseworthy deeds. She would begin the career of duty: she would enjoy boundless equanimity: she would raise her whole being to the level of her sublime passion. She would practise charity, humility, piety, – in fine, all the virtues: together with certain *morceaux* of Beethoven and Chopin. She would walk the earth like one glorified. She would do homage to the best of men by inviolate secrecy. Here, by I know not what gentle transition, as she lay in the quiet darkness, Elizabeth covered her pillow with a flood of tears.

Meanwhile Ford, downstairs, began in this fashion. He was lounging at his manly length on the sofa, in his slippers.

'May I light a pipe, mother?'

'Yes, my love. But please be careful of your ashes. There's a newspaper.'

'Pipes don't make ashes. – Mother, what do you think?' he

continued between the puffs of his smoking; 'I've got a piece of news.'

'Ah?' said Mrs Ford, fumbling for her scissors, 'I hope it's good news.'

'I hope you'll think it so. I've been engaging myself' – puff, – puff – 'to Lizzie Crowe.' A cloud of puffs between his mother's face and his own. When they had cleared away, Jack felt his mother's eyes. Her work was in her lap. 'To be married, you know,' he added.

In Mrs Ford's view, like the king in that of the British Constitution, her only son could do no wrong. Prejudice is a stout bulwark against surprise. Moreover, Mrs Ford's motherly instinct had not been entirely at fault. Still, it had by no means kept pace with fact. She had been silent, partly from doubt, partly out of respect for her son. As long as John did not doubt of himself, he was right. Should he come to do so, she was sure he would speak. And now, when he told her the matter was settled, she persuaded herself that he was asking her advice.

'I've been expecting it,' she said, at last.

'You have? Why didn't you speak?'

'Well, John, I can't say I've been hoping it.'

'Why not?'

'I am not sure of Lizzie's heart,' said Mrs Ford, who, it may be well to add, was very sure of her own.

Jack began to laugh. 'What's the matter with her heart?'

'I think Lizzie's shallow,' said Mrs Ford; and there was that in her tone which betokened some satisfaction with this adjective.

'Hang it! she is shallow,' said Jack. 'But when a thing's shallow, you can see to the bottom. Lizzie doesn't pretend to be deep. I want a wife, mother, that I can understand. That's the only wife I can love. Lizzie's the only girl I ever understood, and the first I ever loved. I love her very much, – more than I can explain to you.'

'Yes, I confess it's inexplicable. It seems to me,' she added, with a bad smile, 'like infatuation.'

Jack did not like the smile; he liked it even less than the remark. He smoked steadily for a few moments, and then he said, –

'Well, mother, love is notoriously obstinate, you know. We shall not be able to take the same view of this subject: suppose we drop it.'

'Remember that this is your last evening at home, my son,' said Mrs Ford.

'I do remember. Therefore I wish to avoid disagreement.'

There was a pause. The young man smoked, and his mother sewed, in silence.

'I think my position, as Lizzie's guardian,' resumed Mrs Ford, 'entitles me to an interest in the matter.'

'Certainly, I acknowledged your interest by telling you of our engagement.'

Further pause.

'Will you allow me to say,' said Mrs Ford, after a while, 'that I think this a little selfish?'

'Allow you? Certainly, if you particularly desire it. Though I confess it isn't very pleasant for a man to sit and hear his future wife pitched into, – by his own mother, too.'

'John, I am surprised at your language.'

'I beg your pardon,' and John spoke more gently. 'You mustn't be surprised at anything from an accepted lover. – I'm sure you misconceive her. In fact, mother, I don't believe you know her.'

Mrs Ford nodded, with an infinite depth of meaning; and from the grimness with which she bit off the end of her thread it might have seemed that she fancied herself to be executing a human vengeance.

'Ah, I know her only too well!'

'And you don't like her?'

Mrs Ford performed another decapitation of her thread.

'Well, I'm glad Lizzie has one friend in the world,' said Jack.

'Her best friend,' said Mrs Ford, 'is the one who flatters her least. I see it all, John. Her pretty face has done the business.'

The young man flushed impatiently.

'Mother,' said he, 'you are very much mistaken. I'm not a boy nor a fool. You trust me in a great many things; why not trust me in this?'

'My dear son, you are throwing yourself away. You deserve for your companion in life a higher character than that girl.'

I think Mrs Ford, who had been an excellent mother, would have liked to give her son a wife fashioned on her own model.

'Oh, come, mother,' said he, 'that's twaddle. I should be thankful if I were half as good as Lizzie.'

'It's the truth, John, and your conduct – not only the step you've taken, but your talk about it – is a great disappointment to me. If I have cherished any wish of late, it is that my darling boy should get a wife worthy of him. The household governed by Elizabeth Crowe is not a home I should desire for anyone I love.'

'It's one to which you should always be welcome, Ma'am,' said Jack.

'It's not a place I should feel at home in,' replied his mother.

'I'm sorry,' said Jack. And he got up and began to walk about the room. 'Well, well, mother,' he said at last, stopping in front of Mrs Ford, 'we don't understand each other. One of these days we shall. For the present let us have done with discussion. I'm half sorry I told you.'

'I'm glad of such a proof of your confidence. But if you hadn't, of course Elizabeth would have done so.'

'No, Ma'am, I think not.'

'Then she is even more reckless of her obligations than I thought her.'

'I advised her to say nothing about it.'

Mrs Ford made no answer. She began slowly to fold up her work.

'I think we had better let the matter stand,' continued her son. 'I'm not afraid of time. But I wish to make a request of you: you won't mention this conversation to Lizzie, will you? or allow her to suppose that you know of our engagement? I have a particular reason.'

Mrs Ford went on smoothing out her work. Then she suddenly looked up.

'No, my dear, I'll keep your secret. Give me a kiss.'

II

I have no intention of following Lieutenant Ford to the seat of war. The exploits of his campaign are recorded in the public journals of the day, where the curious may still peruse them. My own taste has always been for unwritten history, and my present business is with the reverse of the picture.

After Jack went off, the two ladies resumed their old homely life. But the homeliest life had now ceased to be repulsive to Elizabeth. Her common duties were no longer wearisome: for the first time, she experienced the delicious companionship of thought. Her chief task was still to sit by the window knitting soldiers' socks; but even Mrs Ford could not help owning that she worked with a much greater diligence, yawned, rubbed her eyes, gazed up and down the road less, and indeed produced a much more comely article. Ah, me! if half the lovesome fancies that flitted through Lizzie's spirit in those busy hours could have found their way into the texture of the dingy yarn, as it was slowly wrought into shape, the eventual wearer of the socks would have been as light-footed as Mercury. I am afraid I should make the reader sneer, were I to rehearse some of this little fool's diversions. She passed several hours daily in Jack's old chamber: it was in this sanctuary, indeed, at the sunny south window, overlooking the long road, the wood-crowned heights, the gleaming river, that she worked with most pleasure and profit. Here she was removed from the untiring glance of the elder lady, from her jarring questions and common-places; here she was alone with her love, – that greatest common-place in life. Lizzie felt in Jack's room a certain impress of his personality. The idle fancies of her mood were bodied forth in a dozen sacred relics. Some of these articles Elizabeth carefully cherished. It was rather late in the day for her to assert a literary taste, – her reading having begun and ended (naturally enough) with the ancient fiction of the 'Scottish Chiefs.'[4] So she could hardly help smiling, herself, sometimes, at her interest in Jack's old college tomes. She carried several of them to her own apart-ment, and placed them at the foot of her little bed, on a book-shelf adorned, besides, with a pot of spring violets, a portrait of General McClellan,[5] and a likeness of Lieutenant Ford. She had a vague belief that a loving study of their well-thumbed verses would remedy, in some degree, her sad intellectual deficiencies. She was sorry she knew so little: as sorry, that is, as she might be, for we know that she was shallow. Jack's omniscience was one of his most awful attributes. And yet she comforted herself with the thought that, as he had forgiven her ignorance, she herself might surely forget it. Happy Lizzie, I envy you this easy path to knowledge! The volume she most frequently consulted was an old German 'Faust,' over which she used to fumble with a battered lexicon. The secret of this preference was in certain marginal notes in pencil, signed 'J.' I hope they were really of Jack's making.

Lizzie was always a small walker. Until she knew Jack, this had been quite an unsuspected pleasure. She was afraid, too, of the cows, geese, and sheep, – all the agricultural *spectra* of the feminine imagination. But now her terrors were over. Might she not play the soldier, too, in her own humble way? Often with a beating heart, I fear, but still with resolute, elastic steps, she revisited Jack's old haunts; she tried to love Nature as he had seemed to love it; she gazed at his old sunsets; she fathomed his old pools with bright plummet glances, as if seeking some lingering trace of his features in their brown depths, stamped there as on a fond human heart; she sought out his dear name, scratched on the rocks and trees, – and when night came on, she studied, in her simple way, the great starlit canopy, under which, perhaps, her warrior lay sleeping; she wandered through the green glades, singing snatches of his old ballads in a clear voice, made tuneful with love, – and as she sang, there mingled with the everlasting murmur of the trees the faint sound of a muffled bass, borne upon the wind like a distant drum-beat, responsive to a bugle. So she led for some months a very pleasant idyllic life, face to face with a strong, vivid memory, which gave everything and asked nothing. These were doubtless to be (and she half knew it) the happiest days of her life. Has life any bliss so great as this pensive ecstasy? To know that the golden sands are dropping one by one makes servitude freedom, and poverty riches.

In spite of a certain sense of loss, Lizzie passed a very blissful summer. She enjoyed the deep repose which, it is to be hoped, sanctifies all honest betrothals. Possible calamity weighed lightly upon her. We know that when the columns of battle-smoke leave the field, they journey through the heavy air to a thousand quiet homes, and play about the crackling blaze of as many firesides. But Lizzie's vision was never clouded. Mrs Ford might gaze into the thickening summer dusk and wipe her spectacles; but her companion hummed her old ballad-ends with an unbroken voice. She no more ceased to smile under evil tidings than the brooklet ceases to ripple beneath the projected shadow of the roadside willow. The self-given promises of that tearful night of parting were forgotten. Vigilance had no place in Lizzie's scheme of heavenly idleness. The idea of moralizing in Elysium!

It must not be supposed that Mrs Ford was indifferent to Lizzie's mood. She studied it watchfully, and kept note of all its variations. And among the things she learned was, that her companion knew of her scrutiny, and was, on the whole, indifferent to it. Of the full extent of Mrs Ford's observation, however, I think Lizzie was hardly aware. She was like a reveller in a brilliantly lighted room, with a curtainless window, conscious, and yet heedless, of passers-by. And Mrs Ford may not inaptly be compared to the chilly spectator on the dark side of the pane. Very few words passed on the topic of their common thoughts. From the first, as we have seen, Lizzie guessed at her guardian's probable view of her engagement: an abasement incurred by John. Lizzie lacked what is called a sense of duty; and, unlike the majority of such temperaments, which contrive to be buoyant on the glistening bubble of Dignity, she had likewise a modest estimate of her dues. Alack, my poor heroine had no pride! Mrs Ford's silent censure awakened no resentment. It sounded in her ears like a dull, soporific hum. Lizzie was deeply enamoured by what a French book terms her *aises intellectuelles*. Her mental comfort lay in the ignoring of problems. She possessed a certain native insight which revealed many of the horrent inequalities of her pathway; but she found it so cruel and disenchanting a faculty, that blindness was infinitely preferable. She preferred repose to order, and mercy to justice. She was speculative, without being critical. She was continually wondering, but she never inquired. This world was the riddle; the next alone would be the answer.

So she never felt any desire to have an 'understanding' with Mrs Ford. Did the old lady misconceive her? it was her own business. Mrs Ford apparently felt no desire to set herself right. You see, Lizzie was ignorant of her friend's promise. There were moments when Mrs Ford's tongue itched to speak. There were others, it is true, when she dreaded any explanation which would compel her to forfeit her displeasure. Lizzie's happy self-sufficiency was most irritating. She grudged the young girl the dignity of her secret; her own actual knowledge of it rather increased her jealousy, by showing her the importance of the scheme from which she was excluded. Lizzie, being in perfect good-humor with the world and with herself, abated no jot of her personal deference to Mrs Ford. Of Jack, as a good friend and her guardian's son, she spoke very freely. But Mrs Ford was mistrustful of this semi-confidence. She would not, she often said to herself, be wheedled against her principles. Her principles! Oh for some shining blade of purpose to hew down such stubborn stakes! Lizzie had no thought of flattering her companion. She never deceived anyone but herself. She could not bring herself to value Mrs Ford's goodwill. She knew that Jack often suffered from his mother's obstinacy. So her unbroken humility shielded no unavowed purpose. She was patient and kindly from nature, from habit. Yet I think, that, if Mrs Ford would have measured her benignity, she would have preferred, on the whole, the most open defiance. 'Of all things,' she would sometimes mutter, 'to be patronized by that little piece!' It was very disagreeable, for instance, to have to listen to *portions* of her own son's letters.

These letters came week by week, flying out of the South like white-winged carrier-doves. Many and many a time, for very pride, Lizzie would have liked a larger audience. Portions of them certainly deserved publicity. They were far too good for her. Were they not better than that stupid war-correspondence in the 'Times,'[6] which she so often tried to read in vain? They contained long details of movements, plans of campaigns, military opinions and conjectures, expressed with the emphasis habitual to young sub-lieutenants. I doubt whether General Halleck's despatches[7] laid down the law more absolutely than Lieutenant Ford's. Lizzie answered in her own fashion. It must be owned that hers was a dull pen. She told her dearest, dearest Jack how much she loved and honored him, and how much she missed him, and how delightful his last letter was, (with those beautifully drawn diagrams,) and the village gossip, and how stout and strong his mother continued to be, – and again, how she loved, etc., etc., and that she remained his loving L. Jack read these effusions as became one so beloved. I should not wonder if he thought them very brilliant.

The summer waned to its close, and through myriad silent stages began to darken into autumn. Who can tell the story of those red months? I have to chronicle another silent transition. But as I can find no words delicate and fine enough to describe the multifold changes of Nature, so, too, I must be content to give you the spiritual facts in gross.

John Ford became a veteran down by the Potomac. And, to tell the truth, Lizzie became a veteran at home. That is, her love and hope grew to be an old story. She gave way, as the strongest must, as the wisest will, to time. The passion which in her simple, shallow way, she had confided to the woods and waters reflected their outward variations; she thought of her lover less, and with less positive pleasure. The golden sands had run out. Perfect rest was over. Mrs Ford's tacit protest began to be annoying. In a rather resentful spirit, Lizzie forbore to read any more letters aloud. These were as regular as ever. One of them contained a rough camp-photograph of Jack's newly bearded visage. Lizzie declared it was 'too ugly for anything,' and thrust it out of sight. She found herself skipping his military dissertations, which were still as long and written in as handsome a hand as ever. The 'too good,' which used to be uttered rather proudly, was now rather a wearisome truth. When Lizzie in certain critical moods tried to qualify Jack's temperament, she said to herself that he was too literal. Once he gave her a little scolding for not writing oftener. 'Jack can make no allowances,' murmured Lizzie. 'He can understand no feelings but his own. I remember he used to say that moods were diseases. His mind is too healthy for such things; his heart is too stout for ache or pain. The night before he went off he told me that Reason, as he calls it, was the rule of life. I suppose he thinks it the rule of love, too. But his heart is younger than mine, – younger and better. He has lived through awful scenes of danger and bloodshed and cruelty, yet his heart is purer.' Lizzie had a horrible feeling of being *blasée* of this one affection. 'Oh, God bless him!' she cried. She felt much better for the tears in which this soliloquy ended. I fear she had begun to doubt her ability to cry about Jack.

III

Christmas came. The Army of the Potomac had stacked its muskets and gone into winter-quarters. Miss Crowe received an invitation to pass the second fortnight in February at the great manufacturing town of Leatherborough. Leatherborough is on the railroad, two hours south of Glenham, at the mouth of the great river Tan, where this noble stream expands into its broadest smile, or gapes in too huge a fashion to be disguised by a bridge.

'Mrs Littlefield kindly invites you for the last of the month,' said Mrs Ford, reading a letter behind the tea-urn.

It suited Mrs Ford's purpose – a purpose which I have not space to elaborate – that her young charge should now go forth into society and pick up acquaintances.

Two sparks of pleasure gleamed in Elizabeth's eyes. But, as she had taught herself to do of late with her protectress, she mused before answering.

'It is my desire that you should go,' said Mrs Ford, taking silence for dissent.

The sparks went out.

'I intend to go,' said Lizzie, rather grimly. 'I am much obliged to Mrs Littlefield.'

Her companion looked up.

'I intend you shall. You will please to write this morning.'

For the rest of the week the two stitched together over muslins and silks, and were very good friends. Lizzie could scarcely help wondering at Mrs Ford's zeal on her behalf. Might she not have referred it to her guardian's principles? Her wardrobe, hitherto fashioned on the Glenham notion of elegance, was gradually raised to the Leatherborough standard of fitness. As she took up her bedroom candle the night before she left home, she said, –

'I thank you very much, Mrs Ford, for having worked so hard for me, – for having taken so much interest in my outfit. If they ask me at Leatherborough who made my things, I shall certainly say it was you.'

Mrs Littlefield treated her young friend with great kindness. She was a good-natured, childless matron. She found Lizzie very ignorant and very pretty. She was glad to have so great a beauty and so many lions to show.

One evening Lizzie went to her room with one of the maids, carrying half a dozen candles between them. Heaven forbid that I should cross that virgin threshold – for the present! But we will wait. We will allow them two hours. At the end of that time, having gently knocked, we will enter the sanctuary. Glory of glories! The faithful attendant has done her work. Our lady is robed, crowned, ready for worshippers.

I trust I shall not be held to a minute description of our dear Lizzie's person and costume. Who is so great a recluse as never to have beheld young ladyhood in full dress? Many of us have sisters and daughters. Not a few of us, I hope, have female connections of another degree, yet no less dear. Others have looking-glasses. I give you my word for it that Elizabeth made as pretty a show as it is possible to see. She was of course well-dressed. Her skirt was of voluminous white, puffed and trimmed in wondrous sort. Her hair was profusely ornamented with curls and braids of its own rich substance. From her waist depended a ribbon, broad and blue. White with coral ornaments, as she wrote to Jack in the course of the week. Coral ornaments, forsooth! And pray, Miss, what of the other jewels with which your person was decorated, – the rubies, pearls, and sapphires? One by one Lizzie assumes her modest gimcracks: her bracelet, her gloves, her handkerchief, her fan, and then – her smile. Ah, that strange crowning smile!

An hour later, in Mrs Littlefield's pretty drawing-room, amid music, lights, and talk, Miss Crowe was sweeping a grand curtsy before a tall, sallow man, whose name she caught from her hostess's redundant murmur as Bruce. Five minutes later, when the honest matron gave a glance at her newly started enterprise from the other side of the room, she said to herself that really, for a plain country-girl, Miss Crowe did this kind of thing very well. Her next glimpse of the couple showed them whirling round the room to the crashing thrum of the piano. At eleven o'clock she beheld them linked by their fingertips in the dazzling mazes of the reel. At half-past eleven she discerned them charging shoulder to shoulder in the serried columns of the Lancers. At midnight she tapped her young friend gently with her fan.

'Your sash in unpinned, my dear. – I think you have danced often enough with Mr Bruce. If he asks you again, you had better refuse. It's not quite the thing. – Yes, my dear, I know. – Mr Simpson, will you be so good as to take Miss Crowe down to supper?'

I'm afraid young Simpson had rather a snappish partner.

After the proper interval, Mr Bruce called to pay his respects to Mrs Littlefield. He found Miss Crowe also in the drawing-room. Lizzie and he met like old friends. Mrs Littlefield was a willing listener; but it seemed to her that she had come in at the second act of the play. Bruce went off with Miss Crowe's promise to drive with him in the afternoon. In the afternoon he swept up to the door in a prancing, tinkling sleigh. After some minutes of hoarse jesting and silvery laughter in the keen wintry air, he swept away again with Lizzie curled up in the buffalo-robe beside him, like a kitten in a rug. It was dark when they returned. When Lizzie came in to the sitting-room fire, she was congratulated by her hostess upon having made a 'conquest.'

'I think he's a most gentlemanly man,' says Lizzie.

'So he is, my dear,' said Mrs Littlefield; 'Mr Bruce is a perfect gentleman. He's one of the finest young men I know. He's not so young either. He's a little too yellow for my taste; but he's beautifully educated. I wish you could hear his French accent. He has been abroad I don't know how many years. The firm of Bruce and Robertson does an immense business.'

'And I'm so glad,' cries Lizzie, 'he's coming to Glenham in March! He's going to take his sister to the water-cure.'

'Really? – poor thing! She has very good manners.'

'What do you think of his looks?' asked Lizzie, smoothing her feather.

'I was speaking of Jane Bruce. I think Mr Bruce has fine eyes.'

'I must say I like tall men,' says Miss Crowe.

'Then Robert Bruce is your man,' laughs Mr Littlefield. 'He's as tall as a bell-tower. And he's got a bell-clapper in his head, too.'

'I believe I will go and take off my things,' remarks Miss Crowe, flinging up her curls.

Of course it behoved Mr Bruce to call next day and see how Miss Crowe had stood her drive. He set a veto upon her intended departure, and presented an invitation from his sister for the following week. At Mrs Littlefield's instance, Lizzie accepted the invitation, despatched a laconic note to Mrs Ford, and stayed over for Miss Bruce's party. It was a grand affair. Miss Bruce was a very great lady: she treated Miss Crowe with every attention. Lizzie was thought by some persons to look prettier than ever. The vaporous gauze, the sunny hair, the coral, the sapphires, the smile, were displayed with renewed success. The master of the house was unable to dance; he was summoned to sterner duties. Nor could Miss Crowe be induced to perform, having hurt her foot on the ice. This was of course a disappointment; let us hope that her entertainers made it up to her.

On the second day after the party, Lizzie returned to Glenham. Good Mr Littlefield took her to the station, stealing a moment from his precious business-hours.

'There are your checks,' said he; 'be sure you don't lose them. Put them in your glove.'

Lizzie gave a little scream of merriment.

'Mr Littlefield, how can you? I've a reticule, Sir. But I really don't want you to stay.'

'Well, I confess,' said her companion. – 'Hullo! there's your Scottish chief! I'll get him to stay with you till the train leaves. He may be going. Bruce!'

'Oh, Mr Littlefield, don't!' cries Lizzie. 'Perhaps Mr Bruce is engaged.'

Bruce's tall figure came striding towards them. He was astounded to find that Miss Crowe was going by this train. Delightful! He had come to meet a friend who had not arrived.

'Littlefield,' said he, 'you can't be spared from your business. I will see Miss Crowe off.'

When the elder gentleman had departed, Mr Bruce conducted his companion into the car, and found her a comfortable seat, equidistant from the torrid stove and the frigid door. Then he stowed away her shawls, umbrella and reticule. She would keep her muff? She did well. What a pretty fur!

'It's just like your collar,' said Lizzie. 'I wish I had a muff for my feet,' she pursued, tapping the floor.

'Why not use some of those shawls?' said Bruce; 'let's see what we can make of them.'

And he stooped down and arranged them as a rug, very neatly and kindly. And then he called himself a fool for not having used the next seat, which was empty; and the wrapping was done over again.

'I'm so afraid you'll be carried off!' said Lizzie. 'What would you do?'

'I think I should make the best of it. And you?'

'I would tell you to sit down *there*'; and she indicated the seat facing her. He took it. 'Now you'll be sure to,' said Elizabeth.

'I'm afraid I shall, unless I put the newspaper between us.' And he took it out of his pocket. 'Have you seen the news?'

'No,' says Lizzie, elongating her bonnet-ribbons. 'What is it? Just look at that party.'

'There's not much news. There's been a scrimmage on the Rappahannock. Two of our regiments engaged, – the Fifteenth and the Twenty-Eighth. Didn't you tell me you had a cousin or something in the Fifteenth?'

'Not a cousin, no relation, but an intimate friend, – my guardian's son. What does the paper say, please?' inquires Lizzie, very pale.

Bruce cast his eye over the report. 'It doesn't seem to have amounted to much; we drove back the enemy, and recrossed the river at our ease. Our loss only fifty. There are no names,' he added, catching a glimpse of Lizzie's pallor, – 'none in this paper at least.'

In a few moments appeared a newsboy crying the New York journals.

'Do you think the New York papers would have any names?' asked Lizzie.

'We can try,' said Bruce. And he bought a 'Herald,' and unfolded it. 'Yes, there *is* a list,' he continued some time after he had opened out the sheet. 'What's your friend's name?' he asked, from behind the paper.

'Ford, – John Ford, second lieutenant,' said Lizzie.

There was a long pause.

At last Bruce lowered the sheet, and showed a face in which Lizzie's pallor seemed faintly reflected.

'There *is* such a name among the wounded,' he said; and,

folding the paper down, he held it out, and gently crossed to the seat beside her.

Lizzie took the paper, and held it close to her eyes. But Bruce could not help seeing that her temples had turned from white to crimson.

'Do you see it?' he asked; 'I sincerely hope it's nothing very bad.'

'*Severely*,' whispered Lizzie.

'Yes, but that proves nothing. Those things are most unreliable. *Do* hope for the best.'

Lizzie made no answer. Meanwhile passengers had been brushing in, and the car was full. The engine began to puff, and the conductor to shout. The train gave a jog.

'You'd better go, Sir, or you'll be carried off,' said Lizzie, holding out her hand, with her face still hidden.

'May I go on to the next station with you?' said Bruce.

Lizzie gave him a rapid look, with a deepened flush. He had fancied that she was shedding tears. But those eyes were dry; they held fire rather than water.

'No, no, Sir; you must not. I insist. Good bye.'

Bruce's offer had cost him a blush, too. He had been prepared to back it with the assurance that he had business ahead, and, indeed, to make a little business in order to satisfy his conscience. But Lizzie's answer was final.

'Very well,' said he, '*good* bye. You have my real sympathy, Miss Crowe. Don't despair. We shall meet again.'

The train rattled away. Lizzie caught a glimpse of a tall figure with lifted hat on the platform. But she sat motionless, with her head against the windowframe, her veil down, and her hands idle.

She had enough to do to think, or rather to feel. It is fortunate that the utmost shock of evil tidings often comes first. After that everything is for the better. Jack's name stood printed in that fatal column like a stern signal for despair. Lizzie felt conscious of a crisis which almost arrested her breath. Night had fallen at midday: what was the hour? A tragedy had stepped into her life: was she specatator or actor? She found herself face to face with death: was it not her own soul masquerading in a shroud? She sat in a half-stupor. She had been aroused from a dream into a waking nightmare. It was like hearing a murder-shriek while you turn the page of your novel. But I cannot describe these things. In time the crushing sense of calamity loosened its grasp. Feeling lashed her pinions. Thought struggled to rise. Passion was still, stunned, floored. She had recoiled like a receding wave for a stronger onset. A hundred ghastly fears and fancies strutted a moment, pecking at the young girl's naked heart, like sandpipers on the weltering beach. Then, as with a great murmurous rush, came the meaning of her grief. The flood-gates of emotion were opened.

At last passion exhausted itself, and Lizzie thought. Bruce's parting words rang in her ears. She did her best to hope. She reflected that wounds, even severe wounds, did not necessarily mean death. Death might easily be warded off. She would go to Jack; she would nurse him; she would watch by him; she would cure him. Even if Death had already beckoned, she would strike down his hand: if Life had already obeyed she would issue the stronger mandate of Love. She would stanch his wounds; she would unseal his eyes with her kisses; she would call till he answered her.

Lizzie reached home and walked up the garden path. Mrs Ford stood in the parlor as she entered, upright, pale, and rigid. Each read the other's countenance. Lizzie went towards her slowly and giddily. She must of course kiss her patroness. She took her listless hand and bent towards her stern lips. Habitually Mrs Ford was the most undemonstrative of women. But as Lizzie looked closer into her face, she read signs of a grief infinitely more potent than her own. The formal kiss gave way: the young girl leaned her head on the old woman's shoulder and burst into sobs. Mrs Ford acknowledged those tears with a slow inclination of the head, full of a certain grim pathos: she put out her arms and pressed them closer to her heart.

At last Lizzie disengaged herself and sat down.

'I am going to him,' said Mrs Ford.

Lizzie's dizziness returned. Mrs Ford was going, – and she, she?

'I am going to nurse him, and with God's help to save him.'

'How did you hear?'

'I have a telegram from the surgeon of the regiment'; and Mrs Ford held out a paper.

Lizzie took it and read: 'Lieutenant Ford dangerously wounded in the action of yesterday. You had better come on.'

'I should like to go myself,' said Lizzie: 'I think Jack would like to have me.'

'Nonsense! A pretty place for a young girl! I am not going for sentiment; I am going for use.'

Lizzie leaned her head back in her chair, and closed her eyes. From the moment they had fallen upon Mrs Ford, she had felt a certain quiescence. And now it was a relief to have responsibility denied her. Like most weak persons, she was glad to step out of the current of life, now that it had begun to quicken into action. In emergencies, such persons are tacitly counted out; and they as tacitly consent to the arrangement. Even to the sensitive spirit there is a certain meditative rapture in standing on the quiet shore, (beside the ruminating cattle,) and watching the hurrying, eddying flood, which makes up for the loss of dignity. Lizzie's heart resumed its peaceful throbs. She sat, almost dreamily, with her eyes shut.

'I leave in an hour,' said Mrs Ford. 'I am going to get ready. – Do you hear?'

The young girl's silence was a deeper consent than her companion supposed.

IV

It was a week before Lizzie heard from Mrs Ford. The letter, when it came, was very brief. Jack still lived. The wounds were three in number, and very serious; he was unconscious; he had not recognized her; but still the chances either way were thought equal. They would be much greater for his recovery nearer home; but it was impossible to move him. 'I write from the midst of horrible scenes,' said the poor lady. Subjoined was a list of necessary medicines, comforts, and delicacies, to be boxed up and sent.

For a while Lizzie found occupation in writing a letter to Jack, to be read in his first lucid moment, as she told Mrs Ford. This lady's man-of-business came up from the village to superintend the packing of the boxes. Her directions were strictly followed;

and in no point were they found wanting. Mr Mackenzie bespoke
Lizzie's admiration for their friend's wonderful clearness of
memory and judgment. 'I wish we had that woman at the head of
affairs,' said he. ''Gad, I'd apply for a Brigadier-Generalship.' –
'I'd apply to be sent South,' thought Lizzie. When the boxes and
letters were despatched, she sat down to await more news. Sat
down, say I? Sat down, and rose, and wondered, and sat down
again. These were lonely, weary days. Very different are the
idleness of love and the idleness of grief. Very different is it to be
alone with your hope and alone with your despair. Lizzie failed to
rally her musings. I do not mean to say that her sorrow was very
poignant, although she fancied it was. Habit was a great force in
her simple nature; and her chief trouble now was that habit refused
to work. Lizzie had to grapple with the stern tribulation of a
decision to make, a problem to solve. She felt that there was some
spiritual barrier between herself and repose. So she began in her
usual fashion to build up a false repose on the hither side of belief.
She might as well have tried to float on the Dead Sea. Peace
eluding her, she tried to resign herself to tumult. She drank deep
at the well of self-pity, but found its waters brackish. People are
apt to think that they may temper the penalties of misconduct by
self-commiseration, just as they season the long aftertaste of
beneficience by a little spice of self-applause. But the Power of
Good is a more grateful master than the Devil. What bliss to gaze
into the smooth gurgling wake of a good deed, while the comely
bark sails on with floating pennon! What horror to look into the
muddy sediment which floats round the piratic keel! Go, sinner,
and dissolve it with your tears! And you, scoffing friend, there is a
way out! Or would you prefer the window? I'm an honest man
forevermore.

One night Lizzie had a dream, – a rather disagreeable one, –
which haunted her during many waking hours. It seemed to her
that she was walking in a lonely place, with a tall, dark-eyed man
who called her wife. Suddenly, in the shadow of a tree, they came
upon an unburied corpse. Lizzie proposed to dig a grave. They
dug a great hole and took hold the corpse to lift him in; when
suddenly he opened his eyes. Then they saw that he was covered
with wounds. He looked at them intently for some time, turning

his eyes from one to the other. At last he solemnly said, 'Amen!' and closed his eyes. Then she and her companion placed him in the grave, and shovelled the earth over him, and stamped it down with their feet.

He of the dark eyes and he of the wounds were the two constantly recurring figures of Lizzie's reveries. She could never think of John without thinking of the courteous Leatherborough gentleman, too. These were the *data* of her problem. These two figures stood like opposing knights, (the black and the white,) foremost on the great chess-board of fate. Lizzie was the wearied, puzzled player. She would idly finger the other pieces, and shift them carelessly hither and thither; but it was of no avail: the game lay between the two knights. She would shut her eyes and long for some kind hand to come and tamper with the board; she would open them and see the two knights standing immovable, face to face. It was nothing new. A fancy had come in and offered defiance to a fact; they must fight it out. Lizzie generously inclined to the fancy, the unknown champion, with a reputation to make. Call her *blasée*, if you like, this little girl, whose record told of a couple of dances and a single lover, heartless, old before her time. Perhaps she deserves your scorn. I confess she thought herself ill-used. By whom? by what? wherein? These were questions Miss Crowe was not prepared to answer. Her intellect was unequal to the stern logic of human events. She expected two and two to make five: as why should they not for the nonce? She was like an actor who finds himself on the stage with a half-learned part and without sufficient wit to extemporize. Pray, where is the prompter? Alas, Elizabeth, that you had no mother! Young girls are prone to fancy that when once they have a lover, they have everything they need: a conclusion inconsistent with the belief entertained by many persons, that life begins with love. Lizzie's fortunes became old stories to her before she had half read them through. Jack's wounds and danger were an old story. Do not suppose that she had exhausted the lessons, the suggestions of these awful events, their inspirations, exhortations, – that she had wept as became the horror of the tragedy. No: the curtain had not yet fallen, yet our young lady had begun to yawn. To yawn? Aye, and to long for the afterpiece. Since the tragedy

47

dragged, might she not divert herself with that well-bred man beside her?

Elizabeth was far from owning to herself that she had fallen away from her love. For my own part, I need no better proof of the fact than the dull persistency with which she denied it. What accusing voice broke out of the stillness? Jack's nobleness and magnanimity were the hourly theme of her clogged fancy. Again and again she declared to herself that she was unworthy of them, but that, if he would only recover and come home, she would be his eternal bond-slave. So she passed a very miserable month. Let us hope that her childish spirit was being tempered to some useful purpose. Let us hope so.

She roamed about the empty house with her footsteps tracked by an unlaid ghost. She cried aloud and said that she was very unhappy; she groaned and called herself wicked. Then, sometimes, appalled at her moral perplexities, she declared that she was neither wicked nor unhappy; she was contented, patient, and wise. Other girls had lost their lovers: it was the present way of life. Was she weaker than most women? Nay, but Jack was the best of men. If he would only come back directly, without delay, as he was, senseless, dying even, that she might look at him, touch him, speak to him! Then she would say that she could no longer answer for herself, and wonder (or pretend to wonder) whether she were not going mad. Suppose Mrs Ford should come back and find her in an unswept room, pallid and insane? or suppose she should die of her troubles? What if she should kill herself? – dismiss the servants, and close the house, and lock herself up with a knife? Then she would cut her arm to escape from dismay at what she had already done; and then her courage would ebb away with her blood, and, having so far pledged herself to despair, her life would ebb away with her courage: and then, alone, in darkness, with none to help her, she would vainly scream, and thrust the knife into her temple, and swoon to death. And Jack would come back, and burst into the house, and wander through the empty rooms, calling her name, and for all answer get a deathscent! These imaginings were the more creditable or discreditable to Lizzie, that she had never read 'Romeo and Juliet.' At any rate, they served to dissipate time, – heavy, weary time, – the more heavy and weary as it bore dark foreshadowings of some momentous event. If that event would only come, whatever it was, and sever this Gordian knot of doubt!

The days passed slowly: the leaden sands dropped one by one. The roads were too bad for walking; so Lizzie was obliged to confine her restlessness to the narrow bounds of the empty house, or to an occasional journey to the village, where people sickened her by their dull indifference to her spiritual agony. Still they could not fail to remark how poorly Miss Crowe was looking. This was true, and Lizzie knew it. I think she even took a certain comfort in her pallor and in her failing interest in her dress. There was some satisfaction in displaying her white roses amid the apple-cheeked prosperity of Main Street. At last Miss Cooper, the Doctor's sister, spoke to her: –

'How is it, Elizabeth, you look so pale, and thin, and worn out? What you been doing with yourself? Falling in love, eh? It isn't right to be so much alone. Come down and stay with us awhile, – till Mrs Ford and John come back,' added Miss Cooper, who wished to put a cheerful face on the matter.

For Miss Cooper, indeed, any other face would have been difficult. Lizzie agreed to come. Her hostess was a busy, unbeautiful old maid, sister and housekeeper of the village physician. Her occupation here below was to perform the forgotten tasks of her fellowmen, – to pick up their dropped stitches, as she herself declared. She was never idle, for her general cleverness was commensurate with mortal needs. Her own story was, that she kept moving, so that folks couldn't see how ugly she was. And, in fact, her existence was manifest through her long train of good deeds, – just as the presence of a comet is shown by its tail. It was doubtless on the above principle that her visage was agitated by a perpetual laugh.

Meanwhile more news had been coming from Virginia. 'What an absurdly long letter you sent John,' wrote Mrs Ford in acknowledging the receipt of the boxes. 'His first lucid moment would be very short, if he were to take upon himself to read your effusions. Pray keep your long stories till he gets well.' For a fortnight the young soldier remained the same, – feverish, conscious only at intervals. Then came a change for the worse, which, for many weary days, however, resulted in nothing decisive. 'If he could only be moved to Glenham, home, and old sights,' said his mother, 'I should have hope. But think of the journey!' By this time Lizzie had stayed out ten days of her visit.

One day Miss Cooper came in from a walk, radiant with tidings. Her face, as I have observed, wore a continual smile, being dimpled and punctured all over with merriment, – so that, when an unusual cheerfulness was super-diffused, it resembled a tempestuous little pool into which a great stone has been cast.

'Guess who's come,' said she, going up to the piano, which Lizzie was carelessly fingering, and putting her hands on the young girl's shoulders. 'Just guess!'

Lizzie looked up.

'Jack,' she half gasped.

'Oh, dear, no, not that! How stupid of me! I mean Mr Bruce, your Leatherborough admirer.'

'Mr Bruce! Mr Bruce!' said Lizzie. 'Really?'

'True as I live. He's come to bring his sister to the Water-Cure. I met them at the post-office.'

Lizzie felt a strange sensation of good news. Her finger-tips were on fire. She was deaf to her companion's rattling chronicle. She broke into the midst of it with a fragment of some triumphant, jubilant melody. The keys rang beneath her flashing hands. And then she suddenly stopped, and Miss Cooper, who was taking off her bonnet at the mirror, saw that her face was covered with a burning flush.

That evening, Mr Bruce presented himself at Doctor Cooper's, with whom he had a slight acquaintance. To Lizzie he was infinitely courteous and tender. He assured her, in very pretty terms, of his profound sympathy with her in her cousin's danger, – her cousin he still called him, – and it seemed to Lizzie that until that moment no one had begun to be kind. And then he began to rebuke her, playfully and in excellent taste, for her pale cheeks.

'Isn't it dreadful?' said Miss Cooper. 'She looks like a ghost. I guess she's in love.'

'He must be a good-for-nothing lover to make his mistress look so sad. If I were you, I'd give him up, Miss Crowe.'

'I didn't know I looked sad,' said Lizzie.

'You don't now,' said Miss Cooper. 'You're smiling and blushing. A'n't she blushing, Mr Bruce?'

'I think Miss Crowe has no more than her natural color,' said Bruce, dropping his eye-glass. 'What have you been doing all this while since we parted?'

'All this while? It's only six weeks. I don't know. Nothing. What have you?'

'I've been doing nothing, too. It's hard work.'

'Have you been to any more parties?'

'Not one.'

'Any more sleigh-rides?'

'Yes. I took one more dreary drive all alone, – over that same road, you know. And I stopped at the farm-house again, and saw the old woman we had the talk with. She remembered us, and asked me what had become of the young lady who was with me before. I told her you were gone home, but that I hoped soon to go and see you. So she sent you her love' –

'Oh, how nice!' exclaimed Lizzie.

'Wasn't it? And then she made a certain little speech; I won't repeat it, or we shall have Miss Cooper talking about your blushes again.'

'I know,' cried the lady in question: 'she said she was very' –

'Very what?' said Lizzie.

'Very h-a-n-d – what everyone says.'

'Very handy?' asked Lizzie. 'I'm sure no one ever said that.'

'Of course,' said Bruce; 'and I answered what everyone answers.'

'Have you seen Mrs Littlefield lately?'

'Several times. I called on her the day before I left town, to see if she had any message for you.'

'Oh, thank you! I hope she's well.'

'Oh, she's as jolly as ever. She sent you her love, and hoped you would come back to Leatherborough very soon again. I told her, that, however it might be with the first message, the second should be a joint one from both of us.'

'You're very kind. I should like very much to go again. – Do you like Mrs Littlefield?'

'Like her? Yes. Don't you? She's thought a very pleasing woman.'

'Oh, she's very nice. – I don't think she has much conversation.'

'Ah, I'm afraid you mean she doesn't backbite. We've always found plenty to talk about.'

'That's a very significant tone. What, for instance?'

'Well, we *have* talked about Miss Crowe.'

'Oh, you have? Do you call that having plenty to talk about?'

'We *have* talked about Mr Bruce, – haven't we, Elizabeth?' said Miss Cooper, who had her own notion of being agreeable.

It was not an altogether bad notion, perhaps; but Bruce found her interruptions rather annoying, and insensibly allowed them to shorten his visit. Yet, as it was, he sat till eleven o'clock, – a stay quite unprecedented at Glenham.

When he left the house, he went splashing down the road with a very elastic tread, springing over the starlit puddles and trolling out some sentimental ditty. He reached the inn, and went up to his sister's sitting-room.

'Why, Robert, where have you been all this while?' said Miss Bruce.

'At Dr Cooper's.'

'Dr Cooper's? I should think you had! Who's Dr Cooper?'

'Where Miss Crowe's staying.'

'Miss Crowe? Ah, Mrs Littlefield's friend! Is she as pretty as ever?'

'Prettier, – prettier, – prettier. *Ta-ra-ta! tara-ta!*'

'Oh, Robert, do stop that singing! You'll rouse the whole house.'

V

Late one afternoon, at dusk, about three weeks after Mr Bruce's arrival, Lizzie was sitting alone by the fire, in Miss Cooper's parlor, musing, as became the place and hour. The Doctor and his sister came in, dressed for a lecture.

'I'm sorry you won't go, my dear,' said Miss Cooper. 'It's a most interesting subject: "A Year of the War." All the battles and things described, you know.'

'I'm tired of war,' said Lizzie.

'Well, well, if you're tired of the war, we'll leave you in peace.

Kiss me good-bye. What's the matter? You look sick. You are homesick, a'n't you?'

'No, no, – I'm very well.'

'Would you like me to stay at home with you?'

'Oh, no! pray, don't!'

'Well, we'll tell you all about it. Will they have programmes, James? I'll bring her a programme. – But you really feel as if you were going to be ill. Feel of her skin, James.'

'No, you needn't, Sir,' said Lizzie. 'How queer of you, Miss Cooper! I'm perfectly well.'

And at last her friends departed. Before long the servant came with the lamp, ushering, Mr Mackenzie.

'Good evening, Miss,' said he. 'Bad news from Mrs Ford.'

'Bad news?'

'Yes, Miss. I've just got a letter stating that Mr John is growing worse and worse, and that they look for his death from hour to hour. – It's very sad,' he added, as Elizabeth was silent.

'Yes, it's very sad,' said Lizzie.

'I thought you'd like to hear it.'

'Thank you.'

'He was a very noble young fellow,' pursued Mr Mackenzie.

Lizzie made no response.

'There's the letter,' said Mr Mackenzie, handing it over to her.

Lizzie opened it.

'How long she is reading it!' thought her visitor. 'You can't see so far from the light, can you, Miss?'

'Yes,' said Lizzie. – 'His poor mother! Poor woman!'

'Aye, indeed, Miss, – she's the one to be pitied.'

'Yes, she's the one to be pitied,' said Lizzie. 'Well!' and she gave him back the letter.

'I thought you'd like to see it,' said Mackenzie, drawing on his gloves; and then, after a pause, – 'I'll call again, Miss, if I hear anything more. Good night!'

Lizzie got up and lowered the light, and then went back to her sofa by the fire.

Half an hour passed; it went slowly; but it passed. Still lying there in the dark room on the sofa, Lizzie heard a ring at the door-bell, a man's voice and a man's tread in the hall. She rose and went to the lamp. As she turned it up, the parlor door opened. Bruce came in.

'I was sitting in the dark,' said Lizzie, 'but when I heard you coming, I raised the light.'

'Are you afraid of me?' said Bruce.

'Oh, no! I'll put it down again. Sit down.'

'I saw your friends going out,' pursued Bruce; 'so I knew I should find you alone. – What are you doing here in the dark?'

'I've just received bad news from Mrs Ford about her son. He's much worse, and will probably not live.'

'Is it possible?'

'I was thinking about that.'

'Dear me! Well, that's a sad subject. I'm told he was a very fine young man.'

'He was, – very,' said Lizzie.

Bruce was silent awhile. He was a stranger to the young officer, and felt that he had nothing to offer beyond the commonplace expressions of sympathy and surprise. Nor had he exactly the measure of his companion's interest in him.

'If he dies,' said Lizzie, 'it will be under great injustice.'

'Ah! what do you mean?'

'There wasn't a braver man in the army.'

'I suppose not.'

'And, oh, Mr Bruce,' continued Lizzie, 'he was so clever and good and generous! I wish you had known him.'

'I wish I had. But what do you mean by injustice? Were these qualities denied him?'

'No indeed! Everyone that looked at him could see that he was perfect.'

'Where's the injustice, then? It ought to be enough for him that you should think so highly of him.'

'Oh, he knew that,' said Lizzie.

Bruce was a little puzzled by his companion's manner. He watched her, as she sat with her cheek on her hand, looking at the fire. There was a long pause. Either they were too friendly or too thoughtful for the silence to be embarrassing. Bruce broke it at last.

'Miss Crowe,' said he, 'on a certain occasion, some time ago, when you first heard of Mr Ford's wounds, I offered you my company, with the wish to console you as far as I might for what seemed a considerable shock. It was, perhaps, a bold offer for so new a friend; but nevertheless, in it even then my heart spoke. You turned me off. Will you let me repeat it? Now, with a better right, will you let me speak out all my heart?'

Lizzie heard this speech, which was delivered in a slow and hesitating tone, without looking up or moving her head, except, perhaps, at the words 'turned me off'. After Bruce had ceased, she still kept her position.

'You'll not turn me off now?' added her companion.

She dropped her hand, raised her head, and looked at him a moment: he thought he saw the glow of tears in her eyes. Then she sank back upon the sofa with her face in the shadow of the mantelpiece.

'I don't understand you, Mr Bruce,' said she.

'Ah, Elizabeth! am I such a poor speaker. How shall I make it plain? When I saw your friends leave home half an hour ago, and reflected that you would probably be alone, I determined to go right in and have a talk with you that I've long been wanting to have. But first I walked half a mile up the road, thinking hard, – thinking how I should say what I had to say. I made up my mind to nothing, but that somehow or other I should say it. I would trust, – I *do* trust your frankness, kindness, and sympathy, to a feeling corresponding to my own. Do you understand that feeling? Do you know that I love you? I do, I do, I do! You *must* know it. If you don't I solemnly swear it. I solemnly ask you, Elizabeth, to take me for your husband.'

While Bruce said these words, he rose, with their rising passion, and came and stood before Lizzie. Again she was motionless.

'Does it take you so long to think?' said he, trying to read her indistinct features; and he sat down on the sofa beside her and took her hand.

At last Lizzie spoke.

'Are you sure,' said she, 'that you love me?'

'As sure as that I breathe. Now, Elizabeth, make me as sure that I am loved in return.'

'It seems very strange, Mr Bruce,' said Lizzie.

'What seems strange? Why should it? For a month I've been trying, in a hundred dumb ways, to make it plain: and now, when I swear it, it only seems strange!'

'What do you love me for?'

'For? For yourself, Elizabeth.'

'Myself? I am nothing.'

'I love you for what you are, – for your deep, kind heart, – for being so perfectly a woman.'

Lizzie drew away her hand, and her lover rose and stood before her again. But now she looked up into his face, questioning when she should have answered, drinking strength from his entreaties for her replies. There he stood before her, in the glow of the firelight, in all his gentlemanhood, for her to accept or reject. She slowly rose and gave him the hand she had withdrawn.

'Mr Bruce, I shall be very proud to love you,' she said.

And then, as if this effort was beyond her strength, she half staggered back to the sofa again. And still holding her hand, he sat down beside her. And there they were still sitting when they heard the Doctor and his sister come in.

For three days Elizabeth saw nothing of Mr Mackenzie. At last, on the fourth day, passing his office in the village, she went in and asked for him. He came out of his little back parlour with his mouth full and a beaming face.

'Good-day, Miss Crowe, and good news!'

'*Good* news?' cried Lizzie.

'Capital! said he, looking hard at her, while he put on his spectacles. 'She writes that Mr John – won't you take a seat? – has taken a sudden and unexpected turn for the better. Now's the moment to save him; it's an equal risk. They were to start for the North the second day after date. The surgeon comes with them. So they'll be home – of course they'll travel slowly – in four or five days. Yes, Miss, it's a remarkable Providence. And that noble young man will be spared to the country, and to those who love him, as I do.'

'I had better go back to the house and have it got ready,' said Lizzie, for an answer.

'Yes, Miss, I think you had. In fact, Mrs Ford made that request.'

The request was obeyed. That same day Lizzie went home. For two days she found it her interest to overlook, assiduously a general sweeping, scrubbing, and provisioning. She allowed herself no idle moment until bed-time. Then – But I would rather not be the chamberlain of her agony. It was the easier to work, as Mr Bruce had gone to Leatherborough on business.

On the fourth evening, at twilight, John Ford was borne up to the door on his stretcher, with his mother stalking beside him in rigid grief, and kind, silent friends pressing about with helping hands.

> Home they brought her warrior dead,
> She nor swooned nor uttered cry.[8]

It was, indeed, almost a question, whether Jack was not dead. Death is not thinner, paler, stiller. Lizzie moved about like one in a dream. Of course, when there are so many sympathetic friends, a man's family has nothing to do, – except exercise a little self-control. The women huddled Mrs Ford to bed; rest was imperative; she was killing herself. And it was significant of her weakness that she did not resent this advice. On greeting her, Lizzie felt as if she were embracing the stone image on the top of a sepulchre. She, too, had her cares anticipated. Good Doctor Cooper and his sister stationed themselves at the young man's couch.

The Doctor prophesied wondrous things of the change of climate; he was certain of a recovery. Lizzie found herself very shortly dealt with as an obstacle to this consummation. Access to John was prohibited. 'Perfect stillness, you know, my dear,' whispered Miss Cooper, opening his chamber door on a crack, in a pair of very creaking shoes. So for the first evening that her old friend was at home Lizzie caught but a glimpse of his pale, senseless face, as she hovered outside the long train of his attendants. If we may suppose any of these kind people to have had eyes for aught but the sufferer, we may be sure that they saw another visage equally sad and white. The sufferer? It was hardly Jack, after all.

When Lizzie was turned from Jack's door, she took a covering from a heap of draperies that had been hurriedly tossed down in the hall: it was an old army blanket. She wrapped it round her, and went out on the verandah. It was nine o'clock; but the darkness was filled with light. A great wanton wind – the ghost of the raw blast which travels by day – had arisen, bearing long, soft gusts of inland spring. Scattered clouds were hurrying across the white sky. The bright moon, careering in their midst, seemed to have wandered forth in frantic quest of the hidden stars.

Lizzie nestled her head in the blanket, and sat down on the steps. A strange earthy smell lingered in that faded old rug, and with it a faint perfume of tobacco. Instantly the young girl's senses were transported as they had never been before to those far-off Southern battlefields. She saw men lying in swamps, puffing their kindly pipes, drawing their blankets closer, canopied with the same luminous dusk that shone down upon her comfortable weakness. Her mind wandered amid these scenes till recalled to the present by the swinging of the garden gate. She heard a firm, well-known tread crunching the gravel. Mr Bruce came up the path. As he drew near the steps, Lizzie arose. The blanket fell back from her head, and Bruce started at recognizing her.

'Hullo! You, Elizabeth? What's the matter?'

Lizzie made no answer.

'Are you one of Mr Ford's watchers?' he continued, coming up the steps; 'how is he?'

Still she was silent. Bruce put out his hands to take hers, and bent forward as if to kiss her. She half shook him off, and retreated toward the door.

'Good heavens!' cried Bruce; 'what's the matter? Are you moonstruck? Can't you speak?'

'No, – no, – not to-night,' said Lizzie, in a choking voice. 'Go away, – go away!'

She stood holding the door-handle, and motioning him off. He hesitated a moment, and then advanced. She opened the door rapidly, and went in. He heard her lock it. He stood looking at it stupidly for some time, and then slowly turned round and walked down the steps.

The next morning Lizzie arose with the early dawn, and came downstairs. She went to the room where Jack lay, and gently opened the door. Miss Cooper was dozing in her chair. Lizzie crossed the threshold, and stole up to the bed. Poor Ford lay peacefully sleeping. There was his old face, after all, – his strong, honest features refined, but not weakened, by pain. Lizzie softly drew up a low chair, and sat down beside him. She gazed into his face, – the dear honored face into which she had so often gazed in health. It was strangely handsomer: body stood for less. It seemed to Lizzie, that, as the fabric of her lover's soul was more clearly revealed, – the veil of the temple rent wellnigh in twain, – she could read the justification of all her old worship. One of Jack's hands lay outside the sheets, – those strong, supple fingers, once so cunning in workmanship, so frank in friendship, now thinner and whiter than her own. After looking at it for some time, Lizzie gently grasped it. Jack slowly opened his eyes. Lizzie's heart began to throb; it was as if the stillness of the sanctuary had given a sign. At first there was no recognition in the young man's gaze. Then the dull pupils bcgan visibly to brighten. There came to his lips the commencement of that strange moribund smile which seems so ineffably satirical of the things of this world. O imposing spectacle of death! O blessed soul, marked for promotion! What earthly favor is like thine? Lizzie sank down on her knees, and, still clasping John's hand, bent closer over him.

'Jack, – dear, dear Jack,' she whispered, 'do you know me?'

The smile grew more intense. The poor fellow drew out his other hand, and slowly, feebly placed it on Lizzie's head, stroking down her hair with his fingers.

'Yes, yes,' she murmured; 'you know me, don't you? I am Lizzie, Jack. Don't you remember Lizzie?'

Ford moved his lips inaudibly, and went on patting her head.

'This is home, you know,' said Lizzie; 'this is Glenham. You haven't forgotten Glenham? You are with your mother and me and your friends. Dear, darling Jack!'

Still he went on, stroking her head; and his feeble lips tried to emit some sound. Lizzie laid her head down on the pillow beside his own, and still his hand lingered caressingly on her hair.

'Yes, you know me,' she pursued; 'you are with your friends now forever, – with those who will love and take care of you, oh, forever!'

'I'm very badly wounded,' murmured Jack, close to her ear.

'Yes, yes, my dear boy, but your wounds are healing. I will love you and nurse you forever.'

'Yes, Lizzie, our old promise,' said Jack: and his hand fell upon her neck, and with its feeble pressure he drew her closer, and she wet his face with her tears.

Then Miss Cooper, awakening, rose and drew Lizzie away.

'I am sure you excite him, my dear. It is best he should have none of his family near him, – persons with whom he has associations, you know.'

Here the Doctor was heard gently tapping on the window, and Lizzie went round to the door to admit him.

She did not see Jack again all day. Two or three times she ventured into the room, but she was banished by a frown, or a finger raised to the lips. She waylaid the Doctor frequently. He was blithe and cheerful, certain of Jack's recovery. This good man used to exhibit as much moral elation at the prospect of a cure as an orthodox believer at that of a new convert: it was one more body gained from the Devil. He assured Lizzie that the change of scene and climate had already begun to tell: the fever was lessening, the worst symptoms disappearing. He answered Lizzie's reiterated desire to do something by directions to keep the house quiet and the sick-room empty.

Soon after breakfast, Miss Dawes, a neighbor, came in to relieve Miss Cooper, and this indefatigable lady transferred her attention to Mrs Ford. Action was forbidden her. Miss Cooper was delighted for once to be able to lay down the law to her vigorous neighbor, of whose fine judgment she had always stood in awe. Having bullied Mrs Ford into taking her breakfast in the little sitting-room, she closed the doors, and prepared for 'a good long talk.' Lizzie was careful not to break in upon this interview. She had bidden her patroness good morning, asked after her health, and received one of her temperate osculations. As she passed the invalid's door, Doctor Cooper came out and asked her to go and look for a certain roll of bandages, in Mr John's trunk, which had been carried into another room. Lizzie hastened to perform this task. In fumbling through the contents of the trunk, she came across a packet of letters in a well-known feminine hand-writing. She pocketed it, and, after disposing of the bandages, went to her own room, locked the door, and sat down to examine the letters. Between reading and thinking and sighing and (in spite of herself) smiling, this process took the whole morning. As she came down to dinner, she encountered Mrs Ford and Miss Cooper, emerging from the sitting-room, the good long talk being only just concluded.

'How do you feel, Ma'am?' she asked of the elder lady, – 'rested?'

For all answer Mrs Ford gave a look – I had almost said a scowl – so hard, so cold, so reproachful, that Lizzie was transfixed. But suddenly its sickening meaning was revealed to her. She turned to Miss Cooper, who stood pale and fluttering beside the mistress, her everlasting smile glazed over with a piteous, deprecating glance; and I fear her eyes flashed out the same message of angry scorn they had just received. These telegraphic operations are very rapid. The ladies hardly halted: the next moment found them seated at the dinner-table with Miss Cooper scrutinising her napkin-mark and Mrs Ford saying grace.

Dinner was eaten in silence. When it was over, Lizzie returned to her own room. Miss Cooper went home, and Mrs Ford went to her son. Lizzie heard the firm low click of the lock as she closed the door. Why did she lock it? There was something fatal in the silence that followed. The plot of her little tragedy thickened. Be it so: she would act her part with the rest. For the second time in her experience, her mind was lightened by the intervention of Mrs Ford. Before the scorn of her own conscience, (which never came), before Jack's deepest reproach, she was ready to bow down, – but not before that long-faced Nemesis in black silk. The leaven of resentment began to work. She leaned back in her chair, and folded her arms, brave to await results. But before long she fell asleep. She was aroused by a knock at her chamber-door. The afternoon was far gone. Miss Dawes stood without.

'Elizabeth, Mr John wants very much to see you, with his love. Come down very gently: his mother is lying down. Will you sit with him while I take my dinner? – Better? Yes, ever so much.'

Lizzie betook herself with trembling haste to Jack's bedside.

He was propped up with pillows. His pale cheeks were slightly flushed. His eyes were bright. He raised himself, and, for such feeble arms, gave Lizzie a long, strong embrace.

'I've not seen you all day, Lizzie,' said he. 'Where have you been?'

'Dear Jack, they wouldn't let me come near you. I begged and prayed. And I wanted so to go to you in the army; but I couldn't. I wish, I wish I had!'

'You wouldn't have liked it, Lizzie. I'm glad you didn't. It's a bad, bad place.'

He lay quietly, holding her hands and gazing at her.

'Can I do anything for you, dear?' asked the young girl. 'I would work my life out. I'm so glad you're better!'

It was some time before Jack answered, –

'Lizzie,' said he, at last, 'I sent for you to look at you. – You are more wondrously beautiful than ever. Your hair is brown, – like – like nothing; your eyes are blue; your neck is white. Well, well!'

He lay perfectly motionless, but for his eyes. They wandered over her with a kind of peaceful glee, like sunbeams playing on a statue. Poor Ford lay, indeed, not unlike an old wounded Greek, who at falling dusk has crawled into a temple to die, steeping the last dull interval in idle admiration of sculptured Artemis.

'Ah, Lizzie, this is already heaven!' he murmured.

'It will be heaven when you get well,' whispered Lizzie.

He smiled into her eyes: –

'You say more than you mean. There should be perfect truth between us. Dear Lizzie, I am not going to get well. They are all very much mistaken. I am going to die. I've done my work. Death makes up for everything. My great pain is in leaving you. But you, too, will die one of these days; remember that. In all pain and sorrow, remember that.'

Lizzie was able to reply only by the tightening grasp of her hands.

'But there is something more,' pursued Jack. 'Life *is* as good as death. Your heart has found its true keeper; so we shall all three be happy. Tell him I bless him and honor him. Tell him God, too, blesses him. Shake hands with him for me,' said Jack, feebly moving his pale fingers. 'My mother,' he went on – 'be very kind to her. She will have great grief, but she will not die of it. She'll live to a great age. Now, Lizzie, I can't talk any more; I wanted to say farewell. You'll keep me farewell, – you'll stay with me awhile, – won't you? I'll look at you till the last. For a little while you'll be mine, holding my hands – so – until death parts us.'

Jack kept his promise. His eyes were fixed in a firm gaze long after the sense had left them.

In the early dawn of the next day, Elizabeth left her sleepless bed, opened the window, and looked out on the wide prospect, still cool and dim with departing night. It offered freshness and peace to her hot head and restless heart. She dressed herself hastily, crept downstairs, passed the death-chamber, and stole out of the quiet house. She turned away from the still sleeping village and walked towards the open country. She went a long way without knowing it. The sun had risen high when she bethought herself to turn. As she came back along the brightening highway, and drew near home, she saw a tall figure standing beneath the budding trees of the garden, hesitating, apparently, whether to open the gate. Lizzie came upon him almost before he had seen her. Bruce's first movement was to put out his hands, as any lover might; but as Lizzie raised her veil, he dropped them.

'Yes, Mr Bruce,' said Lizzie, 'I'll give you my hand once more, – in farewell.'

'Elizabeth!' cried Bruce, half stupefied, 'in God's name, what do you mean by these crazy speeches?'

'I mean well. I mean kindly and humanely to you. And I mean justice to my old – old love.'

She went to him, took his listless hand, without looking into his wild, smitten face, shook it passionately, and then, wrenching her own from his grasp, opened the gate and let it swing behind her.

'No! no! no!' she almost shrieked, turning about in the path. 'I forbid you to follow me!'

But for all that, he went in.

A Landscape-Painter

Do you remember how, a dozen years ago, a number of our friends were startled by the report of the rupture of young Locksley's engagement with Miss Leary? This event made some noise in its day. Both parties possessed certain claims to distinction: Locksley in his wealth, which was believed to be enormous, and the young lady in her beauty, which was in truth very great. I used to hear that her lover was fond of comparing her to the Venus of Milo; and, indeed, if you can imagine the mutilated goddess with her full complement of limbs, dressed out by Madame de Crinoline, and engaged in small-talk beneath the drawing-room chandelier, you may obtain a vague notion of Miss Josephine Leary. Locksley, you remember, was rather a short man, dark, and not particularly good-looking; and when he walked about with his betrothed it was half a matter of surprise that he should have ventured to propose to a young lady of such heroic proportions. Miss Leary had the gray eyes and auburn hair which I have always attributed to the famous statue. The one defect in her face, in spite of an expression of great candour and sweetness, was a certain lack of animation. What it was besides her beauty that attracted Locksley I never discovered; perhaps, since his attachment was so short-lived, it was her beauty alone. I say that his attachment was of brief duration, because the break was understood to have come from him. Both he and Miss Leary very wisely held their tongues on the matter; but among their friends and enemies it of course received a hundred explanations. That most popular with Locksley's well-wishers was, that he had backed out (these events are discussed, you know, in fashionable circles very much as an expected prize-fight which has miscarried is canvassed in reunions of another kind) only on flagrant evidence of the lady's – what, faithlessness? – on overwhelming proof of the most *mercenary* spirit on the part of Miss Leary. You see, our friend was held capable of doing battle for an 'idea.' It must be owned that this was a novel charge; but, for myself, having long known Mrs Leary, the mother, who was a widow with four daughters, to be an inveterate old screw, it was not impossible for me to believe that her first-born had also shown the cloven foot. I suppose that the young lady's family had, on their own side, a very plausible version of their disappointment. It was, however, soon made up to them by Josephine's marriage with a gentleman of expectations very nearly as brilliant as those of her old suitor. And what was *his* compensation? That is precisely my story.

Locksley disappeared, as you will remember, from public view. The events above alluded to happened in March. On calling at his lodgings in April I was told he had gone to the country. But toward the last of May I met him. He told me that he was on the look-out for a quiet, unfrequented place at the seaside, where he might rusticate and sketch. He was looking very poorly. I suggested Newport,[1] and I remember he hardly had the energy to smile at the simple joke. We parted without my having been able to satisfy him, and for a very long time I quite lost sight of him. He died seven years ago, at the age of thirty-five. For five years, accordingly, he managed to shield his life from the eyes of men. Through circumstances which I need not go into, a good many of his personal belongings have become mine. You will remember that he was a man of what are called cultivated tastes; that is, he was fond of reading, wrote a little, and painted a good deal. He wrote some rather amateurish verse, but he produced a number of remarkable paintings. He left a mass of papers, on many subjects, few of which are calculated to be generally interesting. A few of them, however, I highly prize – that portion which constitutes his private diary. It extends from his twenty-fifth to his thirtieth year, at which period it breaks off suddenly. If you will come to my house I will show you such of his pictures and sketches as I possess, and, I trust, convert you to my opinion that he had in him the stuff of a charming artist. Meanwhile I will place before you the last hundred pages of his diary, as an answer to your inquiry regarding the ultimate view taken by the great Nemesis of his treatment of Miss Leary – his scorn of the magnificent Venus

Victrix.[2] The recent passing away of the one person who had a voice paramount to mine in the disposal of Locksley's effects enables me to act without reserve.

Chowderville,[3] *June 9th.* – I have been sitting some minutes, pen in hand, wondering whether on this new earth, beneath this new sky, I had better resume this occasional history of nothing at all. I think I will at all events make the experiment. If we fail, as Lady Macbeth remarks, we fail. I find my entries have been longest when I have had least to say. I doubt not, therefore, that, once I have had a sufficient dose of dulness, I shall sit scribbling from morning till night. If nothing happens— But my prophetic soul tells me that something *will* happen. I am determined that something shall – if it be nothing else than that I paint a picture.

When I came up to bed half-an-hour ago I was deadly sleepy. Now, after looking out of the window a little, my brain is immensely refreshed, and I feel as if I could write till morning. But, unfortunately, I have nothing to write about. And then, if I expect to rise early, I must turn in betimes. The whole village is asleep, godless metropolitan that I am! The lamps on the square, outside, flicker in the wind; there is nothing abroad but the blue darkness and the smell of the rising tide. I have spent the whole day on my legs, trudging from one side of the peninsula to the other. What a trump is old Mrs Monkhouse, to have thought of this place! I must write her a letter of passionate thanks. Never before have I seen such a pretty little coast – never before have I been so taken with wave and rock and cloud. I am filled with ecstasy at the life, light, and transparency of the air. I am enamoured of all the moods and tenses of the ocean; and as yet, I suppose, I have not seen half of them. I came in to supper hungry, weary, foot-sore, sunburnt, dirty – happier, in short, than I have been for a twelvemonth. And now, if you please, for the prodigies of the brush!

June 11th. – Another day afoot, and also afloat. I resolved this morning to leave this abominable little tavern; I can't stand my feather-bed another night. I determined to find some other prospect than the town-pump and the 'drug-store.' I questioned my host, after breakfast, as to the possibility of getting lodgings in any of the outlying farms and cottages. But my host either did not or would not know anything about the matter. So I resolved to wander forth and seek my fortune – to roam inquisitive through the neighbourhood and appeal to the indigenous sentiment of hospitality. But never have I seen a folk so devoid of this amiable quality. By dinner-time I had given up in despair. After dinner I strolled down to the harbour, which is close at hand. The brightness and breeziness of the water tempted me to hire a boat and resume my explorations. I procured an old tub, with a short stump of a mast, which, being planted quite in the centre, gave the craft much the appearance of an inverted mushroom. I made for what I took to be, and what is, an island, lying long and low, some four or five miles over against the town. I sailed for half-an-hour directly before the wind, and at last found myself aground on the shelving beach of a quiet little cove. Such a dear little cove – so bright, so still, so warm, so remote from Chowderville, which lay in the distance, white and semi-circular! I leaped ashore, and dropped my anchor. Before me rose a steep cliff, crowned with an old ruined fort or tower. I made my way up, and round to the landward entrance. The fort is a hollow old shell; looking upwards, from the beach, you see the harmless blue sky through the gaping loopholes. Its interior is choked with rocks and brambles and masses of fallen masonry. I scrambled up to the parapet, and obtained a noble sea-view. Beyond the broad bay I saw the miniature town and country mapped out before me; and on the other hand, I saw the infinite Atlantic – over which, by the by, all the pretty things are brought from Paris. I spent the whole afternoon in wandering hither and thither on the hills that encircle the little cove in which I had landed, heedless of the minutes and the miles, watching the sailing clouds and the flitting, gleaming sails, listening to the musical attrition of the tidal pebbles, passing the time anyhow. The only particular sensation I remember was that of being ten years old again, together with a general impression of Saturday afternoon, of the liberty to go in wading or even swimming, and of the prospect of limping home in the dusk with a wondrous story of having almost caught a turtle. When I returned I found – but I know very well what I found, and I need hardly repeat it here for my mortification. Heaven knows I never was a practical character. What thought I about the tide? There lay the old tub, high and dry, with the rusty anchor protruding from the flat green stones and the shallow puddles left by the receding wave. Moving the boat an inch, much more a dozen yards, was quite beyond my strength. I slowly reascended the cliff, to see if from its summit any help was discernible. None was within sight, and I was about to go down again, in profound dejection, when I saw a trim little sail-boat shoot out from behind a neighbouring bluff, and advance along the shore. I quickened pace. On reaching the beach I found the newcomer standing out about a hundred yards. The man at the helm appeared to regard me with some interest. With a mute prayer that his disposition might not be hostile – he didn't look like a wild islander – I invited him by voice and gesture to make for a little point of rocks a short distance above us, where I proceeded to join him. I told him my story, and he readily took me aboard. He was a civil old gentleman, of the seafaring sort, who appeared to be cruising about in the evening-breeze for his pleasure. On landing I visited the proprietor of my old tub, related my misadventure, and offered to pay damages if the boat shall turn out in the morning to have sustained any. Meanwhile, I suppose, it is held secure against the next tidal revolution, however violent.

But for my old gentleman. I have decidedly picked up an acquaintance, if not made a friend. I gave him a very good cigar, and before we reached home we had become thoroughly intimate. In exchange for my cigar he gave me his name; and there was that in his tone which seemed to imply that I had by no means the worst of the exchange. His name is Richard Quarterman, 'though most people,' he added, 'call me Cap'n, for respect.' He then proceeded to inquire my own titles and pretensions. I told him no lies, but I told him only half the truth; and if he chooses to indulge mentally in any romantic understatements, why, he is welcome, and bless his simple heart! The fact is, I have simply broken with the past. I have decided, coolly and calmly, as I believe, that it is necessary to my success, or, at any rate, to my happiness, to abjure for a while my conventional self, and to assume a simple, natural character. How can a man be simple and natural who is known to have a large income? That is the supreme curse. It's bad enough to have it; to be known to have it, to be known only because you have it, is most damnable. I suppose I am too proud to be successfully rich. Let me see how poverty will serve my turn. I have taken a fresh start – I have determined to stand upon my merits. If they fail me I shall fall back upon my dollars, but with God's help I will test them, and see what kind of stuff I am made of. To be young, strong and poor – such in this blessed nineteenth century, is the great basis of solid success. I have resolved to take at least one brief draught from the founts of inspiration of my time. I replied to Captain Quarterman with such reservations as a brief survey of these principles dictated. What a luxury to pass in a poor man's mind for his brother! I begin to respect myself. Thus much the Captain knows: that I am an educated man, with a taste for painting; that I have come hither for the purpose of studying and sketching coast-scenery; toning myself up with the sea air. I have reason to believe, moreover, that he suspects me of limited means and of being of a very frugal mind. Amen! *Vogue la galère!*[4] But the point of my story is in his very hospitable offer of lodgings – I had been telling him of my want of success in the morning in the pursuit of the same. He is a queer mixture of the gentleman of the old school and the hot-headed merchant-captain.

'Young man,' said he, after taking several meditative puffs of his cigar, 'I don't see the point of your living in a tavern when there are folks about you with more house-room than they know what to do with. A tavern is only half a house, just as one of these new-fashioned screw-propellers is only half a ship. Suppose you walk round and take a look at my place. I own quite a respectable tenement over yonder to the left of the town. Do you see that old wharf with the tumble-down warehouses, and the long row of elms behind it? I live right in the midst of the elms. We have the sweetest little garden in the world, stretching down to the water's edge. It's all as quiet as anything can be, short of a churchyard. The back windows, you know, overlook the harbour; and you can see twenty miles up the bay, and fifty miles out to sea. You can paint to yourself there the livelong day, with no more fear of intrusion than if you were out yonder at the light-ship. There's no one but myself and my daughter, who's a perfect lady, sir. She teaches music in a young ladies' school. You see, money's an object, as they say. We have never taken boarders yet, because none ever came in our track; but I guess we can learn the ways. I suppose you've boarded before; you can put us up to a thing or two.'

There was something so kindly and honest in the old man's weather-beaten face, something so friendly in his address, that I forthwith struck a bargain with him, subject to his daughter's approval. I am to have her answer to-morrow. This same daughter strikes me as rather a dark spot in the picture. Teacher in a young ladies' school – probably the establishment of which Mrs Monkhouse spoke to me. I suppose she's over thirty. I think I know the species.

June 12th, A.M. – I have really nothing to do but to scribble. 'Barkis is willing.'[5] Captain Quarterman brought me word this morning that his daughter makes no objection. I am to report this evening; but I shall send my slender baggage in an hour or two.

P.M. – Here I am, domiciled, almost domesticated. The house is less than a mile from the inn, and reached by a very pleasant road, which skirts the harbour. At about six o'clock I presented myself; Captain Quarterman had described the place. A very civil old negress admitted me, and ushered me into the garden, where I found my friends watering their flowers. The old man was in his house-coat and slippers – he gave me a cordial welcome. There is something delightfully easy in his manners – and in Miss Quarterman's, too for that matter. She received me very nicely. The late Mrs Quarterman was probably a superior being. As for the young lady's being thirty, she is about twenty-four. She wore a fresh white dress, with a blue ribbon on her neck, and a rosebud in her button-hole – or whatever corresponds to the button-hole on the feminine bosom. I thought I discerned in this costume, a vague intention of courtesy, of gaiety, of celebrating my arrival. I don't believe Miss Quarterman wears white muslin every day. She shook hands with me, and made me a pleasing little speech about their taking me in. 'We have never had any inmates before,' said she; 'and we are consequently new to the business. I don't know what you expect. I hope you don't expect a great deal. You must ask for anything you want. If we can give it, we shall be very glad to do so; if we can't, I give you warning that we shall simply tell you so.' Brava, Miss Quarterman! The best of it is, that she is decidedly beautiful – and in the grand manner; tall, and with roundness in her lines. What is the orthodox description of a pretty girl? – white and red? Miss Quarterman is not a pretty girl, she is a handsome woman. She leaves an impression of black and red; that is, she is a brunette with colour. She has a great deal of wavy black hair, which encircles her head like a dusky glory, a smoky halo. Her eyebrows, too, are black, but her eyes themselves are of a rich blue gray, the colour of those slate-cliffs which I saw yesterday, weltering under the tide. She has perfect teeth, and her smile is almost unnaturally brilliant. Her chin is surpassingly round. She has a capital movement, too, and looked uncommonly well as she strolled in the garden-path with a big spray of geranium lifted to her nose. She has very little to say, apparently; but when she speaks, it is to the point, and if the point suggests it, she doesn't hesitate to laugh very musically. Indeed, if she is not talkative, it is not from timidity. Is it from indifference? Time will elucidate this, as well as other mysteries. I cling to the hypothesis that she is amiable. She is, moreover, intelligent; she is probably fond of keeping herself *to* herself, as the phrase is, and is even, possibly, very proud. She is, in short, a woman of character. There you are, Miss Quarterman, at as full length as I can paint you. After tea she gave us some music in the parlour. I confess that I was more taken with the picture of the dusky little room, lighted by the single candle on the piano, and by her stately way of sitting at the instrument, than by the quality of her playing, though that is evidently high.

June 18th. – I have now been here almost a week. I occupy two very pleasant rooms. My painting-room is a large and rather bare apartment, with a very good north-light. I have decked it out with a few old prints and sketches, and have already grown very fond of it. When I had disposed my artistic odds and ends so as to make it look as much like a studio as possible, I called in my hosts. The Captain snuffed about, silently, for some moments, and then inquired hopefully if I had ever tried my hand at a ship. On learning that I had not yet got to ships, he relapsed into a prudent reserve. His daughter smiled and questioned, very graciously, and called everything beautiful and delightful; which rather disappointed me, as I had taken her to be a woman of some originality. She is rather a puzzle. Or is she, indeed, a very commonplace person, and the fault in me, who am for ever taking women to mean a great deal more than their Maker intended? Regarding Miss Quarterman I have collected a few facts. She is not twenty-four, but twenty-seven years old. She has taught music ever since she was twenty, in a large boarding-school just out of the town, where she originally obtained her education. Her salary in this establishment, which is, I believe, a tolerably flourishing one, and the proceeds of a few additional lessons, constitute the chief revenues of the household. But the Captain fortunately owns his house, and his needs and habits are of the simplest kind. What does he or his daughter know of the great worldly theory of necessities, the great worldly scale of pleasures? The young lady's luxuries are a subscription to the circulating library, and an occasional walk on the beach, which, like one of Miss Brontë's heroines, she paces in company with an old Newfoundland dog. I am afraid she is sadly ignorant. She reads nothing but novels. I am bound to believe, however, that she has derived from the perusal of these works a certain second-hand acquaintance with life. 'I read all the novels I can get,' she said yesterday; 'but I only like the good ones. I do so like *The Missing Bride*, which I have just finished.' I must set her to work at some of the masters. I should like some of those fretful daughters of gold, in New York, to see how this woman lives. I wish, too, that half a dozen of *ces messieurs* of the clubs might take a peep at the present way of life of their humble servant. We breakfast at eight o'clock. Immediately afterwards Miss Quarterman, in a shabby old bonnet and shawl, starts off to school. If the weather is fine the Captain goes a-fishing, and I am left quite to my own devices. Twice I have accompanied the old man. The second time I was lucky enough to catch a big blue-fish, which we had for dinner. The Captain is an excellent specimen of the pure navigator, with his loose blue clothes, his ultra-divergent legs, his crisp white hair, his jolly thick-skinned visage. He comes of a sea-faring English race. There is more or less of the ship's cabin in the general aspect of this antiquated house. I have heard the wind whistle about its walls, on two or three occasions, in true mid-ocean style. And then the illusion is heightened, somehow or other, by the extraordinary intensity of the light. My painting-room is a grand observatory of the clouds. I sit by the half-hour watching them sail past my high uncurtained windows. At the back part of the room something tells you that they belong to an ocean-sky; and there, in truth, as you draw nearer, you behold the vast gray complement of sea. This quarter of the town is perfectly quiet. Human activity seems to have passed over it, never again to return, and to have left a deposit of melancholy resignation. The streets are clean, bright and airy; but this fact only deepens the impression of vanished uses. It seems to say that the protecting heavens look down on their decline and can't help them. There is something ghostly in the perpetual stillness. We frequently hear the rattling of the yards and the issuing of orders on the barks and schooners anchored out in the harbour.

June 28th. – My experiment works far better than I had hoped. I am thoroughly at my ease; my peace of mind quite passeth understanding. I work diligently; I have none but pleasant thoughts. The past has almost lost its bitterness. For a week, now, I have been out sketching daily. The Captain carries me to a certain point on the shore of the bay, I disembark and strike across the uplands to a spot where I have taken a kind of tryst with a particular effect of rock and shadow, which has been tolerably faithful to its appointment. Here I set up my easel, and paint till sunset. Then I retrace my steps and meet the boat. I am in every way much encouraged; the horizon of my work grows perceptibly wider. And then I am inexpressibly happy in the conviction that I am not wholly unfit for a life of (moderate) industry and (comparative) privation. I am quite in love with my poverty, if I may call it so. And why should I not? At this rate I don't spend eight hundred a year.

July 12th. – We have been having a week of bad weather: constant rain, night and day. This is certainly at once the brightest and the blackest spot in New England. The skies can smile, assuredly, but they have also lachrymal moods. I have been painting rather languidly, and at a great disadvantage, at my window. . . .Through all this pouring and pattering Miss Miriam – her name is Miriam, and it exactly fits her – sallies forth to her pupils. She envelops her beautiful head in a great woollen hood, her beautiful figure in a kind of feminine mackintosh; her feet she puts into heavy clogs, and over the whole she balances a cotton umbrella. When she comes home, with the rain-drops glistening on her rich cheeks and her dark lashes, her cloak bespattered with mud and her hands red with the cool damp, she is a very honourable figure. I never fail to make her a very low bow, for which she repays me with a familiar, but not a vulgar, nod. The working-day side of her character is what especially pleases me in Miss Quarterman. This holy working-dress sits upon her with the fine effect of an antique drapery. Little use has she for whale-bones and furbelows. What a poetry there is, after all, in red hands! I kiss yours, Mademoiselle. I do so because you are self-helpful; because you earn your living; because you are honest, simple, and ignorant (for a sensible woman, that is); because you speak and act to the point; because, in short, you are so unlike – certain of your sisters.

July 16th. – On Monday it cleared up generously. When I went to my window, on rising, I found sky and sea looking, for their brightness and freshness, like a clever English water-colour. The ocean is of a deep purple blue; above it, the pure, bright sky looks pale, though it hangs over the island horizon a canopy of denser tissue. Here and there on the dark, breezy water gleams the white cap of a wave, or flaps the white cloak of a fishing-boat. I have been sketching sedulously; I have discovered, within a couple of miles' walk, a large, lonely pond, set in a really grand landscape of barren rocks and grassy slopes. At one extremity is a broad outlook on the open sea; at the other, buried in the foliage of an apple-orchard, stands an old haunted-looking farm-house. To the west of the pond is a wide expanse of rock and grass, of sand and marsh. The sheep browse over it – poorly – as they might upon a Highland moor. Except a few stunted firs and cedars, there is not a tree in sight. When I want shade I have to look for it in the shelter of one of the large stones which hold up to the sun a shoulder coated with delicate gray, figured over with fine, pale, sea-green moss, or else in one of the long, shallow dells where a tangle of blackberry-bushes hedges about a pool that reflects the sky. I am giving my best attention to a plain brown hillside, and trying to make it look like something in nature; and as we have now had the same clear sky for several days, I have almost finished quite a satisfactory little study. I go forth immediately after breakfast. Miss Quarterman supplies me with a little parcel of bread and cold meat, which at the noonday hour, in my sunny solitude, within sight of the slumbering ocean, I voraciously convey to my lips with my discoloured fingers. At seven o'clock I return to tea, at which repast we each tell the story of our day's work. For poor Miss Quarterman it is always the same story: a wearisome round of visits to the school, and to the houses of the mayor, the parson, the butcher, the baker, whose young ladies, of course, all receive instruction on the piano. But she doesn't complain, nor, indeed, does she look very weary. When she has put on a fresh light dress for tea, and arranged her hair anew, and with these improvements flits about with the quiet hither and thither of her gentle footstep, preparing our evening meal, peeping into the teapot, cutting the solid loaf – or when, sitting down on the low door-step, she reads out select scraps from the evening-paper – or else, when tea being over, she folds her arms (an attitude which becomes her mightily) and, still sitting on the door-step, gossips away the evening in comfortable idleness, while her father and I indulge in the fragrant pipe and watch the lights shining out, one by one, in different quarters of the darkening bay: at these moments she is as pretty, as cheerful, as careless as it becomes a sensible woman to be. What a pride the Captain takes in his daughter, and she, in return, how perfect is her devotion to the old man! He is proud of her grace, of her tact, of her good sense, of her wit, such as it is. He believes her to be the most accomplished of women. He waits upon her as if, instead of his old familiar Miriam, she were some new arrival – say a daughter-in-law lately brought home. And à propos of daughters-in-law, if I were his own son he could not be kinder to me. They are certainly – nay, why should I not say it? – we are certainly a very happy little household. Will it last forever? I say we, because both father and daughter have given me a hundred assurances – he direct, and she, if I don't flatter myself, after the manner of her sex, indirect – that I am already a valued friend. It is natural enough that they should like me, because I have tried to please them. The way to the old man's heart is through a studied consideration of his daughter. He knows, I imagine, that I admire Miss Quarterman, but if I should at any time fall below the mark of ceremony, I should have an account to settle with him. All this is as it should be. When people have to economise with the dollars and cents, they have a right to be splendid in their feelings. I have done my best to be nice to the stately Miriam without making love to her. That I haven't done *that*, however, is a fact which I do not, in any degree, set down here to my credit; for I would defy the most impertinent of men (whoever he is) to forget himself with this young lady. Those animated eyes have a power to keep people in their place. I mention the circumstances simply because in future years, when my charming friend shall have become a distant shadow, it will be pleasant, in turning over these pages, to find written testimony to a number of points which I shall be apt to charge solely upon my imagination. I wonder whether Miss Quarterman, in days to come, referring to the tables of her memory for some trivial matter-of-fact, some prosaic date or half-buried landmark, will also encounter this little secret of ours, as I may call it – will decipher an old faint note to this effect, overlaid with the memoranda of intervening years. Of course she will. Sentiment aside, she is a woman of a retentive faculty. Whether she forgives or not I know not; but she certainly doesn't forget. Doubtless, virtue is its own reward; but there is a double satisfaction in being polite to a person on whom it tells!

Another reason for my pleasant relations with the Captain is, that I afford him a chance to rub up his rusty worldly lore and trot out his little scraps of old-fashioned reading, some of which are very curious. It is a great treat for him to spin his threadbare yarns over again to a submissive listener. These warm July evenings, in the sweet-smelling garden, are just the proper setting for his traveller's tales. An odd enough understanding subsists between us on this point. Like many gentlemen of his calling, the Captain is harassed by an irresistible desire to romance, even on the least promising themes; and it is vastly amusing to observe how he will auscultate, as it were, his auditor's inmost mood, to ascertain whether it is in condition to be practised upon. Sometimes his artless fables don't 'take' at all: they are very pretty, I conceive, in the deep and briny well of the Captain's fancy, but they won't bear being transplanted into the dry climate of my land-bred mind. At other times, the auditor being in a dreamy, sentimental, and altogether unprincipled mood, he will drink the old man's salt-water by the bucketful and feel none the worse for it. Which is the worse, wilfully to tell, or wilfully to believe, a pretty little falsehood which will not hurt any one? I suppose you can't believe wilfully; you only pretend to believe. My part of the game, therefore, is certainly as bad as the Captain's. Perhaps I take kindly to his beautiful perversions of fact because I am myself engaged in one, because I am sailing under false colours of the deepest dye. I wonder whether my friends have any suspicion of the real state of the case. How should they? I take for granted that I play my little part pretty well. I am delighted to find it comes so easy. I do not mean that I find little difficulty in foregoing my old luxuries and pleasures – for to these, thank heaven, I was not so indissolubly wedded that one wholesome shock could not loosen my bonds – but that I manage more cleverly than I expected to stifle those innumerable tacit allusions which might serve effectually to belie my character.

Sunday, July 20th. – This has been a very pleasant day for me; although in it, of course, I have done no manner of work. I had this morning a delightful *tête-à-tête* with my hostess. She had sprained her ankle coming down stairs, and so, instead of going forth to Sunday-school and to meeting, she was obliged to remain at home on the sofa. The Captain, who is of a very punctilious piety, went off alone. When I came into the parlour, as the church-bells were ringing, Miss Quarterman asked me if I never went to a place of worship.

'Never when there is anything better to do at home,' said I.

'What is better than going to church?' she asked, with charming simplicity.

She was reclining on the sofa, with her foot on a pillow and her Bible in her lap. She looked by no means afflicted at having to be absent from divine service; and, instead of answering her question, I took the liberty of telling her so.

'I *am* sorry to be absent,' said she. 'You know it's my only festival in the week.'

'So you look upon it as a festival.'

'Isn't it a pleasure to meet one's acquaintance? I confess I am never deeply interested in the sermon, and I very much dislike teaching the children; but I like wearing my best bonnet, and singing in the choir, and walking part of the way home with – '

'With whom?'

'With anyone who offers to walk with me.'

'With Mr Prendergast, for instance,' said I.

Mr Prendergast is a young lawyer in the village, who calls here once a week, and whose attentions to Miss Quarterman have been remarked.

'Yes,' she answered, 'Mr Prendergast will do as an instance.'

'How he will miss you!'

'I suppose he will. We sing off the same book. What are you laughing at? He kindly permits me to hold the book, while he stands with his hands in his pockets. Last Sunday I quite lost patience. "Mr Prendergast," said I, "do hold the book! Where are your manners?" He burst out laughing in the midst of the reading. He will certainly have to hold the book to-day.'

'What a masterful soul he is! I suppose he will call after meeting.'

'Perhaps he will, I hope so.'

'I hope he won't,' said I, frankly. 'I am going to sit down here and talk to you, and I wish our conversation not to be interrupted.'

'Have you anything particular to say?'

'Nothing so particular as Mr Prendergast, perhaps.'

Miss Quarterman has a very pretty affectation of being more matter-of-fact than she really is.

'His rights, then,' she remarked, 'are paramount to yours.'

'Ah, you admit that he has rights?'

'Not at all. I simply assert that you have none.'

'I beg your pardon. I have claims which I mean to enforce. I have a claim upon your undivided attention when I pay you a morning-call.'

'You have had all the attention I am capable of. Have I been so very rude?'

'Not so very rude, perhaps, but rather inconsiderate. You have been sighing for the company of a third person, whom you can't expect me to care much about.'

'Why not, pray? If I, a lady, can put up with Mr Prendergast's society, why shouldn't you, one of his own sex?'

'Because he is so outrageously conceited. You, as a lady, or at any rate as a woman, like conceited men.'

'Ah, yes; I have no doubt that I, as a woman, have all kinds of weak tastes. That's a very old story.'

'Admit, at any rate, that our friend is conceited.'

'Admit it! Why, I have said so a hundred times. I have told him so.'

'Indeed, it has come to that, then?'

'To what, pray?'

'To that critical point in the friendship of a lady and gentleman when they bring against each other all kinds of delightful accusations and rebukes. Take care, Miss Quarterman! A couple of intelligent New-Englanders, of opposite sexes, young, unmarried, are pretty far gone, when they begin to scan each other's faults. So you told Mr Prendergast that he is conceited? And I suppose you added that he was also dreadfully satirical and sceptical? What was his rejoinder? Let me see. Did he ever tell you that you were a wee bit affected?'

'No; he left that for you to say, in this very ingenious manner. Thank you, sir.'

'He left it for me to deny, which is a great deal prettier. Do you think the manner ingenious?'

'I think the matter, considering the day and hour, very profane, Mr Locksley. Suppose you go away and let me peruse my Bible.'

'Meanwhile what shall I do?'

'Go and read yours, if you have one.'

'My Bible,' I said, 'is the female mind.'

I was nevertheless compelled to retire, with the promise of a second audience in half-an-hour. Poor Miss Quarterman owes it to her conscience to read a certain number of chapters. In what a terrible tradition she has been reared, and what an edifying spectacle is the piety of women! Women find a place for everything in their commodious little minds, just as they do in their wonderfully sub-divided trunks when they go on a journey. I have no doubt that this young lady stows away her religion in a corner, just as she does her Sunday-bonnet – and, when the proper moment comes, draws it forth, and reflects, while she puts it on before the glass and blows away the strictly imaginary dust (for what worldly impurity can penetrate through half a dozen layers of cambric and tissue-paper?): 'Dear me, what a comfort it is to have a nice, fresh holiday-creed!' – When I returned to the parlour Miriam was still sitting with her Bible in her lap. Somehow or other I no longer felt in the mood for jesting; so I asked her, without chaffing, what she had been reading, and she answered me in the same tone. She inquired how I had spent my half-hour.

'In thinking good Sabbath thoughts,' I said. 'I have been walking in the garden.' And then I spoke my mind. 'I have been thanking heaven that it has led me, a poor friendless wanderer, into so peaceful an anchorage.'

'Are you so very poor and friendless?'

'Did you ever hear of an art-student who was not poor? Upon my word, I have yet to sell my first picture. Then, as for being friendless, there are not five people in the world who really care for me.'

'*Really* care? I am afraid you look too close. And then I think five good friends is a very large number. I think myself very well-off with half-a-one. But if you are friendless, it's probably your own fault.'

'Perhaps it is,' said I, sitting down in the rocking-chair; 'and also, perhaps it isn't. Have you found me so very difficult to live with? Haven't you, on the contrary, found me rather sociable?'

She folded her arms, and quietly looked at me for a moment, before answering. I shouldn't wonder if I blushed a little.

'You want a lump of sugar, Mr Locksley; that's the long and short of it. I haven't given you one since you have been here. How you must have suffered! But it's a pity you couldn't have waited a little longer, instead of beginning to put out your paws and bark. For an artist, you are very slap-dash. Men never know how to wait. "Have I found you very difficult to live with? haven't I found you sociable?" Perhaps, after all, considering what I have in my mind, it is as well that you asked for your lump of sugar. I have found you very indulgent. You let us off easily, but you wouldn't like us a bit if you didn't pity us. Don't I go deep? Sociable? ah, well, no – decidedly not! You are entirely too particular. You are considerate of me, because you know that I know that you are so. There's the rub, you see: I know that you know that I know it!

Don't interrupt me; I am going to be striking. I want you to understand why I don't consider you sociable. You call poor Mr Prendergast conceited; but, really, I believe he has more humility than you. He envies my father and me – thinks us so cultivated. You don't envy anyone, and yet I don't think you're a saint. You treat us kindly because you think virtue in a lowly station ought to be encouraged. Would you take the same amount of pains for a person you thought your equal, a person equally averse with yourself to being under an obligation? There are differences. Of course it's very delightful to fascinate people. Who wouldn't? There is no harm in it, as long as the fascinator doesn't set up for a public benefactor. If I were a man, a clever man like yourself, who had seen the world, who was not to be dazzled and encouraged, but to be listened to, counted with, would you be equally amiable? It will perhaps seem absurd to you, and it will certainly seem egotistical, but I consider myself sociable, for all that I have only a couple of friends – my father and Miss Blankenberg. That is, I mingle with people without any *arrière-pensée*.[6] Of course the people I see are mainly women. Not that I wish you to do so: on the contrary, if the contrary is agreeable to you. But I don't believe you mingle in the same way with men. You may ask me what I know about it! Of course I know nothing; I simply guess. When I have done, indeed, I mean to beg your pardon for all I have said; but until then, give me a chance. You are incapable of exposing yourself to be bored, whereas I take it as my waterproof takes the rain. You have no idea what heroism I show in the exercise of my profession! Every day I have occasion to pocket my pride and to stifle my sense of the ridiculous – of which of course you think I haven't a bit. It is for instance a constant vexation to me to be poor. It makes me frequently hate rich women; it makes me despise poor ones. I don't know whether you suffer acutely from the smallness of your own means; but if you do, I dare say you shun rich men. I don't, I like to bleed; to go into rich people's houses, and to be very polite to the ladies, especially if they are very much dressed, very ignorant and vulgar. All women are like me in this respect, and all men more or less like you. That is, after all, the text of my sermon. Compared with us it has always seemed to me that you are arrant cowards – that we alone are brave. To be sociable you must have a great deal of patience. You are too fine a gentleman. Go and teach school, or open a corner-grocery, or sit in a law-office all day, waiting for clients: then you will be sociable. As yet you are only selfish. It *is* your own fault if people don't care for you; you don't care for them. That you should be indifferent to their good opinion is all very well; but you don't care for their indifference. You are amiable, you are very kind, and you are also very lazy. You consider that you are working now, don't you? Many persons would not call it work.'

It was now certainly my turn to fold my arms.

'And now,' added my companion, as I did so, 'be so good as to excuse me.'

'This was certainly worth waiting for,' said I. 'I don't know what answer to make. My head swims. Sugar, did you say? I don't know whether you have been giving me sugar or vitriol. So you advise me to open a corner-grocery, do you?'

'I advise you to do something that will make you a little less satirical. You had better marry, for instance.'

'*Je ne demande pas mieux*. Will you have me? I can't afford it.'

'Marry a rich woman.'

I shook my head.

'Why not?' asked Miss Quarterman. 'Because people would accuse you of being mercenary? What of that? I mean to marry the first rich man who offers. Do you know that I am tired of living alone in this weary old way, teaching little girls their scales, and turning and patching my dresses? I mean to marry the first man who offers.'

'Even if he is poor?'

'Even if he is poor and has a hump.'

'I am your man, then. Would you take me if I were to offer?'

'Try and see.'

'Must I get upon my knees?'

'No, you needn't even do that. Am I not on mine? It would be too fine an irony. Remain as you are, lounging back in your chair, with your thumbs in your waistcoat.'

If I were writing a romance now, instead of transcribing facts, I would say that I knew not what might have happened at this juncture had not the door opened and admitted the Captain and Mr Prendergast. The latter was in the highest spirits.

'How are you, Miss Miriam? So you have been breaking your leg, eh? How are you, Mr Locksley? I wish I were a doctor now. Which is it, right or left?'

In this simple fashion he made himself agreeable to Miss Miriam. He stopped to dinner and talked without ceasing. Whether our hostess had talked herself out in her very animated address to myself an hour before, or whether she preferred to oppose no obstacle to Mr Prendergast's fluency, or whether she was indifferent to him, I know not; but she held her tongue with that easy grace, that charming tacit intimation of 'We could if we would,' of which she is so perfect a mistress. This very interesting woman has a number of pretty traits in common with her town-bred sisters; only, whereas in these they are laboriously acquired, in her they are richly natural. I am sure that, if I were to plant her in Madison Square to-morrow, she would, after one quick, all-compassing glance, assume the *nil admirari*[7] in a manner to drive the finest lady of them all to despair. Prendergast is a man of excellent intentions but no haste. Two or three times I looked at Miss Quarterman to see what impression his sallies were making upon her. They seemed to produce none whatever. But I know better, *moi*. Not one of them escaped her. But I suppose she said to herself that her impressions on this point were no business of mine. Perhaps she was right. It is a disagreeable word to use of a woman you admire; but I can't help fancying that she has been a little soured. By what? Who shall say? By some old love-affair, perhaps.

July 24th. – This evening the Captain and I took a half-hour's turn about the port. I asked him frankly, as a friend, whether Prendergast wants to marry his daughter.

'I guess he does,' said the old man, 'and yet I hope he don't. You know what he is: he's smart, promising, and already sufficiently well-off. But somehow he isn't for a man what my Miriam is for a female.'

'That he isn't!' said I; 'and honestly, Captain Quarterman, I don't know who is—'

'Unless it be yourself,' said the Captain.

'Thank you. I know a great many ways in which Mr Prendergast is more worthy of her than I.'

'And I know one in which you are more worthy of her than he – that is in being what we used to call one of the old sort.'

'Miss Quarterman made him sufficiently welcome in her quiet way on Sunday,' I rejoined.

'Oh, she respects him,' said Quarterman. 'As she's situated, she might marry him on that. You see, she's weary of hearing little girls drum on the piano. With her ear for music,' added the Captain, 'I wonder she has borne it so long.'

'She is certainly meant for better things,' said I.

'Well,' answered the Captain, who has an honest habit of deprecating your agreement when it occurs to him that he has obtained it for sentiments which fall somewhat short of the stoical – 'well,' said he, with a very dry, edifying expression, 'she's born to do her duty. We are all of us born for that.'

'Sometimes our duty is rather dismal,' said I.

'So it be; but what's the help for it? I don't want to die without seeing my daughter provided for. What she makes by teaching is a pretty slim subsistence. There was a time when I thought she was going to be fixed for life, but it all blew over. There was a young fellow here, from down Boston way, who came about as near to it as you can come when you actually don't. He and Miriam were excellent friends. One day Miriam came up to me, and looked me in the face, and told me she had passed her word.

'"Who to?" says I, though of course I knew, and Miriam told me as much. "When do you expect to marry?" I asked.

'"When Alfred" – his name was Alfred – "grows rich enough," says she.

'"When will that be?"

'"It may not be for years," said poor Miriam.

'A whole year passed, and, so far as I could see, the young man hadn't accumulated very much. He was for ever running to and fro between this place and Boston. I asked no questions, because I knew that my poor girl wished it so. But at last, one day, I began to think it was time to take an observation, and see whereabouts we stood.

'"Has Alfred made his little pile yet," I asked.

'"I don't know, father," said Miriam.

'"When are you to be married?"

'"Never!" said my poor little girl, and burst into tears. "Please ask me no questions," said she. "Our engagement is over. Ask me no questions."

'"Tell me one thing," said I: "Where is that d—d scoundrel who has broken my daughter's heart?"

'You should have seen the look she gave me.

'"Broken my heart, sir? You are very much mistaken. I don't know who you mean."

'"I mean Alfred Bannister," said I. That was his name.

'"I believe Mr Bannister is in China," says Miriam, as grand as the Queen of Sheba. And there was an end of it. I never learnt the ins and outs of it. I have been told that Bannister is amassing considerable wealth in the China-trade.'

August 7th. – I have made no entry for more than a fortnight. They tell me I have been very ill; and I find no difficulty in believing them. I suppose I took cold, sitting out so late, sketching. At all events, I have had a mild intermittent fever. I have slept so much, however, that the time has seemed rather short. I have been tenderly nursed by this kind old mariner, his daughter, and his black domestic. God bless them, one and all! I say his daughter, because old Cynthia informs me that for half-an-hour one morning, at dawn, after a night during which I had been very feeble, Miss Quarterman relieved guard at my bedside, while I lay sleeping like a log. It is very jolly to see sky and ocean once again. I have got myself into my easy-chair, by the best window, with my shutters closed and the lattice open; and here I sit with my book on my knee, scratching away feebly enough. Now and then I peep from my cool, dark sick-chamber out into the world of light. High noon at midsummer – what a spectacle! There are no clouds in the sky, no waves on the ocean, the sun has it all to himself. To look long at the garden makes the eyes water. And we – 'Hobbs, Nobbs, Stokes and Nokes'[8] – propose to paint that luminosity. *Allons donc!*

The handsomest of women has just tapped, and come in with a plate of early peaches. The peaches are of a gorgeous colour and plumpness; but Miss Quarterman looks pale and thin. The hot weather doesn't agree with her, and besides she is overworked.

Damn her drudgery! Of course I thanked her warmly for her attentions during my illness. She disclaims all gratitude, and refers me to her father and the dusky Cynthia.

'I allude more especially,' I said, 'to that little hour at the end of a weary night when you stole in, like a kind of moral Aurora, and drove away the shadows from my brain. That morning, you know, I began to get better.'

'It was indeed a very little hour,' said Miss Quarterman, colouring. 'It was about ten minutes.' And then she began to scold me for presuming to touch a pen during my convalescence. She laughs at me, indeed, for keeping a diary at all. 'Of all things, a sentimental man is the most despicable!' she exclaimed.

I confess I was somewhat nettled – the thrust seemed gratuitous.

'Of all things a woman without sentiment is the most wanting in sweetness.'

'Sentiment and sweetness are all very well when you have time for them,' said Miss Quarterman. 'I haven't. I am not rich enough. Good morning!'

Speaking of another woman, I would say that she flounced out of the room. But such was the gait of Juno[9] when she moved stiffly over the grass from where Paris stood with Venus holding the apple, gathering up her divine vestment and leaving the others to guess at her face.

Juno has just come back to say that she forgot what she came for half-an-hour ago. What will I be pleased to like for dinner?

'I have just been writing in my diary that you flounced out of the room,' said I.

'Have you, indeed? Now you can write that I have bounced in. There's a nice cold chicken donwstairs,' etc. etc.

August 14th. – This afternoon I sent for a light vehicle, and treated Miss Quarterman to a drive. We went successively over the three beaches. What a spin we had coming home! I shall never forget the breezy trot over Weston's Beach. The tide was very low, and we had the whole glittering, weltering strand to ourselves. There was a heavy blow last night, which has not yet subsided, and the waves have been lashed into a magnificent fury. Trot, trot, trot, trot, we trundled over the hard sand. The sound of the horse's hoofs rang out sharp against the monotone of the thunderous surf, as we drew nearer and nearer to the long line of the cliffs. At our left, almost from the zenith of the pale evening-sky to the high western horizon of the tumultuous dark-green sea, was suspended, so to speak, one of those gorgeous vertical sunsets that Turner sometimes painted. It was a splendid confusion of purple and green and gold – the clouds flying and floating in the wind like the folds of a mighty banner borne by some triumphal fleet which had rounded the curve of the globe. As we reached the point where the cliffs begin I pulled up, and we remained for some time looking at their long, diminishing, crooked perspective, blue and dun as it receded, with the white surge playing at their feet.

August 17th. – This evening, as I lighted my bedroom-candle, I saw that the Captain had something to say to me. So I waited below until my host and his daughter had performed their usual osculation, and the latter had given me that confiding hand-shake which I never fail to extract.

'Prendergast has got his discharge,' said the old man, when he heard his daughter's door close.

'What do you mean?'

He pointed with his thumb to the room above, where we heard, through the thin partition, the movement of Miss Quarterman's light step.

'You mean that he has proposed to Miss Miriam?'

The Captain nodded.

'And has been refused?'

'Flat.'

'Poor fellow!' said I, very honestly. 'Did he tell you himself?'

'Yes, with tears in his eyes. He wanted me to speak for him. I told him it was no use. Then he began to say hard things of my poor girl.'

'What kind of things?'

'A pack of falsehoods. He says she has no heart. She has promised always to regard him as a friend; it's more than I will, hang him!'

'Poor fellow!' said I; and now, as I write, I can only repeat considering what a hope was here disappointed, Poor fellow!

August 23rd. – I have been lounging about all day, thinking of it, dreaming of it, spooning over it, as they say. This is a decided waste of time. I think, accordingly, the best thing for me to do is to sit down and lay the ghost by writing out my little story.

On Thursday evening, Miss Quarterman happened to intimate that she had a holiday on the morrow, it being the birthday of the lady in whose establishment she teaches.

'There is to be a tea-party at four o'clock in the afternoon for the resident pupils and teachers,' Miriam said. 'Tea at four! what do you think of that? And then there is to be a speech-making by the smartest young lady. As my services are not required I propose to be absent. Suppose, father, you take us out in your boat. Will you come, Mr Locksley? We shall have a neat little picnic. Let us go over to old Fort Plunkett, across the bay. We will take our dinner with us, and send Cynthia to spend the day with her sister, and put the house-key in our pocket, and not come home till we please.'

I entered into the project with passion, and it was accordingly carried into execution the next morning, when – about ten o'clock – we pushed off from our little wharf at the garden-foot. It was a perfect summer's day; I can say no more for it; and we made a quiet run over to the point of our destination. I shall never forget the wondrous stillness which brooded over earth and water as we weighed anchor in the lee of my old friend – or old enemy – the ruined fort. The deep, translucent water reposed at the base of the warm sunlit cliff like a great basin of glass, which I half expected to hear shiver and crack as our keel ploughed through it. And how colour and sound stood out in the transparent air! How audibly the little ripples on the beach whispered to the open sky. How our irreverent voices seemed to jar upon the privacy of the little cove! The delicate rocks doubled themselves without a flaw in the clear, dark water. The gleaming white beach lay fringed with its deep deposits of odorous sea-weed, which looked like masses of black lace. The steep, straggling sides of the cliffs lifted their rugged angles against the burning blue of the sky. I remember, when Miss Quarterman stepped ashore and stood upon the beach, relieved against the cool darkness of a recess in the cliff, while her father and I busied ourselves with gathering up our baskets and fastening the anchor – I remember, I say, what a picture she made. There is a certain purity in the air of this place which I have never seen surpassed – a lightness, a brilliancy, a crudity, which allows perfect liberty of self-assertion to each individual object in the landscape. The prospect is ever more or less like a picture which lacks its final process, its reduction to unity. Miss Quarterman's figure, as she stood there on the beach, was almost *criarde*;[10] but how it animated the whole scene! Her light muslin dress, gathered up over her white petticoat, her little black mantilla, the blue veil which she had knotted about her neck, the little silken dome which she poised over her head in one gloved hand, while the other retained her crisp draperies, and which cast down upon her face a sharp circle of shade, where her cheerful eyes shone darkly and her parted lips said things I lost – these are some of the points I hastily noted.

'Young woman,' I cried out, over the water, 'I do wish you might know how pretty you look!'

'How do you know I don't?' she answered. 'I should think I might. You don't look so badly yourself. But it's not I; it's the aerial perspective.'

'Hang it – I am going to become profane!' I called out again.

'Swear ahead,' said the Captain.

'I am going to say you are infernally handsome.'

'Dear me! is that all?' cried Miss Quarterman, with a little light laugh which must have made the tutelar sirens of the cove ready to die with jealousy down in their submarine bowers.

By the time the Captain and I had landed our effects our companion had tripped lightly up the forehead of the cliff – in one place it is very retreating – and disappeared over its crown. She soon returned, with an intensely white pocket-handkerchief added to her other provocations, which she waved to us, as we trudged upward, carrying our baskets. When we stopped to take breath on the summit and wipe our foreheads, we of course rebuked her for roaming about idly with her parasol and gloves.

'Do you think I am going to take any trouble or do any work?' cried Miss Miriam, in the greatest good-humour. 'Is not this my holiday? I am not going to raise a finger, nor soil these beautiful gloves, for which I paid so much at Mr Dawson's at Chowderville.

After you have found a shady place for your provisions, I should like you to look for a spring. I am very thirsty.'

'Find the spring yourself, miss,' said her father. 'Mr Locksley and I have a spring in this basket. Take a pull, sir.'

And the Captain drew forth a stout black bottle.

'Give me a cup, and I will look for some water,' said Miriam. 'Only I'm so afraid of the snakes! If you hear a scream you may know it's a snake.'

'Screaming snakes!' said I; 'that's a new species.'

What cheap fun it all sounds now! As we looked about us shade seemed scarce, as it generally is in this region. But Miss Quarterman, like the very adroit and practical young person she is, for all that she would have me believe the contrary, immediately discovered flowing water in the shelter of a pleasant little dell, beneath a clump of firs. Hither, as one of the young gentlemen who imitate Tennyson would say, we brought our basket, he and I; while Miriam dipped the cup, and held it dripping to our thirsty lips, and laid the cloth, and on the grass disposed the platters round.[11] I should have to be a poet, indeed, to describe half the happiness and the silly sweetness and artless revelry of this interminable summer's day. We ate and drank and talked; we ate occasionally with our fingers, we drank out of the necks of our bottles, and we talked with our mouths full, as befits (and excuses) those who talk perfect nonsense. We told stories without the least point. The Captain and I made atrocious puns. I believe, indeed, that Miss Quarterman herself made one little punkin, as I called it. If there had been any superfluous representative of humanity present to notice the fact, I should say that we made fools of ourselves. But as there was no one to criticise us we were brilliant enough. I am conscious myself of having said several witty things, which Miss Quarterman understood: *in vino veritas*. The dear old Captain twanged the long bow indefatigably. The bright high sun dawdled above us, in the same place, and drowned the prospect with light and warmth. One of these days I mean to paint a picture which, in future ages, when my dear native land shall boast a national school of art, will hang in the Salon Carré of the great central museum (located, let us say, in Chicago) and recall to folks – or rather make them forget – Giorgione, Bordone, and Veronese: A Rural Festival;

three persons feasting under some trees; scene, nowhere in particular; time and hour, problematical. Female figure, a rich *brune*; young man reclining on his elbow; old man drinking. An empty sky, with no end of expression. The whole stupendous in colour, drawing, feeling. Artist uncertain; supposed to be Robinson, 1900.

After dinner the Captain began to look out across the bay, and, noticing the uprising of a little breeze, expressed a wish to cruise about for an hour or two. He proposed to us to walk along the shore to a point a couple of miles northward, and there meet the boat. His daughter having agreed to this proposition, he set off with the lightened hamper, and in less than half-an-hour we saw him standing out from shore. Miss Quarterman and I did not begin our walk for a long, long time. We sat and talked beneath the trees. At our feet a wide cleft in the hills – almost a glen – stretched down to the silent beach; beyond lay the familiar ocean-line. But, as many philosophers have observed, there is an end to all things. At last we got up. My companion remarked that, as the air was freshening, she supposed she ought to put on her shawl. I helped her to fold it into the proper shape, and then I placed it on her shoulders; it being an old shawl of faded red (Canton crape, I believe they call it), which I have seen very often. And then she tied her veil once more about her neck, and gave me her hat to hold, while she effected a partial redistribution of her hair-pins. By way of being humorous, I spun her hat round on my stick; at which she was kind enough to smile, as with downcast face and uplifted elbows she fumbled among her braids. And then she shook out the creases of her dress and drew on her gloves; and finally she said 'Well!' – that inevitable tribute to time and morality which follows upon even the mildest forms of dissipation. Very slowly it was that we wandered down the little glen. Slowly, too, we followed the course of the narrow and sinuous beach, as it keeps to the foot of the low cliffs. We encountered no sign of human life. Our conversation I need hardly repeat. I think I may trust it to the keeping of my memory; it was the sort of thing that comes back to one – after. If something ever happens which I think *may*, that apparently idle hour will seem, as one looks back, very symptomatic, and what we didn't say be perceived to have been more significant than what we did. There was something between us – there *is* something between us and we listened to its impalpable presence – I liken it to the hum (very faint) of an unseen insect – in the golden stillness of the afternoon. I must add that if she expects, foresees, if she waits, she does so with a supreme serenity. If she is my fate (and she has the air of it), she is conscious that it's *her* fate to be so.

September 1st. – I have been working steadily for a week. This is the first day of autumn. Read aloud to Miss Quarterman a little Wordsworth.

September 10th. Midnight. – Worked without interruption – until yesterday, inclusive, that is. But with the day now closing – or opening – begins a new era. My poor vapid old diary, at last you shall hold a *fact*.

For three days past we have been having damp, autumnal weather; dusk has gathered early. This evening, after tea, the Captain went into town – on business, as he said: I believe, to attend some Poorhouse or Hospital Board. Miriam and I went into the parlour. The place seemed cold; she brought in the lamp from the dining-room, and proposed we should have a little fire. I went into the kitchen, procured half-a-dozen logs, and, while she drew the curtains and wheeled up the table, I kindled a lively, crackling blaze. A fortnight ago she would not have allowed me to do this without a protest. She would not have offered to do it herself – not she! – but she would have said I was not here to serve, but to be served, and would at least have made a show of calling the negress. I should have had my own way, but we have changed all that. Miriam went to her piano, and I sat down to a book. I read not a word, but sat considering my fate and watching it come nearer and nearer. For the first time since I have known her (my fate) she had put on a dark, warm dress; I think it was of the material called alpaca. The first time I saw her (I remember such things) she wore a white dress with a blue neck-ribbon; now she wore a black dress with the same ribbon. That is, I remember wondering, as I sat there eyeing her, whether it *was* the same ribbon, or merely another like it. My heart was in my throat; and yet I thought of a number of trivialities of the same kind. At last I spoke.

'Miss Quarterman,' I said, 'do you remember the first evening I passed beneath your roof, last June?'

'Perfectly,' she replied, without stopping.

'You played that same piece.'

'Yes; I played it very badly, too. I only half knew it. But it is a showy piece, and I wished to produce an effect. I didn't know then how indifferent you are to music.'

'I paid no particular attention to the piece. I was intent upon the performer.'

'So the performer supposed.'

'What reason had you to suppose so?'

'I am sure I don't know. Did you ever know a woman to be able to give a reason when she has guessed aright?'

'I think they generally contrive to make up a reason after-wards. Come, what was yours?'

'Well, you stared so hard.'

'Fie! I don't believe it. That's unkind.'

'You said you wished me to invent a reason. If I really had one, I don't remember it.'

'You told me you remembered the occasion in question per-fectly.'

'I meant the circumstances. I remember what we had for tea; I remember what dress I wore. But I don't remember my feelings. They were naturally not very memorable.'

'What did you say when your father proposed that I should come here?'

'I asked how much you would be willing to pay?'

'And then?'

'And then, if you looked respectable.'

'And then?'

'That was all. I told my father to do as he pleased.'

She continued to play, and leaning back in my chair I continued to look at her. There was a considerable pause.

'Miss Quarterman,' said I, at last.

'Well, sir?'

'Excuse me for interrupting you so often. But' – and I got up and went to the piano – 'but, you know, I thank heaven that it has brought you and me together.'

She looked up at me and bowed her head with a little smile, as her hands still wandered over the keys.

'Heaven has certainly been very good to us,' said she.

'How much longer are you going to play?' I asked.

'I'm sure I don't know. As long as you like.'

'If you want to do as I like, you will stop immediately.'

She let her hands rest on the keys a moment, and gave me a rapid, questioning look. Whether she found a sufficient answer in my face I know not; but she slowly rose, and, with a very pretty affectation of obedience, began to close the instrument. I helped her to do so.

'Perhaps you would like to be quite alone,' she said. 'I suppose your own room is too cold.'

'Yes,' I answered, 'you have hit it exactly. I wish to be alone. I wish to monopolise this cheerful blaze. Hadn't you better go into the kitchen and sit with the cook? It takes you women to make such cruel speeches.'

'When we women are cruel, Mr Locksley, it is the merest accident. We are not wilfully so. When we learn that we have been unkind we very humbly ask pardon, without even knowing what our crime has been.' And she made me a very low curtsey.

'I will tell you what your crime has been,' said I. 'Come and sit by the fire. It's rather a long story.'

'A long story? Then let me get my work.'

'Confound your work! Excuse me, but you exasperate me. I want you to listen to me. Believe me, you will need all your attention.'

She looked at me steadily a moment, and I returned her glance. During that moment I was reflecting whether I might put my arm round her waist and kiss her; but I decided that I might do nothing of the sort. She walked over and quietly seated herself in a low chair by the fire. Here she patiently folded her arms. I sat down before her.

'With you, Miss Quarterman,' said I, 'one must be very explicit. You are not in the habit of taking things for granted. You have a great deal of imagination, but you rarely exercise it on behalf of other people.'

'Is that my crime?' asked my companion.

'It's not so much a crime as a vice, and perhaps not so much a vice as a virtue. Your crime is, that you are so stone-cold to a poor devil who loves you.'

She burst into a rather shrill laugh. I wonder whether she thought I meant Prendergast.

'Who are you speaking for, Mr Locksley?' she asked.

'Are there so many? For myself.'

'Honestly?'

'Do you think me capable of deceiving you?'

'What is that French phrase that you are for ever using? I think I may say "*Allons donc!*"'

'Let us speak plain English, Miss Quarterman.'

'"Stone-cold" is certainly very plain English. I don't see the relative importance of the two branches of your proposition. Which is the principal, and which the subordinate clause – that I am stone-cold, as you call it, or that you love me, as you call it?'

'As I call it? What would you have me call it? For pity's sake, Miss Quarterman, be serious, or I shall call it something else. Yes, I love you. Don't you believe it?'

'How can I help believing what you tell me?'

'Dearest, bravest of women,' said I.

And I attempted to take her hand.

'No, no, Mr Locksley,' said she – 'not just yet, if you please.'

'Actions speak louder than words,' said I.

'There is no need of speaking loud. I hear you perfectly.'

'I certainly shall not whisper,' said I; 'although it is the custom, I believe, for lovers to do so. Will you be my wife?'

I don't know whether *she* whispered or not, but before I left her she consented.

September 12th. – We are to be married in about three weeks.

September 19th. – I have been in New York a week, transacting business. I got back yesterday. I find everyone here talking about our engagement. Miriam tells me that it was talked about a month ago, and that there is a very general feeling of disappointment that I am so very poor.

'Really, if you don't mind it,' I remarked, 'I don't see why others should.'

'I don't know whether you are poor or not,' says Miriam, 'but I know that I am rich.'

'Indeed! I was not aware that you had a private fortune,' etc. etc.

This little farce is repeated in some shape every day. I am very idle. I smoke a great deal, and lounge about all day, with my hands in my pockets. I am free from that ineffable weariness of ceaseless *buying* which I suffered from six months ago. That intercourse was conducted by means of little parcels, and I have resolved that this engagement, at all events, shall have no connection with the shops. I was cheated of my poetry once; I shan't be a second time. Fortunately there is not much danger of this, for my mistress is positively lyrical. She takes an enthusiastic interest in her simple outfit – showing me triumphantly certain of her purchases, and making a great mystery about others, which she is pleased to denominate table-cloths and napkins. Last evening I found her sewing buttons on a table-cloth. I had heard a great deal of a certain pink silk dress, and this morning, accordingly, she marched up to me, arrayed in this garment, upon which all the art and taste and eyesight, and all the velvet and lace, of Chowderville have been lavished.

'There is only one objection to it,' said Miriam, parading before the glass in my painting-room: 'I am afraid it is above our station.'

'By Jove! I will paint your portrait in it and make our fortune,' said I. 'And the other men who have handsome wives will bring them to be painted.'

'You mean all the women who have handsome dresses,' Miriam replied, with great humility.

Our wedding is fixed for next Thursday. I tell Miriam that it will be as little of a wedding, and as much of a marriage, as possible. Her father and her good friend Miss Blankenberg (the schoolmistress) alone are to be present. My secret oppresses me considerably; but I have resolved to keep it for the honeymoon, when it may leak out as occasion helps it. I am harassed with a dismal apprehension that if Miriam were to discover it now, the whole thing would have to be done over again. I have taken rooms at a romantic little watering-place called Cragthorpe, ten miles off. The hotel is already quite purged of cockneys,[12] and we shall be almost alone.

September 28th. – We have been here two days. The little transaction in the church went off smoothly. I am truly sorry for the Captain. We drove directly over here, and reached the place at dusk. It was a raw, black day. We have a couple of good rooms, close to the savage sea. I am nevertheless afraid I have made a mistake. It would perhaps have been wiser to go to New York. These things are not immaterial; we make our own heaven, but we scarcely make our own earth. I am writing at a little table by the window, looking out on the rocks, the gathering dusk, the rising fog. My wife has wandered down to the rocky platform in front of the house. I can see her from here, bareheaded, in that old crimson shawl, talking to one of the landlord's little boys. She has just given the infant a kiss, bless her tender heart! I remember her telling me once that she was very fond of little boys; and, indeed, I have noticed that they are seldom too dirty for her to take on her knee. I have been reading over these pages for the first time in – I don't know when. They are filled with *her* – even more in thought than in word. I believe I will show them to her when she comes in. I will give her the book to read, and sit by her, watching her face – watching the great secret dawn upon her.

Later. – Somehow or other, I can write this quietly enough; but I hardly think I shall ever write any more. When Miriam came in I handed her this book.

'I want you to read it,' said I.

She turned very pale, and laid it on the table, shaking her head.

'I know it,' she said.

'What do you know?'

'That you have ever so much money. But believe me, Mr Locksley, I am none the worse for the knowledge. You intimated in one place in your book that I am fitted by nature for wealth and splendour. I verily believe I am. You pretend to hate your money; but you would not have had me without it. If you really love me – and I think you do – you will not let this make any difference. I am not such a fool as to attempt to talk now about what passed through me when you asked me to – to do *this*. But I remember what I said.'

'What do you expect me to do?' I asked. 'Shall I call you some horrible name and cast you off?'

'I expect you to show the same courage that I am showing. I

97

never said I loved you. I never deceived you in that. I said I would be your wife. So I will, faithfully. I haven't so much heart as you think; and yet, too, I have a great deal more. I am incapable of more than one deception – Mercy! didn't you see it? didn't you know it? see that I saw it? know that I knew it? It was diamond cut diamond. You cheated me and I mystified you. Now that you tell me your secret I can tell you mine. *Now* we are free, with the fortune that you know. Excuse me, but it sometimes comes over me! *Now* we can be good and honest and true. It was all a make-believe virtue before.'

'So you read that thing?' I asked: actually – strange as it may seem – for something to say.

'Yes, while you were ill. It was lying with your pen in it, on the table. I read it because I suspected. Otherwise I wouldn't have done so.'

'It was the act of a false woman,' said I.

'A false woman? No, it was the act of any woman – placed as I was placed. You don't believe it?' And she began to smile. 'Come, you may abuse me in your diary if you like – I shall never peep into it again!'

A Day of Days

Mr Herbert Moore, a gentleman of the highest note in the scientific world, and a childless widower, finding himself at last unable to reconcile his sedentary habits with the management of a household, had invited his only sister to come and superintend his domestic affairs. Miss Adela Moore had assented the more willingly to his proposal as by her mother's death she had recently been left without a formal protector. She was twenty-five years of age, and was a very active member of what she and her friends called society. She was almost equally at home in the best company of three great cities, and she had encountered most of the adventures which await a young girl on the threshold of life. She had become rather hastily and imprudently engaged, but she had eventually succeeded in disengaging herself. She had spent a summer or two in Europe, and she had made a voyage to Cuba with a dear friend in the last stage of consumption, who had died at the hotel in the Havana. Although by no means perfectly beautiful in person she was yet thoroughly pleasing, rejoicing in what young ladies are fond of calling an *air*; that is, she was tall and slender, with a long neck, a low forehead, and a handsome nose. Even after six years of the best company, too, she still had excellent manners. She was, moreover, mistress of a very pretty little fortune, and was accounted clever without detriment to her amiability and amiable without detriment to her wit. These facts, as the reader will allow, might have ensured her the very best prospects; but he has seen that she had found herself willing to forfeit her prospects and bury herself in the country. It seemed to her that she had seen enough of the world and of human nature, and that a period of seclusion might yield a fine refreshment. She had begun to suspect that for a girl of her age she was unduly old and wise – and, what is more, to suspect that others suspected as much. A great observer of life and manners, so far as her opportunities went, she conceived that it behoved her to organise the results of her observation into principles of conduct and belief. She was becoming – so she argued – too impersonal, too critical, too intelligent, too contemplative, too just. A woman had no business to be so just. The society of nature, of the great expansive skies and the primeval woods, would check the morbid development of her brain-power. She would spend her time in the fields and merely vegetate; walk and ride, and read the old-fashioned books in Herbert's library.

She found her brother established in a very pretty house, at about a mile's distance from the nearest town, and at about six miles' distance from another town, the seat of a small but ancient college, before which he delivered a weekly lecture. She had seen so little of him of late years that his acquaintance was almost to make; but there were no barriers to break down. Herbert Moore was one of the simplest and least aggressive of men, and one of the most patient and conscientious of students. He had had a vague notion that Adela was a young woman of extravagant pleasures, and that, somehow, on her arrival, his house would be overrun with the train of her attendant revellers. It was not until after they had been six months together that he became aware that his sister led almost an ascetic life. By the time six more months had passed Adela had recovered a delightful sense of youth and *naïveté*. She learned, under her brother's tuition, to walk – nay, to climb, for there were great hills in the neighbourhood – to ride and to botanise. At the end of a year, in the month of August, she received a visit from an old friend, a girl of her own age, who had been spending July at a watering-place, and who was now about to be married. Adela had begun to fear that she had declined into an almost irreclaimable rusticity and had rubbed off the social facility, the 'knowledge of the world' for which she was formerly distinguished; but a week spent in intimate conversation with her friend convinced her not only that she had not forgotten much that she had feared, but had also not forgotten much that she had hoped. For this, and other reasons, her friend's departure left her slightly depressed. She felt lonely and even a little elderly – she had lost another illusion. Laura Benton, for whom a year ago she had entertained a serious regard, now impressed her as a very flimsy little person, who talked about her lover with almost indecent flippancy.

Meanwhile, September was slowly running its course. One morning Mr Moore took a hasty breakfast and started to catch the train for Slowfield, whither a scientific conference called him, which might, he said, release him that afternoon in time for dinner at home, or might, on the other hand, detain him till the night. It was almost the first time during the term of Adela's rustication that she had been left alone for several hours. Her brother's quiet presence was inappreciable enough; yet now that he was at a distance she felt a singular sense of freedom: a return of that condition of early childhood when, through some domestic catastrophe, she had for an infinite morning been left to her own devices. What should she do? she asked herself, with the smile that she reserved for her maidenly monologues. It was a good day for work, but it was a still better one for play. Should she drive into town and call on a lot of tiresome local people? Should she go into the kitchen and try her hand at a pudding for dinner? She felt a delectable longing to do something illicit, to play with fire, to discover some Bluebeard's closet. But poor Herbert was no Bluebeard; if she were to burn down his house he would exact no amends. Adela went out to the verandah, and, sitting down on the steps, gazed across the country. It was apparently the last day of summer. The sky was faintly blue; the woody hills were putting on the morbid colours of autumn; the great pine-grove behind the house seemed to have caught and imprisoned the protesting breezes. Looking down the road toward the village; it occurred to Adela that she might have a visit, and so human was her mood that if any of the local people were to come to her she felt it was in her to humour them. As the sun rose higher she went in and established herself with a piece of embroidery in a deep bow-window, in the second story, which, betwixt its muslin curtains and its external framework of high-creeping plants, commanded most insidiously the principal approach to the house. While she drew her threads she surveyed the road with a deepening conviction that she was destined to have a caller. The air was warm, yet not hot; the dust had been laid during the night by a gentle rain. It had been from the first a source of complaint among Adela's new friends that she was equally gracious to all men, and, what was more remarkable, to all women. Not only had she dedicated herself to no friendships, but she had committed herself to no preferences. Nevertheless, it was with an imagination by no means severely impartial that she sat communing with her open casement. She had very soon made up her mind that, to answer the requirements of the hour, her visitor must be of a sex as different as possible from her own; and as, thanks to the few differences in favour of any individual she had been able to discover among the young males of the country-side, her roll-call in this her hour of need was limited to a single name, so her thoughts were now centred upon the bearer of that name, Mr Weatherby Pynsent, the Unitarian minister. If instead of being Miss Moore's story this were Mr Pynsent's, it might easily be condensed into the simple statement that he was very far gone indeed. Although affiliated to a richer ceremonial than his own she had been so well pleased with one of his sermons, to which she had allowed herself to lend a tolerant ear, that, meeting him some time afterward, she had received him with what she considered a rather knotty doctrinal question; whereupon, gracefully waiving the question, he had asked permission to call upon her and talk over her 'difficulties.' This short interview had enshrined her in the young minister's heart; and the half a dozen occasions on which he had subsequently contrived to see her had each contributed another candle to her altar. It is but fair to add, however, that, although a captive, Mr Pynsent was as yet no captor. He was simply an honourable young parson, who happened at this moment to be the most sympathetic companion within reach. Adela, at twenty-five years of age, had both a past and a future. Mr Pynsent reminded her of the one and gave her a foretaste of the other.

So, at last, when, as the morning waned toward noon, Adela descried in the distance a man's figure treading the grassy margin of the road, and swinging his stick as he came, she smiled to herself with some complacency. But even while she smiled she became conscious that her heart was beating quite idiotically. She rose, and, resenting her gratuitous emotion, stood for a moment half resolved to see no one at all. As she did so she glanced along the road again. Her friend had drawn nearer, and as the distance lessened she began to perceive that he was not her friend. Before many moments her doubts were removed; the gentleman was a stranger. In front of the house three roads went their different ways, and a spreading elm, tall and slim, like the feathery sheaf of a gleaner, with an ancient bench beneath it, made an informal *rond-point*. The stranger came along the opposite side of the highway, and when he reached the elm stopped and looked about him, as if to verify some direction that had been given him. Then he deliberately crossed over. Adela had time to see, unseen, that he was a robust young man, with a bearded chin and a soft white hat. After the due interval Becky the maid came up with a card somewhat rudely superscribed in pencil:

THOMAS LUDLOW,
New York.

Turning it over in her fingers, Adela saw the gentleman had made use of the reverse of a pasteboard abstracted from the basket on her own drawing-room table. The printed name on the other side was dashed out; it ran: *Mr Weatherby Pynsent.*

'He asked me to give you this, ma'am,' said Becky. 'He helped himself to it out of the tray.'

'Did he ask for me by name?'

'No, ma'am; he asked for Mr Moore. When I told him Mr Moore was away, he asked for some of the family. I told him you was all the family, ma'am.'

'Very well,' said Adela, 'I will go down.' But, begging her pardon, we will precede her by a few steps.

Tom Ludlow, as his friends called him, was a young man of twenty-eight, concerning whom you might have heard the most various opinions; for, as far as he was known (which, indeed, was not very far), he was at once one of the best liked and one of the best hated of men. Born in one of the lower walks of New York life, he still seemed always to move in his native element. A certain crudity of manner and aspect proved him to belong to the great vulgar, muscular, popular majority. On this basis, however, he was a sufficiently good-looking fellow: a middle-sized, agile figure, a head so well shaped as to be handsome, a pair of inquisitive, responsive eyes, and a large, manly mouth, constituting the most expressive part of his equipment. Turned upon the world at an early age, he had, in the pursuit of a subsistence, tried his head at everything in succession, and had generally found it to be quite as hard as the opposing substance; and his person may have been thought to reflect this experience in an air of taking success too much for granted. He was a man of strong faculties and a strong will, but it is doubtful whether his feelings were stronger than he. People liked him for his directness, his good-humour, his general soundness and serviceableness, and disliked him for the same qualities under different names; that is, for his impudence, his offensive optimism, his inhuman avidity for facts. When his friends insisted upon his noble disinterestedness, his enemies were wont to reply it was ·'l very well to ignore, to suppress, one's own sensibilities in the pursuit of knowledge, but to trample on the rest of mankind at the same time betrayed an excess of zeal. Fortunately for Ludlow, on the whole, he was no great listener, and even if he had been, a certain plebeian thick-skinnedness would always have saved his tenderer parts; although it must be added that, if, like a genuine democrat, he was very insensitive, like a genuine democrat, too, he was unexpectedly proud. His tastes, which had always been for the natural sciences, had recently led him to the study of fossil remains, the branch cultivated by Herbert Moore; and it was upon business connected with this pursuit that, after a short correspondence, he had now come to see him.

As Adela went to him he came out from the window, where he had been looking at the lawn. She acknowledged the friendly nod which he apparently intended for a greeting.

'Miss Moore, I believe,' said Ludlow.

'Miss Moore,' said Adela.

'I beg your pardon for this intrusion, but as I have come from a distance to see Mr Moore, on business, I thought I might venture either to ask at headquarters how he may most easily be reached, or even to give you a message for him.' These words were accompanied with a smile under the influence of which it had been written on the scroll of Adela's fate that she was to descend from her pedestal.

'Pray make no apologies,' she said. 'We hardly recognise such a thing as intrusion in this simple little place. Won't you sit down? My brother went away only this morning, and I expect him back this afternoon.'

'This afternoon? indeed. In that case I believe I'll wait. It was very stupid of me not to have dropped a word beforehand. But I have been in the city all summer long, and I shall not be sorry to squeeze a little vacation out of this business. I'm tremendously fond of the country, and I have been working for many months in a musty museum.'

'It's possible that my brother may not come home until the evening,' Adela said. 'He was uncertain. You might go to him at Slowfield.'

Ludlow reflected a moment, with his eyes on his hostess. 'If he does return in the afternoon, at what hour will he arrive?'

'Well, about three.'

'And my own train leaves at four. Allow him a quarter of an hour to come from town and myself a quarter of an hour to get there (if he would give me his vehicle back). In that case I should have about half an hour to see him. We couldn't do much talk, but I could ask him the essential questions. I wish chiefly to ask him for some letters – letters of recommendation to some foreign scientists. He is the only man in this country who knows how much I know. It seems a pity to take two superfluous – that is, possibly superfluous – railway-journeys of an hour apiece; for I should probably come back with him, don't you think so?' he asked, very frankly.

'You know best,' said Adela. 'I am not particularly fond of the journey to Slowfield, even when it's absolutely necessary.'

'Yes; and then this is such a lovely day for a good long ramble in the fields. That's a thing I haven't had since I don't know when. I guess I'll remain.' And he placed his hat on the floor beside him.

'I am afraid, now that I think of it,' said Adela, 'that there is no train until so late an hour that you would have very little time left on your arrival to talk with my brother, before the hour at which he himself might have determined to start for home. It's true that you might induce him to stop over till the evening.'

'Dear me! I shouldn't want to do that. It might be very inconvenient for Mr Moore, don't you see? Besides, I shouldn't have time. And then I always like to see a man in his home – or at some place of my own; a man, that is, whom I have any regard for – and I have a very great regard for your brother, Miss Moore. When men meet at a half way house neither feels at his ease. And then this is such an attractive country residence of yours,' pursued Ludlow, looking about him.

'Yes, it's a very pretty place,' said Adela.

Ludlow got up and walked to the window. 'I want to look at your view,' he remarked. 'A lovely little spot. You are a happy woman, Miss Moore, to have the beauties of nature always before your eyes.'

'Yes, if pretty scenery can make one happy, I ought to be happy.' And Adela was glad to regain her feet and stand on the other side of the table, before the window.

'Don't you think it can?' asked Ludlow, turning round. 'I don't know, though; perhaps it can't. Ugly sights can't make you unhappy, necessarily. I have been working for a year in one of the narrowest, darkest, dirtiest, busiest streets in New York, with rusty bricks and muddy gutters for scenery. But I think I can hardly set up to be miserable. I wish I could! It might be a claim on your benevolence.' As he said these words he stood leaning against the window-gutter, outside the curtain, with folded arms. The morning light covered his face, and, mingled with that of his radiant laugh, showed Adela that his was a nature very much alive.

'Whatever else he may be,' she said to herself, as she stood within the shade of the other curtain, playing with the paper-knife, which she had plucked from the table, 'I think he is honest. I am afraid he isn't a gentleman – but he isn't a bore.' She met his eye, freely, for a moment. 'What do you want of my benevolence?' she asked, with an abruptness of which she was perfectly conscious. 'Does he wish to make friends,' she pursued, tacitly, 'or does he merely wish to pay me a vulgar compliment? There is bad taste, perhaps, in either case, but especially in the latter.' Meanwhile her visitor had already answered her.

'What do I want of your benevolence? Why, what does one want of any pleasant thing in life?'

'Dear me, if you never have anything pleasanter than that!' our heroine exclaimed.

'It will do very well for the present occasion,' said the young man, blushing, in a large masculine way, at his own quickness of repartee.

Adela glanced toward the clock on the chimney-piece. She was curious to measure the duration of the acquaintance with this breezy invader of her privacy, with whom she so suddenly found herself bandying jokes so personal. She had known him some eight minutes.

Ludlow observed her movement. 'I am interrupting you and detaining you from your own affairs,' he said; and he moved toward his hat. 'I suppose I must bid you good-morning.' And he picked it up.

Adela stood at the table and watched him cross the room. To express a very delicate feeling in terms comparatively crude, she was loth to see him depart. She divined, too, that he was very sorry to go. The knowledge of this feeling on his side, however, affected her composure but slightly. The truth is – we say it with respect – Adela was an old hand. She was modest, honest and wise; but, as we have said, she had a past – a past of which importunate swains in the guise of morning-callers had been no inconsiderable part; and a great dexterity in what may be called outflanking these gentlemen was one of her registered accomplishments. Her liveliest emotion at present, therefore, was less one of annoyance at her companion than of surprise at her own mansuetude, which was yet undeniable. 'Am I dreaming?' she asked herself. She looked out of the window, and then back at Ludlow, who stood grasping his hat and stick, contemplating her face. Should she give him leave to remain? 'He is honest,' she repeated; 'why should I not be honest for once? I am sorry you are in a hurry,' she said, aloud.

'I am in no hurry,' he answered.

Adela turned her face to the window again, and toward the opposite hills. There was a moment's pause.

'I thought *you* were in a hurry,' said Ludlow.

Adela shifted her eyes back to where they could see him. 'My brother would be very glad that you should stay as long as you like. He would expect me to offer you what little hospitality is in my power.'

'Pray, offer it then.'

'That is very easily done. This is the parlour, and there, beyond the hall, is my brother's study. Perhaps you would like to look at his books and collections. I know nothing about them, and I should be a very poor guide. But you are welcome to go in and use your discretion in examining what may interest you.'

'This, I take it, would be but another way of separating from you.'

'For the present, yes.'

'But I hesitate to take such liberties with your brother's things as you recommend.'

'Recommend? I recommend nothing.'

'But if I decline to penetrate into Mr Moore's sanctum, what alternative remains?'

'Really – you must make your own alternative.'

'I think you mentioned the parlour. Suppose I choose that.'

'Just as you please. Here are some books, and if you like I will bring you some periodicals. There are ever so many scientific papers. Can I serve you in any other way? Are you tired by your walk? Would you like a glass of wine?'

'Tired by my walk? – not exactly. You are very kind, but I feel no immediate desire for a glass of wine. I think you needn't trouble yourself about scientific periodicals either. I am not exactly in the mood to read.' And Ludlow pulled out his watch and compared it with the clock. 'I am afraid your clock is fast.'

'Yes,' said Adela; 'very likely.'

'Some ten minutes. Well, I suppose I had better be walking.' And, coming toward Adela, he extended his hand.

She gave him hers. 'It is a day of days for a long, slow ramble,' she said.

Ludlow's only rejoinder was his hand-shake. He moved slowly toward the door, half accompanied by Adela. 'Poor fellow!' she said to herself. There was a summer-door, composed of lattices painted green, like a shutter; it admitted into the hall a cool, dusky light, in which Adela looked pale. Ludlow pushed its wings apart with his stick, and disclosed a landscape, long, deep, and bright, framed by the pillars of the porch. He stopped on the threshold, swinging his cane. 'I hope I shall not lose my way,' he said.

'I hope not. My brother will not forgive me if you do.'

Ludlow's brows were slightly contracted by a frown, but he contrived to smile with his lips. 'When shall I come back?' he asked, abruptly.

Adela found but a low tone – almost a whisper – at her command to answer – 'Whenever you please.'

The young man turned round, with his back to the bright doorway, and looked into Adela's face, which was now covered with light. 'Miss Moore,' said he, 'it's very much against my will that I leave you at all!'

Adela stood debating within herself. After all, what if her companion should stay with her? It would, under the circumstances, be an adventure; but was an adventure necessarily a criminal thing? It lay wholly with herself to decide. She was her own mistress, and she had hitherto been a just mistress. Might she not for once be a generous one? The reader will observe in Adela's meditation the recurrence of this saving clause 'for once.' It was produced by the simple fact that she had begun the day in a romantic mood. She was prepared to be interested; and now that an interesting phenomenon had presented itself, that it stood before her in vivid human – nay, manly – shape, instinct with reciprocity, was she to close her hand to the liberality of fate? To do so would be only to expose herself the more, for it would imply a gratuitous insult to human nature. Was not the man before her redolent of good intentions, and was that not enough? He was not what Adela had been used to call a gentleman; at this conviction she had arrived by a rapid diagonal, and now it served as a fresh starting-point. 'I have seen all the gentlemen can show me' (this was her syllogism): 'let us try something new! I see no reason why you should run away so fast, Mr Ludlow,' she said, aloud.

'I think it would be the greatest piece of folly I ever committed!' cried the young man.

'I think it would be rather a pity,' Adela remarked.

'And you invite me into your parlour again? I come as *your* visitor, you know. I was your brother's before. It's a simple enough matter. We are old friends. We have a solid common ground in your brother. Isn't that about it?'

'You may adopt whatever theory you please. To my mind it is indeed a very simple matter.'

'Oh, but I wouldn't have it too simple,' said Ludlow, with a genial smile.

'Have it as you please!'

Ludlow leaned back against the doorway. 'Look here, Miss Moore; your kindness makes me as gentle as a little child. I am passive; I am in your hands; do with me what you please. I can't help contrasting my fate with what it might have been but for you. A quarter of an hour ago I was ignorant of your existence; you were not in my programme. I had no idea your brother had a sister. When your servant spoke of "Miss Moore," upon my word I expected something rather elderly – something venerable – some rigid old lady, who would say, "exactly," and "very well, sir," and leave me to spend the rest of the morning tilting back in a chair on the piazza of the hotel. It shows what fools we are to attempt to forecast the future.'

'We must not let our imagination run away with us in any direction,' said Adela, sententiously.

'Imagination? I don't believe I have any. No, madam' – and Ludlow straightened himself up – 'I live in the present. I write my programme from hour to hour – or, at any rate, I will in the future.'

'I think you are very wise,' said Adela. 'Suppose you write a programme for the present hour. What shall we do? It seems to me a pity to spend so lovely a morning indoors. There is something in the air – I can't imagine what – which seems to say it is the last day of summer. We ought to commemorate it. How should you like to take a walk?' Adela had decided that, to reconcile her aforesaid benevolence with the proper maintenance of her dignity, her only course was to be the perfect hostess. This decision made, very naturally and gracefully she played her part. It was the one possible part; and yet it did not preclude those delicate sensations with which so rare an episode seem charged: it simply legitimated them. A romantic adventure on so conventional a basis would assuredly hurt no one.

'I should like a walk very much,' said Ludlow; 'a walk with a halt at the end of it.'

'Well, if you will consent to a short halt at the beginning of it,' Adela rejoined, 'I will be with you in a very few minutes.' When she returned, in her little hat and jacket, she found her friend seated on the steps of the verandah. He arose and gave her a card.

'I have been requested, in your absence, to hand you this.'

Adela read with some compunction the name of Mr Weatherby Pynsent.

'Has he been here?' she asked. 'Why didn't he come in?'

'I told him you were not at home. If it wasn't true then, it was going to be true so soon that the interval was hardly worth taking account of. He addressed himself to me, as I seemed from my position to be quite in possession; that is, I put myself in his way, as it were, so that he had to speak to me: but I confess he looked at me as if he doubted my word. He hesitated as to whether he should confide his name to me, or whether he should ring for the servant. I think he wished to show me that he suspected my veracity, for he was making rather grimly for the doorbell when I, fearing that once inside the house he might encounter the living truth, informed him in the most good-humoured tone possible that I would take charge of his little tribute, if he would trust me with it.'

'It seems to me, Mr Ludlow, that you are a strangely un-scrupulous man. How did you know that Mr Pysent's business was not urgent?'

'I didn't know it! But I knew it could be no more urgent than mine. Depend upon it, Miss Moore, you have no case against me. I only pretend to be a man; to have admitted that sweet little cleric – isn't he a cleric, eh? – would have been the act of an angel.'

Adela was familiar with a sequestered spot, in the very heart of the fields, as it seemed to her, to which she now proposed to conduct her friend. The point was to select a goal neither too distant nor too near, and to adopt a pace neither too rapid nor too slow. But although Adela's happy valley was at least two miles away, and they had dawdled immensely over the interval, yet their arrival at a certain little rustic gate, beyond which the country grew vague and gently wild, struck Adela as sudden. Once on the road she felt a precipitate conviction that there could be no evil in an excursion so purely pastoral and no guile in a spirit so deeply sensitive to the influences of nature, and to the melancholy aspect of incipient autumn, as that of her companion. A man with an unaffected relish for small children is a man to inspire young women with a confidence; and so, in a less degree, a man with a genuine feeling for the unsophisticated beauties of a casual New England landscape may not unreasonably be regarded by the daughters of the scene as a person whose motives are pure. Adela was a great observer of the clouds, the trees, and the streams, the sounds and colours, the transparent airs and blue horizons of her adopted home; and she was reassured by Ludlow's appreciation of these modest phenomena. His enjoyment of them, deep as it was, however, had to struggle against the sensuous depression natural to a man who has spent the summer looking over dry specimens in a laboratory, and against an impediment of a less material order – the feeling that Adela was a remarkably attractive woman. Still, naturally a great talker, he uttered his various satisfactions with abundant humour and point. Adela felt that he was decidedly a companion for the open air – he was a man to make use even to abuse, of the wide horizon and the high ceiling of nature. The freedom of his gestures, the sonority of his voice, the keenness of his vision, the general vivacity of his manners, seemed to necessitate and to justify a universal absence of resisting surfaces. They passed through the little gate and wandered over empty pastures, until the ground began to rise, and stony surfaces to crop through the turf; when, after a short ascent, they reached a broad plateau, covered with boulders and shrubs, which lost itself on one side in a short, steep cliff, whence fields and marshes stretched down to the opposite river, and on the other, in scattered clumps of cedar and maple, which gradually thickened and multiplied, until the horizon in that quarter was purple with mild masses of forest. Here was both sun and shade – the unobstructed sky, or the whispering dome of a circle of trees which had always reminded Adela of the stone-pines of the Villa Borghese.[1] Adela led the way to a sunny seat among the rocks which commanded the course of the river, where the murmuring cedars would give them a kind of human company.

'It has always seemed to me that the wind in the trees is always the voice of coming changes,' Ludlow said.

'Perhaps it is,' Adela replied. 'The trees are for ever talking in this melancholy way, and men are for ever changing.'

'Yes, but they can only be said to express the foreboding of coming events – that is what I mean – when there is someone there to hear them; and more especially someone in whose life a change is, to his knowledge, about to take place. Then they are quite prophetic. Don't you know Longfellow says so?'[2]

'Yes, I know Longfellow says so. But you seem to speak from your own inspiration.'

'Well, I rather think I do.'

'Is there some great change hanging over you?'

'Yes, rather an important one.'

'I believe that's what men say when they are going to be married,' said Adela.

'I am going to be divorced, rather. I am going to Europe.'

'Indeed! soon?'

'To-morrow,' said Ludlow, after an instant's pause.

'Oh!' exclaimed Adela. 'How I envy you!'

Ludlow, who sat looking over the cliff and tossing stones down into the plain, observed a certain inequality in the tone of his companion's two exclamations. The first was nature, the second art. He turned his eyes upon her, but she had directed hers away into the distance. Then, for a moment, he retreated within himself and thought. He rapidly surveyed his position. Here was he, Tom Ludlow, a hard-headed son of toil; without fortune, without credit, without antecedents, whose lot was cast exclusively with vulgar males, and who had never had a mother, a sister, nor a well-bred sweetheart, to pitch his voice for the feminine tympanum, who had seldom come nearer an indubitable lady than, in a favouring crowd, to receive a mechanical 'thank you' (as if he were a policeman) for some accidental assistance: here he found himself up to his neck in a sudden pastoral with a young woman who was evidently altogether superior. That it was in him to enjoy the society of such a person (provided, of course, she were not a chit) he very well knew; but he had never happened to suppose that he should find it open to him. Was he now to infer that this brilliant gift was his – the gift of which is called in the relation between the sexes success? The inference was at least logical. He had made a good impression. Why else should an eminently discriminating girl have fraternised with him at such a rate? It was with a little thrill of satisfaction that Ludlow reflected upon the directness of his course. 'It all comes back to my old theory that a process can't be too simple. I used no arts. In such an enterprise I shouldn't have known where to begin. It was my ignorance of the regular way that saved me. Women like a gentleman, of course; but they like a man better.' It was the little touch of nature he had detected in Adela's tone that set him thinking; but as compared with the frankness of his own attitude it betrayed after all no undue emotion. Ludlow had accepted the fact of his adaptability to the idle mood of a cultivated woman in a thoroughly rational spirit, and he was not now tempted to exaggerate its bearings. He was not the man to be intoxicated by a triumph after all possibly superficial. 'If Miss Moore is so wise – or so foolish – as to like me half an hour for what I am, she is welcome,' he said to himself. 'Assuredly,' he added, as he glanced at her intelligent profile, 'she will not like me for what I am not.' It needs a woman, however, far more intelligent than (thank heaven!) most women are – more intelligent, certainly, than Adela was – to guard her happiness against a clever man's consistent assumption of her intelligence; and doubtless it was from a sense of this general truth that, as Ludlow continued to observe his companion, he felt an emotion of manly tenderness. 'I wouldn't offend her for the world,' he thought. Just then Adela, conscious of his contemplation, looked about; and before he knew it, Ludlow had repeated aloud, 'Miss Moore, I wouldn't offend you for the world.'

Adela eyed him for a moment with a little flush that subsided into a smile. 'To what dreadful impertinence is that the prelude?' she inquired.

'It's a prelude to nothing. It refers to the past – to any possible displeasure I may have caused you.'

'Your scruples are unnecessary, Mr Ludlow. If you had given me offence, I should not have left you to apologise for it. I should not have left the matter to occur to you as you sat dreaming charitably in the sun.'

'What would you have done?'

'Done? nothing. You don't imagine I would have scolded you –

or snubbed you – or answered you back, I take it. I would have left undone – what, I can't tell you. Ask yourself what I *have* done. I am sure I hardly know myself,' said Adela, with some intensity. 'At all events, here I am sitting with you in the fields, as if you were a friend of many years. Why do you speak of offence?' And Adela (an uncommon accident with her) lost command of her voice, which trembled ever so slightly. 'What an odd thought! why should you offend me? Do I seem so open to that sort of thing?' Her colour had deepened again, and her eyes had brightened. She had forgotten herself, and before speaking had not, as was her wont, sought counsel of that staunch conservative, her taste. She had spoken from a full heart – a heart which had been filling rapidly, since the outset of their walk, with a feeling almost passionate in its quality, and which that little puff of the actual conveyed in Mr Ludlow's announcement of his departure had caused to overflow. The reader may give this feeling whatever name he chooses. We will content ourselves with saying that Adela had played with fire so effectually that she had been scorched. The slight violence of the speech just quoted may represent her sensation of pain.

'You pull one up rather short, Miss Moore,' said Ludlow. 'A man says the best he can.'

Adela made no reply – for a moment she hung her head. Was she to cry out because she was hurt? Was she to thrust her injured heart into a company in which there was, as yet at least, no question of hearts? No! here our reserved and contemplative heroine is herself again. Her part was still to be the youthful woman of the world, the perfect young lady. For our own part, we can imagine no figure more engaging than this civilised and disciplined personage under such circumstances; and if Adela had been the most accomplished of coquettes she could not have assumed a more becoming expression than the air of judicious consideration which now covered her features. But having paid this generous homage to propriety, she felt free to suffer in secret. Raising her eyes from the ground, she abruptly addressed her companion.

'By the way, Mr Ludlow, tell me something about yourself.'

Ludlow burst into a laugh. 'What shall I tell you?'

'Everything.'

'Everything? Excuse me, I'm not such a fool. But do you know that's a very tempting request you make? I suppose I ought to blush and hesitate; but I never yet blushed or hesitated in the right place.'

'Very good. There is one fact. Continue. Begin at the beginning.'

'Well, let me see. My name you know. I am twenty-eight years old.'

'That's the end,' said Adela.

'But you don't want the history of my babyhood, I take it. I imagine that I was a very big, noisy, ugly baby – what's called a "splendid infant." My parents were poor, and, of course, honest. They belonged to a very different set – or "sphere," I suppose you call it – from any you probably know. They were working people. My father was a chemist, in a small way of business, and I suspect my mother was not above using her hands to turn a penny. But although I don't remember her, I am sure she was a good, sound woman; I feel her occasionally in my own sinews. I myself have been at work all my life, and a very good worker I am, let me tell you. I am not patient, as I imagine your brother to be – although I have more patience than you might suppose – but I don't let go easily. If I strike you as very egotistical, remember 'twas you began it. I don't know whether I am clever, and I don't much care; that's a kind of metaphysical, sentimental, vapid word. But I know what I want to know, and I generally manage to find it out. I don't know much about my moral nature; I have no doubt I am beastly selfish. Still, I don't like to hurt peoples' feelings, and I am rather fond of poetry and flowers. I don't believe I am very "high-toned," all the same. I should not be at all surprised to discover I was prodigiously conceited; but I am afraid the discovery wouldn't cut me down much. I am remarkably hard to keep down, I know. Oh, you would think me a great brute if you knew me. I shouldn't recommend anyone to count too much on my being of an amiable disposition. I am often very much bored with people who are fond of me – because some of them are, really; so I am afraid I am ungrateful. Of course, as a man speaking to a woman, there's nothing for it but to say I am very low; but I hate to talk about things you can't prove. I have got very little "general culture," you know, but first and last I have read a great many books – and, thank heaven, I remember things. And I have some tastes, too. I am very fond of music. I have a good young voice of my own; *that* I can't help knowing; and I am not one to be bullied about pictures. I know how to sit on a horse, and how to row a boat. Is that enough? I am conscious of a great inability to say anything to the point. To put myself in a nutshell, I am a greedy specialist – and not a bad fellow. Still, I am only what I am – a very common creature.'

'Do you call yourself a very common creature because you really believe yourself to be one, or because you are weakly tempted to disfigure your rather flattering catalogue with a great final blot?'

'I am sure I don't know. You show more subtlety in that one question than I have shown in a whole string of affirmations. You women are strong on asking embarrassing questions. Seriously, I believe I *am* second-rate. I wouldn't make such an admission to every one though. But to you, Miss Moore, who sit there under your parasol as impartial as the muse of history, to you I owe the truth. I am no man of genius. There is something I miss; some final distinction I lack; you may call it what you please. Perhaps it's humility. Perhaps you can find it in Ruskin, somewhere. Perhaps it's delicacy – perhaps it's imagination. I am very vulgar, Miss Moore. I am the vulgar son of vulgar people. I use the word, of course, in its literal sense. So much I grant you at the outset, but it's my last concession!'

'Your concessions are smaller than they sound. Have you any sisters?'

'Not a sister; and no brothers, nor cousins, nor uncles, nor aunts.'

'And you sail for Europe to-morrow?'

'To-morrow, at ten o'clock.'

'To be away how long?'

'As long as I can. Five years, if possible.'

'What do you expect to do in those five years?'

'Well, study.'

'Nothing but study?'

'It will all come back to that, I guess. I hope to enjoy myself considerably, and to look at the world as I go. But I must not waste time; I am growing old.'

'Where are you going?'

'To Berlin. I wanted to get some letters of introduction from your brother.'

'Have you money? Are you well off?'

'Well off? Not I, heaven forgive me! I am very poor. I have in hand a little money that has just come to me from an unexpected quarter: an old debt owing my father. It will take me to Germany and keep me for six months. After that I shall work my way.'

'Are you happy? Are you contented?'

'Just now I am pretty comfortable, thank you.'

'But shall you be so when you get to Berlin?'

'I don't promise to be contented; but I am pretty sure to be happy.'

'Well,' said Adela, 'I sincerely hope you will succeed in everything.'

'Thank you, awfully,' said Ludlow.

Of what more was said at this moment no record may be given here. The reader has been put into possession of the key of our friends' conversation; it is only needful to say that in this key it was prolonged for half an hour more. As the minutes elapsed Adela found herself drifting further and further away from her anchorage. When at last she compelled herself to consult her watch and remind her companion that there remained but just time enough for them to reach home in anticipation of her brother's arrival, she knew that she was rapidly floating seaward. As she descended the hill at her companion's side she felt herself suddenly thrilled by an acute temptation. Her first instinct was to close her eyes upon it, in the trust that when she should open them again it would have vanished; but she found that it was not to be so uncompromisingly dismissed. It pressed her so hard that before she walked a mile homeward she had succumbed to it, or had at least given it the pledge of that quickening of the heart which accompanies a bold resolution. This little sacrifice allowed her no breath for idle words, and she accordingly advanced with a bent and listening head. Ludlow marched along, with no apparent diminution of his habitual buoyancy of mien, talking as fast and

loud as at the outset. He risked a prophecy that Mr Moore would
not have returned, and charged Adela with a comical message of
regrets. Adela had begun by wondering whether the approach of
their separation had wrought within him any sentimental depression at all commensurate with her own, with that which sealed her
lips and weighed upon her heart; and now she was debating as to
whether his express declaration that he felt 'awfully blue' ought
necessarily to remove her doubts. Ludlow followed up this declaration with a very pretty review of the morning, and a leave-taking
speech which, whether intensely sincere or not, struck Adela as at
least in very good taste. He might be a common creature – but he
was certainly a very uncommon one. When they reached the
garden-gate it was with a fluttering heart that Adela scanned the
premises for some accidental sign of her brother's presence. She
felt that there would be an especial fitness in his not having
returned. She led the way in. The hall table was bare of his usual
hat and overcoat, his silver-headed stick was not in the corner.
The only object that struck her was Mr Pynsent's card, which she
had deposited there on her exit. All that was represented by that
little white ticket seemed a thousand miles away. She looked for
Mr Moore in his study, but it was empty.

As Adela went back from her quest into the drawing-room she
simply shook her head at Ludlow, who was standing before the
fire-place; and as she did so she caught her reflection in the mantel-
glass. 'Verily,' she said to herself, 'I have travelled far.' She had
pretty well unlearned her old dignities and forms, but she was to
break with them still more completely. It was with a singular
hardihood that she prepared to redeem the little pledge which had
been extorted from her on her way home. She felt that there was
no trial to which her generosity might now be called which she
would not hail with enthusiasm. Unfortunately, her generosity was
not likely to be challenged; although she nevertheless had the
satisfaction of assuring herself at this moment that, like the mercy
of the Lord, it was infinite. Should she satisfy herself of her
friend's? or should she leave it delightfully uncertain? These had
been the terms of what has been called her temptation, at the foot
of the hill.

'Well, I have very little time,' said Ludlow; 'I must get my dinner and pay my bill and drive to the train.' And he put out his hand.

Adela gave him her own, without meeting his eyes. 'You are in a great hurry,' she said, rather casually.

'It's not I who am in a hurry. It's my confounded destiny. It's the train and the steamer.'

'If you really wished to stay you wouldn't be bullied by the train and the steamer.'

'Very true – very true. But *do* I really wish to stay?'

'That's the question. That's exactly what I want to know.'

'You ask difficult questions, Miss Moore.'

'Difficult for me – yes.'

'Then, of course, you are prepared to answer easy ones.'

'Let me hear what you call easy.'

'Well then, do you wish me to stay? All I have to do is to throw down my hat, sit down, and fold my arms for twenty minutes. I lose my train and my ship. I remain in America, instead of going to Europe.'

'I have thought of all that.'

'I don't mean to say it's a great deal. There are attractions on both sides.'

'Yes, and especially on one. It *is* a great deal.'

'And you request me to give it up – to renounce Berlin?'

'No; I ought not to do that. What I ask of you is whether, if I *should* so request you, you would say "yes."'

'That *does* make the matter easy for you, Miss Moore. What attractions do you hold out?'

'I hold out nothing whatever, sir.'

'I suppose that means a great deal.'

'A great deal of absurdity.'

'Well, you are certainly a most interesting woman, Miss Moore – a charming woman.'

'Why don't you call me irresistible at once, and bid me good morning?'

'I don't know but that I shall have to come to that. But I will give you no answer that leaves you at an advantage. Ask me to stay – order me to stay, if that suits you better – and I will see how it sounds. Come, you must not trifle with a man.' He still held

Adela's hand, and now they were looking watchfully into each other's eyes. He paused, waiting for an answer.

'Goodbye, Mr Ludlow,' said Adela. 'God bless you!' And she was about to withdraw her hand; but he held it.

'Are we friends?' said he.

Adela gave a little shrug of her shoulders. 'Friends of three hours!'

Ludlow looked at her with some sternness. 'Our parting could at best hardly have been sweet,' said he; 'but why should you make it bitter, Miss Moore?'

'If it's bitter, why should you try to change it?'

'Because I don't like bitter things.'

Ludlow had caught a glimpse of the truth – that truth of which the reader has had a glimpse – and he stood there at once thrilled and annoyed. He had both a heart and a conscience. 'It's not my fault,' he murmured to the latter; but he was unable to add, in all consistency, that it was his misfortune. It would be very heroic, very poetic, very chivalric, to lose his steamer, and he felt that he could do so for sufficient cause – at the suggestion of a fact. But the motive here was less than a fact – an idea; less than an idea – a mere guess. 'It's a very pretty little romance as it is,' he said to himself. 'Why spoil it? She's a different sort from any I have met, and just to have seen her like this – that is enough for me!' He raised her hand to his lips, pressed them to it, dropped it, reached the door, and bounded out of the garden gate.

A Light Man[1]

'And I – what I seem to my friend, you see –
   What I soon shall seem to his love, you guess.
What I seem to myself, do you ask of me?
   No hero, I confess.'

                    A Light Woman – Browning's Men and Women[2]

April 4, 1857 – I have changed my sky without changing my mind.
I resume these old notes in a new world. I hardly know of what
use they are; but it's easier to stick to the habit than to drop it. I
have been at home now a week – at home, forsooth! And yet, after
all, it is home. I am dejected, I am bored, I am blue. How can a
man be more at home than that? Nevertheless, I am the citizen of
a great country, and for that matter, of a great city. I walked to-
day some ten miles or so along Broadway, and on the whole I don't
blush for my native land. We are a capable race and a good-looking
withal; and I don't see why we shouldn't prosper as well as
another. This, by the way, ought to be a very encouraging
reflection. A capable fellow and a good-looking withal; I don't see
why he shouldn't die a millionaire. At all events he must do
something. When a man has, at thirty-two, a net income of
considerably less than nothing, he can scarcely hope to overtake a
fortune before he himself is overtaken by age and philosophy –
two deplorable obstructions. I am afraid that one of them has
already planted itself in my path. What am I? What do I wish?
Whither do I tend? What do I believe? I am constantly beset by
these impertinent whisperings. Formerly it was enough that I was
Maximus Austin; that I was endowed with a cheerful mind and a
good digestion; and one day or another, when I had come to the
end, I should return to America and begin at the beginning; that,
meanwhile, existence was sweet in – in the Rue Tronchet. But

now? Has the sweetness really passed out of life? Have I eaten the plums and left nothing but the bread and milk and corn-starch, or whatever the horrible concoction is? – I had it to-day for dinner. Pleasure, at least, I imagine – pleasure pure and simple, pleasure crude, brutal and vulgar – this poor flimsy delusion has lost all its charm. I shall never again care for certain things – and indeed for certain persons. Of such things or such persons, I firmly maintain, however, that I was never an enthusiastic votary. It would be more to my credit, I suppose, if I had been. More would be forgiven me if I had loved a little more, if into all my folly and egotism I had put a little more *naïveté* and sincerity. Well, I did the best I could, I was at once too bad and too good for it all. At present, it's far enough off; I have put the sea between us; I am stranded. I sit high and dry, scanning the horizon for a friendly sail, or waiting for a high tide to set me afloat. The wave of pleasure has deposited me here in the sand. Shall I owe my rescue to the wave of pain? At moments I feel a kind of longing to expiate my stupid little sins. I see, as through a glass, darkly, the beauty of labor and love. Decidedly, I am willing to work. It's written.

7th – My sail is in sight; it's at hand; I have all but boarded the vessel. I received this morning a letter from the best man in the world. Here it is:

DEAR MAX: I see this very moment, in an old newspaper which had already passed through my hands without yielding up its most precious item, the announcement of your arrival in New York. To think of your having perhaps missed the welcome you had a right to expect from me! Here it is dear Max – as cordial as you please. When I say I have just read of your arrival, I mean that twenty minutes have elapsed by the clock. These have been spent in conversation with my excellent friend Mr Sloane – we having taken the liberty of making you the topic. I haven't time to say more about Frederick Sloane than that he is very anxious to make your acquaintance, and that, if your time is not otherwise engaged, he would like you very much to spend a month with him. He is an excellent host, or I shouldn't be here myself. It appears that he knew your mother very intimately, and he has a taste for visiting the amenities of the parents upon the children; the original ground of my own connection with him was that he had been a particular friend of my father. You may have heard your mother speak of him. He is a very strange old fellow, but you will like him, Whether or no you come for his sake, come for mine.

Yours always,
THEODORE LISLE

Theodore's letter is of course very kind, but it's remakably obscure. My mother may have had the highest regard for Mr Sloane, but she never mentioned his name in my hearing. Who is he, what is he, and what is the nature of his relations with Theodore? I shall learn betimes. I have written to Theodore that I gladly accept (I believe I suppressed the 'gladly' though) his friend's invitation, and that I shall immediately present myself. What can I do that is better? Speaking sordidly, I shall obtain food and lodging while I look about me. I shall have a base of operations. D., it appears, is a long day's journey, but enchanting when you reach it. I am curious to see an enchanting American town. And to stay a month! Mr Frederick Sloane, whoever you are, *vous faites bien les choses*, and the little that I know of you is very much to your credit. You enjoyed the friendship of my dear mother, you possess the esteem of the virtuous Theodore, you commend yourself to my own affection. At this rate, I shall not grudge it.

D – , 14th. – I have been here since Thursday evening – three days. As we rattled up to the tavern in the village, I perceived from the top of the coach in the twilight, Theodore beneath the porch, scanning the vehicle, with all his amiable disposition in his eyes. He has grown older, of course, in these five years, but less so than I had expected. His is one of those smooth, unwrinkled souls that keep their bodies fair and fresh. As tall as ever, moreover, and as lean and clean. How short and fat and dark and debauched he makes one feel! By nothing he says or means, of course, but merely by his old unconscious purity and simplicity – that slender straightness which makes him remind you of the spire of an English abbey. He greeted me with smiles, and stares, and alarming blushes. He assures me that he never would have known me, and that five years have altered me – *sehr!* I asked him if it were for the better? He looked at me hard for a moment, with his eyes of blue, and then, for an answer, he blushed again.

On my arrival we agreed to walk over from the village. He dismissed his wagon with my luggage, and we went arm-in-arm through the dusk. The town is seated at the foot of certain mountains, whose names I have yet to learn, and at the head of a big sheet of water, which, as yet, too, I know only as 'the Lake.' The road hitherward soon leaves the village and wanders in rural loveliness by the margin of this expanse. Sometimes the water is hidden by clumps of trees, behind which we heard it lapping and gurgling in the darkness; sometimes it stretches out from your feet in shining vagueness, as if it were tired of making, all day, a million little eyes at the great stupid hills. The walk from the tavern takes some half an hour, and in this interval Theodore made his position a little more clear. Mr Sloane is a rich old widower; his age is seventy-two, and as his health is thoroughly broken, is practically even greater; and his fortune – Theodore, characteristically, doesn't know anything definite about that. It's probably about a million. He has lived much in Europe, and in the 'great world'; he has had adventures and passions and all that sort of thing; and now, in the evening of his days, like an old French diplomatist, he takes it into his head to write his memoirs. To this end he has lured poor Theodore to his gruesome side, to mend his pens for him. He has been a great scribbler, says Theodore, all his days, and he proposes to incorporate a large amount of promiscuous literary matter into these *souvenirs intimes*. Theodore's principal function seems to be to get him to leave things out. In fact, the poor youth seems troubled in conscience. His patron's lucubrations have taken the turn of many other memoirs, and have ceased to address themselves *virginibus puerisque*. On the whole, he declares they are a very odd mixture – a medley of gold and tinsel, of bad taste and a good sense. I can readily understand it. The old man bores me, puzzles me, and amuses me.

He was in waiting to receive me. We found him in his library – which, by the way, is simply the most delightful apartment that I ever smoked a cigar in – a room arranged for a lifetime. At one end stands a great fireplace, with a florid, fantastic mantelpiece in carved white marble – an importation, of course, and, as one may say, an interpolation; the groundwork of the house, the 'fixtures,' being throughout plain, solid and domestic. Over the mantel-shelf is a large landscape, a fine Gainsborough, full of the complicated harmonies of an English summer. Beneath it stands a row of bronzes of the Renaissance and potteries of the Orient. Facing the door as you enter, is an immense window set in a recess, with cushioned seats and large clear panes, stationed as it were at the very apex of the lake (which forms an almost perfect oval) and commanding a view of its whole extent. At the other end, opposite the fireplace, the wall is studded, from floor to ceiling, with choice foreign paintings, placed in relief against the orthodox crimson screen. Elsewhere the walls are covered with books, arranged neither in formal regularity nor quite helter-skelter, but in a sort of genial incongruity, which tells that sooner or later each volume feels sure of leaving the ranks and returning into different company. Mr Sloane makes use of his books. His two passions, according to Theodore, are reading and talking; but to talk he must have a book in his hand. The charm of the room lies in the absence of certain pedantic tones – the browns, blacks and grays – which distinguish most libraries. The apartment is of the feminine gender. There are half a dozen light colors scattered about – pink in the carpet, tender blue in the curtains, yellow in the chairs. The result is a general look of brightness and lightness; it expresses even a certain cynicism. You perceive the place to be the home, not of a man of learning, but of a man of fancy.

He rose from his chair – the man of fancy, to greet me – the man of fact. As I looked at him, in the lamplight, it seemed to me, for the first five minutes, that I had seldom seen an uglier little person. It took me five minutes to get the point of view; then I began to admire. He is diminutive, or at best of my own moderate stature, and bent and contracted with his seventy years; lean and delicate, moreover, and very highly finished. He is curiously pale, with a kind of opaque yellow pallor. Literally, it's a magnificent yellow. His skin is of just the hue and apparent texture of some old crumpled Oriental scroll. I know a dozen painters who would give more than they have to arrive at the exact 'tone' of his thick-veined, bloodless hands, his polished ivory knuckles. His eyes are circled with red, but in the battered little setting of their orbits they have the lustre of old sapphires. His nose, owing to the falling away of other portions of his face, has assumed a grotesque, unnatural prominence; it describes an immense arch, gleaming like a piece of parchment stretched on ivory. He has, apparently, all his teeth, but has muffled his cranium in a dead black wig; of course he's clean shaven. In his dress he has a muffled, wadded look and an apparent aversion to linen, inasmuch as none is visible on his person. He seemed neat enough, but not fastidious. At first, as I say, I fancied him monstrously ugly; but on further acquaint-ance I perceived that what I had taken for ugliness is nothing but the incomplete remains of remarkable good looks. The line of his features is pure; his nose, *cœteris paribus*, would be extremely handsome; his eyes are the oldest eyes I ever saw, and yet they are wonderfully living. He has something remarkably insinuating.

He offered his two hands, as Theodore introduced me; I gave him my own, and he stood smiling at me like some quaint old image in ivory and ebony, scanning my face with a curiosity which he took no pains to conceal. 'God bless me,' he said, at last, 'how much you look like your father!' I sat down, and for half an hour we talked of many things – of my journey, of my impressions of America, of my reminiscences of Europe, and, by implication, of my prospects. His voice is weak and cracked, but he makes it express everything. Mr Sloane is not yet in his dotage – oh no! He nevertheless makes himself out a poor creature. In reply to an inquiry of mine about his health, he favored me with a long list of his infirmities (some of which are very trying, certainly) and assured me that he was quite finished.

'I live out of mere curiosity,' he said.

'I have heard of people dying from the same motive.'

He looked at me a moment, as if to ascertain whether I were laughing at him. And then, after a pause, 'Perhaps you don't know that I disbelieve in a future life,' he remarked, blandly.

At these words Theodore got up and walked to the fire.

'Well, we shan't quarrel about that,' said I. Theodore turned round, staring.

'Do you mean that you agree with me?' the old man asked.

'I certainly haven't come here to talk theology! Don't ask me to disbelieve, and I'll never ask you to believe.'

'Come,' cried Mr Sloane, rubbing his hands, 'you'll not persuade me you are a Christian – like your friend Theodore there.'

'Like Theodore – assuredly not.' And then, somehow, I don't know why, at the thought of Theodore's Christianity I burst into a laugh. 'Excuse me, my dear fellow,' I said, 'you know, for the last ten years I have lived in pagan lands.'

'What do you call pagan?' asked Theodore, smiling.

I saw the old man, with his hands locked, eyeing me shrewdly, and waiting for my answer. I hesitated a moment, and then I said, 'Everything that makes life tolerable!'

Hereupon Mr Sloane began to laugh till he coughed. Verily, I thought, if he lives for curiosity, he's easily satisfied.

We went into dinner, and this repast showed me that some of his curiosity is culinary. I observed, by the way, that for a victim of neuralgia, dyspepsia, and a thousand other ills, Mr Sloane plies a most inconsequential knife and fork. Sauces and spices and condiments seem to be the chief of his diet. After dinner he dismissed us, in consideration of my natural desire to see my friend in private. Theodore has capital quarters – a downy bedroom and a snug little *salon*. We talked till near midnight – of ourselves, of each other, and of the author of the memoirs, down stairs. That is, I spoke of myself, and Theodore listened; and then Theodore descanted upon Mr Sloane, and I listened. His commerce with the old man has sharpened his wits. Sloane has taught him to observe and judge, and Theodore turns round, observes, judges – him! He has become quite the critic and analyst. There is something very pleasant in the discriminations of a conscientious mind, in which criticism is tempered by an angelic charity. Only, it may easily end by acting on one's nerves. At midnight we repaired to the library, to take leave of our host till the morrow – an attention which, under all circumstances, he rigidly exacts. As I gave him my hand he held it again and looked at me as he had done on my arrival. 'Bless my soul,' he said, at last, 'how much you look like your mother!'

To-night, at the end of my third day, I begin to feel decidedly at home. The fact is, I am remarkably comfortable. The house is pervaded by an indefinable, irresistible love of luxury and privacy. Mr Frederick Sloane is a horribly corrupt old mortal. Already in his relaxing presence I have become heartily reconciled to doing nothing. But with Theodore on one side – standing there like a tall interrogation-point – I honestly believe I can defy Mr Sloane on the other. The former asked me this morning, with visible solicitude, in allusion to the bit of dialogue I have quoted above on matters of faith, whether I am really a materialist – whether I don't believe something? I told him I would believe anything he liked. He looked at me a while, in friendly sadness. 'I hardly know whether you are not worse than Mr Sloane,' he said.

But Theodore is, after all, in duty bound to give a man a long rope in these matters. His own rope is one of the longest. He reads Voltaire with Mr Sloane, and Emerson in his own room. He is the stronger man of the two; he has the larger stomach. Mr Sloane delights, of course, in Voltaire, but he can't read a line of Emerson. Theodore delights in Emerson, and enjoys Voltaire, though he thinks him superficial. It appears that since we parted in Paris, five years ago, his conscience has dwelt in many lands. *C'est tout une histoire* – which he tells very prettily. He left college determined to enter the church, and came abroad with his mind full of theology and Tübingen.[3] He appears to have studied, not wisely but too well. Instead of faith full-armed and serene, there sprang from the labor of his brain a myriad sickly questions, piping for answers. He went for a winter to Italy, where, I take it, he was not quite so much afflicted as he ought to have been at the sight of the beautiful spiritual repose that he had missed. It was after this that we spent those three months together in Brittany – the best-spent months of my long residence in Europe. Theodore inoculated me, I think with some of his seriousness, and I just touched him with my profanity; and we agreed together that there were a few good things left – health, friendship, a summer sky, and the lovely byways of an old French province. He came home, searched the Scriptures once more, accepted a 'call,' and made an attempt to respond to it. But the inner voice failed him. His outlook was cheerless enough. During his absence his married sister, the elder one, had taken the other to live with her, relieving Theodore of the charge of contribution to her support. But suddenly, behold the husband, the brother-in-law, dies, leaving a mere figment of property; and the two ladies, with their two little girls, are afloat in the wide world. Theodore finds himself at twenty-six without an income, without a profession, and with a family of four females to support. Well, in his quiet way he draws on his courage. The history of the two years that passed before he came to Mr Sloane is really absolutely edifying. He rescued his sisters and nieces from the deep waters, placed them high and dry, established them somewhere in decent gentility – and then found at last that his strength had left him – had dropped dead like an overridden horse. In short, he had worked himself to the bone. It was now his sisters' turn. They nursed him with all the added tenderness of gratitude for the past and terror of the future, and brought him safely through a grievous malady. Meanwhile Mr Sloane having decided to treat himself to a private secretary and suffered dreadful mischance in three successive experiments, had heard of Theodore's situation and his merits; had furthermore recognized in him the son of an early and intimate friend, and had finally offered him the very comfortable position he now occupies. There is a decided incongruity between Theodore as a man – as Theodore, in fine – and the dear fellow as the intellectual agent, confidant, complaisant, purveyor, pander – what you will – of a battered old cynic and dilettante – a worldling if there ever was one. There seems at first sight a perfect want of agreement between his character and his function. One is gold and the other brass, or something very like it. But on reflection I can enter into it – his having, under the circumstances, accepted Mr Sloane's offer and been content to do his duties. *Ce que c'est de nous!*[4] Theodore's contentment in such a case is a theme for the moralist – a better moralist than I. The best and purest mortals are an odd mixture, and in none of us does honesty exist on its own terms. Ideally, Theodore hasn't the smallest business *dans cette galère*.[5] It offends my sense of propriety to find him here. I feel that I ought to notify him as a friend that he has knocked at the wrong door, and that he had better retreat before he is brought to the blush. However, I suppose he might as well be here as reading Emerson 'evenings' in the back parlor, to those two very plain sisters – judging from their photographs. Practically it hurts no one not to be too much of a prig. Poor Theodore was weak, depressed, out of work. Mr Sloane offers him a lodging and a salary in return for – after all, merely a little tact. All he has to do is to read to the old man, lay down the book a while, with his finger in the place, and let him talk; take it up again, read another dozen pages and submit to another commentary. Then to write a dozen pages under his dictation – to suggest a word, polish off a period, or help him out with a complicated idea or a half-remembered fact. This is all, I say; and yet this is much. Theodore's apparent success proves it to be much, as well as the old man's satisfaction. It is a part; he has to simulate. He has to 'make believe' a little – a good deal; he has to put his pride in his pocket and send his conscience to the wash. He has to be accommodating – to listen and pretend and flatter; and he does it as well as many a worse man – does it far better than I. I might bully the old man, but I don't think I could humor him. After all, however, it is not a matter of comparative merit. In every son of woman there are two men – the practical man and the dreamer. We live for our dreams – but, meanwhile, we live by our wits. When the dreamer is a poet, the other fellow is an artist. Theodore, at bottom is only a man of taste. If he were not destined to become a high priest among moralists, he might be a prince among connoisseurs. He plays his part, therefore, artistically, with spirit, with originality, with all his native refinement. How can Mr Sloane fail to believe that he possesses a paragon? He is no such fool as not to appreciate a *nature distinguée* when it comes in his way. He confidentially assured me this morning that Theodore has the most charming mind in the world, but that it's a pity he's so simple as not to suspect it. If he only doesn't ruin him with his flattery!

19th. – I am certainly fortunate among men. This morning when, tentatively, I spoke of going away, Mr Sloane rose from his seat in horror and declared that for the present I must regard his house as my home. 'Come, come,' he said, 'when you leave this place where do you intend to go?' Where, indeed? I graciously allowed Mr Sloane to have the best of the argument. Theodore assures me that he appreciates these and other affabilities, and that I have made what he calls a 'conquest' of his venerable heart. Poor, battered, bamboozled old organ! he would have one believe that it has a most tragical record of capture and recapture. At all events, it appears that I am master of the citadel. For the present I have no wish to evacuate. I feel, nevertheless, in some far-off corner of my soul, that I ought to shoulder my victorious banner and advance to more fruitful triumphs.

I blush for my beastly laziness. It isn't that I am willing to stay here a month, but that I am willing to stay here six. Such is the charming, disgusting truth. Have I really outlived the age of energy? Have I survived my ambition, my integrity, my self-respect? Verily, I ought to have survived the habit of asking myself silly questions. I made up my mind long ago to go in for nothing but present success; and I don't care for that sufficiently to secure it at the cost of temporary suffering. I have a passion for nothing – not even for life. I know very well the appearance I make in the world. I pass for a clever, accomplished, capable, good-natured fellow, who can do anything if he would only try. I am supposed to be rather cultivated, to have latent talents. When I was younger I used to find a certain entertainment in the spectacle of human affairs. I liked to see men and women hurrying on each other's heels across the stage. But I am sick and tired of them now; not that I am a misanthrope, God forbid! They are not worth hating. I never knew but one creature who was, and her I went and loved. To be consistent, I ought to have hated my mother, and now I ought to detest Theodore. But I don't – truly, on the whole, I don't – any more than I dote on him. I firmly believe that it makes a difference to him, his idea that I *am* fond of him. He believes in that, as he believes in all the rest of it – in my culture, my latent talents, my underlying 'earnestness,' my sense of beauty and love of truth. Oh, for a *man* among them all – a fellow with eyes in his head – eyes that would know me for what I am and let me see they had guessed it. Possibly such a fellow as that might get a 'rise' out of me.

In the name of bread and butter, what am I to do? (I was obliged this morning to borrow fifty dollars from Theodore, who remembered gleefully that he has been owing me a trifling sum for the past four years, and in fact has preserved a note to this effect.) Within the last week I have hatched a desperate plan: I have made up my mind to take a wife – a rich one, *bien entendu*. Why not accept the goods of the gods? It is not my fault, after all, if I pass for a good fellow. Why not admit that practically, mechanically – as I may say – maritally, I *may* be a good fellow? I warrant myself kind. I should never beat my wife; I don't think I should even contradict her. Assume that her fortune has the proper number of zeros and that she herself is one of them, and I can even imagine her adoring me. I really think this is my only way. Curiously, as I look back upon my brief career, it all seems to tend to this consummation. It has its graceful curves and crooks, indeed, and here and there a passionate tangent; but on the whole, if I were to unfold it here *à la* Hogarth, what better legend could I scrawl beneath the series of pictures than So-and-So's Progress to a Mercenary Marriage?

Coming events do what we all know with their shadows. My noble fate is, perhaps, not far off. I already feel throughout my person a magnificent languor – as from the possession of many dollars. Or is it simply my sense of well-being in this perfectly appointed house? Is it simply the contact of the highest civilization I have known? At all events, the place is of velvet, and my only complaint of Mr Sloane is that, instead of an old widower, he's not an old widow (or a young maid), so that I might marry him, survive him, and dwell forever in this rich and mellow home. As I write here, at my bedroom table, I have only to stretch out an arm and raise the window-curtain to see the thick-planted garden budding and breathing and growing in the silvery silence. Far above in the liquid darkness rolls the brilliant ball of the moon; beneath, in its light, lies the lake, in murmuring, troubled sleep; round about, the mountains, looking strange and blanched, seem to bare their heads and undrape their shoulders. So much for midnight. To-morrow the scene will be lovely with the beauty of day. Under one aspect or another I have it always before me. At the end of the garden is moored a boat, in which Theodore and I have indulged in an immense deal of irregular navigation. What lovely landward coves and bays – what alder-smothered creeks – what lily-sheeted pools – what sheer steep hillsides, making the water dark and quiet where they hang. I confess that in these excursions Theodore looks after the boat and I after the scenery. Mr Sloane avoids the water – on account of the dampness, he says; because he's afraid of drowning, I suspect.

22nd. – Theodore is right. The *bonhomme* has taken me into his favor. I protest I don't see how he was to escape it. *Je l'ai bien soigné,*[6] as they say in Paris. I don't blush for it. In one coin or another I must repay his hospitality – which is certainly very liberal. Theodore dots his *i*'s, crosses his *t*'s, verifies his quotations; while I set traps for that famous 'curiosity.' This speaks vastly well for my powers. He pretends to be surprised at nothing, and to possess in perfection – poor, pitiable old fop – the art of keeping his countenance; but repeatedly, I know, I have made him stare. As for his corruption, which I spoke of above, it's a very pretty piece of wickedness, but it strikes me as a purely intellectual matter. I imagine him never to have had any real senses. He may have been unclean; morally, he's not very tidy now; but he never can have been what the French call a *viveur*. He's too delicate, he's of a feminine turn; and what woman was ever a *viveur*? He likes to sit in his chair and read scandal, talk scandal, make scandal, so far as he may without catching a cold or bringing on a headache. I already feel as if I had known him a lifetime. I read him as clearly as if I had. I know the type to which he belongs; I have encountered, first and last, a good many specimens of it. He's neither more nor less than a gossip – a gossip flanked by a coxcomb and an egotist. He's shallow, vain, cold, superstitious, timid, pretentious, capricious; a pretty list of foibles! And yet, for all this, he has his good points. His caprices are sometimes generous, and his rebellion against the ugliness of life frequently makes him do kind things. His memory (for trifles) is remarkable, and (where his own performances are not involved) his taste is excellent. He has no courage for evil more than for good. He is the victim, however, of more illusions with regard to himself than I ever knew a single brain to shelter. At the age of twenty, poor, ignorant and remarkably handsome, he married a woman of immense wealth, many years his senior. At the end of three years she very considerately took herself off and left him to the enjoyment of his freedom and riches. If he had remained poor he might from time to time have rubbed at random against the truth, and would be able to recognize the touch of it. But he wraps himself in his money as in a wadded dressing-gown, and goes trundling through life on his little gold wheels. The greater part of his career, from the time of his marriage till about ten years ago, was spent in Europe, which, superficially, he knows very well. He has lived in fifty places, known thousands of people, and spent a very large fortune. At one time, I believe, he spent considerably too much, trembled for an instant on the verge of a pecuniary crash, but recovered himself, and found himself more frightened than hurt, yet audibly recommended to lower his pitch. He passed five years in a species of penitent seclusion on the lake of – I forget what (his genius seems to be partial to lakes), and laid the basis of his present magnificent taste for literature. I can't call him anything but magnificent in this respect, so long as he must have his punctuation done by a *nature distinguée*. At the close of this period, by economy, he had made up his losses. His turning the screw during those relatively impecunious years represents, I am pretty sure, the only act of resolution of his life. It was rendered possible by his morbid, his actually pusillanimous dread of poverty; he doesn't feel safe without half a million between him and starvation. Meanwhile he had turned from a young man into an old man; his health was broken, his spirit was jaded, and I imagine, to do him justice, that he began to feel certain natural, filial longings for this dear American mother of us all. They say the most hopeless truants and triflers have come to it. He came to it, at all events; he packed up his books and pictures and gimcracks, and bade farewell to Europe. This house which he now occupies belonged to his wife's estate. She had, for sentimental reasons of her own, commended it to his particular care. On his return he came to see it, liked it, turned a parcel of carpenters and upholsterers into it, and by inhabiting it for nine years transformed it into the perfect dwelling which I find it. Here he has spent all his time, with the exception of a usual winter's visit to New York – a practice recently discontinued, owing to the increase of his ailments and the projection of these famous memoirs. His life has finally come to be passed in comparative solitude. He tells of various distant relatives, as well as intimate friends of both sexes, who used formerly to be entertained at his cost; but with each of them, in the course of time, he seems to have succeeded in quarrelling. Throughout life, evidently, he has had capital fingers for plucking off parasites. Rich, lonely, and vain, he must have been fair game for the race of social sycophants and cormorants; and it's much to the credit of his sharpness and that instinct of self-defence which nature bestows even on the weak, that he has not been despoiled and *exploité*. Apparently they have all been bunglers. I maintain that something is to be done with him still. But one must work in obedience to certain definite laws. Doctor Jones, his physician, tells me that in point of fact he has had for the past ten years an unbroken series of favourites, *protégés*, heirs presumptive; but that each in turn, by some fatally false movement, has spilled his pottage. The doctor declares, moreover, that they were mostly very common people. Gradually the old man seems to have developed a preference for two or three strictly exquisite intimates, over a throng of your vulgar pensioners. His tardy literary schemes, too – fruit of his all but sapless senility – have absorbed more and more of his time and attention. The end of it all is, therefore, that Theodore and I have him quite to ourselves, and that it behooves us to hold our porringers straight.

Poor, pretentious old simpleton! It's not his fault, after all, that he fancies himself a great little man. How are you to judge of the stature of mankind when men have forever addressed you on their knees? Peace and joy to his innocent fatuity! He believes himself the most rational of men; in fact, he's the most superstitious. He fancies himself a philosopher, an inquirer, a discoverer. He has not yet discovered that he is a humbug, that Theodore is a prig, and that I am an adventurer. He prides himself on his good manners, his urbanity, his knowing a rule of conduct for every occasion in life. My private impression is that his skinny old bosom contains unsuspected treasures of impertinence. He takes his stand on his speculative audacity – his direct, undaunted gaze at the universe; in truth, his mind is haunted by a hundred dingy old-world spectres and theological phantasms. He imagines himself one of the most solid of men; he is essentially one of the hollowest. He thinks himself ardent, impulsive, passionate, magnanimous – capable of boundless enthusiasm for an idea or a sentiment. It is clear to me that on no occasion of disinterested action can he ever have done anything in time. He believes, finally, that he has drained the cup of life to the dregs; that he has known, in its bitterest intensity, every emotion of which the human spirit is capable; that he has loved, struggled, suffered. Mere vanity, all of it. He has never loved any one but himself; he has never suffered from anything but an undigested supper or an exploded preten-sion; he has never touched with the end of his lips the vulgar bowl from which the mass of mankind quaffs its floods of joy and sorrow. Well, the long and short of it all is, that I honestly pity him. He may have given sly knocks in his life, but he can't hurt any one now. I pity his ignorance, his weakness, his pusillanimity. He has tasted the real sweetness of life no more than its bitterness; he has never dreamed, nor experimented, nor dared; he has never known any but mercenary affection; neither men nor women have risked aught for *him* – for his good spirits, his good looks, his empty pockets. How I should like to give him, for once, a real sensation!

26th. – I took a row this morning with Theodore a couple of miles along the lake, to a point where we went ashore and lounged away an hour in the sunshine, which is still very comfortable. Poor Theodore seems troubled about many things. For one, he is troubled about me; he is actually more anxious about my future than I myself; he thinks better of me than I do of myself; he is so deucedly conscientious, so scrupulous, so averse to giving offence or to *brusquer*[7] any situation before it has played itself out, that he shrinks from betraying his apprehensions or asking direct questions. But I know that he would like very much to extract from me some intimation that there is something under the sun I should like to do. I catch myself in the act of taking – heaven forgive me! – a half-malignant joy in confounding his expectations – leading his generous sympathies off the scent by giving him momentary glimpses of my latent wickedness. But in Theodore I have so firm a friend that I shall have a considerable job if I ever find it needful to make him change his mind about me. He admires me – that's absolute; he takes my low moral tone for an eccentricity of genius; and it only imparts an extra flavor – a *haut goût* – to the charm of my intercourse. Nevertheless, I can see that he is disappointed. I have even less to show, after all these years, than he had hoped. Heaven help us! little enough it must strike him as being. What a contradiction there is in our being friends at all! I believe we shall end with hating each other. It's all very well now – our agreeing to differ, for we haven't opposed interests. But if we should *really* clash, the situation would be warm! I wonder, as it is, that Theodore keeps his patience with me. His education since we parted should tend logically to make him despise me. He has studied, thought, suffered, loved – loved those very plain sisters and nieces. Poor me! how should I be virtuous? I have no sisters, plain or pretty! – nothing to love, work for, live for. My dear Theodore, if you are going one of these days to despise me and drop me – in the name of comfort, come to the point at once, and make an end of our state of tension.

He is troubled, too, about Mr Sloane. His attitude toward the *bonhomme* quite passes my comprehension. It's the queerest jumble of contraries. He penetrates him, disapproves of him – yet respects and admires him. It all comes of the poor boy's shrinking New England conscience. He's afraid to give his perceptions a fair chance, lest, forsooth, they should look over his neighbor's wall. He'll not understand that he may as well sacrifice the old reprobate for a lamb as for a sheep. His view of the gentleman, therefore, is a perfect tissue of cobwebs – a jumble of half-way sorrows, and wire-drawn charities, and hair-breadth 'scapes from utter damnation, and sudden platitudes of generosity – fit, all of it, to make an angel curse!

'The man's a perfect egoist and fool,' say I, 'but I like him.' Now Theodore likes him – or rather wants to like him; but he can't reconcile it to his self-respect – fastidious deity! – to like a fool. Why the deuce can't he leave it alone altogether? It's a purely practical matter. He ought to do the duties of his place all the better for having his head clear of officious sentiment. I don't believe in disinterested service; and Theodore is too desperately bent on preserving his disinterestedness. With me it's different. I am perfectly free to love the *bonhomme* – for a fool. I'm neither a scribe nor a Pharisee; I am simply a student of the art of life.

And then, Theodore is troubled about his sisters. He's afraid he's not doing his duty by them. He thinks he ought to be with them – to be getting a larger salary – to be teaching his nieces. I am not versed in such questions. Perhaps he ought.

May 3rd. – This morning Theodore sent me word that he was ill and unable to get up; upon which I immediately went in to see him. He had caught cold, was sick and a little feverish. I urged him to make no attempt to leave his room, and assured him that I would do what I could to reconcile Mr Sloane to his absence. This

I found an easy matter. I read to him for a couple of hours, wrote four letters – one in French – and then talked for a while – a good while. I have done more talking, by the way, in the last fortnight, than in any previous twelve months – much of it, too, none of the wisest, nor, I may add, of the most superstitiously veracious. In a little discussion, two or three days ago with Theodore, I came to the point and let him know that in gossiping with Mr Sloane I made no scruple, for our common satisfaction, of 'coloring' more or less. My confession gave him 'that turn,' as Mrs Gamp[8] would say, that his present illness may be the result of it. Nevertheless, poor dear fellow, I trust he will be on his legs to-morrow. This afternoon, somehow, I found myself really in the humour of talking. There was something propitious in the circumstances, a hard, cold rain without, a wood-fire in the library, the *bonhomme* puffing cigarettes in his arm-chair, beside him a portfolio of newly imported prints and photographs, and – Theodore tucked safely away in bed. Finally, when I brought our *tête-à-tête* to a close (taking good care not to overstay my welcome) Mr Sloane seized me by both hands and honored me with one of his venerable grins. 'Max,' he said – 'you must let me call you Max – you are the most delightful man I ever knew.'

Verily, there's some virtue left in me yet. I believe I almost blushed.

'Why didn't I know you ten years ago?' the old man went on. 'There are ten years lost.'

'Ten years ago I was not worth your knowing,' Max remarked.

'But I did know you!' cried the *bonhomme*. 'I knew you in knowing your mother.'

Ah! my mother again. When the old man begins that chapter I feel like telling him to blow out his candle and go to bed.

'At all events,' he continued, 'we must make the most of the years that remain. I am a rotten old carcass, but I have no intention of dying. You won't get tired of me and want to go away?'

'I am devoted to you, sir,' I said. 'But I must be looking for some occupation, you know.'

'Occupation? bother! I'll give you occupation. I'll give you wages.'

'I am afraid that you will want to give me the wages without the work.' And then I declared that I must go up and look at poor Theodore.

The *bonhomme* still kept my hands. 'I wish very much that I could get you to be as fond of me as you are of poor Theodore.'

'Ah, don't talk about fondness, Mr Sloane. I don't deal much in that article.'

'Don't you like my secretary?'

'Not as he deserves.'

'Nor as he likes you, perhaps?'

'He likes me more than I deserve.'

'Well, Max,' my host pursued, 'we can be good friends all the same. We don't need a hocus-pocus of false sentiment. We are *men*, aren't we? – men of sublime good sense.' And just here, as the old man looked at me, the pressure of his hands deepened to a convulsive grasp, and the bloodless mask of his countenance was suddenly distorted with a nameless fear. 'Ah, my dear young man!' he cried, 'come and be a son to me – the son of my age and desolation! For God's sake, don't leave me to pine and die alone!'

I was greatly surprised – and I may add I was moved. Is it true, then, that this dilapidated organism contains such measureless depths of horror and longing? He has evidently a mortal fear of death. I assured him on my honor that he may henceforth call upon me for any service.

8th. – Theodore's little turn proved more serious than I expected. He has been confined to his room till to-day. This evening he came down to the library in his dressing-gown. Decidedly, Mr Sloane is an eccentric, but hardly, as Theodore thinks, a 'charming' one. There is something extremely curious in his humors and fancies – the incongruous fits and starts, as it were, of his taste. For some reason, best known to himself, he took it into his head to regard it as a want of delicacy, of respect, of *savoir-vivre* – of heaven knows what – that poor Theodore, who is still weak and languid, should enter the sacred precinct of his study in the vulgar drapery of a dressing-gown. The sovereign trouble with the *bonhomme* is an absolute lack of the instinct of justice. He's of the real feminine turn – I believe I have written it before – without the redeeming fidelity of the sex. I honestly believe that I might come into his study in my night-shirt and he would smile at it as a picturesque *déshabillé*. But for poor Theodore to-night there was nothing but scowls and frowns, and barely a civil inquiry about his health. But poor Theodore is not such a fool, either; he will not die of a snubbing; I never said he was a weakling. Once he fairly saw from what quarter the wind blew, he bore the master's brutality with the utmost coolness and gallantry. Can it be that Mr Sloane really wishes to drop him? The delicious old brute! He understands favor and friendship only as a selfish rapture – a reaction, an infatuation, an act of aggressive, exclusive patronage. It's not a bestowal, with him, but a transfer, and half his pleasure in causing his sun to shine is that – being wofully near its setting – it willl produce certain long fantastic shadows. He wants to cast my shadow, I suppose, over Theodore; but fortunately I am not altogether an opaque body. Since Theodore was taken ill he has been into his room but once, and has sent him none but a dry little message or two. I, too have been much less attentive than I should have wished to be; but my time has not been my own. It has been, every moment of it, at the disposal of my host. He actually runs after me; he devours me; he makes a fool of himself, and is trying hard to make one of me. I find that he will bear – that, in fact, he actually enjoys – a sort of unexpected contradiction. He likes anything that will tickle his fancy, give an unusual tone to our relations, remind him of certain historical characters whom he thinks he resembles. I have stepped into Theodore's shoes, and done – with what I feel in my bones to be very inferior skill and taste – all the reading, writing, condensing, transcribing and advising that he has been accustomed to do. I have driven with the *bonhomme*; played chess and cribbage with him; beaten him, bullied him, contradicted him; forced him into going out on the water under my charge. Who shall say, after this, that I haven't done my best to discourage his advances, put myself in a bad light? As yet, my efforts are vain; in fact they quite turn to my own confusion. Mr Sloane is so thankful at having escaped from the lake with his life that he looks upon me as a preserver and protector. Confound it all; it's a bore! But one thing is certain, it can't last forever. Admit that he *has* cast Theodore out and taken me in. He will speedily discover that he has made a pretty mess of it, and he had much better have left well enough alone. He likes my reading and writing now, but in a month he will begin to hate them. He will miss Theodore's better temper and better knowledge – his healthy impersonal judgment. What an advantage that well-regulated youth has over me, after all! I am for days, he is for years; he for the long run, I for the short. I, perhaps, am intended for success, but he is adapted for happiness. He has in his heart a tiny sacred particle which leavens his whole being and keeps it pure and sound – a faculty of admiration and respect. For him human nature is still a wonder and mystery; it bears a divine stamp – Mr Sloane's tawdry composition as well as the rest.

13th. – I have refused, of course, to supplant Theodore further, in the exercise of his functions, and he has resumed his morning labors with Mr Sloane. I, on my side, have spent these morning hours in scouring the country on that capital black mare, the use of which is one of the perquisites of Theodore's place. The days have been magnificent – the heat of the sun tempered by a murmuring, wandering wind, the whole north a mighty ecstasy of sound and verdure, the sky a far-away value of bended blue. Not far from the mill at M., the other end of the lake, I met, for the third time, that very pretty young girl who reminds me so forcibly of A. L. She makes so lavish a use of her eyes that I ventured to stop and bid her good-morning. She seems nothing loath to an acquaintance. She's a pure barbarian in speech, but her eyes are quite articulate. These rides do me good; I was growing too pensive.

There is something the matter with Theodore; his illness seems to have left him strangely affected. He has fits of silent stiffness, alternating with spasms of extravagant gayety. He avoids me at times for hours together, and then he comes and looks at me with an inscrutable smile, as if he were on the verge of a burst of confidence – which again is swallowed up in the immensity of his dumbness. Is he hatching some astounding benefit to his species? Is he working to bring about my removal to a higher sphere of action? *Nous verrons bien.*

18th. – Theodore threatens departure. He received this morning a letter from one of his sisters – the young widow – announcing her engagement to a clergyman whose acquaintance she has recently made, and intimating her expectation of an immediate union with the gentleman – a ceremony which would require Theodore's attendance. Theodore, in high good humor, read the letter aloud at breakfast – and, to tell the truth, it was a charming epistle. He then spoke of his having to go on to the wedding, a proposition to which Mr Sloane graciously assented – much more than assented. 'I shall be sorry to lose you, after so happy a connection,' said the old man. Theodore turned pale, stared a moment, and then, recovering his color and his composure, declared that he should have no objection in life to coming back.

'Bless your soul!' cried the *bonhomme*, 'you don't mean to say you will leave your other sister all alone?'

To which Theodore replied that he would arrange for her and her little girl to live with the married pair. 'It's the only proper thing,' he remarked, as if it were quite settled. Has it come to this, then, that Mr Sloane actually wants to turn him out of the house? The shameless old villain! He keeps smiling an uncanny smile, which means, as I read it, that if the poor young man once departs he shall never return on the old footing – for all his impudence!

20th. – This morning, at breakfast, we had a terrific scene. A letter arrives for Theodore, he opens it, turns white and red, frowns, falters, and then informs us that the clever widow has broken off her engagement. No wedding, therefore, and no departure for Theodore. The *bonhomme* was furious. In his fury he took the liberty of calling poor Mrs Parker (the sister) a very uncivil name. Theodore rebuked him, with perfect good taste, and kept his temper.

'If my opinions don't suit you, Mr Lisle,' the old man broke out, 'and my mode of expressing them displeases you, you know you can easily protect yourself.'

'My dear Mr Sloane,' said Theodore, 'your opinions, as a general thing, interest me deeply, and have never ceased to act beneficially upon the formation of my own. Your mode of expressing them is always brilliant, and I wouldn't for the world, after all our pleasant intercourse, separate from you in bitterness. Only, I repeat, your qualification of my sister's conduct is perfectly uncalled for. If you knew her, you would be the first to admit it.'

There was something in Theodore's look and manner, as he said these words, which puzzled me all the morning. After dinner, finding myself alone with him, I told him I was glad he was not obliged to go away. He looked at me with the mysterious smile I have mentioned, thanked me, and fell into meditation. As this bescribbled chronicle is the record of my follies as well of my *hauts faits*, I needn't hesitate to say that for a moment I was a good deal vexed. What business has this angel of candor to deal in signs and portents, to look unutterable things? What right has he to do so with me especially, in whom he has always professed an absolute confidence? Just as I was about to cry out, 'Come, my dear fellow, this affectation of mystery has lasted quite long enough – favor me at last with the result of your cogitations!' – as I was on the point of thus expressing my impatience of his ominous behavior, the oracle at last addressed itself to utterance.

'You see, my dear Max,' he said, 'I can't, in justice to myself, go away in obedience to the sort of notice that was served on me this morning. What do you think of my actual footing here?'

Theodore's actual footing here seems to me impossible; of course I said so.

'No, I assure you it's not,' he answered. 'I should, on the contrary, feel very uncomfortable to think that I had come away, except by my own choice. You see a man can't afford to cheapen himself. What are you laughing at?'

'I am laughing, in the first place, my dear fellow, to hear on your lips the language of cold calculation; and in the second place, at your odd notion of the process by which a man keeps himself up in the market.'

'I assure you it's the correct notion. I came here as a particular favor to Mr Sloane; it was expressly understood so. The sort of work was odious to me; I had regularly to break myself in. I had to trample on my convictions, preferences, prejudices. I don't take such things easily; I take them hard; and when once the effort has been made, I can't consent to have it wasted. If Mr Sloane needed me then, he needs me still. I am ignorant of any change having taken place in his intentions, or in his means of satisfying them. I came, not to amuse him, but to do a certain work; I hope to remain until the work is completed. To go away sooner is to make a confession of incapacity which, I protest, costs me too much. I am too conceited, if you like.'

Theodore spoke these words with a face which I have never seen him wear – a fixed, mechanical smile; a hard, dry glitter in his eyes; a harsh, strident tone in his voice – in his whole physiognomy a gleam, as it were, a note of defiance. Now I confess that for defiance I have never been conscious of an especial relish. When I am defied I am beastly. 'My dear man,' I replied, 'your sentiments do you prodigious credit. Your very ingenious theory of your present situation, as well as your extremely pronounced sense of your personal value, are calculated to insure you a degree of practical success which can very well dispense with the furtherance of my poor good wishes.' Oh, the grimness of his visage as he listened to this, and, I suppose I may add, the grimness of mine! But I have ceased to be puzzled. Theodore's conduct for the past ten days is suddenly illumined with a backward, lurid ray. I will note down here a few plain truths which it behooves me to take to heart – commit to memory. Theodore is jealous of Maximus Austin. Theodore hates the said Maximus. Theodore has been seeking for the past three months to see his name written, last but not least, in a certain testamentary document: 'Finally, I bequeath to my dear young friend, Theodore Lisle, in return for invaluable service and unfailing devotion, the bulk of my property, real and personal consisting of – ' (hereupon follows an exhaustive enumeration of houses, lands, public securities, books, pictures, horses, and dogs). It is for this that he has toiled, and watched, and prayed; submitted to intellectual weariness and spiritual torture; accommodated himself to levity, blasphemy and insult. For this he sets his teeth and tightens his grasp; for this he'll fight. Dear me, it's an immense weight off one's mind! There are nothing, then, but vulgar, common laws; no sublime exceptions, no transcendent anomalies. Theodore's a knave, a hypo – nay, nay; stay, irreverent hand! – Theodore's a *man*! Well, that's all I want. *He* wants fight – he shall have it. Have I got, at last my simple, natural emotion?

21st. – I have lost no time. This evening, late, after I had heard Theodore go to his room (I had left the library early, on the pretext of having letters to write), I repaired to Mr Sloane, who had not yet gone to bed, and informed him I should be obliged to leave him at once, and pick up a subsistence somehow in New York. He felt the blow; it brought him straight down on his marrow-bones. He went through the whole gamut of his arts and graces; he blustered, whimpered, entreated, flattered. He tried to drag in Theodore's name; but this I, of course, prevented. But finally, why, *why*, WHY, after all my promises of fidelity, must I thus cruelly desert him? Then came my trump card: I have spent my last penny; while I stay, I'm a beggar. The remainder of this extraordinary scene I have no power to describe: how the *bon-homme*, touched, inflamed, inspired, by the thought of my destitution, and at the same time annoyed, perplexed, bewildered at having to commit himself to doing anything for me, worked himself into a nervous frenzy which deprived him of a clear sense of the value of his words and his actions; how I, prompted by the irresistible spirit of my desire to leap astride of his weakness and ride it hard to the goal of my dreams, cunningly contrived to keep his spirit at the fever-point, so that strength and reason and resistance should burn themselves out. I shall probably never again have such a sensation as I enjoyed to-night – actually feel a heated human heart throbbing and turning and struggling in my grasp; know its pants, its spasms, its convulsions, and its final senseless quiescence. At half-past one o'clock Mr Sloane got out of his chair, went to his secretary, opened a private drawer, and took out a folded paper. 'This is my will,' he said, 'made some seven weeks ago. If you will stay with me I will destroy it.'

'Really, Mr Sloane,' I said, 'if you think my purpose is to exert any pressure upon your testamentary inclinations – '

'I will tear it in pieces,' he cried; 'I will burn it up! I shall be as sick as a dog to-morrow; but I will do it. A-a-h!'

He clapped his hand to his side, as if in sudden, overwhelming pain, and sank back fainting into his chair. A single glance assured me that he was unconscious. I possessed myself of the paper, opened it, and perceived that he had left everything to his saintly secretary. For an instant a savage, puerile feeling of hate popped up in my bosom, and I came within a hair's-breadth of obeying my foremost impulse – that of stuffing the document into the fire. Fortunately, my reason overtook my passion, though for a moment it was an even race. I put the paper back into the bureau, closed it, and rang the bell for Robert (the old man's servant). Before he came I stood watching the poor, pale remnant of mortality before me, and wondering whether those feeble life-gasps were numbered. He was as white as a sheet, grimacing with pain – horribly ugly. Suddenly he opened his eyes; they met my own; I fell on my knees and took his hands. They closed on mine with a grasp strangely akin to the rigidity of death. Nevertheless, since then he has revived, and has relapsed again into a comparatively healthy sleep. Robert seems to know how to deal with him.

22nd. – Mr Sloane is seriously ill – out of his mind and unconscious of people's indentity. The doctor has been here, off and on, all day, but this evening reports improvement. I have kept out of the old man's room, and confined myself to my own, reflecting largely upon the chance of his immediate death. Does Theodore know of the will? Would it occur to him to divide the property? Would it occur to me, in his place? We met at dinner, and talked in a grave, desultory, friendly fashion. After all, he's an excellent fellow. I don't hate him. I don't even dislike him. He jars on me, *il m'agace*;[9] but that's no reason why I should do him an evil turn. Nor shall I. The property is a fixed idea, that's all. I shall get it if I can. We are fairly matched. Before heaven, no, we are not fairly matched! Theodore has a conscience.

23rd. – I am restless and nervous – and for good reasons. Scribbling here keeps me quiet. This morning Mr Sloane is better; feeble and uncertain in mind, but unmistakably on the rise. I may confess now that I feel relieved of a horrid burden. Last night I hardly slept a wink. I lay awake listening to the pendulum of my clock. It seemed to say, 'He lives – he dies.' I fully expected to hear it stop suddenly at *dies*. But it kept going all the morning, and to a decidedly more lively tune. In the afternoon the old man sent for me. I found him in his great muffled bed, with his face the color of damp chalk, and his eyes glowing faintly, like torches half stamped out. I was forcibly struck with the utter loneliness of his lot. For all human attendance, my villainous self grinning at his bedside and old Robert without, listening, doubtless, at the keyhole. The *bonhomme* stared at me stupidly; then seemed to know me, and greeted me with a sickly smile. It was some

moments before he was able to speak. At last he faintly bade me to
descend into the library, open the secret drawer of the secretary
(which he contrived to direct me how to do so), possess myself of
his will, and burn it up. He appears to have forgotten his having
taken it out night before last. I told him that I had an insurmount-
able aversion to any personal dealings with the document. He
smiled, patted the back of my hand, and requested me, in that
case, to get it, at least, and bring it to him. I couldn't deny him
that favor? No, I couldn't indeed. I went down to the library,
therefore, and on entering the room found Theodore standing by
the fireplace with a bundle of papers. The secretary was open. I
stood still, looking from the violated cabinet to the documents in
his hand. Among them I recognized, by its shape and size, the
paper of which I had intended to possess myself. Without delay I
walked straight up to him. He looked surprised, but not confused.
'I am afraid I shall have to trouble you to surrender one of those
papers,' I said.

'Surrender, Maximus? To anything of your own you are perfectly welcome. I didn't know that you made use of Mr Sloane's
secretary. I was looking for some pages of notes which I have made
myself and in which I conceive I have a property.'

'This is what I want, Theodore,' I said; and I drew the will,
unfolded, from between his hands. As I did so his eyes fell upon
the superscription, 'Last Will and Testament. March. F.S.' He
flushed an extraordinary crimson. Our eyes met. Somehow – I
don't know how or why, or for that matter why not – I burst into
a violent peal of laughter. Theodore stood staring, with two hot,
bitter tears in his eyes.

'Of course you think I came to ferret out that thing,' he said.

I shrugged my shoulders – those of my body only. I confess,
morally, I was on my knees with contrition, but there was a
fascination in it – a fatality. I remembered that in the hurry of my
movements the other evening I had slipped the will simply into
one of the outer drawers of the cabinet, among Theodore's own
papers. 'Mr Sloane sent me for it,' I remarked.

'Very good; I am glad to hear he's well enough to think of such
things.'

'He means to destroy it.'

'I hope, then, he has another made.'

'Mentally, I suppose he has.'

'Unfortunately, his weakness isn't mental – or exclusively so.'

'Oh, he will live to make a dozen more,' I said. 'Do you know the purport of this one?'

Theodore's color, by this time, had died away into plain white. He shook his head. The doggedness of the movement provoked me, and I wished to arouse his curiosity. 'I have his commission to destroy it.'

Theodore smiled very grandly. 'It's not a task I envy you,' he said.

'I should think not – especially if you knew the import of the will.' He stood with folded arms, regarding me with cold, detached eyes. I couldn't stand it. 'Come, it's your property! You are sole legatee. I give it to you.' And I thrust the paper into his hand.

He received it mechanically, but after a pause, bethinking himself, he unfolded it and cast his eyes over the contents. Then he slowly smoothed it together and held it a moment with a tremulous hand. 'You say that Mr Sloane directed you to destroy it?' he finally inquired.

'I say so.'

'And that you know the contents?'

'Exactly.'

'And that you were about to do what he asked you?'

'On the contrary, I declined.'

Theodore fixed his eyes for a moment on the superscription and then raised them again to my face. 'Thank you, Max,' he said. 'You have left me a real satisfaction.' He tore the sheet across and threw the bits into the fire. We stood watching them burn. 'Now he can make another,' said Theodore.

'Twenty others,' I replied.

'No,' said Theodore, 'you will take care of that.'

'You are very bitter,' I said, sharply enough.

'No, I am perfectly indifferent. Farewell.' And he put out his hand.

'Are you going away?'

'Of course I am. Good-bye.'

'Good-bye, then. But isn't your departure rather sudden?'

'I ought to have gone three weeks ago – three weeks ago.' I had
taken his hand, he pulled it away; his voice was trembling – there
were tears in it.

'Is *that* indifference?' I asked.

'It's something you will never know!' he cried. 'It's shame! I am
not sorry you should see what I feel. It will suggest to you,
perhaps, that my heart had never been in this filthy contest. Let
me assure you, at any rate, that it hasn't; that it has had nothing
but scorn for the base perversion of my pride and my ambition. I
could easily shed tears of joy at their return – the return of the
prodigals! Tears of sorrow – sorrow – '

He was unable to go on. He sank into a chair, covering his face
with his hands.

'For God's sake, stick to the joy!' I exclaimed.

He rose to his feet again. 'Well,' he said, 'it was for your sake
that I parted with my self-respect; with your assistance I recover
it.'

'How for my sake?'

'For whom but you would I have gone as far as I did? For what
other purpose than that of keeping our friendship whole would I
have borne your company into this narrow pass? A man whom I
cared for less I would long since have parted with. You were
needed – you and something you have about you that always takes
me so – to bring me to this. You ennobled, exalted, enchanted the
struggle. I *did* value my prospect of coming into Mr Sloane's
property. I valued it for my poor sisters' sake as well as for my
own, so long as it was the natural reward of conscientious service,
and not the prize of hypocrisy and cunning. With another man
than you I never would have contested such a prize. But you
fascinated me, even as my rival. You played with me, deceived
me, betrayed me. I held my ground, hoping you would see that
what you were doing was not fair. But if you have seen it, it has
made no difference with you. For Mr Sloane, from the moment
that, under your magical influence, he revealed his nasty little
nature, I had nothing but contempt.'

'And for me now?'

'Don't ask me. I don't trust myself.'

'Hate, I suppose.'

'Is that the best you can imagine? Farewell.'

'Is it a serious farewell – farewell forever?'

'How can there be any other?'

'I am sorry this should be your point of view. It's characteristic. All the more reason then that I should say a word in self-defence. You accuse me of having "played with you, deceived you, betrayed you." It seems to me that you are quite beside the mark. You say you were such a friend of mine; if so, you ought to be one still. It was not to my fine sentiments you attached yourself, for I never had any or pretended to any. In anything I have done recently, therefore, there has been no inconsistency. I never pretended to take one's friendship so seriously. I don't understand the feeling of affection between men. To me it means quite another thing. You give it a meaning of your own; you enjoy the profit of your invention; it's no more than just that you should pay the penalty. Only it seems to me rather hard that *I* should pay it.' Theodore remained silent, but he looked quite sick. 'Is it still a "serious farewell"?' I went on. 'It seems a pity. After this clearing up, it appears to me that I shall be on better terms with you. No man can have a deeper appreciation of your excellent parts, a keener enjoyment of your society. I should very much regret the loss of it.'

'Have we, then, all this while understood each other so little?' said Theodore.

'Don't say "we" and "each other." I think I have understood you.'

'Very likely. It's not for my having kept anything back.'

'Well, I do you justice. To me you have always been over generous. Try now and be just.'

Still he stood silent, with his cold, hard frown. It was plain that, if he was to come back to me, it would be from the other world – if there be one! What he was going to answer I knew not. The door opened, and Robert appeared, pale, trembling, his eyes starting in his head.

'I verily believe that poor Mr Sloane is dead in his bed!' he cried.

There was a moment's perfect silence. 'Amen,' said I. 'Yes, old boy, try and be just.' Mr Sloane had quietly died in my absence.

24th. – Theodore went up to town this morning, having shaken hands with me in silence before he started. Doctor Jones, and Brooks the attorney, have been very officious, and, by their advice, I have telegraphed to a certain Miss Meredith, a maiden lady, by their account the nearest of kin; or, in other words, simply a discarded niece of the defunct. She telegraphs back that she will arrive in person for the funeral. I shall remain till she comes. I have lost a fortune, but have I irretrievably lost a friend? I am sure I can't say. Yes, I shall wait for Miss Meredith.

Master Eustace

I

Having handed me my cup of tea, she proceeded to make her own – an operation she performed with an old-maidish precision I delighted to observe.

The story is not my own (she then began), but that of persons with whom for a time I was intimately connected. I have led a quiet life; that is my only romance – and it's the romance of others. When I was a young woman of twenty-two my poor mother died, after a long, weary illness, and I found myself obliged to seek a new home. Making a home requires time and money. I had neither to spare, so I advertised for a 'situation,' rating my accomplishments modestly, and asking rather for kind treatment than high wages. Mrs Garnyer immediately answered my advertisement. She offered me a fair salary and a peaceful asylum. I was to teach her little boy the rudiments of my slender stock of science and to make myself generally useful. Something in her tone and manner assured me that in accepting this latter condition, I was pledging myself to no very onerous servitude, and I never found reason to repent of my bargain. I had always valued my freedom before all things, and it seemed to me that in trading it away even partially I was surrendering a priceless treasure; but Mrs Garnyer made bondage very easy. I liked her from the first, and I doubt if she ever fully appreciated my fidelity and affection. She knew she could trust me, and she always spoke of me as a 'good creature'; but she never measured the trouble I saved her, or the little burdens I lifted from her pretty, feeble shoulders. Both in her position and her person there was something singularly appealing. She was in those days – indeed she always remained – a very attractive woman; but she had grace even more than beauty. She was young, and looked even

153

younger than her years; slight, fluttering, with frequent gestures and not many words, and fairer, whiter, purer, in complexion than any woman I have seen. She reminded me of a sketch from which the 'shading' has been omitted. She had her shadows indeed, as well as her lights; but they were all turned inward. She might have been made up of the airy substance of lights and shadows. Nature in putting her together had left out the harder, heavier parts, the selfishness, the ambition, the power to insist and to calculate. Experience, however, had given her a burden to carry; she was evidently sorrow-laden. She shifted the cruel weight from shoulder to shoulder, she ached and sighed under it, and in the depths of her sweet natural smile you saw it pressing the tears from her very soul. Mrs Garnyer's distresses, I confess, were in my eyes an added charm. I was desperately fond of a bit of romance, and as I was plainly never to have one of my own, I made the most of my neighbour's. This secret sadness would have covered more sins than I ever had to forgive her. At first, naturally, I connected it with the death of her husband; but, as time went on, I found reason to believe that there had been little love between the pair. She had been married against her will; Mr Garnyer was fifteen years her senior, and, as she frankly mentioned, coarsely and cruelly dissipated. Their married life had lasted but three years, and had come to an end to her great and manifest relief. Had he done her while it lasted some irreparable wrong? I suspected so; she was like a garden rose with half its petals plucked. He had left her with diminished means, though her property (mostly her own) was still ample for her needs. These, with those of her son, were extremely simple. To certain little luxuries she was obstinately attached; but her manner of life was so monotonous and frugal that she must have spent but a fraction of her income. It was her single son – the heir of her hopes, the apple of her eye – that she entrusted to my care. He was five years old, and she had taught him his letters – a great feat she seemed to think; she was as proud of it as if she had invented the alphabet for the occasion. She had called him Eustace, for she meant that he should have the best of everything – the prettiest clothes, the prettiest playthings and the prettiest name. He was himself as pretty as his name, though not at all in the manner of his mother. He was slight like her, but far more nervous and decided, and he had neither her features nor her colouring. Least of all had he her expression. Mrs Garnyer's attitude was one of tender, pensive sufferance modified by hopes – a certain half-mystical hope which seemed akin to religion, but which was not all religion, for the heaven she dreamed of was situated here below. The boy from his early childhood presented himself as a little man who would take a line of his own. He was not one who would ever wait for things, good or evil; he would snatch boldly at the one sort and snap his fingers at the other. He had a pale, dark skin, not altogether healthy in tone; a mass of fine brown hair, which seemed given him just to emphasise by its dancing sweep the petulant little nods and shakes of his head; and a deep, wilful, malicious eye. His eye told me from the first that I should have no easy work with him, and with every possible relaxation of the nursery-code my place never became in the least a sinecure. His wits were so quick, however, and his imagination so lively, that I gradually managed to fill out his mother's meagre little programme of study. This had been drawn up with a sparing hand; her only fear was of his being over-worked. The poor lady had but a dim conception of what a man of the world is expected to know. She thought, I believe, that with his handsome face, his handsome property, and his doting mother, he would need to know little more than how to sign that pretty name of Eustace to replies to invitations to dinner. I wonder now that with her constant interference I contrived to set the child intellectually on his legs. Later, when he had a tutor, I received a compliment for my perseverance.

The truth is, I became fond of him; his very imperfections fascinated me. He would soon enough have to take his chance of the world's tolerance, and society would cease to consist for him of a couple of coaxing women. I told Mrs Garnyer that there was never an easier child to spoil, and that those fondling hands of hers would sow a crop of formidable problems for future years. But Mrs Garnyer was utterly incapable of taking a rational view of matters, or of sacrificing to-day to to-morrow; and her folly was the more incurable as it was founded on a strange, perverse little principle – a crude, passionate theory – that love, love, pure love, is the sum and substance of maternal duty, and that the love which reasons and requires and refuses is cruel and wicked. 'I know you think I am a silly goose,' she said, 'and not fit to have a child at all. But you are wrong – I promise you you are wrong. I am very reasonable, I am very patient; I have a great deal to bear – more than you know – and I bear it very well. But one can't be always on the stretch – always hard and wise and good. In some things one must break down and be one's poor natural, lonely self. Eustace can't turn out wrong; it's impossible; it would be too cruel. You must not say it nor hint it. I shall do with him what my heart bids me; he is all I have; he consoles me.'

My notions perhaps were a little old-fashioned; but surely it will never altogether go out of fashion to teach a child that he is not to have the moon by crying for it. Now Eustace had a particular fancy for the moon, for everything bright, inaccessible and absurd. His will was as sharp as a steel spring, and it was vain to attempt to bend it or break it. He had an indefeasible conviction that he was number one among men; and if he had been born in the purple, as they say, of some far-off Eastern court, or found himself the final morbid little offshoot of a long line of despots, he couldn't have had a greater idea of his prerogative. The poor child had no sense of justice – he had the extra virtues, but not the regular ones. He could condescend, he could forgive, he could allow things, if his leave had been asked, but he couldn't endure the hint of a conflicting right. He could love, love passionately; but he was so jealous and exacting that his love cost you very much more than it was worth. If he liked me and confided in me, I had worked hard for it – I had to 'live up' to it. He thought it a very great honour that he should care to harness me up as his horse, to throw me his ball by the hour, to make me joggle with him on the see-saw (sitting close to the middle) till my poor bones ached. Nevertheless, in this frank, childish arrogance there was an almost irresistible charm and, I was absurdly flattered at his liking me. Poor me! at twenty-three I was his first 'conquest' – the first in a long list, as I believe it came to be. If he required a great margin, he used it with a peculiar grace of his own, and he admitted the corresponding obligation of being clever and brilliant. As a child even, he had a kind of personal distinction. His talents were excellent, and teaching him, whatever it may have been, was at least not dull work. It was indeed less to things really needful than to the luxuries of learning that he took most kindly. He had an excellent ear for music; and though he never practised properly he turned off an air with wonderful expression. In this he resembled his mother, who was a natural musician. She, however, was always at the piano, and whenever I think of her in those early years I see her sitting before it musingly, half sadly, with her pretty head on one side, her fair braids thrust behind her ears – ears from which a couple of small but admirable diamonds were never absent – and her white hands wandering over the notes, seeking vaguely for a melody they seemed hardly to dare to remember. Eustace had an unsatiable appetite for stories, though he was one of the coolest and most merciless of critics. I can imagine him now at my knee, with his big eyes fastened on my lips, demanding more wonders and more, till my short-winded invention had to cry for breath. Do my best, I could never startle him; my giants were never big enough and my fairies never small enough, my enchanters, dragons, dungeons and castles never on the really grand scale of his own imaginative needs. I felt dreadfully below the mark. At last he would open his wilful little mouth and yawn in my face, with a dreadfully dry want of conviction. I felt flattered when by chance I had pleased him, for, by a precocious instinct, he knew tinsel from gold. 'Look here,' he would say, 'you are remarkably ugly; what makes you so ugly? Your nose is so big at the end.' (You needn't protest; I *was* ugly. Like most very plain women, I have improved with time.) Of course I used to rebuke him for his rudeness; though I was secretly thankful, because it taught me a number of things. Once he said something, I forget what, that made me burst into tears. It was the first time, and the last; for I found that, instead of exciting his pity, tears only moved his contempt, and apparently a kind of cynical, physical disgust. The best way was to turn the tables on him by pretending to be indifferent and superior. In that case he himself would condescend to tears – bitter, wrathful tears. Then you had perhaps gained nothing, but you had lost nothing. In every other case you *had* lost.

II

Of course these close relations lasted but a couple of years. I had made him very much wiser than myself; he was growing tall and boyish and terribly inquisitive. My poor little stories ceased to have any illusion for him, and he would spend hours lying on his face on the carpet, kicking up his neat little legs and poring over the *Arabian Nights*, the *Fairy Queen*, the other prime enchanters of childhood. My advice would have been to pack him off to school; but I might as well have asked his mother to send him to the penitentiary. He was to be educated *en prince;*[1] he was to have an instructor to himself. I thought sympathetically of the worthy pedagogue who was to minister to Eustace without competition. But such a one was easily found – in fact, he was found three times over. Three private tutors came and went successively. They fell in love, punctually, with Mrs Garnyer. Their love indeed she might have put up with; but unhappily, unlike Viola, they 'told' it – by letter – with an offer of their respective hands. Their letters were different, but to Mrs Garnyer their hands were all alike, all very untidy paws. 'The horrid creatures!' was her invariable commentary. 'I wouldn't speak to them for the world. My dear, you must do it.' And I, who had never declined an offer on my own account, went to work in this wholesale manner for my friend! You will say that, young as she was – pretty, independent, lonely – Mrs Garnyer would have looked none the worse for a spice of coquetry. But she never would have forgiven herself a flirtation. Her greatest charm for me was her scorn for this sort of levity, and indeed her general contempt for cheap sentimental effects. It was as if, from having drunk at the crystal head-spring, she had lost her taste for standing water. She was absolutely indifferent to attention; it inspired her, in fact, with a kind of terror. She had not a trace of personal vanity; she was even without visible desire to please. Unfortunately, as you see, she pleased in spite of herself. As regards love, she had an imposing arrays of principles; on this one point she was always very explicit. 'It's either a passion,' she said, 'or it's nothing. You can know it by being willing to give up everything for it – name and fame, past and future, this world and the next. Do you keep back a feather's weight of tenderness or trust? Then you are not in love. You must risk everything, for you get everything – if you are happy. I can't understand a woman trifling with such feelings. They talk about the unpardonable sin; that's it, it seems to me. Do you know the word in the language I most detest? – *Flirtation*. Poh! it makes me ill.' When Mrs Garnyer uttered this hint of an esoteric doctrine, her clear blue eyes would become clouded with the gathered mists of memory. In this matter she understood herself and meant what she said.

Impatient as she was of being 'made up to,' she exposed herself very little to such dangers, and almost never went into the world. She met her few friends but two or three times a year, and was without a single intimate. As time went on she came to care more for me than any one. When Eustace had outgrown my teaching she insisted on my remaining in any capacity I chose – as housekeeper, companion, seamstress, guest; I might make my own terms. I became a little of each of these, and with the increasing freedom of our intercourse grew to regard her as a younger and weaker sister. I gave her, for what it was worth, my best judgment on all things. Her own confidence always stopped short of a certain point; a little curtain of reticence was always suspended between us. Sometimes it appeared to grow thinner and thinner, becoming almost transparent and revealing the figures behind it. Sometimes it seemed to move and flutter in the murmur of our talk, as if in a moment it might drop away or melt away into air. But it was a magical web; it played a hundred tormenting tricks, and year after year it hung in its place. Of course I had fits of immense curiosity, but I can't say more for the disinterested affection I felt for Mrs Garnyer than that I never pried, never pressed her. I lingered near the door of her Blue-Beard's chamber, but I never peeped through the keyhole. She was a poor lady with a secret; I took her into my heart, secret and all. She insisted that her isolation was her own choice, and pretended to be exceedingly glad that society let her so well alone. She made her widowhood serve as a motive for her monotonous years, and declared that her boy's education amply filled them. She was a widow, however, who never of her own accord mentioned her husband's name, and she wore her weeds very lightly. She was very fond of white, and for six months of the year was rarely seen in a dark dress. Occasionally, on certain fixed days, she would flame forth in some old-fashioned piece of finery from a store which she religiously preserved, and would flash about the house in rose-colour or blue. One day – her boy's birthday – she kept with extraordinary solemnity. It fell in the middle of September. On this occasion she would put on a faded ball-dress, overload herself with jewels and trinkets, dress her hair with flowers. Eustace, too, she would trick out in a suit of crimson velvet, and in this singular guise the pair would walk with prodigious gravity about the garden and up and down the avenue. Every now and then she would stoop and give him a convulsive hug. The child himself seemed to feel the magnitude of this festival, and played his part with precocious effect. He would appear at dusk with the curl still in his hair, his velvet trousers unstained, his ruffles uncrumpled. In the evening the coachman let off rockets in the garden; we feasted on ice-cream and a bottle of champagne was sent to the kitchen. No wonder Master Eustace carried himself like an heir-apparent! Once, I remember, the mother and son were overtaken in their festal promenade by some people who had come to live in the neighbourhood and, who drove up, rather officiously, to leave their cards. They stared, in amazement, from the carriage-window, and were told Mrs Garnyer was not at home. A few days later we heard that Mrs Garnyer was out of her mind; she had been found masquerading in her grounds with her little boy, in the most indecent costume. From time to time she received an invitation, and occasionally she accepted one. When she went out she made her mourning more marked, and she always came home in a fret. 'It is the last house I will go to,' she used to say, as I helped her to undress. 'People's neglect I can bear, and thank them for it; but heaven deliver me from their kindness! I won't be patronised – I won't, I won't! Shall I, my boy? We will wait till you grow up, shan't we, my darling? Then his poor little mother shan't be patronised, shall she, my brave little man?' The child was constantly dangling at his mother's skirts, and was seldom beyond the reach of some such passionate appeal.

A preceptor had at last been found of a less inflammable composition than the others – a worthy, elderly German of fair attainments, with a stout, sentimental wife – she gave music-lessons in town – who monopolised his ardour. He was a mild, patient man; a nose of wax, as the saying is – a pretty nose it grew to be in Eustace's supple fingers! I will answer for it that in all those years he never carried a single point. I believe that, like me, he had begun with tears; but finding this an altogether losing game, he was content now to take off his spectacles, drop his head on one side, look imploringly at his pupil with his weak blue eyes, and then exhale his renunciation in a plaintive *Lieber Gott!* Under this discipline the boy bloomed like a flower; but it was to my sense a kind of hot-house growth. His tastes were sedentary, and he lived most of the time within doors. He kept a horse, and took long lonely rides; but there were whole days that he spent lounging over a book, trifling at the piano, or fretting over a water-colour sketch which he was sure to throw aside in disgust. One amusement he pursued with unwearying constancy, it was a sign of especial good-humour, and I never knew it to fail him. He would sit for hours lounging in a chair, with his head thrown back and his legs extended, staring at vacancy, or what seemed to us so: but a vacancy filled with the silent revel of his imagination and the scenes it presented to him. What was the substance of these csctatic visions? The broad, happy life on which he would enter some day, the great world whose far-off murmur caressed his ear – the joys of prosperous manhood – pleasure, success, popularity – a kind of triumphant and transfigured egotism. His reveries swarmed with tinted pictures and transcendent delights; his handsome young face, his idle insolent smile, wore the cold reflection of their brightness. His mother, after watching him for a while in these moods, would steal up behind him and kiss him softly on the forehead, as if to marry his sweet illusions to sweeter reality. For my part, I wanted to divorce them. It was a sad pity, I thought that desire and occasion, in the lad's life, played so promptly into each other's hands. I longed to spoil the game, to shuffle the cards afresh and give him a taste of bad luck. I felt as if between them – she by her measureless concessions, he by his consuming arrogance – they were sowing a crop of dragon's teeth. This sultry summer of youth couldn't last for ever, and I knew that the poor lady would be the first to suffer by a change of weather. He would turn some day, in his passionate vanity, and rend the gentle creature who had fed it with the delusive wine of her love. And yet he had a better angel as well as a worse, and it was a marvel to see how this superior spirit (a sort of human conscience) tussled with the fiend and, in spite of bruises and ruffled pinions, returned again and again to the onset. There were days when his generous, boyish gaiety – the natural sunshine of youth and cleverness – warmed our women's hearts and kindled our most trusting smiles. Me, as he grew older, he treated as a licensed old-time friend. I was the prince's jester – I used to tell him his truths, as the French say. He believed them just enough to feel an agreeable irritation in listening; for the rest, doubtless, they seemed as vague and remote as the croaking of the frogs in the pond. There were moments, I think, when the eternal blue sky of his mother's temper wearied his capricious brain. At such times he would come and sprawl on the sofa near my little work-table, clipping my threads, mixing my reels, mislaying my various utensils, and criticising my work without reserve – chattering, gossiping, complaining, boasting. With all his faults, Eustace had one sovereign merit – that merit without which even the virtues he lacked lose half their charm; he was magnificently candid. He was only too transparent. The light of truth played through his interlaced pretensions, and against it they stood relieved in their hard tenacity, like fine young trees against a sunrise. He expressed his passions – expressed them only too loudly; you received ample notice of his revenges. They came as a matter of course; he never took them out in talk; but you were warned.

III

If these intense meditations of which I have spoken followed exclusively the train of his personal fortunes, his conversation was hardly more disinterested. It was altogether about himself – his ambitions, his ailments, his dreams, his opinions, his intentions. He talked a great deal of his property, and though he had a great aversion to figures he knew the amount of his expectations before he was out of jackets. He had a keen relish for luxury, and indeed, as he respected pretty things and used them with a degree of tenderness which he by no means lavished upon animate objects, saving, sparing, and preserving them, this seemed to me one of his most human traits, though, I admit, an expensive virtue – and he promised to spend his fortune in books and pictures, in art and travel. His mother was frequently called upon to do the honours of his castles in the air. She would look at him always with her doting smile, and with a little glow of melancholy in her eyes – a faint tribute to some shadowy chance that even her Eustace might reckon without his host. She would shake her head tenderly, or lean it on his shoulder and murmur, 'Who knows, who knows? It's perhaps as foolish, my son, to try and anticipate our happiness as to attempt to take the measure of our misery. We know them each when they come. Whatever comes to us, at all events, we shall meet it together.' Resting in this delicious contact, with her arm round his neck and her cheek on his hair, she would close her eyes in a sort of mild ecstacy. As I have never had a son myself I can speak of maternity but by hearsay; but I feel as if I knew some of its secrets, as if I had gained from Mrs Garnyer a revelation of maternal passion. The perfect humility of her devotion, indeed, seemed to me to point to some motive deeper than common motherhood. It looked like a kind of penance, a kind of pledge. Had she done him some early wrong? Did she meditate some wrong to come? Did she wish to purchase pardon for the past or impunity for the future? One might have supposed from the lad's calm relish of her incense – as if it were the fumes of some perfumed chibouque[2] palpitating lazily through his own lips – that he had a gratified sense of something to forgive. In fact, he had something to forgive us all – our dulness, our vulgarity, our not guessing his unuttered desires, the want of a pre-established harmony between our wills and his. It seemed to me, however, that there were even moments when he turned dizzy on the edge of this awful gulf of his mother's self-sacrifice. Fixing his eyes, then, an instant, to steady himself, he took comfort in the thought that she had ceased to suffer – her personal ambitions lay dead at the bottom. He could vaguely see them – distant, dim, motionless. It was to be hoped that no adventurous ghost of those shuffled-off passions would climb upward to the light.

A frequent source of complaint, with Eustace, when he had no more handy dissatisfaction, was that he had not known his father. He had formed a mental image of the late Mr Garnyer which I am afraid hardly tallied at all points with the original. The boy knew that he had been a man of pleasure, and he had painted his portrait in ideal hues. What a charming father – a man of pleasure, Eustace thought, as if he had believed that gentlemen of this stamp take their pleasure in the nursery. What pleasures they might have shared; what rides, what talks, what games, what adventures – what far other hours than those he passed in the deserted billiard-room (this had been one of Mr Garnyer's most marked tastes), clicking the idle balls in the stillness. He learned to talk very early of arranging his life to resemble his father's. What he had done his son would do. A dozen odds and ends which had belonged to Mr Garnyer he carried to his room, where he paraded them on his mantel-shelf like relics on a high altar. When he was seventeen years old he began to smoke an old silver-mounted pipe which had his father's initials embossed on the bowl. 'It would be a great blessing,' he said, as he puffed this pipe – it made him dismally sick, for he hated tobacco – 'to have some man in the house. It's so fearfully womanish here. No one but you two and Hauff, and what's he but an old woman? Mother, why have you always lived in this way? What's the matter with you? You have no *savoir vivre*. What are you blushing about? That comes of moping here all your days – that you blush for nothing. I don't want my mother to blush for anything or anyone, not even for me. But I give you notice, I can stand it no longer. Now I'm seventeen it's time I should see the world. I am going to travel. My father travelled; he went all over Europe. There's a little French book upstairs, the poems of Parny[3] – it's awfully French, too – with "Henry Garnyer, Paris, 1802," on the fly-leaf. I must go to Paris; I shan't go to college. I have never been to school. I want to be complete – privately educated altogether. Very few Americans are; it's quite a distinction. Besides, I know all I want to know. Hauff brought me out some college-catalogues. They're absurd; he laughs at them. We did all that three years ago. I know more about books than most young fellows; what I want is knowledge of the world. My father had it, and you haven't, mother. But he had plenty of taste, too. Hauff says that little edition of Parny is very rare. I shall bring home lots of such things. *Vous allez voir!*' Mrs Garnyer listened to such effusions of filial emulation in sad, embarrassed silence. I couldn't but pity her. She knew that her husband was no proper model for her child; yet she couldn't in decency turn his heart against his father's memory. She took refuge in that tremulous reserve which committed her neither to condemnation of her husband nor to approval with her son.

She had recourse at this period, as I had known her to do before, to a friend attached to a mercantile house in India – an old friend, she had told me; 'in fact,' she had added, 'my only friend – a man to whom I am under immense obligations.' Once in six months there came to her from this distant benefactor a large square letter, heavily sealed and covered with foreign post-marks. I used to believe it to be a kind of bulletin of advice for the coming half-year. Advice about what? Her cares were so few, her habits so simple, that they offered scanty matter for discussion. But now, of course, came a packet of good counsel in regard to these plans of Eustace's. I knew that she dreaded it; but, since her oracle had spoken, she put on a brave face. She was certainly a very faithful believer. She concealed from Eustace the extent of her dependence on this far-away monitor, for the boy would have resented such interference, even though it should fall in with his own projects. She had always read her friend's letters in secret; this was the only practice of her life she failed to share with her son. Me she now for the first time admitted into her confidence. 'Mr Cope strongly recommends my letting him go,' she said. 'He says it will make a man of him. He needs to rub against other men. I suppose, at least,' she cried, with her usual sweet fatuity, 'it will do other men no harm! Perhaps I don't love him as I ought, and I must lose him awhile to learn to prize him. If I only get him back again! It would be monstrous that I shouldn't! But why are we cursed with these perpetual scruples and fears? It's a weary life!' She would have said more if she had known that it was not his departure but his return that was to be cruel.

The excellent Mr Hauff was too limp and battered to be a bear-leader in distant lands; but a companion was secured in the person of his nephew, an amiable young German, who was represented to know the world as well as he knew books. For a week before he left us Eustace was so friendly and good-humoured that we cried for him in advance. 'I give her into your care,' he said to me. 'If anything happens to her I shall hold you responsible. She is very woe-begone just now, but will cheer up as soon as I am out of sight. But, mother, you are not to be too cheerful, mind. You are not to forget me an instant. If you do I will never forgive you. I insist on being missed. There's little enough merit in loving me when I am here; I wish to be loved in my absence.' For many weeks after he left he might have been satisfied. His mother wandered about like a churchyard-ghost keeping watch near a buried treasure. When his letters began to come she read them over a dozen times, and sat for hours, with her eyes closed, holding them in her hand. They were wretchedly meagre and hurried, but their very brevity gratified her. He was prosperous and happy, and could snatch but odd moments from the recreations of his age.

One morning, after he had been away some three months, there came two letters, one from Eustace, the other from India, the latter very much in advance of its time. Mrs Garnyer opened the Indian letter first. I was pouring out tea; I observed her from behind the urn. As her eyes ran over the pages she turned deadly pale; then, raising her glance, she met mine. Immediately her paleness turned to crimson. She rose to her feet and hurried out of the room, leaving Eustace's letter untouched on the table. This little fact was eloquent, and my curiosity was excited. Later in the day it was partially satisfied. She came to me with a singular, conscious look – the look of a sort of oppression of happiness – and announced Mr Cope was coming home. He had obtained release from his engagement in India, and would arrive in a fortnight. She uttered no words of rejoicing, and I could see that her joy was of the unutterable sort. As the days elapsed, however, her emotion betrayed itself in a restless, aimless flutter of movement, so violent as to be painful to behold. She roamed about the house, singing to herself, gazing out of the windows, shifting the chairs and tables, smoothing the curtains, trying vaguely to brighten the faded look of things. Before every mirror she paused and inspected herself, with that frank audacity of pretty women which I have always envied, tucking up a curl of her fair hair or smoothing a crease in those muslins which she always kept so fresh. Of Eustace for the moment she rarely spoke; the boy's prediction had not been so very much amiss. Who was this wonderful Mr Cope, this mighty magician?

I very soon learned. He arrived on the day he had fixed, and took up his residence in the house. From the moment I looked at him I felt that he was a man I should like. I suppose I was flattered by the notice he took of so humble a personage. He had often heard of me, he said; he knew how good a friend I had been to Mrs Garnyer; he hoped very much I would be indulgent to him. I felt as if I were amply repaid for my years of domestic service. But, in spite of this pleasant assurance, I had a sense of being for the moment altogether *de trop*. He was united to his friend by a closer bond than I had suspected. I left them alone with their old memories and references, and confined myself to my own room; though indeed I had noticed between them a sort of sentimental intelligence in which words might pass without audible speech. Mrs Garnyer underwent a singular change; I seemed to know her now for the first time. It was as if she had flung aside a veil which muffled her tones and blurred her features. There was a new decision in her tread, a deeper meaning in her smile; so, at thirty-eight her girlhood had come back to her! She was as full of blushes and random prattle and foolish falterings for very pleasure as a young bride. Upon Mr Cope the years had set a more ineffaceable seal. He was a man of forty-five, but you might easily have given him ten years more. He had that look which I have always liked, of people who have lived in hot climates; a bronzed complexion and a cool, deliberate gait, as if he had learned to think twice before moving. He was tall and lean, yet very powerful, like a large man somewhat 'reduced.' His hair was thin and perfectly white, and he wore a grizzled moustache. He dressed in loose, light-coloured garments of those fine Eastern stuffs. I had a singular impression of having seen him before, but I could never say when or where. He was extremely deaf – so deaf that I had to force my voice; though I observed that Mrs Garnyer easily made him hear by speaking slowly and looking at him. He had, peculiarly, that patient, appealing air which you find in very deaf persons less frequently than in the blind, but which is more touching when the eye is alive and sees what the ear loses. He had been obliged to make good company of himself, and the glimpses that one got of this resigned fellowship in stillness were of a kind to make one long to enter into it. But with others, too, he was a charming talker, though he was obliged to keep the talk in his own hands. He took your response for granted with a kind of conciliating brightness, guessed your opinion with a glance, and phrased it usually better than you would have done.

IV

For ten years I had been pitying Mrs Garnyer; it was odd now to find myself envying her. Patient waiting is no loss, and at last her day had come. I had always rather wondered at her patience; but, after all, it was spiced with private reasons. She had lived by precept and example, by chapter and verse; for *his* sake it was easy to be wise. I say for 'his' sake, because as matter of course, I now connected her visitor with that element of mystery which had been one of my earliest impressions of Mrs Garnyer. Mr Cope's presence renewed my memory of it. I fitted the key to the lock, but on coming to open the casket I was disappointed to find that the principal part of the secret had evaporated. I made up my mind that Mr Cope had been her first and only love. Her parents had frowned on him and forced her into a marriage with poor dissolute Mr Garnyer – a course the more revolting as he had already spent half his own property and was likely to make sad havoc with his wife's. He had a high social value, which the girl's own family, who were plain enough people to have had certain primitive scruples in larger measure, deemed a compensation for his vices. The discarded lover, thinking she had not resisted as firmly as she might, embarked for India, and there, half in spite, half in despair, married as sadly amiss as herself. He had trifled with his happiness; he lived to repent. His wife lived, as well, to perpetuate his misery; it was my belief that she had only recently died, and that this event was the occasion of his return. When he arrived he wore a weed on his hat; the next day it had disappeared. Reunion had come to the pair in the afternoon of life, when the tricks and graces of passion are no longer becoming; but when these have spent themselves something of passion still is left, and this my companions were free to enjoy. They had begun to enjoy it with the chastened eagerness of which I caught the aroma. Such was my reading of the riddle. Right or not, at least it made sense.

I had promised Eustace to write to him, and one afternoon as I

sat alone, well pleased to have a theme, I despatched him a long
letter, full of the praises of Mr Cope, and, by implication, of his
mother's improved condition. I wished to anticipate his possible
suspicions and reconcile him with the altered situation. But after I
had posted my letter it seemed to me that I had been too
precipitate. I doubted whether, even amid the larger life of the
grand tour, he had unlearned the old trick of jealousy. Jealousy
surely would have been quite misplaced, for Mr Cope's affection
for his hostess embraced the boy, embraced everything that
concerned her. He regretted the lad's absence; he manifested the
kindliest interest in everything that spoke of him; he turned over
his books, he looked at his sketches, he examined and compared
the half dozen portraits which the fond mother had caused to be
executed at various stages of his growth. One sultry day, when
poor Mr Hauff travelled out from town for news of his pupil, he
made a point of being introduced and of shaking his hand. The
tutor stayed to dinner, and on Mr Cope's proposition we drank the
boy's health in brimming glasses. The old German of course wept
profusely; it was Eustace's mission to make people cry. I thought
too I saw a tear on Mr Cope's lid. The cup of his contentment was
full; at a touch it overflowed. On the whole, however, he took this
bliss of reunion more quietly than his friend. He was a melancholy
man. He had the air of one for whom the moral of this fable of life
has greater charms than the plot, and who has made up his mind
to ask no favours of destiny. When he met me he used to smile
gently, frankly, saying little; but I had a great liking for his smile.
It seemed to say much – to murmur, 'Receive my compliments.
You and I are a couple of tested souls; we understand each other.
We are not in a flutter with the privilege of existence, like charity-
children on a picnic. We have had, each of us, to live for years
without the thing we once fancied gave life its only value. We have
tasted of servitude; and patience, taken up as a means, has grown
grateful as an end. It has cured us of eagerness.' So wisely it
gossiped, the smile of our guest. No wonder I liked it.

One evening, a month after his advent, Mrs Garnyer came to
me with a strange, embarrassed air. 'I have something to tell you,'
she said; 'something that will surprise you. Do you consider me a
very old woman? I am old enough to be wiser, you will say. But I

have never been so wise as to-day. I am engaged to be married to
Mr Cope. There! make the best of it. I have no apologies to make
to any one,' she went on, almost defiantly. 'It's between ourselves.
If we suit each other, it's no one's business. I know what I am
about. He means to remain in this country; we should be constantly together and extremely intimate. As he says, I am young
enough to be – what do they call it? – compromised. Of course,
therefore, I am young enough to marry. It will make no difference
with you; you will stay with me all the same. Who cares, after all,
what I do? No one but Eustace, and he will thank me for giving
him such a father. Ah, I shall do well by my boy!' she cried,
clasping her hands in ecstacy. 'I shall do better than he knows. My
property, it appears, is dreadfully entangled. Mr Garnyer did as
he pleased with it; I was given to him with my hands tied. Mr
Cope has been looking into it, and he tells me that it will be a long
affair to put things to rights. I have been living all these years at
the mercy of unprincipled agents. But now I have given up
everything to Mr Cope. *He* will drive the money-changers from
the temple! It's a small reward to marry him. Eustace has no head
for money-matters; he only knows how to spend. For years now
he needn't think of them – Mr Cope is our providence. Don't be
afraid; Eustace won't object, and at last he will have a companion
– the best, the wisest, the kindest. You know how he used to long
for one – how tired he was of me and you. It will be a new life.
Oh, I'm a happy mother – at last – at last! Don't look at me so
hard; I am a blushing bride, remember. Smile, laugh, kiss me.
There! You are a good creature. I shall make my boy a present –
the handsomest that ever was made. Poor Mr Cope – I am happier
than he! I have had my boy all these years, and he has had none.
He has the heart of a father – he has longed for a son. Do you
know,' she added, with a strange smile, 'that I think he marries
me as much for my son's sake as for my own? He marries me at all
events – boy and all!' This speech was uttered with a forced and
hurried animation which betrayed the effort to cheat herself into
pure enthusiasm. The matter was not quite so simple as she tried
to believe. Nevertheless, I was exceedingly pleased, and I kissed
her in genuine sympathy. The more I thought of it the better I
liked the marriage. It relieved me personally of a burdensome

sense of ineffectual care, and it filled out solidly a kind of defenceless breach which had always existed on the worldly face of Mrs Garnyer's position. Moreover, it promised to be full of advantages for Eustace. It was a pity indeed that Eustace had but a slender relish for things that were good for him. I venture to hope, however, that his worship of his father's memory had been, at bottom, the expression of a need for some higher authority and of a capacity to be respectful when there was something really to respect. Yet I took the liberty of suggesting to Mrs Garnyer that she perhaps counted too implicitly on her son's concurrence; that he was always in opposition; that a margin should be left for his possible perversity. Of course I was called a suspicious wretch for my pains.

'For what do you take him?' she cried. 'I shall just put them face to face. Eustace has delicacy. A word to the wise, says the proverb. I know what I am about.'

She knew it, I think, hardly so well as she declared. I had deemed it my duty to make a modest little speech of congratulation to the bridegroom elect. He blushed – somewhat to my surprise – but he answered me with a few proper, grateful words. He was much preoccupied; Mrs Garnyer was of a dozen different minds about her wedding-day. I had taken for granted that they would wait for Eustace's return; but I was somewhat startled on learning that Mr Cope disapproved of further delay. They had waited twenty years! Mrs Garnyer told me that she had not announced the news to Eustace – she wished it to be a 'surprise.' She seemed, however, not altogether to believe in her surprise. Poor lady! she had made herself a restless couch. One evening, coming into the library, I found Mr Cope pleading his cause. For the first time I saw him excited, and he turned appealingly to me. 'You have great influence with this lady,' he said. 'Argue my case. Are we people to care for Mrs Grundy? Has she been so very civil to us? We don't marry to please her; I don't see why she should arrange the wedding. Mrs Garnyer has no trousseau to buy, no cards to send. Indeed, I think any more airs and graces are rather ridiculous. They don't belong to our years. There's little Master Grundy, I know,' he went on, smiling – 'a highly honourable youth! But I will take charge of him. I should like immensely, of course, to have him at the wedding; but one of these days I shall make up for the breach of ceremony by punctually attending his own.' It was only an hour before this, as it happened, that I had received Eustace's answer to my letter. It was brief and hasty, but he had found time to insert some such words as this: 'I don't at all thank you for your news of Mr Cope. I knew that my mother only wanted a chance to forget me and console herself, as they say in France. Demonstrative mothers always do. I am like Hamlet – I don't approve of mothers consoling themselves. Mr Cope may be an excellent fellow – I have no doubt he is; but I do hope he will have finished his visit by the time I get back. The house isn't large enough for both of us. You will find me a bigger man than when I left home, I give you warning. I have got a bristling black moustache, and I am proportionately fiercer.' I said nothing about this letter, and a week later my companions were married. The time will always be memorable to me, apart from this matter of my story, for the intense and overwhelming heat which then prevailed. It had lasted several days when the nuptials took place; it bade fair to last all summer. The ceremony was performed by the little old Episcopal clergyman whose ministrations Mrs Garnyer had regularly attended, and who had always given her a vague parochial countenance. His sister, a mature spinster who wore her hair cut short and called herself 'strong-minded,' and, thus qualified, had made overtures to Mrs Garnyer – this lady and myself were the only witnesses. The marriage had nothing of a festive air; it seemed a solemn sacrifice to the unknown god. Mrs Garnyer was very much oppressed by the heat; in the vestibule, on leaving the church, she fainted. They had arranged to go for a week to the seaside to a place they had known of old. When she had revived we placed her in the carriage, and they immediately started. I, of course, remained in charge of the empty house, greatly envying them their cooling breezes.

V

On the morning after the wedding, sitting alone in the darkened library, I heard a rapid tread in the hall. My first thought, of course, was of burglars – my second of Eustace. In a moment he came striding into the room. His step, his glance, his whole outline, foretold trouble. He was extraordinarily changed, and all for the better. He seemed taller, older, manlier. He was bronzed by travel and dressed with great splendour. The moustache he had mentioned, though but a slender thing as yet, gave him, to my eye, a formidable foreign look. He gave me no greeting.

'Where's my mother?' he cried.

My heart rose to my throat; his tone seemed to put us horribly in the wrong. 'She's away – for a day,' I said. 'But you' – and I took his hand – 'pray where have you dropped from?'

'From New York, from shipboard, from Southampton. Is this the way my mother receives me?'

'Why, she never dreamed you were coming.'

'She got no letter? I wrote from New York.'

'Your letter never came. She left town yesterday, for a week.'

He looked at me hard. 'How comes it you are not with her?'

'I am not needed. She has – she has – ' But I faltered.

'Say it – say it!' he cried; and he stamped his foot. 'She has a companion.'

'Mr Cope went with her,' I said, in a still small voice. I was ashamed of my trepidation, I was outraged by his imperious manner, but the thought of worse to come unnerved me.

'Mr Cope – ah!' he answered, with an indefinable accent. He looked about the room as if he wanted to pick out some offensive trace of Mr Cope's passage. Then flinging himself into a chair, 'What infernal heat!' he went on. 'What a horrible climate you have got here! Do bring me a glass of water.'

I brought him his glass, and stood before him as he quickly drank it. 'Don't think you are not welcome if I ask what has brought you home so suddenly,' I ventured to say.

He gave me another hard look over the top of his glass. 'A suspicion. It's none too soon. Tell me what is going on between my mother and Mr Cope.'

'Eustace,' I said, 'before I answer you, let me remind you of the respect which, under all circumstances, you owe your mother.'

He sprang from his chair. 'Respect! I am right then – they mean to marry! Speak!' And as I hesitated, 'You needn't speak,' he cried, 'I see it in your face. Thank God, I'm here!'

His violence roused me. 'If you have a will to enforce in the matter, you are indeed none too soon. You are too late – your mother is married.' I spoke passionately, but in a moment I repented of my words.

'*Married!*' the poor boy shouted, 'MARRIED, you say!' He turned deadly pale, and stood staring at me with his mouth wide open. Then, trembling in all his limbs, he dropped into a chair. For some moments he was silent, gazing at me with a kind of fierce stupefaction, overwhelmed by the treachery of fate. 'Married,' he went on. 'When, where, how? Without me – without notice – without shame! And you stood and watched it, as you stand and tell me now! I called you friend!' he cried, with the bitterest reproach. 'But if my mother betrays me, what can I expect of *you?* Married!' he repeated. 'Is the devil in it? I'll unmarry her! When – when – when?' And he seized me by the arm.

'Yesterday, Eustace. I entreat you to be calm.'

'Calm? Is it a case for calmness? *She* was calm enough – that she couldn't wait for her son?' He flung aside the hand I had laid upon his to soothe him, and began a furious march about the room. 'What has come to her? Is she mad? Has she lost her head, her heart, her memory – all that made her mine? You are joking – come, it's a horrible dream!' And he stopped before me, glaring through fiery tears. 'Did she hope to keep it a secret? Did she hope to hide away her husband in a cupboard? Her husband! And I – I – I – what has she done with me? Where am I in this devil's game? Standing here crying like a schoolboy for a cut finger – for the bitterest of disappointments! She has blighted my life – she has blasted my rights. She has insulted me – dishonoured me. Am I a man to treat in that fashion? Am I a man to be made light of? Brought up as a flower and trampled as a weed! Wrapped in cotton and then exposed – you needn't speak' – I had tried, for pity, to remonstrate – 'you can say nothing that is not idiotic. There's nothing to be said but this – that I'm *insulted*. Do you understand?' He uttered the word with a concentrated rancour of vanity. 'I guessed it from the first. I knew it was coming. Mr Cope – Mr Cope – always Mr Cope! It poisoned my journey – it poisoned my pleasure – it poisoned Italy. You don't know what that means. But what matter, so long as it has poisoned my home? I held my tongue

– I swallowed my rage; I was patient, I was gentle, I forbore. And for this! I could have damned him with a word! At the seaside, hey? Enjoying the breezes – splashing in the surf – picking up shells. It's idyllic, it's ideal: great heavens, it's fabulous, it's monstrous! It's well she's not here. I don't answer for myself. Yes, you goose, stare, stare – wring your hands! You see an angry man, an outraged man, but a man, mind you! He means to act as one.'

This sweeping torrent of unreason I had vainly endeavoured to arrest. He pushed me aside, strode out of the room, and went bounding upstairs to his own chamber, where I heard him close the door with a terrible bang and turn the key. My hope was that his passion would expend itself in this first explosion; I was glad to bear the brunt of it. But I regarded it as my duty to communicate with his mother. I wrote her a hurried line: 'Eustace is back – very ill. Come home.' This I entrusted to the coachman, with injunctions to carry it in person to the place where she was staying. I believed that if she should start as soon as she received it she might reach home late at night. Those were the days of private conveyances. Meanwhile I did my best to pacify the poor young man. There was something almost insane in his resentment; he seemed absolutely rabid. This was the sweet compliance, the fond assent, on which his mother had counted; this was the 'surprise'! I went repeatedly to the door of his room with soft speeches and urgent prayers and offers of luncheon, of wine, of vague womanly comfort. But there came no answer but shouts and imprecations, and finally a sullen silence. Late in the day I heard him, from the window, order the gardener to saddle his horse; and in a short time he came stamping down stairs, booted and spurred, pale, dishevelled, with bloodshot eyes. 'Where are you going,' I said, 'in this awful heat?'

'To ride – ride – ride myself cool!' he cried. 'There's nothing so hot as my rage!' And in a moment he was in the saddle and bounding out of the gate. I went up to his room. Its wild disorder told me how he had raved up and down. A dozen things were strewn, broken, on the floor; old letters were lying crumpled and torn; I was sickened by the sight of a pearl necklace, snatched from his gaping valise, and evidently purchased as a present to his mother, ground into fragments on the carpet, as if by his boot-heels. His father's relics were standing in a row, untouched, on the mantelshelf, save for a couple of pistols, mounted with his initials, in silver, which were tossed upon the table. I made a courageous effort to thrust them into a drawer and turn the key, but to my eternal regret I was afraid to touch them. Evening descended and wore away; but neither Eustace nor his mother returned. I sat gloomily enough on the verandah, listening for wheels or hoofs. Towards midnight a carriage rattled over the gravel; my friend descended, with her husband, at the door. She fluttered into my arms with a kind of shrinking eagerness. 'Where is he – how is he?' she cried.

I was spared the pain of answering, for at the same moment I heard Eustace's horse clatter into the stable-yard. He had rapidly dismounted, and he passed into the house by one of the lateral windows, which opened from the piazza into the drawing-room. There the lamps were lighted; I led in my companions. Eustace had crossed the threshold of the window; the lamplight fell upon him, relieving him against the darkness. His mother, with a shriek, flung herself toward him, but in an instant, with a deeper cry, she stopped short, pressing her hand to her heart. He had raised his hand, and, with a gesture which had all the spiritual force of a blow, he had cast her off. 'Ah, my son, my son!' she cried, with a piteous moan, and looking round at us in wild bewilderment.

'I am not your son!' said the boy, in a voice half stifled with passion, 'I give you up! You are not my mother! Don't touch me! You have cheated me – betrayed me – dishonoured me!' In this mad peal of imprecations it was still the note of vanity which rang clearest.

I looked at Mr Cope – he was deadly pale. He had seen the lad's gesture; he was unable to hear his words. He sat down in the nearest chair and eyed him wonderingly. I hurried to his poor wife's relief; she seemed smitten with a sudden tremor, a deadly chill. She clasped her hands, but she could barely find her voice. 'Eustace – my boy – my darling – my own – do you know what you say? Listen, listen, Eustace. It's all for you – that you should love me more. I have done my best. I seem to have been hasty, but hasty to do for you – to do for you – ' Her strength deserted her; she burst into tears. 'He curses me – he denies me!' she cried. 'He has killed me!'

'Cry, cry!' Eustace retorted; 'cry as I have been crying! But don't be falser than you have been. That you couldn't even wait! And you prate of my happiness! Is my happiness in a ruined home – in a disputed heart – in a bullying step-father! You have chosen him big and strong! Cry your eyes out – you are no mother of mine.'

'He's killing me – he's killing me,' groaned his mother. 'Oh heavens, if I dared to speak I should kill *him!*' She turned to her husband. 'Go to him – go to him?' she cried. He's ill, he's mad – he doesn't know what he says. Take his hand in yours – look at him, soothe him, cure him. It's the hot weather,' she rambled on. 'Let him feel your touch! Eustace, Eustace, be cured!'

Poor Mr Cope had risen to his feet, passing his handkerchief over his forehead, on which the perspiration stood in great drops. He went slowly towards the young man, bending his eyes on him half in entreaty, half in command. Before him he stopped and frankly held out his hand. Eustace glared at him defiantly, from head to foot, him and his proffered friendship, pressed upon him as it was in the kindest, wisest, firmest way. Then pushing his hand savagely down, 'Hypocrite!' he roared close to his face – 'can you hear that?' and marched straight out of the room. Mr Cope shook his head with a world of tragic meaning, and for an instant exchanged with his wife a long look, brimming with anguish. She fell upon his neck with passionate sobs. But soon recovered herself, 'Go to him,' she repeated, 'follow him; say everything, spare nothing. No matter for me; I have got *my* blow.'

VI

I helped her up to her room; her strength had completely left her; she only half undressed and let me lay her on her bed. She was in a state of the intensest excitement; every nerve in her body was thrilling and quivering. She kept murmuring to herself, with a kind of heartbreaking incoherency. 'Nothing can hurt me now; I needn't be spared. Nothing can disgrace me – or grace me. I have got my blow. It's my fault – all, all, all! I heaped up folly on folly and weakness on weakness. My heart's broken; it will never be of any use again. You have been right, my dear – I perverted him, I taught him to strike. Oh what a blow! He's hard – he's hard. He's cruel. He has no heart. He is blind with vanity and egotism. But it matters little now; I shan't live to suffer. I have suffered enough. I am dying, my friend, I am dying.'

In this broken strain the poor lady poured out the bitterness of her grief. I used every art to soothe and console her, but I felt that the tenderest spot in her gentle nature had received an irreparable bruise. 'I don't want to live,' she murmured. 'I have seen something too dreadful. It could never be patched up; we should never be the same. He has shown his character – isn't it his character? It's bad!'

In spite of my efforts to restore her to calmness she became, not more excited – for her strength seemed to be ebbing and her voice was low – but more painfully and incoherently talkative. Nevertheless, from her distressing murmur I gathered the glimmer of a meaning. She seemed to wish to make a kind of supreme confession. I sat on the edge of her bed, with her hand in mine. From time to time, above her loud whispers, I heard the sound of the two gentlemen's voices. Adjoining her chamber was a large dressing-room; beyond this was Eustace's apartment. The three rooms opened upon a long, uncovered balcony.

Mr Cope had followed the young man to his own room, and was addressing him in a low, steady voice. Eustace apparently was silent; but there was something sullen and portentious to my ear in this unnatural absence of response.

'What have you thought of me, my friend, all these years?' his mother asked. 'Have I seemed to you like other women? I haven't been like others. I have tried to be so – and you see – you see! Let me tell you. It don't matter whether you despise me – I shan't know it. These are my last words; let them be frank.'

They were not, however so frank as she intended. She seemed to lose herself in a dim wilderness of memories; her faculty wandered, faltered, stumbled, Not from her words – they were ambiguous – but from her silence and from the rebound of my own quickened sympathy, as it were, I guessed the truth. It blossomed into being, vivid and distinct; it flashed a long, illuminating glow upon the past – a lurid light upon the present. Strange it seemed now that my suspicions had been so late to bear fruit; but our imagination is always too timid. Now all things were clear! Heaven knows that in this unpitying light I felt no contempt for the poor woman who lay before me, panting with a supreme disappointment.

Poor victims of destiny – if I could only bring them to terms! For the moment, however, the unhappy mother and wife demanded all my attention. I left her and passed along the balcony, intending to make her husband come to her. The light in Eustace's room showed me the young man and his companion. They sat facing each other, silent for the moment. Mr Cope's two hands were on his knees, his eyes were fixed on the carpet, his teeth were set – as if, baffled, irate, desperate, he was preparing to play his last card. Eustace was looking at him hard, with a terribly vicious expression. It made me sick. I was on the point of rushing in and forcing them somehow apart, when suddenly Mr Cope raised his eyes and exchanged with the boy a look with which he seemed to read his very soul. He waved his hand in the air as if to say that he had been patient enough.

'If you were to see yourself as I see you,' he said, 'you would be immensely surprised; you would know your absurd appearance. Young as you are, you are rotten with arrogance and pride. What would you say if I were to tell you that, least of men, you have reason to be proud? Your stable-boy there has more. There's a leak in your vanity, there's a blot on your scutcheon! You force me to take strong measures. Let me tell you, in the teeth of your monstrous egotism, what you are. You're a – '

I knew what was coming, but I hadn't the heart to hear it. The word, ringing out, overtook my ear as I hurried back to Mrs Cope. It was followed by a loud, incoherent cry, the sound, prolonged for some moments, of a scuffle, and then the report of a pistol. This was lost in the noise of crashing glass. Mrs Cope rose erect in bed and shrieked aloud, 'He has killed him – and me!' I caught her in my arms; she drew her last breath. I laid her gently on the bed and made my trembling way, by the balcony, to Eustace's room. The first glance reassured me. Neither of the men were visibly injured; the pistol lay smoking on the floor. Eustace had sunk into a chair, with his head buried in his hands. I saw his face burning red through his fingers.

'It's not murder,' Mr Cope said to me as I crossed the threshold, 'but it has just missed being suicide. It has been fatal only to the looking-glass.' The mirror was shivered.

'It *is* murder,' I answered, seizing Eustace by the arm and forcing him to rise. 'You have killed your mother. This is your father!'

My friend paused and looked at me with a triumphant air, as if she was very proud of her effect. Of course I had foreseen it half-an-hour ago. 'What a dismal tale!' I said. 'But it's interesting. Of course Mrs Cope recovered.'

She was silent an instant. 'You are like me,' she answered; 'your imagination is timid.'

'I confess,' I rejoined, 'I am rather at a loss how to dispose of our friend Eustace. I don't see how the two could very well shake hands – nor yet how they couldn't.'

'They did once – and but once. They were for years, each in his way, lonely men. They were never reconciled. The trench had been dug too deep. Even the poor lady buried there didn't avail to fill it up. Yet the son was forgiven – the father never!'

The Sweetheart of M. Briseux

The little picture gallery at M— is a typical *musée de province* –
cold, musty, unvisited, and enriched chiefly with miniature works
by painters whose maturity was not to be powerful. The floors are
tiled in brick, and the windows draped in faded moreen; the very
light seems pale and neutral, as if the dismal lack-lustre atmosphere
of the pictures were contagious. The subjects represented are of
course of the familiar academic sort – the Wisdom of Solomon and
the Fureurs d'Oreste; together with a few elegant landscapes
exhibiting the last century view of nature, and half a dozen neat
portraits of French gentlefolks of that period, in the act, as one
may say, of taking the view in question. To me, I confess, the
place had a melancholy charm, and I found none of the absurd old
paintings too absurd to enjoy. There is always an agreeable finish
in the French touch, even when the hand is not a master's. The
catalogue, too, was prodigiously queer; a bit of very ancient
literature, with comments, in the manner of the celebrated M. La
Harpc.[1] I wondered, as I turned its pages, into what measure of
reprobation pictures and catalogue together had been compressed
by that sole son of M—, who has achieved more than local renown
in the arts. Conjecture was pertinent, for it was in these crepuscular
halls that this deeply original artist must have heard the first early
bird-notes of awakening genius: first, half credulously, as we may
suppose, on festal Sundays, with his hand in his father's, gazing
rosy and wide-eyed at the classical wrath of Achilles and the sallow
flesh-tints of Dido; and later, with his hands in his pockets, an
incipient critical frown and the mental vision of an Achilles
somehow more in earnest and a Dido more deeply desirable. It
was indeed doubly pertinent, for the little Musée had at last, after
much watching and waiting and bargaining, become possessor of
one of Briseux's pictures. I was promptly informed of the fact by

the *concierge*, a person much reduced by years and chronic catarrh, but still robust enough to display his aesthetic culture to a foreigner presumably of distinction. He led me solemnly into the presence of the great work, and placed a chair for me in the proper light. The famous painter had left this native town early in life, before making his mark, and an inappreciative family – his father was a small apothecary with a proper admiration of the arts, but a horror of artists – had been at no pains to preserve his boyish sketches. The more fools they! The merest scrawl with his signature now brought hundreds of francs, and there were those of his blood still in the town with whom the francs were scarce enough. To obtain a serious picture had of course been no small affair, and little M—, though with the yearning heart of a mother, happened to have no scanty maternal savings. Yet the thing had been managed by subscription, and the picture paid for. To make the triumph complete, a fortnight after it had been hung on its nail, M. Briseux succumbs to a fever in Rome and his pictures rise to the most fantastic prices! This was the very work which had made the painter famous. The portrait of a Lady in a Yellow Shawl in the Salon of 1836 had *fait époque*. Every one had heard of the Yellow Shawl; people talked of it as they did of the Chapeau de Paille of Rubens, or the 'Torn Glove' of Titian; or if they didn't, posterity would! Such was the discursive murmur of the concierge as I examined this precious specimen of Briseux's first manner; and there was a plaintive cadence in this last assurance, which seemed to denote a too vivid prevision of the harvest of tributary francs to be reaped by his successors in office. It would be graceless praise to say that a glimpse of the picture is worth your franc. It is a superb performance, and I spent half an hour before it in such serene enjoyment that I forgot the concierge was a bore.

It is a half-length portrait representing a young woman, not exactly beautiful, yet very far from plain, draped with a singularly simple elegance in a shawl of yellow silk embroidered with fantastic arabesque. She is dark and grave, her dress is dark, the background is of a sober tone, and this brilliant scarf glows splendidly by contrast. It seems indeed to irradiate luminous color, and makes the picture brilliant in spite of its sombre accessories; and yet it leaves their full value to the tenderly glowing flesh portions. The portrait lacks a certain harmonious finish, that masterly interfusion of parts which the painter afterwards practised; the touch is hasty, and here and there a little heavy; but its splendid vivacity and energy, and the almost boyish good faith of some of its more venturesome strokes, make it a capital example of that momentous point in the history of genius when still tender promise blooms – in a night, as it were – into perfect force. It was little wonder that the picture had made a noise: judges of the more penetrating sort must have felt that it contained that invaluable something which an artist gives but once – the prime outgush of his effort – the flower of his originality. As I continued to look, however, I began to wonder whether it did not contain something better still – the reflection of a countenance very nearly as deep and ardent as the artist's talent. In spite of the expressive repose of the figure the brow and mouth wore a look of smothered agitation, the dark gray eye almost glittered, and the flash in the check burned ominously. Evidently this was the picture of something more than a yellow shawl. To the analytic eye it was the picture of a mind, or at least of a mood. 'Who was the lady?' I asked of my companion.

He shrugged his shoulders, and for an instant looked uncertain. But, as a Frenchman, he produced his hypothesis as follows: 'Mon Dieu! a sweetheart of M. Briseux! – *Ces artistes!*'

I left my place and passed into the adjoining rooms, where, as I have said, I found half an hour's diversion. On my return, my chair was occupied by a lady, apparently my only fellow-visitor. I noticed her no further than to see that, though comely, she was no longer young, that she was dressed in black, and that she was looking intently at the picture. Her intentness indeed at last attracted me, and while I lingered to gather a final impression, I covertly glanced at her. She was so far from being young that her hair was white, but with that charming and often premature brilliancy which belongs to fine brunettes. The concierge hovered near, narrating and expounding, and I fancied that her brief responses (for she asked no questions) betrayed an English accent. But I had doubtless no business to fancy anything, for my companion, as if with a sudden embarrassing sense of being watched, gathered her shawl about her, rose, and prepared to turn away. I should have immediately retreated, but that with this movement of hers our eyes met, and in the light of her rapid, just slightly deprecating glance, I read something which helped curiosity to get the better of politeness. She walked away, and I stood staring; and as she averted her head it seemed to me that my rather too manifest surprise had made her blush. I watched her slowly cross the room and pass into the next one, looking very vaguely at the pictures; and then addressed a keenly questioning glance at the Lady with the Yellow Shawl. Her startlingly vivid eyes answered my question most distinctly. I was satisfied, and I left the Musée.

It would perhaps be more correct to say that I was wholly unsatisfied. I strolled at haphazard through the little town, and emerged, as a matter of course, on the local promenade. The promenade at M— is a most agreeable spot. It stretches along the top of the old town wall, over whose sturdy parapet, polished by the peaceful showers of many generations, you enjoy a view of the pale-hued but charming Provencal landscape. The middle of the rampart is adorned with a row of close-clipped lime-trees, with benches in the spaces between them; and, as you sit in the shade, the prospect is framed to your vision by the level parapet and the even limit of the far-projecting branches. What you see is therefore a long horizontal strip of landscape – a radiant stretch of white rocks and vaporous olives, scintillating in the southern light. Except a *bonne* or two, with a couple of children grubbing in the gravel, an idle apprentice in a blouse dozing on a bench, and a couple of red-legged soldiers leaning on the wall, I was the only lounger on the rampart, and this was a place to relish solitude. By nature a very sentimental traveller, there is nothing I like better than to light a cigar and lose myself in a meditative perception of local color. I love to ruminate the picturesque, and the scene before me was redolent of it. On this occasion however, the shady rampart and the shining distance were less interesting than a figure, disembodied but distinct, which soon obtruded itself on my attention. The mute assurance gathered before leaving the Musée had done as much to puzzle as to enlighten me. Was that modest and venerable person, then, the sweetheart of the illustrious Briseux? one of *ces artistes*, as rumor loudly proclaimed him, in the invidious as well as in the most honorable sense of the term. Plainly, she was the original of the portrait. In the days when her complexion would bear it, she had worn the yellow shawl. Time had changed, but not transformed her, as she must have fancied it had, to come and contemplate thus frankly this monument of her early charms. Why had she come? Was it accident, or was it vanity? How did it seem to her to find herself so strangely lifted out of her own possession and made a helpless spectator of her survival to posterity? The more I consulted my impression of her, the more certain I felt that she was no Frenchwoman, but a modest spinster of my own transatlantic race, on whom posterity had as little claim as this musty Musée, which indeed possessed much of that sepulchral chill which clings to such knowledge of us as posterity enjoys. I found it hard to reconcile the lady with herself, and it was with the restlessness of conjecture that I left my place and strolled to the further end of the rampart. Here conjecture paused, amazed at its opportunities; for M. Briseux's sweetheart was seated on a bench under the lime-trees. She was gazing almost as thoughtfully on the distant view as she had done on her portrait; but as I passed, she gave me a glance from which embarrassment seemed to have vanished. I slowly walked the length of the rampart again, and as I went an impulse, born somehow of the delicious mild air, the light-bathed landscape of rock and olive, and of the sense of a sort of fellowship in isolation in the midst of these deeply foreign influences, as well as of a curiosity which was after all but the frank recognition of an obvious fact, was transmuted into a decision sufficiently remarkable in a bashful man. I proceeded gravely to carry it out. I approached my companion and bowed. She acknowledged my bow with a look which, though not exactly mistrustful, seemed to demand an explanation. To give it, I seated myself beside her. Something in her face made explanation easy. I was sure that she was an old maid, and gently but frankly eccentric. Her age left her at liberty to be as frank as she chose, and though I was somewhat her junior, I had gray hairs enough in my moustache to warrant her in smiling at my almost ardent impatience. Her smile, when she perceived that my direct appeal was deeply respectful, broke into a genial laugh which completed our introduction. To her inner sense, as well, evidently, the gray indifference of the historic rampart, the olive-sown landscape, the sweet foreign climate, left the law very much in our own hands;

and then moreover, as something in her eyes proclaimed, the well of memory in her soul had been so strongly stirred that it naturally overflowed. I fancy that she looked more like her portrait for that hour or two than she had done in twenty years. At any rate, it had come to seem, before many minutes, a delightful matter of course that I should sit there – a perfect stranger – listening to the story into which her broken responses to my first questions gradually shaped themselves. I should add that I had made a point of appearing a zealous student of the lamented Briseux. This was no more than the truth, and I proved categorically that I knew his works. We were thus pilgrims in the same faith, and licensed to discuss its mysteries. I repeat her story literally, and I surely don't transgress the proper limits of editorial zeal in supplying a single absent clause: she must in those days have been a wonderfully charming girl.

I have been spending the winter (she said) with my niece at Cannes, where I accidentally heard from an English gentleman interested in such matters, that Briseux's 'Yellow Shawl' had been purchased by this little Musée. He had stopped to see it on his way from Paris, and, though a famous *connoisseur*, poor man, do you know he never discovered what it took you but a moment to perceive? I didn't enlighten him, in spite of his kindness in explaining, 'Bradshaw' in hand, just how I might manage to diverge on my way to Paris and give a day to M—. I contented myself with telling him that I had known M. Briseux thirty years ago, and had chanced to have the first glimpse of his first masterpiece. Even this suggested nothing. But in fact, why should it have suggested anything? As I sat before the picture just now, I felt in all my pulses that I am *not* the person who stands masquerading there with that strangely cynical smile. That poor girl is dead and buried; I should tell no falsehood in saying I'm not she. Yet as I looked at her, time seemed to roll backward and experience to repeat itself. Before me stood a pale young man in a ragged coat, with glowing dark eyes, brushing away at a great canvas, with gestures more like those of inspiration than any I have ever seen. I seemed to see myself – to *be* myself – muffled in that famous shawl, *posing* there for hours in a sort of fever that made me unconscious of fatigue. I've often wondered whether, during those memorable hours, I was more or less myself than usual, and whether the singular episode they brought forth was an act of folly or of transcendent reason. Perhaps you can tell me.

It was in Paris, in my twenty-first year. I had come abroad with Mrs Staines, an old and valued friend of my mother's, who during the last days of her life, a year before, had consigned me appealingly to this lady's protection. But for Mrs Staines, indeed, I should have been homeless. My brother had recently married, but not happily, and experiment had shown me that under his roof I was an indifferent peacemaker. Mrs Staines was what is called a very superior person – a person with an aquiline nose, who wore gloves in the house, and gave you her ear to kiss. My mother, who considered her the wisest of women, had written her every week since their schooldays a crossed letter beginning 'My dearest Lucretia'; but it was my poor mother's nature to like being patronized and bullied. Mrs Staines would send her by return of mail a budget of advice adapted to her 'station' – this being a considerate mode of allusion to the fact that she had married a very poor clergyman. Mrs Staines received me, however, with such substantial kindness, that I should have had little grace to complain that the manner of it was frigid. When I knew her better I forgave her frigidity, for it was that of a disappointed woman. She was ambitious, and her ambitions had failed. She had married a very clever man, a rising young lawyer, of political tendencies, who promised to become famous. She would have enjoyed above all things being the wife of a legal luminary, and she would have insisted on his expanding to the first magnitude. She believed herself born, I think, to be the lawful Egeria[2] of a cabinet minister. A cabinet minister poor Mr Staines might have become if he had lived; but he broke down at thirty-five from overwork, and a year later his wife had to do double mourning. As time went on she transferred her hopes to her only boy; but here her disappointment lay the heavier on her heart that maternal pride had bidden it be forever dumb. He would never tread in his father's steps, nor redeem his father's pledges. His genius – if genius it was – was bent in quite another way, and he was to be, not a useful, but an ornamental member of society. Extremely ornamental he seemed likely to become, and his mother found partial comfort as he grew older. He did his duty apparently in growing up so very handsome that, whatever else he might do, he would be praised less for that than for his good looks. They were those of a decorous young Apollo. When I first saw him, as he was leaving college, he might well have passed for an incipient great man. He had in perfection the *air* of distinction, and he carried it out in gesture and manner. Never was a handsomer, graver, better-bred young man. He was tall, slender, and fair, with the finest blonde hair curling close about his shapely head; a blue eye, as clear and cold as a winter's morning; a set of teeth so handsome that his infrequent smile might have seemed almost a matter of modesty; and a general expression of discretion and maturity which seemed to protest against the imputation of foppishness. After a while, probably, you would have found him too imperturbably neat and polite, and have liked him better if his manner had been sometimes at fault and his cravat occasionally awry. Me, I confess, he vastly impressed from the first, and I secretly worshipped him. I had never seen so fine a gentleman, and I doubted if the world contained such another. My experience of the world was small, and I had lived among what Harold Staines would have considered very shabby people – several of whom wore ill-brushed hats. I was, therefore, not sorry to find that I appreciated merit of the most refined sort; and in fact, ignorant though I was, my judgment was not at fault. Harold was perfectly honorable and amiable, and his only fault was that he looked wiser than he could reasonably be expected to be. In the evening especially, in a white cravat, leaning in a doorway, and overtopping the crowd by his whole handsome head, he seemed some inscrutable young diplomatist whose skepticism hadn't undermined his courtesy.

He had, through his mother, expectation of property sufficient to support him in ample ease; but though he had elegant tastes, idleness was not one of them, and he agreed with his mother that he ought to choose a profession. Then it was that she fully measured her disappointment. There had been nothing in her family but judges and bishops, and anything else was of questionable respectability. There was a great deal of talk on the matter between them; for superficially at least they were a most united pair, and if Harold had not asked her opinion from conviction he would have done so from politeness. In reality, I believe, there was but one person in the world whose opinion he greatly cared for – and that person was not Mrs Staines; nor had it yet come to pass that he pretended for a while it was I. It was so far from being Mrs Staines that one day, after a long talk, I found her leaving him in tears; and tears with this superior woman were an event of portentous rarity. Harold on the same day was not at home at dinner, and I thought the next day held his handsome head even higher than usual. I asked no questions, but a little later my curiosity was satisfied. Mrs Staines informed me, with an air of dignity which evidently cost her some effort and seemed intended to deprecate criticism, that Harold had determined to be an – artist. 'It's not the career I should have preferred,' she said, 'but my son has talent – and respectability – which will make it honorable.' That Harold would do anything more for the profession of the brush than Raphael and Rembrandt had done, I was perhaps not prepared to affirm; but I answered that I was very glad, and that I wished him all success. Indeed, I was not surprised, for Mr Staines had what in any one else would have been called a mania for pictures and bronzes, old snuff-boxes and candle-sticks. He had not apparently used his pencil very freely; but he had recently procured – indeed, I think he had himself designed – a 'sketching apparatus' of the most lavish ingenuity. He was now going to use it in earnest, and I remember reflecting with a good deal of satisfaction that the great white umbrella which formed its principal feature was large enough to protect his handsome complexion from the sun.

It was at this time I came to Mrs Staines to stay indefinitely – with doubts and fears so few that I must have been either very ignorant or very confident. I had indeed an ample measure of the blessed simplicity of youth; but if I judged my situation imperfectly, I did so at any rate with a conscience. I was stoutly determined to receive no favors that I couldn't repay, and to be as quietly useful and gracefully agreeable as I could modestly devise occasion for. I was a homeless girl, but I was not a poor relation. My fortune was slender, but I was ready to go out into the world and seek a better, rather than fall into an attitude of irresponsive dependence. Mrs Staines thought at first that I was dull and amiable, and that as a companion I would do no great credit to anything but her benevolence. Later, for a time, as I gave proofs of some sagacity and perhaps of some decision, I think she fancied me a schemer and – Heaven forgive her! – a hypocrite. But at last, evidently – although to the end, I believe, she continued to compliment my shrewdness at the expense of that feminine sweetness by which I should have preferred to commend myself – she decided that I was a person of the best intentions, and – here comes my story – that I would make a suitable wife for her son.

To this unexpectedly flattering conclusion, of course, she was slow in coming; it was the result of the winter we passed together after Harold had 'turned his attention,' as his mother always publicly phrased it, 'to art.' He had declared that we must immediately go abroad that he might study the works of the masters. His mother, I believe, suggested that he might begin with the rudiments nearer home. But apparently he had mastered the rudiments, for she was overruled and we went to Rome. I don't know how many of the secrets of the masters Harold learned; but we passed a delightful winter. He began his studies with the solemn promptitude which he used in all things, and devoted a great deal of time to copying from the antique in the Vatican and the Capitol. He worked slowly, but with extraordinary precision and neatness, and finished his drawings with exquisite care. He was openly very little of a dogmatist, but on coming to know him you found that he had various principles of which he was extremely tenacious. Several of these related to the proportions of the human body, as ascertained by himself. They constituted, he affirmed, an infallible method for learning to draw. If other artists didn't know it, so much the worse for them. He applied this rare method persistently all winter, and carried away from Rome a huge portfolio full of neatly shaded statues and statuesque *contadini*. At first he had gone into a painter's studio with several other pupils, but he took no fancy to either his teacher or his companions, and came home one day in disgust, declaring that he had washed his hands of them. As he never talked about disagreeable things, he said nothing as to what had vexed him; but I guessed that he had received some mortal offence, and I was not surprised that he shouldn't care to fraternize with the common herd of art-students. They had long, untidy hair, and smoked bad tobacco; they lay no one knew where, and borrowed money and took liberties. Mr Staines certainly was not a man to refuse a needy friend a napoleon, but he couldn't forgive a liberty. He took none with himself! We became very good friends, and it was especially for this that I liked him. Nothing is truer than that in the long run we like our opposites; they're a change and a rest from ourselves. I confess that my good intentions sometimes clashed with a fatal light-headedness, of which a fair share of trouble had not cured me. In moments of irritation I had a trick of giving the reins to my 'sarcasm;' so at least my partners in quadrilles had often called it. At my leisure I was sure to repent, and frank public amends followed fast on the heels of offence. Then I believe I was called generous – not only by my partners in quadrilles. But I had a secret admiration for people who were just, from the first and always, and whose demeanor seemed to shape itself with a sort of harmonious unity, like the outline of a beautiful statue. Harold Staines was a finished gentleman, as we used to say in those days, and I admired him the more that I still had ringing in my ears that eternal refrain of my schoolroom days – 'My child, my child, when will you ever learn to be a lady?' He seemed to me an embodiment of the serene amenities of life, and I didn't know how very great a personage I thought him until I once overheard a young man in a crowd at St Peter's call him *that confounded prig*. Then I came to the conclusion that it was a very coarse and vulgar world, and that Mr Staines was too good for it.

This impression was not removed by – I hardly know what to call it – the gallant propriety of his conduct toward me. He had treated me at first with polite condescension, as a very young and rather humble person, whose presence in the house rested on his mother's somewhat eccentric benevolence, rather than on any very obvious merits of her own. But later, as my native merit, whatever it was, got the better of my shyness, he approached me, especially in company, with a sort of ceremonious consideration which seemed to give notice to the world that if his mother and he treated me as their equal – why, I *was* their equal. At last, one fine day in Rome, I learned that I had the honor to please him. It had seemed

to me so little of a matter of course that I should captivate Mr
Staines, that for a moment I was actually disappointed, and felt
disposed to tell him that I had expected more of his taste. But as I
grew used to the idea, I found no fault with it, and I felt
prodigiously honored. I didn't take him for a man of genius, but
his admiration pleased me more than if it had come in chorus from
a dozen of the men of genius whom I had had pointed out to me at
archæological picnics. They somehow were covered with the
world's rust and haunted with the world's errors, and certainly on
any vital question could not be trusted to make their poor wives
the same answers two days running. Besides, they were dreadfully
ugly. Harold was consistency itself, and his superior manner and
fine blond beauty seemed a natural result of his spiritual serenity.
The way he declared himself was very characteristic, and to some
girls might have seemed prosaic. To my mind it had a peculiar
dignity. I had asked him, a week before, as we stood on the
platform before the Lateran,[3] some question about the Claudian
aqueduct, which he had been unable to answer at the moment,
although on coming to Rome he had laid in a huge provision of
books of reference which he consulted with unfailing diligence.
'I'll look it up,' he said gravely; but I thought no more about it,
and a few days afterwards, when he asked me to ride with him on
the Campagna, I never supposed I was to be treated to an
archæological lecture. It was worthy of a wiser listener. He led the
way to a swelling mound, overlooking the long stretch of the
aqueduct, and poured forth the result of his researches. This was
surely not a trivial compliment; and it seemed to me a finer sort of
homage than if he had offered me a fifty-franc bouquet or put his
horse at a six-foot wall. He told me the number of the arches, and
very possibly of the stones; his story bristled with learning. I
listened respectfully and stared hard at the long ragged ruin, as if
it had suddenly become intensely interesting. But it was Mr Staines
who was interesting: all honor to the man who kept his polite
promises so handsomely! I said nothing when he paused, and after
a few minutes was going to turn away my horse. Then he laid his
hand on the bridle, and, in the same tone, as if he were still talking
of the aqueduct, informed me of the state of his affections. I, in
my unsuspectingness, had enslaved them, and it was proper that I

should know he adored me. Proper! I have always remembered the word, though I was far from thinking then that it clashed with his eloquence. It often occurred to me afterwards as the key-note of his character. In a moment more, he formally offered himself.

Don't be surprised at these details: to be just I must be perfectly frank, and if I consented to tell you my story, it is because I fancied I should find profit in hearing it myself. As I speak my words come back to me. I left Rome engaged to Mr Staines, subject to his mother's approval. He might dispense with it, I told him, but I could not, and as yet I had no reason to expect it. She would, of course, wish him to marry a woman of more consequence. Mine of late had risen in her eyes, but she could hardly regard me as yet as a possible daughter-in-law. With time I hoped to satisfy her and to receive her blessing. Then I would ask for no further delay. We journeyed slowly up from Rome along the Mediterranean, stopping often for several days to allow Harold to sketch. He depicted mountains and villages with the same diligence as the statues in the Vatican, and presumably with the same success. As his winter's practice had given him great facility, he would dash off a magnificent landscape in a single morning. I always thought it strange that, being very sober in his speech and manner, he should be extremely fond of color in art. Such at least was the fact, and these rapid water-colors were a wonderful medley. Crimson and azure, orange and emerald – nothing less would satisfy him. But, for that matter, nature in those regions has a dazzling brightness. So at least it had for a lively girl of twenty, just engaged. So it had for a certain time afterwards. I'll not deny, the lustrous sea and sky began vaguely to reflect my own occasionally sombre mood. How to explain to you the process of my feeling at this time is more than I can say; how especially to make you believe that I was neither perverse nor capricious. I give it up; I can only assure you that I observed my emotions, even before I understood them, with painful surprise. I was not disillusioned, but an end had suddenly come to my elation. It was as if my heart had had wings, which had been suddenly clipped. I have never been especially fond of my own possessions, and I have learned that if I wish to admire a thing in peace, I must remain at a respectful distance. My happiness in Harold's affection reached its climax too suddenly, and before I knew it I found myself wondering, questioning, and doubting. It was no fault of his, certainly, and he had promised me nothing that he was not ready to bestow. He was all attention and decorous devotion. If there was a fault, it was mine, for having judged like the very young and uninformed person I was. Since my engagement I felt five years older, and the first use I made of my maturity – cruel as it may seem – was to turn round and look keenly at my lover and revise my judgment. His rigid urbanity was still extremely impressive, but at times I could have fancied that I was listening to a musical symphony, of which only certain brief, unresonant notes were audible. Was this all, and were there no others? It occurred to me more than once, with a kind of dull dismay, in the midst of my placid expectancy, that Harold's grave notes were the beginning and the end of his character. If the human heart were a less incurable skeptic, I might have been divinely happy. I sat by my lover's side while he worked, gazing at the loveliest landscape in the world, and admiring the imperturbable audacity with which he attacked it. Sooner than I expected, these rather silent interviews, as romantic certainly as scenery could make them, received Mrs Staines's sanction. She had guessed our secret, and disapproved of nothing but its secrecy. She was satisfied with her son's choice, and declared with great emphasis that she was not ambitious. She was kindness itself (though, as you see, she indulged in no needless flattery), and I wondered that I could ever have thought her stern. From this time forward she talked to me a great deal about her son; too much, I might have thought, if I had cared less for the theme. I have said I was not perverse. Do I judge myself too tenderly? Before long I found something oppressive – something almost irritating – in the frequency and complacency of Mrs Staines's maternal disquisitions. One day, when she had been reminding me at greater length than usual of what a prize I had drawn, I abruptly changed the subject in the midst of a sentence, and left her staring at my petulance. She was on the point, I think of administering a reprimand, but she suppressed it and contented herself with approaching the topic more cautiously in future. Here is another reminiscence. One morning (it was near Spezia, I think) Harold had been sketching under a tree, not far from the inn, and

I sitting by and reading aloud from Shelley, whom one might feel
a kindness for there if nowhere else. We had had a little difference
of opinion about one of the poems – the beautiful 'Stanzas written
in Dejection near Naples,' which you probably remember. Harold
pronounced them childish. I thought the term ill-chosen, and
remember saying, to reinforce my opinion, that though I was no
judge of painting, I pretended to be of poetry. He told me (I have
not forgotten his words) that 'I lacked cultivation in each department,' and I believe I replied that I would rather lack cultivation
than imagination. For a pair of lovers it was a very pretty quarrel
as it stood. Shortly afterwards he discovered that he had left one
of his brushes at the inn, and went off in search of it. He had
trouble in finding it, and was absent for some time. His verdict on
poor Shelley rang in my ears as I sat looking out on the blue
iridescence of the sea, and murmuring the lines in which the poet
has so wonderfully suggested it.[4] Then I went and sat down on
Harold's stool to see how he had rendered this enchanting effect.
The picture was nearly finished, but unfortunately I had too little
cultivation to enjoy it. The blue sea, however, seemed in all
conscience blue enough. While I was comparing it with the far-
fading azure of the original, I heard a voice behind me, and
turning, saw two gentlemen from the inn, one of whom had been
my neighbor the evening before at dinner. He was a foreigner, but
he spoke English. On recognizing me he advanced gallantly,
ushering his companion, and immediately fell into ecstasies over
my picture. I informed him without delay that the picture was not
mine; it was the work of Mr Staines. Nothing daunted, he
declared, that it was pretty enough to be mine, and that I must
have given suggestions; but his companion, a less superficial
character apparently, and extremely near-sighted, after examining
it minutely with his nose close to the paper, exclaimed with an
annoying smile, 'Monsieur Staines? Surprising! I should have
sworn it was the work of a *jeune fille*.'

The compliment was doubtful, and not calculated to restore my
equanimity. As a *jeune fille* I suppose I ought to have been gratified,
but as a betrothed I should have preferred Harold to paint like a
man. I don't know how long after this it was that I allowed myself
to wonder, by way of harmless conjecture, how a woman might

feel who should find herself married to an ineffective mediocrity. Then I remembered – as if the case were my own – that I had never heard any one talk about his pictures, and that when I had seen them handed about before company by his mother, the buzz of admiration usual on such occasions seemed rather heavy-winged. But I quickly reminded myself that it was not because he painted better or worse that I cared for him, but because personally and morally he was the pink of perfection. This being settled, I fell to wondering whether one mightn't grow weary of perfection – whether (Heaven forgive me!) I was not already the least bit out of patience with Harold's. I could fancy him a trifle too absolute, too imperturbable, too prolific in cut-and-dried opinions. Had he settled everything, then, in his mind? Yes, he had certainly made the most of his time, and I could only admire his diligence. From the moment that I observed that he wasted no time in moods, or reveries, or intellectual pleasantry of any sort, I decided without appeal that he was not a man of genius; and yet, to listen to him at times, you would have vowed at least that he might be. He dealt out his opinions as if they were celestial manna, and nothing was more common than for him to say, 'You remember, a month ago, I told you so-and-so;' meaning that he had laid down the law on some point and expected me to engrave it on my heart. It often happened that I had forgotten the lesson, and was obliged to ask him to repeat it; but it left me more unsatisfied than before. Harold would settle his shirt collar as if he considered that he had exhausted the subject, and I would take refuge in a silence which from day to day covered more treacherous conjectures. Nevertheless (strange as you may think it), I believe I should have decided that, Harold being a paragon, my doubts were immoral, if Mrs Staines, after his cause might have been supposed to be gained, had not persisted in pleading it in season and out. I don't know whether she suspected my secret falterings, but she seemed to wish to secure me beyond relapse. I was so very modest a match for her son, that if I had been more worldly-wise, her enthusiasm might have alarmed me. Later I understood it; then I only understood that there was a general flavor of insinuation in her talk which made me vaguely uneasy. I did the poor lady injustice, and if I had been quicker-witted (and possibly harder-hearted) we might have become sworn allies. She judged her son less with a mother's tenderness than with a mother's zeal, and foresaw the world's verdict – which I won't anticipate! She perceived that he must depend upon a clever wife to float him into success; he would never prosper on his own merits. She did me the honor to believe me socially a sufficiently buoyant body for this arduous purpose, and must have felt it a thousand pities that she couldn't directly speak her mind. A thousand pities indeed! My answer would have been to the point, and would have saved us all a vast deal of pain. Meanwhile, trying half to convince and half to entangle me, she did everything to hasten our marriage.

If there had been anything less than the happiness of a life-time at stake, I think I should have felt that I owed Harold a sort of reparation for thinking him too great a man, and should still have offered him an affection none the less genuine for being transposed into a minor key. But it was hard for a girl who had dreamed blissfully of a grandly sentimental union, to find herself suddenly face to face with a sternly rational one. When, therefore, Harold mentioned a certain day as the latest for which he thought it proper to wait, I found it impossible to assent, and asked for another month's delay. What I wished to wait for I could hardly have told. Possibly for the first glow of illusion to return; possibly for the last uneasy throb which told that illusion was ebbing away. Harold received this request very gravely, and inquired whether I doubted of his affection.

'No,' I said, 'I believe it's greater than I deserve.'

'Why then,' he asked, 'should you wait?'

'Suppose I were to doubt of my own?'

He looked as if I had said something in very bad taste, and I was almost frightened at his sense of security. But he at last consented to the delay. Perhaps on reflection he was alarmed, for the grave politeness with which he discharged his attentions took a still more formal turn, as if to remind me at every hour of the day that his was not a sentiment to be trifled with. To trifle, Heaven knows, was far enough from my thoughts; for I was fast losing my spirits, and I woke up one morning with the conviction that I was decidedly not happy.

We were to be married in Paris, where Harold had determined to spend six months in order that he might try his fortune again in the studio of a painter whom he especially esteemed – a certain Monsieur Martinet, an old man, and belonging, I believe, to a rather antiquated school of art. During our first days in Paris I went with Harold a great deal to the Louvre, where he was a very profitable companion. He had the history of the schools at his fingers' ends, and, as the phrase is, he knew what he liked. We had a fatal habit of not liking the same things; but I pretended to no critical insight, and desired nothing better than to agree with him. I listened devoutly to everything that could be said for Guido and Caravaggio. One day we were standing before the inscrutable 'Joconde' of Leonardo, a picture disagreeable to most women. I had been expressing my great aversion to the lady's countenance, which Harold on this occasion seemed to share. I was surprised therefore, when, after a pause, he said quietly, 'I believe I'll copy her.'

I hardly knew why I should have smiled, but I did, apparently to his annoyance. 'She must be very difficult,' I said. 'Try something easier.'

'I want something difficult,' he answered sternly.

'Truly?' I said. 'You mean what you say?'

'Why not?'

'Why then copy a portrait when you can copy an original?'

'What original?'

'Your betrothed! Paint my portrait. I promise to be difficult enough. Indeed, I'm surprised you should never have proposed it.' In fact the idea had just occurred to me; but I embraced it with a sort of relief. It seemed to me that it would somehow test my lover, and that if he succeeded, I might believe in him irremissibly. He stared a moment as if he had hardly understood me, and I completed my thought. 'Paint my portrait, and the day you finish it I'll fix our wedding day.'

The proposal was after all not very terrible, and before long he seemed to relish it. The next day he told me that he had composed his figure mentally, and that we might begin immediately. Circumstances favored us, for he had for the time undisturbed all of M. Martinet's studio. This gentleman had gone into the country to paint a portrait, and Harold just then was his only pupil. Our first sitting took place without delay. At his request I brought with me a number of draperies among which was the yellow shawl you have just been admiring. We wore such things then, just as we played on the harp and read 'Corinne.'[5] I tried on my scarfs and veils, one after the other, but Harold was satisfied with none. The yellow shawl, in especial, he pronounced a meretricious ornament, and decided that I should be represented in a plain dark dress, with as few accessories as possible. He quoted with a bow the verse about beauty when unadorned,[6] and began his work.

After the first day or two it progressed slowly, and I felt at moments as if I had saddled him with a cruel burden. He expressed no irritation, but he often looked puzzled and wearied, and sometimes would lay aside his brushes, fold his arms, and stand gazing at his work with a sort of vacant scowl which tried my patience. 'Frown at me,' I said more than once; 'don't frown at that blameless sheet of canvas. Don't spare me, though I confess it's not my fault if I'm hard to paint.' Thus admonished, he would turn toward me without smiling, often shading his eyes with his hand, and would walk slowly round the room, examining me at a distance. Then coming back to his easel, he would make half a dozen strokes and pause again, as if his impetus had already expired. For some time I was miserable; it seemed to me that I had been wonderfully wise to withhold my hand till the picture was finished. He begged I would not look at it, but I knew it was standing still. At last, one morning, after gazing at his work for some time in silence, he laid down his palette gravely, but with no further sign of discomposure than that he gently wiped his forehead with his pocket-handkerchief. 'You make me nervous,' he suddenly declared.

I fancied there was a tremor in his voice, and I began to pity him. I left my place and laid my hand on his arm. 'If it wearies you,' I said, 'give it up.'

He turned away and for some time made no answer. I knew what he was thinking about, and I suppose he knew that I knew it, and was hesitating to ask me seriously whether in giving up his picture he gave up something more. He decided apparently to give up nothing, but grasped his palette, and, with the short incisive gesture habitual to him, motioned me back to my seat. 'I'll bother no longer over the drawing,' he said; 'I'll begin to paint.' With his colors he was more prosperous, for the next day he told me that we were progressing fast.

We generally went together to the studio, but it happened one day that he was to be occupied during the early morning at the other end of Paris, and he arranged to meet me there. I was punctual, but he had not arrived, and I found myself face to face with my reluctant image. Opportunity served too well, and I looked at it in spite of his prohibition, meaning of course to confess my fault. It brought me less pleasure than faults are reputed to bring. The picture, as yet very slight and crude, was unpromising and unflattering. I chiefly distinguished a long white face with staring black eyes, and a terribly angular pair of arms. Was it in this unlovely form that I had impressed myself on Harold's vision? Absorbed by the question, it was some moments before I perceived that I was not alone. I heard a sound, looked round, and discovered a stranger, a young man, gazing over my shoulder at Harold's canvas. His gaze was intense and not expressive of pleasure, and some moments passed before he perceived that I had noticed him. He reminded me strongly of certain dishevelled copyists whom I had seen at work in the Louvre, and as I supposed he had some lawful errand in the studio, I contented myself with thinking that he hadn't the best manners in the world, and walked to the other end of the room. At last, as he continued to betray no definite intentions, I ventured to look at him again. He was young – twenty-five at most – and excessively shabby. I remember, among other details, that he had a black cravat wound two or three times round his neck without any visible linen. He was short, thin, pale, and hungry-looking. As I turned toward him, he passed his hand through his hair, as if to do what he could to make himself presentable, and called my attention to his prodigious shock of thick black curls – a real *coiffure de rapin*.[7] His face would have been meagre and vulgar, if from beneath their umbrageous locks there had not glanced an extraordinary pair of eyes – eyes really of fire. They were not tender nor appealing, but they glittered with a sort of feverish intelligence and penetration, and stamped their possessor not, as the French say, the first comer.[8] He almost glared at me and stopped my words short.

'That's your portrait?' he asked, with a toss of his head. I assented with dignity.

'It's bad, bad, bad!' he cried. 'Excuse my frankness, but it's really too bad. It's a waste of colors, of money, of time.'

His frankness certainly was extreme; but his words had an accent of ardent conviction which doesn't belong to commonplace impertinence. 'I don't know who you are that I should value your opinion,' I said.

'Who am I? I'm an artist, mademoiselle. If I had money to buy visiting-cards, I would present you with one. But I haven't even money to buy colors – hardly to buy bread. I've talent – I've imagination – too much! – I've ideas – I've promise – I've a future; and yet the machine won't work – for want of fuel! I have to roam about with my hands in my pockets – to keep them warm – for want of the very tools of my trade. I've been a fool – an ignoble fool; I've thrown precious hours to the dogs and made enemies of precious friends. Six months ago I quarrelled with the père Martinet, who believed in me and would have been glad to keep me. *Il faut que jeunesse se passe!*⁹ Mine has passed at a rattling pace, ill-mounted though it was; we have parted company forever. Now I only ask to do a man's work with a man's will. Meanwhile the père Martinet, justly provoked, has used his tongue so well that not a colorman in Paris will trust me. There's a situation! And yet what could I do with ten francs' worth of paint? I want a room and light and a model, and a dozen yards of satin tumbling about her feet. Bah! I shall have to want! There are things I want more. Behold the force of circumstances. I've come back with my pride in my pocket to make it up with the venerable author of the "Apotheosis of Molière," and ask him to lend me a louis.'

I arrested this vehement effusion by informing him that M. Martinet was out of town, and that for the present the studio was – private. But he seemed too much irritated to take my hint. 'That's not his work?' he went on, turning to the portrait. 'Martinet is bad, but is not as bad as that. *Quel genre!*¹⁰ You deserve, mademoiselle, to be better treated; you're an excellent model. Excuse me, once for all; I know I'm atrociously impudent. But I'm an artist, and I find it pitiful to see a fine great canvas besmeared in such a fashion as that! There ought to be a society for the protection of such things.'

I was at loss what to reply to this extraordinary explosion of contempt. Strange to say – it's the literal truth – I was neither annoyed nor disgusted; I simply felt myself growing extremely curious. This impudent little Bohemian was forcing me somehow to respect his opinion; he spoke with penetrating authority. Don't say that I was willing to be convinced; if you had been there, you would have let him speak. It would have been, of course, the part of propriety to request him in a chilling voice to leave the room, or to ring for the concierge, or to flee in horror. I did none of these things: I went back to the picture, and tried hard to see something in it which would make me passionately contradict him. But it seemed to exhale a mortal chill, and all I could say was: 'Bad – bad? How bad?'

'Ridiculously bad; impossibly bad! You're an angel of charity, mademoiselle, not to see it!'

'Is it weak – cold – ignorant?'

'Weak, cold, ignorant, stiff, empty, hopeless! And, on top of all, pretentious – oh, pretentious as the *façade* of the Madeleine!'

I endeavored to force a skeptical smile. 'After all, monsieur, I'm not bound to believe you.'

'Evidently!' And he rubbed his forehead and looked gloomily round the room. 'But one thing I can tell you' – fixing me suddenly with his extraordinary eyes, which seemed to expand and glow with the vividness of prevision – 'the day will come when people will fight for the honor of having believed me, and of having been the first. "I discovered him – I always said so. But for me you'd have let the poor devil starve!" You'll hear the chorus! So now's your chance, mademoiselle! Here I stand, a man of genius if there ever was one, without a sou, without a friend, without a ray of reputation. Believe in me now, and you'll be the first, by many a day. You'd find it easier, you'll say, if I had a little more modesty. I assure you I don't go about blowing my trumpet in this fashion every day. This morning I'm in a kind of fever, and I've reached a crisis. I must do something – even make an ass of myself! I can't go on devouring my own heart. You see for these three months I've been *à sec*.[11] I haven't dined every day. Perhaps a sinking at

202

the stomach is propitious to inspiration: certainly, week by week, my brain has grown clearer, my imagination more restless, my desires more boundless, my visions more splendid! Within the last fortnight my last doubt has vanished, and I feel as strong as the sun in heaven! I roam about the streets and lounge in the public gardens for want of a better refuge, and everything I look at – the very sunshine in the gutter, the chimney-pots against the sky – seems a picture, a subject, an opportunity! I hang over the balustrade that runs before the pictures at the Louvre, and Titian and Correggio seem to turn pale, like people when you've guessed their secret. I don't know who the author of this masterpiece may be, but I fancy he would have more talent if he weren't so sure of his dinner. Do you know how I learned to look at things and use my eyes? By staring at the *charcutier*'s windows when my pockets were empty. It's a great lesson to learn even the shape of a sausage and the color of a ham. This gentleman, it's easy to see, hasn't noticed such matters. He goes by the sense of taste. *Voilà le monde!* I – I – I – ' – and he slapped his forehead with a kind of dramatic fury – 'here as you see me – ragged, helpless, hopeless, with my soul aching with ambition and my fingers itching for a brush – and *he*, standing up here after a good breakfast, in this perfect light, among pictures and tapestries and carvings, with you in your blooming beauty for a model, and painting that – sign-board.'

His violence was startling; I didn't know what might come next, and I took up my bonnet and mantle. He immediately protested with ardor. 'A moment's reflection, mademoiselle, will tell you that, with the appearance I present, I don't talk about your beauty *pour vous faire la cour*.[12] I repeat with all respect, you're a model to make a painter's fortune. I doubt if you've many attitudes or much flexibility; but for once – the portrait of Mlle X. – you're perfect.'

'I'm obliged to you for your – information,' I answered gravely. 'You see my artist is chosen. I expect him here at any moment, and I won't answer for his listening to you as patiently as I have done.'

'He's coming?' cried my visitor. '*Quelle chance!* I shall be charmed to meet him. I shall vastly enjoy seeing the human head from which that conception issued. I see him already: I construct the author from the work. He's tall and blond, with eyes very much the color of his own china-blue there. He wears straw-colored whiskers, and doubtless he paints in straw-colored gloves. In short, he's *un homme magnifique!*'

This was sarcasm run mad; but I listened to it and resented it as little as I enjoyed it. My companion seemed to possess a sort of demonic veracity of which the influence was irresistible. I questioned his sincerity so little that, if I offered him charity, it was with no intention of testing it. 'I dare say you've immense talent,' I said, 'but you've horrible manners. Nevertheless, I believe you will perceive that there is no reason why our conversation should continue; and I should pay you a poor compliment in thinking that you need to be bribed to withdraw. But since M. Martinet isn't here to lend you a louis, let me act for him.' And I laid the piece of gold on the table.

He looked at it hard for a moment and then at me, and I wondered whether he thought the gift too meagre. 'I won't go so far as to say that I'm proud,' he answered at last. 'But from a lady, *ma foi!* it's beggarly – it's humiliating. Excuse me then if I refuse; I mean to ask for something else. To do me justice, remember that I speak to you not as a man, but as an artist. Bestow your charity on the artist, and if it costs you an effort, remember that that is the charity which is of most account with heaven. Keep your louis; go and stand as you've been standing for this picture, in the same light and the same attitude, and then let me look at you for three little minutes.' As he spoke he drew from his pocket a ragged notebook and the stump of a pencil. 'The few scrawls I shall make here will be your alms.'

He spoke of effort, but it is a fact that I made little to comply. While I resumed my familiar attitude in front of Harold's canvas, he walked rapidly across the room and stooped over a chair upon which a mass of draperies had been carelessly tossed. In a moment I saw what had attracted him. He had caught a glimpse of the famous yellow scarf, glowing splendidly beneath a pile of darker stuffs. He pulled out the beautiful golden-hued tissue with furious alacrity, held it up before him and broke into an ecstasy of admiration. 'What a tone – what a glow – what a texture! In Heaven's name, put it on!' And without further ceremony he tossed it over my shoulders. I need hardly tell you that I obeyed but a natural instinct in gathering it into picturesque folds. He rushed away, and stood gazing and clapping his hands. 'The harmony is perfect – the effect sublime! You possess that thing and you bury it out of sight? Wear it, wear it, I entreat you – and your portrait – but ah!' and he glared angrily askance at the picture: 'you'll never wear it there!'

'We thought of using it, but it was given up.'

'Given up? *Quelle horreur!* He hadn't the pluck to attack it! Oh, if I could just take a brush at it and rub it in for him!' And, as if possessed by an uncontrollable impulse, he seized poor Harold's palette. But I made haste to stop his hand. He flung down the brushes, buried his face in his hands, and pressed back, I could fancy, the tears of baffled eagerness. 'You'll think me crazy!' he cried.

He was not crazy, to my sense; but he was a raging, aimless force, which I suddenly comprehended that I might use. I seemed to measure the full proportions of Harold's inefficiency and to foresee the pitiful result of his undertaking. He wouldn't succumb, but he would doggedly finish his task and present me, in evidence of his claim, with a dreadful monument of his pretentious incapacity. Twenty strokes from this master-hand would make a difference; ten minutes' work would carry the picture forward. I thrust the palette into the young man's grasp again and looked at him solemnly. 'Paint away for your life,' I said; 'but promise me this: to succeed!'

He waved his hand in the air, despatched me with a glance to my place, and let himself loose on the canvas; there are no other words for his tremulous eagerness. A quarter of an hour passed in silence. As I watched his motions grow every moment broader and more sweeping, I could fancy myself listening to some ardent pianist, plunging deeper into a passionate symphony and devouring the key-board with outstretched arms. Flushed and dishevelled, consuming me almost with his ardent stare, daubing, murmuring, panting, he seemed indeed to be painting for life.

At last I heard a tread in the vestibule. I knew it was Harold's, and I hurried to look at the picture. How would he take it? I confess I was prepared for the worst. The picture spoke for itself. Harold's work had disappeared with magical rapidity, and even my unskilled eye perceived that a graceful and expressive figure had been powerfully sketched in. As Harold appeared, I turned to meet him. He seemed surprised at not finding me alone, and I laid my finger gravely on my lips and led him to the front of the canvas. The position of things was so singular that for some moments it baffled his comprehension. My companion finished what he was immediately concerned with; then with an obsequious bow laid down his brushes. 'It was a loan, monsieur,' he said. 'I return it with interest.'

Harold flushed to his eyes, and sat down in silence. I had expected him to be irritated; but this was more than irritation. At last: 'Explain this extraordinary performance,' he said in a low voice.

I felt pain, and yet somehow I felt no regret. The situation was tense, as the phrase is, and yet I almost relished it. 'This gentleman is a great artist,' I said boldly. 'Look for yourself. Your picture was lost; he has redeemed it.'

Harold looked at the intruder slowly from head to foot. 'Who is this person?' he demanded, as if he had not heard me.

The young man understood no English, but he apparently guessed at the question. 'My name is Pierre Briseux; let *that*' (pointing to his work) 'denote my profession. If you're affronted, monsieur, don't visit your displeasure on mademoiselle; I alone am responsible. You had got into a tight place; I wished to help you out of it; *sympathie de confrère!* I've done you no injury. I've made you a present of half a masterpiece. If I could only trust you not to spoil it!'

Harold's face betrayed his invincible disgust, and I saw that my offence was mortal. He had been wounded in his tenderest part, and his self-control was rapidly ebbing. His lips trembled, but he was too angry even to speak. Suddenly he seized a heavy brush which stood in a pot of dusky varnish, and I thought for a moment he was going to fling it at Briseux. He balanced it an instant, and then tossed it full in the face of the picture. I raised my hands to my face as if I felt the blow. Briseux, at least, felt it sorely.

'*Malheureux!*' he cried. 'Are you blind as well? Don't you know a good thing when you see it? That's what I call a waste of material. *Allons*, you're very angry; let me explain. In meddling with your picture I certainly took a great liberty. My misery is my excuse. You have money, materials, models – everything but talent. No, no, you're no painter; it's impossible! There isn't an intelligent line on your canvas. I, on the other hand, am a born painter. I've talent and nothing more. I came here to see M. Martinet; learning he was absent, I staid for very envy! I looked at your work, and found it a botch; at your empty stool and idle palette, and found them an immense temptation; at mademoiselle, and found her a perfect model. I persuaded, frightened, convinced her, and out of charity she gave me a five minutes' sitting. Once the brush in my hand, I felt the divine afflatus; I hoped for a miracle – that you'd never come back, that you'd be run over in the street, or have an attack of apoplexy. If you had only let me go on, I should have served you up a great work, monsieur – a work to which, in spite of your natural irritation, you wouldn't have dared to do a violence. You'd have been afraid of it. That's the sort of thing I meant to paint. If you could only believe me, you'd not regret it. Give me a start, and ten years hence I shall see you buying my pictures, and not thinking them dear. Oh, I thought I had my foot in the stirrup; I dreamed I was in the saddle and riding hard. But I've turned a somersault!'

I doubt that Harold, in his resentment, either understood M. Briseux's words or appreciated his sketch. He simply felt that he had been the victim of a monstrous aggression, in which I, in some painfully inexplicable way, had been half dupe and half accomplice. I was watching his anger and weighing its ominous significance. His cold fury, and the expression it threw into his face and gestures, told me more about him than weeks of placid love-making had done, and, following close upon my vivid sense of his incapacity, seemed suddenly to cut the knot that bound us together, and over which my timid fingers had been fumbling. 'Put on your bonnet,' he said to me; 'get a carriage and go home.'

I can't describe his tone. It contained an assumption of my confusion and compliance, which made me feel that I ought to lose no time in undeceiving him. Nevertheless I felt cruelly perplexed, and almost afraid of his displeasure. Mechanically I took up my bonnet. As I held it in my hand, my eyes met those of our terrible companion, who was evidently trying to read the riddle of my relations with Harold. Planted there with his trembling lips, his glittering, searching eyes, an indefinable something in his whole person that told of joyous impulse arrested, but pausing only for a more triumphant effort, he seemed a strangely eloquent embodiment of youthful genius. I don't know whether he read in my glance a ray of sympathy, but his lips formed a soundless '*Restez, madame,*' which quickened the beating of my heart. The feeling that then invaded it I despair of making you understand; yet it must help in your eyes to excuse me, and it was so profound that often in memory it seems more real and poignant than the things of the present. Poor little Briseux, ugly, shabby, disreputable, seemed to me some appealing messenger from the mysterious immensity of life; and Harold, beside him, comely, elegant, imposing, justly indignant, seemed to me simply his narrow, personal, ineffectual self. This was a wider generalization than the feminine heart is used to. I flung my bonnet on the floor and burst into tears.

'This is not an exhibition for a stranger,' said Harold grimly. 'Be so good as to follow me.'

'You must excuse me; I can't follow you; I can't explain. I have something more to say to M. Briseux. He's less of a stranger than you think.'

'I'm to leave you here?' stammered Harold.

'It's the simplest way.'

'With that dirty little Frenchman?'

'What should I care for his being clean? It's his genius that interests me.'

Harold stared in dark amazement. 'Are you insane? Do you know what you're doing?'

'An act, I believe, of real charity.'

'Charity begins at home. It's an act of desperate folly. Must I *command* you to leave?'

'You've done that already. I can't obey you. If I were to do so, I should pretend what isn't true; and, let me say it, it's to undeceive you that I refuse.'

'I don't understand you,' cried Harold, 'nor to what spell this meddlesome little beggar has subjected you! But I'm not a man to be trifled with, you know, and this is my last request; my last, do you understand? If you prefer the society of this abandoned person, you're welcome, but you forfeit mine forever. It's a choice! You give up the man who has offered you an honorable affection, a name, a fortune, who has trusted and cherished you, who stands ready to make you a devoted husband. What you get the Lord knows!'

I had sunk into a chair. I listened in silence, and for some time answered nothing. His words were vividly true. He offered me much, and I gave up everything. He had played an honorable part, and I was playing a very strange one. I asked myself sternly whether I was ready to rise and take his arm and let him lead me blindfold through life. When I raised my eyes Briseux stood before me, and from the expression of his face I could have fancied he had guessed at the meaning of Harold's words. 'I'll make you immortal,' he murmured; 'I'll delight mankind – and I'll begin my own career!'

An ineffable prevision of the truth which after the lapse of years has brought about our meeting here seemed to raise me as if on wings, and made decision easy. We women are so habitually condemned by fate to act simply in what is called the domestic sphere, that there is something intoxicating in the opportunity to exert a far-reaching influence outside of it. To feel the charms of such an opportunity, one must perhaps be of a reprehensibly fanciful turn. Such at any rate was my mood for that hour. I seemed to be the end of an electric chain, of which the rest was throbbing away through time. I seemed to hold in my hand an immeasurable gift. 'We had better part on the spot,' I said to Harold. 'I've foreseen our parting for weeks, only it has come more abruptly. Forgive the abruptness. To myself the pretext seems better than to you; perhaps some day you'll appreciate it. A single question,' I added. 'Could you ever have finished my portrait?'

He looked at me askance for some moments, with a strange mistrust, as if I had suddenly developed some monstrous and sinister slyness; then catching his breath with a little groan – almost a shudder – he marched out of the room.

Briseux clasped his hands in ecstasy. 'You're magnificent!' he cried. 'If you could only look so for three hours!'

'To business,' I said sternly. 'If you don't paint a perfect picture, you're the most shameless of impostors.'

He had but a single sitting, but it was a long one; though how many hours it lasted, I doubt that either of us could have told. He painted till dusk, and then we had lamps. Before I left him I looked at the picture for the last and only time before seeing it to-day. It seemed to me as perfect as it seemed this morning, and I felt that my choice was justified and that Briseux's fortune was made. It gave me all the strength I needed for the immediate future. He was evidently of the same opinion and profoundly absorbed in it. When I bade him farewell, in very few words, he answered me almost absently. I had served his purpose and had already passed into that dusky limbo of unhonored victims, the experience – intellectual and other – of genius. I left him the yellow shawl, that he might finish this part of his work at his leisure, and, as for the picture, I told him to keep it, for that I should have little pleasure in seeing it again. Then he stared a moment, but the next he was painting hard.

I had the next morning what under other circumstances I might call an explanation with Mr Staines, an explanation in which I explained nothing to his satisfaction but that he had been hideously wronged, and that I was a demon of inconstancy. He wrapped himself in an icy silence, and, I think, expected some graceful effusion of humility. I may not have been humble, but I was considerate, and I perceived, for my reward, that the sore point with him was not that he had lost me, but that I had ventured to judge him. Mrs Staines's manner, on the other hand, puzzled me, so strange a mixture was it of half-disguised elation and undisguised sarcasm. At last I guessed her meaning. Harold, after all, had had an escape; instead of being the shrewd, practical girl she had thought me, I was a terribly romantic one! Perhaps she was right; I was romantic enough to make no further claim on her hospitality, and with as little delay as possible I returned home. A month later I received an enclosure of half a dozen cuttings from newspapers, scrawled boldly across with the signature of Pierre Briseux. The Paris *salon* had opened and the critics had spoken. They had not neglected the portrait of Mademoiselle X—. The picture was an immense success, and M. Briseux was famous.

There were a few protesting voices, but it was evident that his career had begun. For Mademoiselle X— herself, I believe, there were none but compliments, several of which took the form of gallant conjecture as to her real identity. Mademoiselle X— was an assumed name, and according to more than one voice the lady was an imperious Russian princess with a distaste for vulgar publicity. You know the rest of M. Briseux's history. Since then he has painted real princesses by the dozen. He has delighted mankind rarely. As for his having made me immortal, I feel as if it were almost true. It must be an eternity since the thing happened – so very unreservedly I've described it!

Madame de Mauves

I

The view from the terrace at Saint-Germain-en-Laye is immense and famous. Paris lies spread before you in dusky vastness, domed and fortified, glittering here and there through her light vapors, and girdled with her silver Seine. Behind you is a park of stately symmetry, and behind that a forest, where you may lounge through turfy avenues and light-checkered glades, and quite forget that you are within half an hour of the boulevards. One afternoon, however, in mid-spring, some five years ago, a young man seated on the terrace had chosen not to forget this. His eyes were fixed in idle wistfulness on the mighty human hive before him. He was fond of rural things, and he had come to Saint-Germain a week before to meet the spring half-way; but though he could boast of a six months' acquaintance with the great city, he never looked at it from his present standpoint without a feeling of painfully unsatisfied curiosity. There were moments when it seemed to him that not to be there just then was to miss some thrilling chapter of experience. And yet his winter's experience had been rather fruitless, and he had closed the book almost with a yawn. Though not in the least a cynic, he was what one may call a disappointed observer; and he never chose the right-hand road without beginning to suspect after an hour's wayfaring that the left would have been the interesting one. He now had a dozen minds to go to Paris for the evening, to dine at the Café Brébant, and to repair afterwards to the Gymnase and listen to the latest exposition of the duties of the injured husband. He would probably have risen to execute this project, if he had not observed a little girl who, wandering along the terrace, had suddenly stopped short and begun to gaze at him with round-eyed frankness. For a moment he was simply amused, for the child's face denoted helpless wonderment; the next he was agreeably surprised. 'Why, this is my friend Maggie,' he said; 'I see you have not forgotten me.'

Maggie, after a short parley, was induced to seal her remembrance with a kiss. Invited then to explain her appearance at Saint-Germain, she embarked on a recital in which the general, according to the infantine method, was so fatally sacrificed to the particular, that Longmore looked about him for a superior source of information. He found it in Maggie's mamma, who was seated with another lady at the opposite end of the terrace; so, taking the child by the hand, he led her back to her companions.

Maggie's mamma was a young American lady, as you would immediately have perceived, with a pretty and friendly face and an expensive spring toilet. She greeted Longmore with surprised cordiality, mentioned his name to her friend, and bade him bring a chair and sit with them. The other lady, who, though equally young and perhaps even prettier, was dressed more soberly, remained silent, stroking the hair of the little girl, whom she had drawn against her knee. She had never heard of Longmore, but she now perceived that her companion had crossed the ocean with him, had met him afterwards in travelling, and (having left her husband in Wall Street) was indebted to him for various small services.

Maggie's mamma turned from time to time and smiled at her friend with an air of invitation; the latter smiled back, and continued gracefully to say nothing.

For ten minutes Longmore felt a revival of interest in his interlocutress; then (as riddles are more amusing than commonplaces) it gave way to curiosity about her friend. His eyes wandered; her volubility was less suggestive than the latter's silence.

The stranger was perhaps not obviously a beauty nor obviously an American, but essentially both, on a closer scrutiny. She was slight and fair, and, though naturally pale, delicately flushed, apparently with recent excitement. What chiefly struck Longmore in her face was the union of a pair of beautifully gentle, almost languid gray eyes, with a mouth peculiarly expressive and firm. Her forehead was a trifle more expansive than belongs to classic types, and her thick brown hair was dressed out of the fashion, which was just then very ugly. Her throat and bust were slender, but all the more in harmony with certain rapid, charming movements of the head, which she had a way of throwing back every now and then, with an air of attention and a sidelong glance from her dove-like eyes. She seemed at once alert and indifferent, contemplative and restless; and Longmore very soon discovered that if she was not a brilliant beauty, she was at least an extremely interesting one. This very impression made him magnanimous. He perceived that he had interrupted a confidential conversation, and he judged it discreet to withdraw, having first learned from Maggie's mamma – Mrs Draper – that she was to take the six-o'clock train back to Paris. He promised to meet her at the station.

He kept his appointment, and Mrs Draper arrived betimes, accompanied by her friend. The latter, however, made her farewells at the door and drove away again, giving Longmore time only to raise his hat. 'Who is she?' he asked with visible ardor, as he brought Mrs Draper her tickets.

'Come and see me to-morrow at the Hôtel de l'Empire,' she answered, 'and I will tell you all about her.' The force of this offer in making him punctual at the Hôtel de l'Empire Longmore doubtless never exactly measured; and it was perhaps well that he did not, for he found his friend, who was on the point of leaving Paris, so distracted by procrastinating milliners and perjured lingères that she had no wits left for disinterested narrative. 'You must find Saint-Germain dreadfully dull,' she said, as he was going. 'Why won't you come with me to London?'

'Introduce me to Madame de Mauves,' he answered, 'and Saint-Germain will satisfy me.' All he had learned was the lady's name and residence.

'Ah! she, poor woman, will not make Saint-Germain cheerful for you. She's very unhappy.'

Longmore's further inquiries were arrested by the arrival of a young lady with a bandbox; but he went away with the promise of a note of introduction, to be immediately despatched to him at Saint-Germain.

He waited a week, but the note never came; and he declared that it was not for Mrs Draper to complain of her milliner's treachery. He lounged on the terrace and walked in the forest, studied suburban street life, and made a languid attempt to investigate the records of the court of the exiled Stuarts; but he spent most of his time in wondering where Madame de Mauves lived, and whether she never walked on the terrace. Sometimes, he finally discovered; for one afternoon toward dusk he perceived her leaning against the parapet, alone. In his momentary hesitation to approach her, it seemed to him that there was almost a shade of trepidation; but his curiosity was not diminished by the consciousness of this result of a quarter of an hour's acquaintance. She immediately recognized him on his drawing near, with the manner of a person unaccustomed to encounter a confusing variety of faces. Her dress, her expression, were the same as before; her charm was there, like that of sweet music on a second hearing. She soon made conversation easy by asking him for news of Mrs Draper. Longmore told her that he was daily expecting news, and, after a pause, mentioned the promised note of introduction.

'It seems less necessary now,' he said – 'for me, at least. But for you – I should have liked you to know the flattering things Mrs Draper would probably have said about me.'

'If it arrives at last,' she answered, 'you must come and see me and bring it. If it doesn't, you must come without it.'

Then, as she continued to linger in spite of the thickening twilight, she explained that she was waiting for her husband, who was to arrive in the train from Paris, and who often passed along the terrace on his way home. Longmore well remembered that Mrs Draper had pronounced her unhappy, and he found it convenient to suppose that this same husband made her so. Edified by his six months in Paris – 'What else is possible,' he asked himself, 'for a sweet American girl who marries an unclean Frenchman?'

But this tender expectancy of her lord's return undermined his hypothesis, and it received a further check from the gentle eagerness with which she turned and greeted an approaching figure. Longmore beheld in the fading light a stoutish gentleman, on the fair side of forty, in a high light hat, whose countenance, indistinct against the sky, was adorned by a fantastically pointed mustache. M. de Mauves saluted his wife with punctilious gallantry, and having bowed to Longmore, asked her several questions in French. Before taking his proffered arm to walk to their carriage, which was in waiting at the terrace gate, she introduced our hero as a friend of Mrs Draper, and a fellow-countryman, whom she hoped to see at home. M. de Mauves responded briefly, but civilly, in very fair English, and led his wife away.

Longmore watched him as he went, twisting his picturesque mustache, with a feeling of irritation which he certainly would have been at a loss to account for. The only conceivable cause was the light which M. de Mauves's good English cast upon his own bad French. For reasons involved apparently in the very structure of his being, Longmore found himself unable to speak the language tolerably. He admired and enjoyed it, but the very genius of awkwardness controlled his phraseology. But he reflected with satisfaction that Madame de Mauves and he had a common idiom, and his vexation was effectually dispelled by his finding on his table that evening a letter from Mrs Draper. It enclosed a short, formal missive to Madame de Mauves, but the epistle itself was copious and confidential. She had deferred writing till she reached London, where for a week, of course, she had found other amusements.

'I think it is these distracting Englishwomen,' she wrote, 'with their green barege gowns and their white-stitched boots, who have reminded me in self-defence of my graceful friend at Saint-Germain and my promise to introduce you to her. I believe I told you that she was unhappy, and I wondered afterwards whether I had not been guilty of a breach of confidence. But you would have found it out for yourself, and besides, she told me no secrets. She declared she was the happiest creature in the world, and then, poor thing, she burst into tears, and I prayed to be delivered from such happiness. It's the miserable story of an American girl, born to be neither a slave nor a toy, marrying a profligate Frenchman, who believes that a woman must be one or the other. The silliest American woman is too good for the best foreigner, and the poorest of us have moral needs a Frenchman can't appreciate. She was romantic and wilful, and thought Americans were vulgar. Matrimonial felicity perhaps *is* vulgar; but I think nowadays she wishes she were a little less elegant. M. de Mauves cared, of course, for nothing but her money, which he's spending royally on his *menus plaisirs*. I hope you appreciate the compliment I pay you when I recommend you to go and console an unhappy wife. I have never given a man such a proof of esteem, and if you were to disappoint me I should renounce the world. Prove to Madame de Mauves that an American friend may mingle admiration and respect better than a French husband. She avoids society and lives quite alone, seeing no one but a horrible French sister-in-law. Do let me hear that you have drawn some of the sadness from that desperate smile of hers. Make her smile with a good conscience.'

These zealous admonitions left Longmore slightly disturbed. He found himself on the edge of a domestic tragedy from which he instinctively recoiled. To call upon Madame de Mauves with his present knowledge seemed a sort of fishing in troubled waters. He was a modest man, and yet he asked himself whether the effect of his attentions might not be to add to her tribulation. A flattering sense of unwonted opportunity, however, made him, with the lapse of time, more confident, – possibly more reckless. It seemed a very inspiring idea to draw the sadness from his fair country-woman's smile, and at least he hoped to persuade her that there was such a thing as an agreeable American. He immediately called upon her.

II

She had been placed for her education, fourteen years before, in a Parisian convent, by a widowed mamma, fonder of Homburg and Nice than of letting out tucks in the frocks of a vigorously growing daughter. Here, besides various elegant accomplishments, – the art of wearing a train, of composing a bouquet, of presenting a cup of tea, – she acquired a certain turn of the imagination which might have passed for a sign of precocious worldliness. She dreamed of marrying a title, – not for the pleasure of hearing herself called Mme la Vicomtesse (for which it seemed to her that she should never greatly care), but because she had a romantic belief that the best birth is the guaranty of an ideal delicacy of feeling. Romances are rarely shaped in such perfect good faith, and Euphemia's excuse was in the radical purity of her imagination. She was profoundly incorruptible, and she cherished this pernicious conceit as if it had been a dogma revealed by a white-winged angel. Even after experience had given her a hundred rude hints, she found it easier to believe in fables, when they had a certain nobleness of meaning, than in well-attested but sordid facts. She believed that a gentleman with a long pedigree must be of necessity a very fine fellow, and that the consciousness of a picturesque family tradition imparts an exquisite tone to the character. *Noblesse oblige*, she thought, as regards yourself, and insures, as regards your wife. She had never spoken to a nobleman in her life, and these convictions were but a matter of transcendent theory. They were the fruit, in part, of the perusal of various ultramontane works of fiction[1] – the only ones admitted to the convent library – in which the hero was always a legitimist vicomte who fought duels by the dozen, but went twice a month to confession; and in part of the perfumed gossip of her companions, many of them *filles de haut lieu*, who in the convent garden, after Sundays at home, depicted their brothers and cousins as Prince Charmings and young Paladins. Euphemia listened and said nothing; she shrouded her visions of matrimony under a coronet in religious mystery. She was not of that type of young lady who is easily induced to declare that her husband must be six feet high and a little near-sighted, part his hair in the middle, and have amber lights in his beard. To her companions she seemed to have a very pallid fancy; and even the fact that she was a sprig of the transatlantic democracy never sufficiently explained her apathy on social questions. She had a mental image of that son of the Crusaders who was to suffer her to adore him, but like many an artist who has produced a masterpiece of idealization, she shrank from exposing it to public criticism. It was the portrait of a gentleman rather ugly than handsome, and rather poor than rich. But his ugliness was to be nobly expressive, and his poverty delicately proud. Euphemia had a fortune of her own, which, at the proper time, after fixing on her in eloquent silence those fine eyes which were to soften the feudal severity of his visage, he was to accept with a world of stifled protestations. One condition alone she was to make, – that his blood should be of the very finest strain. On this she would stake her happiness.

It so chanced that circumstances were to give convincing color to this primitive logic.

Though little of a talker, Euphemia was an ardent listener, and there were moments when she fairly hung upon the lips of Mademoiselle Marie de Mauves. Her intimacy with this chosen schoolmate was, like most intimacies, based on their points of difference. Mademoiselle de Mauves was very positive, very shrewd, very ironical, very French, – everything that Euphemia felt herself unpardonable in not being. During her Sundays *en ville* she had examined the world and judged it, and she imparted her impressions to our attentive heroine with an agreeable mixture of enthusiasm and scepticism. She was moreover a handsome and well-grown person, on whom Euphemia's ribbons and trinkets had a trick of looking better than on their slender proprietress. She had, finally, the supreme merit of being a rigorous example of the virtue of exalted birth, having, as she did, ancestors honorably mentioned by Joinville and Commines,[2] and a stately grandmother with a hooked nose, who came up with her after the holidays from a veritable *castel* in Auvergne. It seemed to Euphemia that these attributes made her friend more at home in the world than if she had been the daughter of even the most prosperous grocer. A certain aristocratic impudence Mademoiselle de Mauves abundantly possessed, and her raids among her friend's finery were quite in the spirit of her baronial ancestors in the twelfth century, – a spirit which Euphemia considered but a large way of understanding friendship, – a freedom from small deference to the world's opinions which would sooner or later justify itself in acts of surprising magnanimity. Mademoiselle de Mauves perhaps enjoyed but slightly that easy attitude toward society which Euphemia envied her. She proved herself later in life such an accomplished schemer that her sense of having further heights to scale must have awakened early. Our heroine's ribbons and trinkets had much to do with the other's sisterly patronage, and her appealing pliancy of character even more; but the concluding motive of Marie's writing to her grandmamma to invite Euphemia for a three weeks' holiday to the *castel* in Auvergne, involved altogether superior considerations. Mademoiselle de Mauves was indeed at this time seventeen years of age, and presumably capable of general views; and Euphemia, who was hardly less, was a very well-grown subject for experiment, besides being pretty enough almost to pre-assure success. It is a proof of the sincerity of Euphemia's aspirations that the *castel* was not a shock to her faith. It was neither a cheerful nor a luxurious abode, but the young girl found it as delightful as a play. It had battered towers and an empty moat, a rusty drawbridge and a court paved with crooked, grass-grown slabs, over which the antique coach-wheels of the old lady with the hooked nose seemed to awaken the echoes of the seventeenth century. Euphemia was not frightened out of her dream; she had the pleasure of seeing it assume the consistency of a flattering presentiment. She had a taste for old servants, old anecdotes, old furniture, faded household colors, and sweetly stale odors, – musty treasures in which the Château de Mauves abounded. She made a dozen sketches in water-colors, after her conventual pattern; but sentimentally, as one may say, she was forever sketching with a freer hand.

Old Madame de Mauves had nothing severe but her nose, and she seemed to Euphemia, as indeed she was, a graciously venerable relic of a historic order of things. She took a great fancy to the young American, who was ready to sit all day at her feet and listen to anecdotes of the *bon temps* and quotations from the family chronicles. Madame de Mauves was a very honest old woman, and uttered her thoughts with antique plainness. One day, after pushing back Euphemia's shining locks and blinking at her with some tenderness from under her spectacles, she declared, with an energetic shake of the head, that she didn't know what to make of her. And in answer to the young girl's startled blush, – 'I should like to advise you,' she said, 'but you seem to me so all of a piece that I am afraid that if I advise you, I shall spoil you. It's easy to see that you're not one of us. I don't know whether you're better, but you seem to me to listen to the murmur of your own young spirit, rather than to the voice from behind the confessional or to the whisper of opportunity. Young girls, in my day, when they were stupid, were very docile, but when they were clever, were very sly. You're clever enough, I imagine, and yet if I guessed all your secrets at this moment, is there one I should have to frown at? I can tell you a wickeder one than any you have discovered for yourself. If you expect to live in France, and you want to be happy, don't listen too hard to that little voice I just spoke of, – the voice that is neither the curé's nor the world's. You'll fancy it saying things that it won't help your case to hear. They'll make you sad, and when you're sad you'll grow plain, and when you're plain you'll grow bitter, and when you're bitter you'll be very disagreeable. I was brought up to think that a woman's first duty was to please, and the happiest women I've known have been the ones who performed this duty faithfully. As you're not a Catholic, I suppose you can't be a dévote; and if you don't take life as a fifty years' mass, the only way to take it is as a game of skill. Listen: not to lose, you must, – I don't say cheat; but don't be too sure your neighbor won't, and don't be shocked out of your self-possession if he does. Don't lose, my dear; I beseech you, don't lose. Be neither suspicious nor credulous; but if you find your neighbor peeping, don't cry out, but very politely wait your own chance. I've had my *revanche* more than once in my day, but I'm not sure that the sweetest I could take against life as a whole would be to have your blessed innocence profit by my experience.'

This was rather awful advice, but Euphemia understood it too little to be either edified or frightened. She sat listening to it very much as she would have listened to the speeches of an old lady in a comedy, whose diction should picturesquely correspond to the pattern of her mantilla and the fashion of her head-dress. Her indifference was doubly dangerous, for Madame de Mauves spoke at the prompting of coming events, and her words were the result of a somewhat troubled conscience, – a conscience which told her at once that Euphemia was too tender a victim to be sacrificed to an ambition, and that the prosperity of her house was too precious a heritage to be sacrificed to a scruple. The prosperity in question had suffered repeated and grievous breaches, and the house of De Mauves had been pervaded by the cold comfort of an establishment in which people were obliged to balance dinner-table allusions to feudal ancestors against the absence of side dishes; a state of things the more regrettable as the family was now mainly represented by a gentleman whose appetite was large, and who justly maintained that its historic glories were not established by underfed heroes.

Three days after Euphemia's arrival, Richard de Mauves came

down from Paris to pay his respects to his grandmother, and treated our heroine to her first encounter with a gentilhomme in the flesh. On coming in he kissed his grandmother's hand, with a smile which caused her to draw it away with dignity, and set Euphemia, who was standing by, wondering what had happened between them. Her unanswered wonder was but the beginning of a life of bitter perplexity, but the reader is free to know that the smile of M. de Mauves was a reply to a certain postscript affixed by the old lady to a letter promptly addressed to him by her granddaughter, after Euphemia had been admitted to justify the latter's promises. Mademoiselle de Mauves brought her letter to her grandmother for approval, but obtained no more than was expressed in a frigid nod. The old lady watched her with a sombre glance as she proceeded to seal the letter, and suddenly bade her open it again and bring her a pen.

'Your sister's flatteries are all nonsense,' she wrote; 'the young lady is far too good for you, *mauvais sujet*. If you have a conscience you'll not come and take possession of an angel of innocence.'

The young girl, who had read these lines, made up a little face as she redirected the letter; but she laid down her pen with a confident nod, which might have seemed to mean that, to the best of her belief, her brother had not a conscience.

'If you meant what you said,' the young man whispered to his grandmother on the first opportunity, 'it would have been simpler not to let her send the letter!'

It was perhaps because she was wounded by this cynical insinuation, that Madame de Mauves remained in her own apartment during a greater part of Euphemia's stay, so that the latter's angelic innocence was left entirely to the Baron's mercy. It suffered no worse mischance, however, than to be prompted to intenser communion with itself. M. de Mauves was the hero of the young girl's romance made real, and so completely accordant with this creature of her imagination, that she felt afraid of him, very much as she would have been of a supernatural apparition. He was thirty-five years old, – young enough to suggest possibilities of ardent activity, and old enough to have formed opinions which a simple woman might deem it an intellectual privilege to listen to. He was perhaps a trifle handsomer than Euphemia's rather grim, Quixotic ideal, but a very few days reconciled her to his good looks, as they would have reconciled her to his ugliness. He was quiet, grave, and eminently distinguished. He spoke little, but his speeches, without being sententious, had a certain nobleness of tone which caused them to re-echo in the young girl's ears at the end of the day. He paid her very little direct attention, but his chance words – if he only asked her if she objected to his cigarette – were accompanied by a smile of extraordinary kindness.

It happened that shortly after his arrival, riding an unruly horse, which Euphemia with shy admiration had watched him mount in the castle yard, he was thrown with a violence which, without disparaging his skill, made him for a fortnight an interesting invalid, lounging in the library with a bandaged knee. To beguile his confinement, Euphemia was repeatedly induced to sing to him, which she did with a little natural tremor in her voice, which might have passed for an exquisite refinement of art. He never overwhelmed her with compliments, but he listened with unwandering attention, remembered all her melodies, and sat humming them to himself. While his imprisonment lasted, indeed, he passed hours in her company, and made her feel not unlike some unfriended artist who has suddenly gained the opportunity to devote a fortnight to the study of a great model. Euphemia studied with noiseless diligence what she supposed to be the 'character' of M. de Mauves, and the more she looked the more fine lights and shades she seemed to behold in this masterpiece of nature. M. de Mauves's character indeed, whether from a sense of being generously scrutinized, or for reasons which bid graceful defiance to analysis, had never been so amiable; it seemed really to reflect the purity of Euphemia's interpretation of it. There had been nothing especially to admire in the state of mind in which he left Paris, – a hard determination to marry a young girl whose charms might or might not justify his sister's account of them, but who was mistress, at the worst, of a couple of hundred thousand francs a year. He had not counted out sentiment; if she pleased him, so much the better; but he had left a meagre margin for it, and he would hardly have admitted so excellent a match could be improved by it. He was a placid sceptic, and it was a singular fate for a man who believed in nothing to be so tenderly believed in. What his original faith had been he could hardly have told you; for as he came back to his childhood's home to mend his fortunes by pretending to fall in love, he was a thoroughly perverted creature, and overlaid with more corruptions than a summer day's questioning of his conscience would have released him from. Ten years' pursuit of pleasure, which a bureau full of unpaid bills was all he had to show for, had pretty well stifled the natural lad, whose violent will and generous temper might have been shaped by other circumstances to a result which a romantic imagination might fairly accept as a late-blooming flower of hereditary honor. The Baron's violence had been subdued, and he had learned to be irreproachably polite; but he had lost the edge of his generosity, and his politeness, which in the long run society paid for, was hardly more than a form of luxurious egotism, like his fondness for cambric handkerchiefs, lavender gloves, and other fopperies by which shopkeepers remained out of pocket. In after years he was terribly polite to his wife. He had formed himself, as the phrase was, and the form prescribed to him by the society into which his birth and his tastes introduced him was marked by some peculiar features. That which mainly concerns us is its classification of the fairer half of humanity as objects not essentially different – say from the light gloves one soils in an evening and throws away. To do M. de Mauves justice, he had in the course of time encountered such plentiful evidence of this pliant, glove-like quality in the feminine character, that idealism naturally seemed to him a losing game.

Euphemia, as he lay on his sofa, seemed by no means a refutation; she simply reminded him that very young women are generally innocent, and that this, on the whole, was the most charming stage of their development. Her innocence inspired him with profound respect, and it seemed to him that if he shortly became her husband it would be exposed to a danger the less. Old Madame de Mauves, who flattered herself that in this whole matter she was being laudably rigid, might have learned a lesson from his gallant consideration. For a fortnight the Baron was almost a blushing boy again. He watched from behind the 'Figaro,' and admired, and held his tongue. He was not in the least disposed toward a flirtation; he had no desire to trouble the waters he proposed to transfuse into the golden cup of matrimony. Sometimes a word, a look, a movement of Euphemia's, gave him the oddest sense of being, or of seeming at least, almost bashful; for she had a way of not dropping her eyes, according to the mysterious virginal mechanism, of not fluttering out of the room when she found him there alone, of treating him rather as a benignant than as a pernicious influence, – a radiant frankness of demeanor, in fine, in spite of an evident natural reserve, which it seemed equally graceless not to make the subject of a compliment and indelicate not to take for granted. In this way there was wrought in the Baron's mind a vague, unwonted resonance of soft impressions, as we may call it, which indicated the transmutation of 'sentiment' from a contingency into a fact. His imagination enjoyed it; he was very fond of music, and this reminded him of some of the best he had ever heard. In spite of the bore of being laid up with a lame knee, he was in a better humor than he had known for months; he lay smoking cigarettes and listening to the nightingales, with the comfortable smile of one of his country neighbors whose big ox should have taken the prize at a fair. Every now and then, with an impatient suspicion of the resemblance, he declared that he was pitifully *bête*; but he was under a charm which braved even the supreme penalty of seeming ridiculous. One morning he had half an hour's tête-à-tête with his grandmother's confessor, a soft-voiced old abbé, whom, for reasons of her own, Madame de Mauves had suddenly summoned, and had left waiting in the drawing-room while she rearranged her curls. His reverence, going up to the old lady, assured her that M. le Baron was in a most edifying state of mind, and a promising subject for the operation of grace. This was a pious interpretation of the Baron's momentary good-humor. He had always lazily wondered what priests were good for, and he now remembered, with a sense of especial obligation to the abbé, that they were excellent for marrying people.

A day or two after this he left off his bandages, and tried to walk. He made his way into the garden and hobbled successfully along one of the alleys; but in the midst of his progress he was seized with a spasm of pain which forced him to stop and call for help. In an instant Euphemia came tripping along the path and offered him her arm with the frankest solicitude.

'Not to the house,' he said, taking it; 'farther on, to the bosquet.' This choice was prompted by her having immediately confessed that she had seen him leave the house, had feared an accident, and had followed him on tiptoe.

'Why didn't you join me?' he had asked, giving her a look in which admiration was no longer disguised, and yet felt itself half at the mercy of her replying that a *jeune fille* should not be seen following a gentleman. But it drew a breath which filled its lungs for a long time afterward, when she replied simply that if she had overtaken him he might have accepted her arm out of politeness, whereas she wished to have the pleasure of seeing him walk alone.

The bosquet was covered with an odorous tangle of blossoming vines, and a nightingale overhead was shaking out love-notes with a profuseness which made the Baron consider his own conduct the perfection of propriety.

'In America,' he said, 'I have always heard that when a man wishes to marry a young girl, he offers himself simply, face to face, without any ceremony, – without parents, and uncles, and cousins sitting round in a circle.'

'Why, I believe so,' said Euphemia, staring, and too surprised to be alarmed.

'Very well, then,' said the Baron, 'suppose our bosquet here to be America. I offer you my hand, à l'Américaine. It will make me intensely happy to have you accept it.'

Whether Euphemia's acceptance was in the American manner is more than I can say; I incline to think that for fluttering, grateful, trustful, softly-amazed young hearts, there is only one manner all over the world.

That evening, in the little turret chamber, which it was her happiness to inhabit, she wrote a dutiful letter to her mamma, and had just sealed it when she was sent for by Madame de Mauves. She found this ancient lady seated in her boudoir, in a lavender satin gown, with all her candles lighted, as if to celebrate her grandson's betrothal. 'Are you very happy?' Madame de Mauves demanded, making Euphemia sit down before her.

'I'm almost afraid to say so,' said the young girl, 'lest I should wake myself up.'

'May you never wake up, *belle enfant*,' said the old lady, solemnly. 'This is the first marriage ever made in our family in this way, – by a Baron de Mauves proposing to a young girl in an arbor, like Jeannot and Jeannette. It has not been our way of doing things, and people may say it wants frankness. My grandson tells me he considers it the perfection of frankness. Very good. I'm a very old woman, and if your differences should ever be as frank as your agreement, I shouldn't like to see them. But I should be sorry to die and think you were going to be unhappy. You can't be, beyond a certain point; because, though in this world the Lord sometimes makes light of our expectations, he never altogether ignores our deserts. But you're very young and innocent, and easy to deceive. There never was a man in the world – among the saints themselves – as good as you believe the Baron. But he's a *galant homme* and a gentleman, and I've been talking to him to-night. To you I want to say this, – that you're to forget the worldly rubbish I talked the other day about frivolous women being happy. It's not the kind of happiness that would suit you. Whatever befalls you, promise me this: to be yourself. The Baronne de Mauves will be none the worse for it. Yourself, understand, in spite of everything, – bad precepts and bad examples, bad usage even. Be persistently and patiently yourself, and a De Mauves will do you justice!'

Euphemia remembered this speech in after years, and more than once, wearily closing her eyes, she seemed to see the old woman sitting upright in her faded finery and smiling grimly, like one of the Fates who sees the wheel of fortune turning up her favorite event. But at the moment it seemed to her simply to have the proper gravity of the occasion; this was the way, she supposed, in which lucky young girls were addressed on their engagement by wise old women of quality.

At her convent, to which she immediately returned, she found a letter from her mother, which shocked her far more than the remarks of Madame de Mauves. Who were these people, Mrs Cleve demanded, who had presumed to talk to her daughter of marriage without asking her leave? Questionable gentlefolk, plainly; the best French people never did such things. Euphemia would return straightway to her convent, shut herself up, and await her own arrival.

It took Mrs Cleve three weeks to travel from Nice to Paris, and during this time the young girl had no communication with her lover beyond accepting a bouquet of violets, marked with his initials and left by a female friend. 'I've not brought you up with such devoted care,' she declared to her daughter at their first interview, 'to marry a penniless Frenchman. I will take you straight home, and you will please to forget M. de Mauves.'

Mrs Cleve received that evening at her hotel a visit from the Baron which mitigated her wrath, but failed to modify her decision. He had very good manners, but she was sure he had horrible morals; and Mrs Cleve, who had been a very good-natured censor on her own account, felt a genuine spiritual need to sacrifice her daughter to propriety. She belonged to that large class of Americans who make light of America in familiar discourse, but are startled back into a sense of moral responsibility when they find Europeans taking them at their word. 'I know the type, my dear,' she said to her daughter with a sagacious nod. 'He'll not beat you; sometimes you'll wish he would.'

Euphemia remained solemnly silent; for the only answer she felt capable of making her mother was that her mind was too small a measure of things, and that the Baron's 'type' was one which it took some mystical illumination to appreciate. A person who confounded him with the common throng of her watering-place acquaintance was not a person to argue with. It seemed to Euphemia that she had no cause to plead; her cause was in the Lord's hands and her lover's.

M. de Mauves had been irritated and mortified by Mrs Cleve's opposition, and hardly knew how to handle an adversary who failed to perceive that a De Mauves of necessity gave more than he received. But he had obtained information on his return to Paris which exalted the uses of humility. Euphemia's fortune, wonderful to say, was greater than its fame, and in view of such a prize, even a De Mauves could afford to take a snubbing.

The young man's tact, his deference, his urbane insistence, won a concession from Mrs Cleve. The engagement was to be suspended and her daughter was to return home, be brought out and receive the homage she was entitled to, and which would but too surely take a form dangerous to the Baron's suit. They were to exchange neither letters, nor mementos, nor messages; but if at the end of two years Euphemia had refused offers enough to attest the permanence of her attachment, he should receive an invitation to address her again.

This decision was promulgated in the presence of the parties interested. The Baron bore himself gallantly, and looked at the young girl, expecting some tender protestation. But she only looked at him silently in return, neither weeping, nor smiling, nor putting out her hand. On this they separated; but as the Baron walked away, he declared to himself that, in spite of the confounded two years, he was a very happy fellow, – to have a fiancée who, to several millions of francs, added such strangely beautiful eyes.

How many offers Euphemia refused but scantily concerns us, – and how the Baron wore his two years away. He found that he needed pastimes, and, as pastimes were expensive, he added heavily to the list of debts to be cancelled by Euphemia's millions. Sometimes, in the thick of what he had once called pleasure with a keener conviction than now, he put to himself the case of their failing him after all; and then he remembered that last mute assurance of her eyes, and drew a long breath of such confidence as he felt in nothing else in the world save his own punctuality in an affair of honor.

At last, one morning, he took the express to Havre with a letter of Mrs Cleve's in his pocket, and ten days later made his bow to mother and daughter in New York. His stay was brief, and he was apparently unable to bring himself to view what Euphemia's uncle, Mr Butterworth, who gave her away at the altar, called our great experiment in democratic self-government in a serious light. He smiled at everything, and seemed to regard the New World as a colossal *plaisanterie*. It is true that a perpetual smile was the most natural expression of countenance for a man about to marry Euphemia Cleve.

III

Longmore's first visit seemed to open to him so large an opportunity for tranquil enjoyment, that he very soon paid a second, and, at the end of a fortnight, had spent a great many hours in the little drawing-room which Madame de Mauves rarely quitted except to drive or walk in the forest. She lived in an old-fashioned pavilion, between a high-walled court and an excessively artificial garden, beyond whose enclosure you saw a long line of tree tops. Longmore liked the garden, and in the mild afternoons used to move his chair through the open window to the little terrace which overlooked it, while his hostess sat just within. After a while she came out and wandered through the narrow alleys and beside the thin-spouting fountain, and last introduced him to a little gate in the garden wall, opening upon a lane which led into the forest. Hitherward, more than once, she wandered with him, bare-headed and meaning to go but twenty rods, but always strolling good-naturedly farther, and often taking a generous walk. They discovered a vast deal to talk about, and to the pleasure of finding the hours tread inaudibly away, Longmore was able to add the satisfaction of suspecting that he was a 'resource' for Madame de Mauves. He had made her acquaintance with the sense, not altogether comfortable, that she was a woman with a painful secret, and that seeking her acquaintance would be like visiting at a house where there was an invalid who could bear no noise. But he very soon perceived that her sorrow, since sorrow it was, was not an aggressive one; that it was not fond of attitudes and ceremonies, and that her earnest wish was to forget it. He felt that even if Mrs Draper had not told him she was unhappy, he would have guessed it; and yet he could hardly have pointed to his evidence. It was chiefly negative, – she never alluded to her husband. Beyond this it seemed to him simply that her whole being was pitched on a lower key than harmonious Nature meant; she was like a powerful singer who had lost her high notes. She never drooped nor sighed nor looked unutterable things; she indulged in no dusky sarcasms against fate; she had in short, none of the coquetry of unhappiness. But Longmore was sure that her gentle gayety was the result of strenuous effort, and that she was trying to interest herself in his thoughts to escape from her own. If she had wished to irritate his curiosity and lead him to take her confidence by storm, nothing could have served her purpose better than this ingenuous reserve. He declared to himself that there was a rare magnanimity in such ardent self-affacement, and that but one woman in ten thousand was capable of merging an intensely personal grief in thankless outward contemplation. Madame de Mauves, he instinctively felt, was not sweeping the horizon for a compensation or a consoler; she had suffered a personal deception which had disgusted her with persons. She was not striving to balance her sorrow with some strongly flavored joy; for the present, she was trying to live with it, peaceably, reputably, and without scandal, – turning the key on it occasionally, as you would on a companion liable to attacks of insanity. Longmore was a man of fine senses and of an active imagination, whose leading-strings had never been slipped. He began to regard his hostess as a figure haunted by a shadow which was somehow her intenser, more authentic self. This hovering mystery came to have for him an extraordinary charm. Her delicate beauty acquired to his eye the serious cast of certain blank-browed Greek statues, and sometimes, when his imagination, more than his ear, detected a vague tremor in the tone in which she attempted to make a friendly question seem to have behind it none of the hollow resonance of absentmindedness, his marvelling eyes gave her an answer more eloquent, though much less to the point, than the one she demanded.

She gave him indeed much to wonder about, and, in his ignorance, he formed a dozen experimental theories upon the history of her marriage. She had married for love and staked her whole soul on it; of that he was convinced. She had not married a Frenchman to be near Paris and her base of supplies of millinery; he was sure she had seen conjugal happiness in a light of which her present life, with its conveniences for shopping and its moral aridity, was the absolute negation. But by what extraordinary process of the heart – through what mysterious intermission of that moral instinct which may keep pace with the heart, even when that organ is making unprecedented time – had she fixed her affections on an arrogantly frivolous Frenchman? Longmore needed no telling; he knew M. de Mauves was frivolous; it was stamped on his eyes, his nose, his mouth, his carriage. For French women Longmore had but a scanty kindness, or at least (what with him was very much the same thing) but a scanty gallantry; they all seemed to belong to the type of certain fine lady to whom he had ventured to present a letter of introduction, and whom, directly after his first visit to her, he had set down in his note-book as 'metallic.' Why should Madame de Mauves have chosen a French woman's lot, – she whose character had a perfume which doesn't belong to even the brightest metals? He asked her one day frankly if it had cost her nothing to transplant herself, – if she was not oppressed with a sense of irreconcilable difference from 'all these people.' She was silent awhile, and he fancied that she was hesitating as to whether she should resent so unceremonious an allusion to her husband. He almost wished she would; it would seem a proof that her deep reserve of sorrow had a limit.

'I almost grew up here,' she said at last, 'and it was here for me that those dreams of the future took shape that we all have when we cease to be very young. As matters stand, one may be very American and yet arrange it with one's conscience to live in Europe. My imagination perhaps – I had a little when I was younger – helped me to think I should find happiness here. And after all, for a woman, what does it signify? This is not America, perhaps, about me, but it's quite as little France. France is out there, beyond the garden, in the town, in the forest; but here, close about me, in my room and' – she paused a moment – 'in my mind, it's a nameless country of my own. It's not her country,' she added, 'that makes a woman happy or unhappy.'

Madame Clairin, Euphemia's sister-in-law, might have been supposed to have undertaken the graceful task of making Longmore ashamed of his uncivil jottings about her sex and nation. Mademoiselle de Mauves, bringing example to the confirmation of precept, had made a remunerative match and sacrificed her name to the millions of a prosperous and aspiring wholesale druggist, – a gentleman liberal enough to consider his fortune a moderate price for being towed into circles unpervaded by pharmaceutic odors. His system, possibly, was sound, but his own application of it was unfortunate. M. Clairin's head was turned by his good luck. Having secured an aristocratic wife, he adopted an aristocratic vice and began to gamble at the Bourse. In an evil hour he lost heavily and staked heavily to recover himself. But he overtook his loss only by a greater one. Then he let everything go, – his wits, his courage, his probity, – everything that had made him what his ridiculous marriage had so promptly unmade. He walked up the Rue Vivienne one day with his hands in his empty pockets, and stood for half an hour staring confusedly up and down the glittering boulevard. People brushed against him, and half a dozen carriages almost ran over him, until at last a policeman, who had been watching him for some time, took him by the arm and led him gently away. He looked at the man's cocked hat and sword with tears in his eyes; he hoped he was going to interpret to him the wrath of Heaven, – to execute the penalty of his dead-weight of self-abhorrence. But the sergent de ville only stationed him in the embrasure of a door, out of harm's way, and walked away to supervise a financial contest between an old lady and a cabman. Poor M. Clairin had only been married a year, but he had had time to measure the lofty spirit of a De Mauves. When night had fallen, he repaired to the house of a friend and asked for a night's lodging; and as his friend, who was simply his old head book-keeper and lived in a small way, was put to some trouble to accommodate him, – 'You must excuse me,' Clairin said, 'but I can't go home. I'm afraid of my wife!' Toward morning he blew his brains out. His widow turned the remnants of his property to better account than could have been expected, and wore the very handsomest mourning. It was for this latter reason, perhaps, that she was obliged to retrench at other points and accept a temporary home under her brother's roof.

Fortune had played Madame Clairin a terrible trick, but had found an adversary and not a victim. Though quite without beauty, she had always had what is called the grand air, and her air from this time forward was grander than ever. As she trailed about in her sable furbelows, tossing back her well-dressed head, and holding up her vigilant eye-glass, she seemed to be sweeping the whole field of society and asking herself where she should pluck her revenge. Suddenly she espied it, ready made to her hand, in poor Longmore's wealth and amiability. American dollars and American complaisance had made her brother's fortune; why shouldn't they make hers? She overestimated Longmore's wealth and misinterpreted his amiability; for she was sure that a man could not be so contented without being rich, nor so unassuming without being weak. He encountered her advances with a formal politeness which covered a great deal of unflattering discomposure. She made him feel acutely uncomfortable; and though he was at a loss to conceive how he could be an object of interest to a shrewd Parisienne, he had an indefinable sense of being enclosed in a magnetic circle, like the victim of an incantation. If Madame Clairin could have fathomed his Puritanic soul, she would have laid by her wand and her book and admitted that he was an impossible subject. She gave him a kind of moral chill, and he never mentally alluded to her save as that dreadful woman, – that terrible woman. He did justice to her grand air, but for his pleasure he preferred the small air of Madame de Mauves; and he never made her his bow, after standing frigidly passive for five minutes to one of her gracious overtures to intimacy, without feeling a peculiar desire to ramble away into the forest, fling himself down on the warm grass, and, staring up at the blue sky, forget that there were any women in nature who didn't please like the swaying tree-tops. One day, on his arrival, she met him in the court and told him that her sister-in-law was shut up with a headache, and that his visit must be for her. He followed her into the drawing-room with the best grace at his command, and sat twirling his hat for half an hour. Suddenly he understood her; the caressing cadence of her voice was a distinct invitation to solicit the incomparable honor of her hand. He blushed to the roots of his hair and jumped up with uncontrollable alacrity; then, dropping a glance at Madame Clairin, who sat watching him with hard eyes over the edge of her smile, as it were, perceived on her brow a flash of unforgiving wrath. It was not becoming, but his eyes lingered a moment, for it seemed to illuminate her character. What he saw there frightened him, and he felt himself murmuring, 'Poor Madame de Mauves!' His departure was abrupt, and this time he really went into the forest and lay down on the grass.

After this he admired Madame de Mauves more than ever; she seemed a brighter figure, dogged by a darker shadow. At the end of a month he received a letter from a friend with whom he had arranged a tour through the Low Countries, reminding him of his promise to meet him promptly at Brussels. It was only after his answer was posted that he fully measured the zeal with which he had declared that the journey must either be deferred or abandoned, – that he could not possibly leave Saint-Germain. He took a walk in the forest, and asked himself if this was irrevocably true. If it was, surely his duty was to march straight home and pack his trunk. Poor Webster, who, he knew, had counted ardently on this excursion, was an excellent fellow; six weeks ago he would have gone through fire and water to join Webster. It had never been in his books to throw overboard a friend whom he had loved for ten years for a married woman whom for six weeks he had – admired. It was certainly beyond question that he was lingering at Saint-Germain because this admirable married woman was there; but in the midst of all this admiration what had become of prudence? This was the conduct of a man prepared to fall utterly in love. If she was as unhappy as he believed, the love of such a man would help her very little more than his indifference; if she was less so, she needed no help and could dispense with his friendly offices. He was sure, moreover, that if she knew he was staying on her account, she would be extremely annoyed. But this very feeling had much to do with making it hard to go; her displeasure would only enhance the gentle stoicism which touched him to the heart. At moments, indeed, he assured himself that to linger was simply impertinent; it was indelicate to make a daily study of such a shrinking grief. But inclination answered that some day her self-support would fail, and he had a vision of this admirable creature calling vainly for help. He would be her friend, to any length; it was unworthy of both of them to think about consequences. But he was a friend who carried about with him a muttering resentment that he had not known her five years earlier, and a brooding hostility to those who had anticipated him. It seemed one of fortune's most mocking strokes, that she should be surrounded by persons whose only merit was that they threw the charm of her character into radiant relief.

Longmore's growing irritation made it more and more difficult for him to see any other merit than this in the Baron de Mauves. And yet, disinterestedly, it would have been hard to give a name to the portentous vices which such an estimate implied, and there were times when our hero was almost persuaded against his finer judgment that he was really the most considerate of husbands, and that his wife liked melancholy for melancholy's sake. His manners were perfect, his urbanity was unbounded, and he seemed never to address her but, sentimentally speaking, hat in hand. His tone to Longmore (as the latter was perfectly aware) was that of a man of the world to a man not quite of the world; but what it lacked in deference it made up in easy friendliness. 'I can't thank you enough for having overcome my wife's shyness,' he more than once declared. 'If we left her to do as she pleased, she would bury herself alive. Come often, and bring some one else. She'll have nothing to do with my friends, but perhaps she'll accept yours.'

The Baron made these speeches with a remorseless placidity very amazing to our hero, who had an innocent belief that a man's head may point out to him the shortcomings of his heart and make him ashamed of them. He could not fancy him capable both of neglecting his wife and taking an almost humorous view of her suffering. Longmore had, at any rate, an exasperating sense that the Baron thought rather less of his wife than more, for that very same fine difference of nature which so deeply stirred his own sympathies. He was rarely present during Longmore's visits, and made a daily journey to Paris, where he had 'business,' as he once mentioned, – not in the least with a tone of apology. When he appeared, it was late in the evening, and with an imperturbable air of being on the best of terms with every one and everything, which was peculiarly annoying if you happened to have a tacit quarrel with him. If he was a good fellow, he was surely a good fellow spoiled. Something he had, however, which Longmore vaguely envied – a kind of superb positiveness – a manner rounded and polished by the traditions of centuries – an amenity exercised for his own sake and not his neighbors' – which seemed the result of something better than a good conscience – of a vigorous and unscrupulous temperament. The Baron was plainly not a moral man, and poor Longmore, who was, would have been glad to learn the secret of his luxurious serenity. What was it that enabled him, without being a monster with visibly cloven feet, exhaling brimstone, to misprize so cruelly a lovely wife, and to walk about the world with a smile under his mustache? It was the essential grossness of his imagination, which had nevertheless helped him to turn so many neat compliments. He could be very polite, and

he could doubtless be supremely impertinent; but he was as unable
to draw a moral inference of the finer strain, as a school-boy who
has been playing truant for a week to solve a problem in algebra.
It was ten to one he didn't know his wife was unhappy; he and his
brilliant sister had doubtless agreed to consider their companion a
Puritanical little person, of meagre aspirations and slender accomplishments, contented with looking at Paris from the terrace, and,
as an especial treat, having a countryman very much like herself to
supply her with homely transatlantic gossip. M. de Mauves was
tired of his companion: he relished a higher flavor in female
society. She was too modest, too simple, too delicate; she had too
few arts, too little coquetry, too much charity. M. de Mauves,
some day, lighting a cigar, had probably decided she was stupid.
It was the same sort of taste, Longmore moralized, as the taste for
Gérôme in painting, and for M. Gustave Flaubert[3] in literature.
The Baron was a pagan and his wife was a Christian, and between
them, accordingly, was a gulf. He was by race and instinct a *grand
seigneur*. Longmore had often heard of this distinguished social
type, and was properly grateful for an opportunity to examine it
closely. It had certainly a picturesque boldness of outline, but it
was fed from spiritual sources so remote from those of which he
felt the living gush in his own soul, that he found himself gazing
at it, in irreconcilable antipathy, across a dim historic mist. 'I'm a
modern *bourgeois*,' he said, 'and not perhaps so good a judge of
how far a pretty woman's tongue may go at supper without
prejudice to her reputation. But I've not met one of the sweetest
of women without recognizing her and discovering that a certain
sort of character offers better entertainment than Thérésa's songs,
sung by a dissipated duchess. Wit for wit, I think mine carries me
further.' It was easy indeed to perceive that, as became a *grand
seigneur*, M. de Mauves had a stock of rigid notions. He would not
especially have desired, perhaps, that his wife should compete in
amateur operettas with the duchesses in question, chiefly of recent
origin; but he held that a gentleman may take his amusement
where he finds it, that he is quite at liberty not to find it at home;
and that the wife of a De Mauves who should hang her head and
have red eyes, and allow herself to make any other response to
officious condolence than that her husband's amusements were his

own affair, would have forfeited every claim to having her finger-tips bowed over and kissed. And yet in spite of these sound principles, Longmore fancied that the Baron was more irritated than gratified by his wife's irreproachable reserve. Did it dimly occur to him that it was self-control and not self-effacement? She was a model to all the inferior matrons of his line, past and to come, and an occasional 'scene' from her at a convenient moment would have something reassuring, – would attest her stupidity a trifle more forcibly than her inscrutable tranquillity.

Longmore would have given much to know the principle of her submissiveness, and he tried more than once, but with rather awkward timidity, to sound the mystery. She seemed to him to have been long resisting the force of cruel evidence, and, though she had succumbed to it at last, to have denied herself the right to complain, because if faith was gone her heroic generosity remained. He believed even that she was capable of reproaching herself with having expected too much, and of trying to persuade herself out of her bitterness by saying that her hopes had been illusions and that this was simply – life. 'I hate tragedy,' she once said to him; 'I have a really pusillanimous dread of moral suffering. I believe that – without base concessions – there is always some way of escaping from it. I had almost rather never smile all my life than have a single violent explosion of grief.' She lived evidently in nervous apprehension of being fatally convinced, – of seeing to the end of her deception. Longmore, when he thought of this, felt an immense longing to offer her something of which she could be as sure as of the sun in heaven.

IV

His friend Webster lost no time in accusing him of the basest infidelity, and asking him what he found at Saint-Germain to prefer to Van Eyck and Memling, Rubens and Rembrandt. A day or two after the receipt of Webster's letter, he took a walk with Madame de Mauves in the forest. They sat down on a fallen log, and she began to arrange into a bouquet the anemones and violets she had gathered. 'I have a letter,' he said at last, 'from a friend whom I some time ago promised to join at Brussels. The time has come, – it has passed. It finds me terribly unwilling to leave Saint-Germain.'

She looked up with the candid interest which she always displayed in his affairs, but with no disposition, apparently, to make a personal application of his words. 'Saint-Germain is pleasant enough,' she said; 'but are you doing yourself justice? Won't you regret in future days that instead of travelling and seeing cities and monuments and museums and improving your mind, you sat here – for instance – on a log, pulling my flowers to pieces?'

'What I shall regret in future days,' he answered after some hesitation, 'is that I should have sat here and not spoken the truth on the matter. I am fond of museums and monuments and of improving my mind, and I'm particularly fond of my friend Webster. But I can't bring myself to leave Saint-Germain without asking you a question. You must forgive me if it's unfortunate, and be assured that curiosity was never more respectful. Are you really as unhappy as I imagine you to be?'

She had evidently not expected his question, and she greeted it with a startled blush. 'If I strike you as unhappy,' she said, 'I have been a poorer friend to you than I wished to be.'

'I, perhaps, have been a better friend of yours than you have supposed. I've admired your reserve, your courage, your studied gayety. But I have felt the existence of something beneath them that was more *you* – more you as I wished to know you – than they were; something that I have believed to be a constant sorrow.'

She listened with great gravity, but without an air of offence, and he felt that while he had been timorously calculating the last consequences of friendship, she had placidly accepted them. 'You surprise me,' she said slowly, and her blush still lingered. 'But to refuse to answer you would confirm an impression which is evidently already too strong. An unhappiness that one can sit comfortably talking about, is an unhappiness with distinct limitations. If I were examined before a board of commissioners for investigating the felicity of mankind, I'm sure I should be pronounced a very fortunate woman.'

There was something delightfully gentle to him in her tone, and its softness seemed to deepen as she continued: 'But let me add, with all gratitude for your sympathy, that it's my own affair altogether. It needn't disturb you, Mr Longmore, for I have often found myself in your company a very contented person.'

'You're a wonderful woman,' he said, 'and I admire you as I never have admired any one. You're wiser than anything I, for one, can say to you; and what I ask of you is not to let me advise or console you, but simply thank you for letting me know you.' He had intended no such outburst as this, but his voice rang loud, and he felt a kind of unfamiliar joy as he uttered it.

She shook her head with some impatience. 'Let us be friends, – as I supposed we were going to be, – without protestations and fine words. To have you making bows to my wisdom, – that would be real wretchedness. I can dispense with your admiration better than the Flemish painters can, – better than Van Eyck and Rubens, in spite of all their worshippers. Go join your friend, – see everything, enjoy everything, learn everything, and write me an excellent letter, brimming over with your impressions. I'm extremely fond of the Dutch painters,' she added with a slight faltering of the voice, which Longmore had noticed once before, and which he had interpreted as the sudden weariness of a spirit self-condemned to play a part.

'I don't believe you care about the Dutch painters at all,' he said with an unhesitating laugh. 'But I shall certainly write you a letter.'

She rose and turned homeward, thoughtfully rearranging her flowers as she walked. Little was said; Longmore was asking himself, with a tremor in the unspoken words, whether all this meant simply that he was in love. He looked at the rooks wheeling against the golden-hued sky, between the tree-tops, but not at his companion, whose personal presence seemed lost in the felicity she had created. Madame de Mauves was silent and grave, because she was painfully disappointed. A sentimental friendship she had not desired; her scheme had been to pass with Longmore as a placid creature with a good deal of leisure, which she was disposed to devote to profitable conversation of an impersonal sort. She liked him extremely, and felt that there was something in him to which, when she made up her girlish mind that a needy French baron was the ripest fruit of time, she had done very scanty justice. They went through the little gate in the garden wall and approached the house. On the terrace Madame Clairin was entertaining a friend, – a little elderly gentleman with a white mustache, and an order in his button-hole. Madame de Mauves chose to pass round the house into the court; whereupon her sister-in-law, greeting Longmore with a commanding nod, lifted her eye-glass and stared at them as they went by. Longmore heard the little old gentleman uttering some old-fashioned epigram about 'la vieille galanterie Française,' and then, by a sudden impulse, he looked at Madame de Mauves and wondered what she was doing in such a world. She stopped before the house, without asking him to come in. 'I hope,' she said, 'you'll consider my advice, and waste no more time at Saint-Germain.'

For an instant there rose to his lips some faded compliment about his time not being wasted, but it expired before the simple sincerity of her look. She stood there as gently serious as the angel of disinterestedness, and Longmore felt as if he should insult her by treating her words as a bait for flattery. 'I shall start in a day or two,' he answered, 'but I won't promise you not to come back.'

'I hope not,' she said simply. 'I expect to be here a long time.'

'I shall come and say good by,' he rejoined; on which she nodded with a smile, and went in.

He turned away, and walked slowly homeward by the terrace. It seemed to him that to leave her thus, for a gain on which she herself insisted, was to know her better and admire her more. But he was in a vague ferment of feeling which her evasion of his question half an hour before had done more to deepen than to allay. Suddenly, on the terrace, he encountered M. de Mauves, who was leaning against the parapet finishing a cigar. The Baron, who, he fancied, had an air of peculiar affability, offered him his fair, plump hand. Longmore stopped; he felt a sudden angry desire to cry out to him that he had the loveliest wife in the world; that he ought to be ashamed of himself not to know it; and that for all his shrewdness he had never looked into the depths of her eyes. The Baron, we know, considered that he had; but there was something in Euphemia's eyes now that was not there five years before. They talked for a while about various things, and M. de Mauves gave a humorous account of his visit to America. His tone was not soothing to Longmore's excited sensibilities. He seemed to consider the country a gigantic joke, and his urbanity only went so far as to admit that it was not a bad one. Longmore was not, by habit, an aggressive apologist for our institutions; but the Baron's narrative confirmed his worst impressions of French superficiality. He had understood nothing, he had felt nothing, he had learned nothing; and our hero, glancing askance at his aristocratic profile, declared that if the chief merit of a long pedigree was to leave one so vaingloriously stupid, he thanked his stars that the Longmores had emerged from obscurity in the present century, in the person of an enterprising lumber merchant. M. de Mauves dwelt of course on that prime oddity of ours, – the liberty allowed to young girls; and related the history of his researches into the 'opportunities' it presented to French noblemen, – researches in which, during a fortnight's stay, he seemed to have spent many agreeable hours. 'I am bound to admit,' he said, 'that in every case I was disarmed by the extreme candor of the young lady, and that they took care of themselves to better purpose than I have seen some mammas in France take care of them.' Longmore greeted this handsome concession with the grimmest of smiles, and damned his impertinent patronage.

Mentioning at last that he was about to leave Saint-Germain, he was surprised, without exactly being flattered, by the Baron's quickened attention. 'I'm very sorry,' the latter cried. 'I hoped we had you for the summer.' Longmore murmured something civil, and wondered why M. de Mauves should care whether he stayed or went. 'You were a diversion to Madame de Mauves,' the Baron added. 'I assure you I mentally blessed your visits.'

'They were a great pleasure to me,' Longmore said gravely. 'Some day I expect to come back.'

'Pray do,' and the Baron laid his hand urgently on his arm. 'You see I have confidence in you!' Longmore was silent for a moment, and the Baron puffed his cigar reflectively and watched the smoke. 'Madame de Mauves,' he said at last, 'is a rather singular person.'

Longmore shifted his position, and wondered whether he was going to 'explain' Madame de Mauves.

'Being as you are her fellow-countryman,' the Baron went on, 'I don't mind speaking frankly. She's just a little morbid, – the most charming woman in the world, as you see, but a little fanciful, – a little *exaltée*. Now you see she has taken this extraordinary fancy for solitude. I can't get her to go anywhere, – to see any one. When my friends present themselves she's polite, but she's freezing. She doesn't do herself justice, and I expect every day to hear two or three of them say to me, "Your wife's *jolie à croquer:*[4] what a pity she hasn't a little *esprit*." You must have found out that she has really a great deal. But to tell the whole truth, what she needs is to forget herself. She sits alone for hours poring over her English books and looking at life through that terrible brown fog which they always seem to me to fling over the world. I doubt if your English authors,' the Baron continued, with a serenity which Longmore afterwards characterized as sublime, 'are very sound reading for young married women. I don't pretend to know much about them; but I remember that, not long after our marriage, Madame de Mauves undertook to read me one day a certain Wordsworth, – a poet highly esteemed, it appears, *chez vous*. It seemed to me that she took me by the nape of the neck and forced my head for half an hour over a basin of *soupe aux choux*, and that one ought to ventilate the drawing-room before any one called. But I suppose you know him, – *ce génie là*. I think my wife never forgave me, and that it was a real shock to her to find she had married a man who had very much the same taste in literature as in cookery. But you're a man of general culture,' said the Baron, turning to Longmore and fixing his eyes on the seal on his watch-guard. 'You can talk about everything, and I'm sure you like Alfred de Musset as well as Wordsworth. Talk to her about everything, Alfred de Musset included. Bah! I forgot you're going. Come back then as soon as possible and talk about your travels. If Madame de Mauves too would travel for a couple of months, it would do her good. It would enlarge her horizon,' – and M. de Mauves made a series of short nervous jerks with his stick in the air, – 'it would wake up her imagination. She's too rigid, you know, – it would show her that one may bend a trifle without breaking.' He paused a moment and gave two or three vigorous puffs. Then turning to his companion again, with a little nod and a confidential smile: – 'I hope you admire my candor. I wouldn't say all this to one of *us*.'

Evening was coming on, and the lingering light seemed to float in the air in faintly golden motes. Longmore stood gazing at these luminous particles; he could almost have fancied them a swarm of humming insects, murmuring as a refrain, 'She has a great deal of *esprit*, – she has a great deal of *esprit*.' 'Yes, she has a great deal,' he said mechanically, turning to the Baron. M. de Mauves glanced at him sharply, as if to ask what the deuce he was talking about. 'She has a great deal of intelligence,' said Longmore, deliberately, 'a great deal of beauty, a great many virtues.'

M. de Mauves busied himself for a moment in lighting another cigar, and when he had finished, with a return of his confidential smile, 'I suspect you of thinking,' he said, 'that I don't do my wife justice. Take care, – take care, young man; that's a dangerous assumption. In general, a man always does his wife justice. More than justice,' cried the Baron with a laugh, – 'that we keep for the wives of other men!'

Longmore afterwards remembered it in favor of the Baron's grace of address that he had not measured at this moment the dusky abyss over which it hovered. But a sort of deepening subterranean echo lingered on his spiritual ear. For the present his keenest sensation was a desire to get away and cry aloud that M. de Mauves was an arrogant fool. He bade him an abrupt good-night, which must serve also, he said, as good by.

'Decidedly, then, you go?' said M. de Mauves, almost peremptorily.

'Decidedly.'

'Of course you'll come and say good by to Madame de Mauves.' His tone implied that the omission would be most uncivil; but there seemed to Longmore something so ludicrous in his taking a lesson in consideration from M. de Mauves, that he burst into a laugh. The Baron frowned, like a man for whom it was a new and most unpleasant sensation to be perplexed. 'You're a queer fellow,' he murmured, as Longmore turned away, not forseeing that he would think him a very queer fellow indeed before he had done with him.

Longmore sat down to dinner at his hotel with his usual good intentions; but as he was lifting his first glass of wine to his lips, he suddenly fell to musing and set down his wine untasted. His revery lasted long, and when he emerged from it, his fish was cold;

but this mattered little, for his appetite was gone. That evening he packed his trunk with a kind of indignant energy. This was so effective that the operation was accomplished before bedtime, and as he was not in the least sleepy, he devoted the interval to writing two letters; one was a short note to Madame de Mauves, which he intrusted to a servant, to be delivered the next morning. He had found it best, he said, to leave Saint-Germain immediately, but he expected to be back in Paris in the early autumn. The other letter was the result of his having remembered a day or two before that he had not yet complied with Mrs Draper's injunction to give her an account of his impressions of her friend. The present occasion seemed propitious, and he wrote half a dozen pages. His tone, however, was grave, and Mrs Draper, on receiving them, was slightly disappointed, – she would have preferred a stronger flavor of rhapsody. But what chiefly concerns us is the concluding sentences.

'The only time she ever spoke to me of her marriage,' he wrote, 'she intimated that it had been a perfect love-match. With all abatements, I suppose most marriages are; but in her case this would mean more, I think, than in that of most women; for her love was an absolute idealization. She believed her husband was a hero of rose-colored romance, and he turns out to be not even a hero of very sad-colored reality. For some time now she has been sounding her mistake, but I don't believe she has touched the bottom of it yet. She strikes me as a person who is begging off from full knowledge, – who has struck a truce with painful truth, and is trying awhile the experiment of living with closed eyes. In the dark she tries to see again the gilding on her idol. Illusion of course is illusion, and one must always pay for it; but there is something truly tragical in seeing an earthly penalty levied on such divine folly as this. As for M. de Mauves, he's a Frenchman to his fingers' ends; and I confess I should dislike him for this if he were a much better man. He can't forgive his wife for having married him too sentimentally and loved him too well; for in some uncorrupted corner of his being he feels, I suppose, that as she saw him, so he ought to have been. It's a perpetual vexation to him that a little American bourgeoise should have fancied him a finer fellow than he is, or than he at all wants to be. He hasn't a glimmering of real acquaintance with his wife; he can't understand the stream of passion flowing so clear and still. To tell the truth, I hardly can myself; but when I see the spectacle I can admire it furiously. M. de Mauves, at any rate, would like to have the comfort of feeling that his wife was as corruptible as himself; and you'll hardly believe me when I tell you that he goes about intimating to gentlemen whom he deems worthy of the knowledge, that it would be a convenience to him to have them make love to her.'

V

On reaching Paris, Longmore straightway purchased a Murray's 'Belgium,' to help himself to believe that he would start on the morrow for Brussels; but when the morrow came, it occurred to him that, by way of preparation, he ought to acquaint himself more intimately with the Flemish painters in the Louvre. This took a whole morning, but it did little to hasten his departure. He had abruptly left Saint-Germain, because it seemed to him that respect for Madame de Mauves demanded that he should allow her husband no reason to suppose that he had understood him; but now that he had satisfied this immediate need of delicacy, he found himself thinking more and more ardently of Euphemia. It was a poor expression of ardor to be lingering irresolutely on the deserted boulevards, but he detested the idea of leaving Saint-Germain five hundred miles behind him. He felt very foolish, nevertheless, and wandered about nervously, promising himself to take the next train; but a dozen trains started, and Longmore was still in Paris. This sentimental tumult was more than he had bargained for, and, as he looked in the shop windows, he wondered whether it was a 'passion.' He had never been fond of the word, and had grown up with a kind of horror of what it represented. He had hoped that when he fell in love, he should do it with an excellent conscience, with no greater agitation than a mild general glow of satisfaction. But here was a sentiment compounded of pity and anger, as well as admiration, and bristling with scruples and doubts. He had come abroad to enjoy the Flemish painters and all others; but what fair-tressed saint of Van Eyck or Memling was so appealing a figure as Madame de Mauves? His restless steps carried him at last out of the long villa-bordered avenue which leads to the Bois de Boulogne.

Summer had fairly begun, and the drive beside the lake was empty, but there were various loungers on the benches and chairs, and the great café had an air of animation. Longmore's walk had given him an appetite, and he went into the establishment and demanded a dinner, remarking for the hundredth time, as he observed the smart little tables disposed in the open air, how much better they ordered this matter in France.

'Will monsieur dine in the garden, or in the salon?' asked the waiter. Longmore chose the garden; and observing that a great vine of June roses was trained over the wall of the house, placed himself at a table near by, where the best of dinners was served him on the whitest of linen, in the most shining of porcelain. It so happened that his table was near a window, and that as he sat he could look into a corner of the salon. So it was that his attention rested on a lady seated just within the window, which was open, face to face apparently to a companion who was concealed by the curtain. She was a very pretty woman, and Longmore looked at her as often as was consistent with good manners. After a while he even began to wonder who she was, and to suspect that she was one of those ladies whom it is no breach of good manners to look at as often as you like. Longmore, too, if he had been so disposed, would have been the more free to give her all his attention, that her own was fixed upon the person opposite to her. She was what the French call a *belle brune*, and though our hero, who had rather a conservative taste in such matters, had no great relish for her bold outlines and even bolder coloring, he could not help admiring her expression of basking contentment.

She was evidently very happy, and her happiness gave her an air of innocence. The talk of her friend, whoever he was, abundantly suited her humor, for she sat listening to him with a broad, lazy smile, and interrupted him occasionally, while she crunched her bon-bons, with a murmured response, presumably as broad, which seemed to deepen his eloquence. She drank a great deal of champagne and ate an immense number of strawberries, and was plainly altogether a person with an impartial relish for strawberries, champagne, and what she would have called *bêtises*.

They had half finished dinner when Longmore sat down, and he was still in his place when they rose. She had hung her bonnet on a nail above her chair, and her companion passed round the table to take it down for her. As he did so, she bent her head to look at a wine stain on her dress, and in the movement exposed the greater part of the back of a very handsome neck. The gentleman observed it, and observed also, apparently, that the room beyond them was empty; that he stood within eyeshot of Longmore, he failed to observe. He stooped suddenly and imprinted a gallant kiss on the fair expanse. Longmore then recognized M. de Mauves. The recipient of this vigorous tribute put on her bonnet, using his flushed smile as a mirror, and in a moment they passed through the garden on their way to their carriage.

Then, for the first time, M. de Mauves perceived Longmore. He measured with a rapid glance the young man's relation to the open window, and checked himself in the impulse to stop and speak to him. He contented himself with bowing with great gravity as he opened the gate for his companion.

That evening Longmore made a railway journey, but not to Brussels. He had effectually ceased to care about Brussels; the only thing he now cared about was Madame de Mauves. The atmosphere of his mind had had a sudden clearing up; pity and anger were still throbbing there, but they had space to rage at their pleasure, for doubts and scruples had abruptly departed. It was little, he felt, that he could interpose between her resignation and the unsparing harshness of her position; but that little, if it involved the sacrifice of everything that bound him to the tranquil past, it seemed to him that he could offer her with a rapture which at last made reflection a wofully halting substitute for faith. Nothing in his tranquil past had given such a zest to consciousness as the sense of tending with all his being to a single aim which bore him company on his journey to Saint-Germain. How to justify his return, how to explain his ardor, troubled him little. He was not sure, even, that he wished to be understood; he wished only to feel that it was by no fault of his that Madame de Mauves was alone with the ugliness of fate. He was conscious of no distinct desire to 'make love' to her; if he could have uttered the essence of his longing, he would have said that he wished her to remember that in a world colored gray to her vision by disappointment, there was one vividly honest man. She might certainly have remembered it, however, without his coming back to remind her; and it is not to be denied that, as he packed his valise that evening, he wished immensely to hear the sound of her voice.

He waited the next day till his usual hour of calling, – the late afternoon; but he learned at the door that Madame de Mauves was not at home. The servant offered the information that she was walking in the forest. Longmore went through the garden and out of the little door into the lane, and, after half an hour's vain exploration, saw her coming toward him at the end of a green by-path. As he appeared, she stopped for a moment, as if to turn aside; then recognizing him, she slowly advanced, and he was soon shaking hands with her.

'Nothing has happened,' she said, looking at him fixedly. 'You're not ill?'

'Nothing, except that when I got to Paris I found how fond I had grown of Saint-Germain.'

She neither smiled nor looked flattered; it seemed indeed to Longmore that she was annoyed. But he was uncertain, for he immediately perceived that in his absence the whole character of her face had altered. It told him that something momentous had happened. It was no longer self-contained melancholy that he read in her eyes, but grief and agitation which had lately struggled with that passionate love of peace of which she had spoken to him, and forced it to know that deep experience is never peaceful. She was pale, and she had evidently been shedding tears. He felt his heart beating hard; he seemed now to know her secrets. She continued to look at him with a contracted brow, as if his return had given her a sense of responsibility too great to be disguised by a commonplace welcome. For some moments, as he turned and walked beside her, neither spoke; then abruptly, – 'Tell me truly, Mr Longmore,' she said, 'why you have come back.'

He turned and looked at her with an air which startled her into a certainty of what she had feared. 'Because I've learned the real answer to the question I asked you the other day. You're not happy, – you're too good to be happy on the terms offered you. Madame de Mauves,' he went on with a gesture which protested against a gesture of her own, 'I can't be happy if you're not. I don't care for anything so long as I see such a depth of unconquerable sadness in your eyes. I found during three dreary days in Paris that the thing in the world I most care for is this daily privilege of seeing you. I know it's absolutely brutal to tell you I admire you; it's an insult to you to treat you as if you had complained to me or appealed to me. But such a friendship as I waked up to there,' – and he tossed his head toward the distant city – 'is a potent force, I assure you; and when forces are compressed they explode. But if you had told me every trouble in your heart, it would have mattered little; I couldn't say more than I must say now, – that if that in life from which you've hoped most has given you least, *my* devoted respect will refuse no service and betray no trust.'

She had begun to make marks in the earth with the point of her parasol; but she stopped and listened to him in perfect immobility. Rather, her immobility was not perfect; for when he stopped speaking a faint flush had stolen into her cheek. It told Longmore that she was moved, and his first perceiving it was the happiest instant of his life. She raised her eyes at last, and looked at him with what at first seemed a pleading dread of excessive emotion.

'Thank you – thank you!' she said, calmly enough; but the next moment her own emotion overcame her calmness, and she burst into tears. Her tears vanished as quickly as they came, but they did Longmore a world of good. He had always felt indefinably afraid of her; her being had somehow seemed fed by a deeper faith and a stronger will than his own; but her half-dozen smothered sobs showed him the bottom of her heart, and assured him that she was weak enough to be grateful.

'Excuse me,' she said, 'I'm too nervous to listen to you. I believe I could have faced an enemy to-day, but I can't endure a friend.'

'You're killing yourself with stoicism, – that's my belief,' he cried. 'Listen to a friend for his own sake, if not for yours. I have never ventured to offer you an atom of compassion, and you can't accuse yourself of an abuse of charity.'

She looked about her with a kind of weary confusion which promised a reluctant attention. But suddenly perceiving by the wayside the fallen log on which they had rested a few evenings before, she went and sat down on it in impatient resignation, and looked at Longmore, as he stood silent, watching her, with a glance which seemed to urge that, if she was charitable now, he must be very wise.

'Something came to my knowledge yesterday,' he said as he sat down beside her, 'which gave me a supreme sense of your moral isolation. You are truth itself, and there is no truth about you. You believe in purity and duty and dignity, and you live in a world in which they are daily belied. I sometimes ask myself with a kind of rage how you ever came into such a world, – and why the perversity of fate never let me know you before.'

'I like my "world" no better than you do, and it was not for its own sake I came into it. But what particular group of people is worth pinning one's faith upon? I confess it sometimes seems to me that men and women are very poor creatures. I suppose I'm romantic. I have a most unfortunate taste for poetic fitness. Life is hard prose, which one must learn to read contentedly. I believe I once thought that all the prose was in America, which was very foolish. What I thought, what I believed, what I expected, when I was an ignorant girl, fatally addicted to falling in love with my own theories, is more than I can begin to tell you now. Sometimes, when I remember certain impulses, certain illusions of those days, they take away my breath, and I wonder my bedazzled visions didn't lead me into troubles greater than any I have now to lament. I had a conviction which you would probably smile at if I were to attempt to express it to you. It was a singular form for passionate faith to take, but it had all of the sweetness and the ardor of passionate faith. It led me to take a great step, and it lies behind me now in the distance like a shadow melting slowly in the light of experience. It has faded, but it has not vanished. Some feelings, I am sure, die only with ourselves; some illusions are as much the condition of our life as our heart-beats. They say that life itself is an illusion, – that this world is a shadow of which the reality is yet to come. Life is all of a piece, then, and there is no shame in being miserably human. As for my "isolation," it doesn't greatly matter;

it's the fault, in part, of my obstinacy. There have been times when I have been frantically distressed, and, to tell you the truth, wretchedly homesick, because my maid – a jewel of a maid – lied to me with every second breath. There have been moments when I have wished I was the daughter of a poor New England minister, living in a little white house under a couple of elms, and doing all the housework.'

She had begun to speak slowly, with an air of effort; but she went on quickly, as if talking were a relief. 'My marriage introduced me to people and things which seemed to me at first very strange and then very horrible, and then, to tell the truth, very contemptible. At first I expended a great deal of sorrow and dismay and pity on it all; but there soon came a time when I began to wonder whether it was worth one's tears. If I could tell you the eternal friendships I've seen broken, the inconsolable woes consoled, the jealousies and vanities leading off the dance, you would agree with me that tempers like yours and mine can understand neither such losses nor such compensations. A year ago, while I was in the country, a friend of mine was in despair at the infidelity of her husband; she wrote me a most tragical letter, and on my return to Paris I went immediately to see her. A week had elapsed, and, as I had seen stranger things, I thought she might have recovered her spirits. Not at all; she was still in despair, – but at what? At the conduct, the abandoned shameless conduct of Mme de T. You'll imagine, of course, that Mme de T. was the lady whom my friend's husband preferred to his wife. Far from it; he had never seen her. Who, then, was Mme de T.? Mme de T. was cruelly devoted to M. de V. And who was M. de V.? M. de V. – in two words, my friend was cultivating two jealousies at once. I hardly know what I said to her; something, at any rate, that she found unpardonable, for she quite gave me up. Shortly afterwards my husband proposed we should cease to live in Paris, and I gladly assented, for I believe I was falling into a state of mind that made me a detestable companion. I should have preferred to go quite into the country, into Auvergne, where my husband has a place. But to him Paris, in some degree, is necessary, and Saint-Germain has been a sort of compromise.'

'A sort of compromise!' Longmore repeated. 'That's your whole life.'

'It's the life of many people, of most people of quiet tastes, and it is certainly better than acute distress. One is at a loss theoretically to defend a compromise; but if I found a poor creature clinging to one from day to day, I should think it poor friendship to make him lose his hold.' Madame de Mauves had no sooner uttered these words than she smiled faintly, as if to mitigate their personal application.

'Heaven forbid,' said Longmore, 'that one should do that unless one has something better to offer. And yet I am haunted by a vision of a life in which you should have found no compromises, for they are a perversion of natures that tend only to goodness and rectitude. As I see it, you should have found happiness serene, profound, complete; a *femme de chambre* not a jewel perhaps, but warranted to tell but one fib a day; a society possibly rather provincial, but (in spite of your poor opinion of mankind) a good deal of solid virtue; jealousies and vanities very tame, and no particular iniquities and adulteries. A husband,' he added after a moment, – 'a husband of your own faith and race and spiritual substance, who would have loved you well.'

She rose to her feet, shaking her head. 'You are very kind to go to the expense of visions for me. Visions are vain things; we must make the best of the reality.'

'And yet,' said Longmore, provoked by what seemed the very wantonness of her patience, 'the reality, if I'm not mistaken, has very recently taken a shape that keenly tests your philosophy.'

She seemed on the point of replying that his sympathy was too zealous; but a couple of impatient tears in his eyes proved that it was founded on a devotion to which it was impossible not to defer. 'Philosophy?' she said. 'I have none. Thank Heaven!' she cried with vehemence, 'I have none. I believe, Mr Longmore,' she added in a moment, 'that I have nothing on earth but a conscience, – it's a good time to tell you so, – nothing but a dogged, clinging, inexpugnable conscience. Does that prove me to be indeed of your faith and race, and have you one for which you can say as much? I don't say it in vanity, for I believe that if my conscience will prevent me from doing anything very base, it will effectually prevent me from doing anything very fine.'

'I am delighted to hear it,' cried Longmore. 'We are made for each other. It's very certain I too shall never do anything fine. And yet I have fancied that in my case this inexpugnable organ you so eloquently describe might be blinded and gagged awhile, in a fine cause, if not turned out of doors. In yours,' he went on with the same appealing irony, 'is it absolutely invincible?'

But her fancy made no concession to his sarcasm. 'Don't laugh at your conscience,' she answered gravely; 'that's the only blasphemy I know.'

She had hardly spoken when she turned suddenly at an unexpected sound, and at the same moment Longmore heard a footstep in an adjacent by-path which crossed their own at a short distance from where they stood.

'It's M. de Mauves,' said Euphemia directly, and moved slowly forward. Longmore, wondering how she knew it, had overtaken her by the time her husband advanced into sight. A solitary walk in the forest was a pastime to which M. de Mauves was not addicted, but he seemed on this occasion to have resorted to it with some equanimity. He was smoking a fragrant cigar, and his thumb was thrust into the armhole of his waistcoat, with an air of contemplative serenity. He stopped short with surprise on seeing his wife and her companion, and Longmore considered his surprise impertinent. He glanced rapidly from one to the other, fixed Longmore's eye sharply for a single instant, and then lifted his hat with formal politeness.

'I was not aware,' he said, turning to Madame de Mauves, 'that I might congratulate you on the return of monsieur.'

'You should have known it,' she answered gravely, 'if I had expected Mr Longmore's return.'

She had become very pale, and Longmore felt that this was a first meeting after a stormy parting. 'My return was unexpected to myself,' he said. 'I came last evening.'

M. de Mauves smiled with extreme urbanity. 'It's needless for me to welcome you. Madame de Mauves knows the duties of hospitality.' And with another bow he continued his walk.

Madame de Mauves and her companion returned slowly home, with few words, but, on Longmore's part at least, many thoughts. The Baron's appearance had given him an angry chill; it was a dusky cloud reabsorbing the light which had begun to shine between himself and his companion.

He watched Euphemia narrowly as they went, and wondered what she had last had to suffer. Her husband's presence had checked her frankness, but nothing indicated that she had accepted the insulting meaning of his words. Matters were evidently at a crisis between them, and Longmore wondered vainly what it was on Euphemia's part that prevented an absolute rupture. What did she suspect? – how much did she know? To what was she resigned? – how much had she forgiven? How, above all, did she reconcile with knowledge, or with suspicion, that ineradicable tenderness of which she had just now all but assured him? 'She has loved him once,' Longmore said with a sinking of the heart, 'and with her to love once is to commit one's being forever. Her husband thinks her too rigid! What would a poet call it?'

He relapsed with a kind of aching impotence into the sense of her being somehow beyond him, unattainable, immeasurable by his own fretful spirit. Suddenly he gave three passionate switches in the air with his cane, which made Madame de Mauves look round. She could hardly have guessed that they meant that where ambition was so vain, it was an innocent compensation to plunge into worship.

Madame de Mauves found in her drawing-room the little elderly Frenchman, M. de Chalumeau, whom Longmore had observed a few days before on the terrace. On this occasion, too, Madame Clairin was entertaining him, but as her sister-in-law came in she surrendered her post and addressed herself to our hero. Longmore, at thirty, was still an ingenuous youth, and there was something in this lady's large coquetry which had the power of making him blush. He was surprised at finding he had not absolutely forfeited her favor by his deportment at their last interview, and a suspicion of her meaning to approach him on another line completed his uneasiness.

'So you've returned from Brussels,' she said, 'by way of the forest.'

'I've not been to Brussels, I returned yesterday from Paris by the only way, – by the train.'

Madame Clairin stared and laughed. 'I've never known a young man to be so fond of Saint-Germain. They generally declare it's horribly dull.'

'That's not very polite to you,' said Longmore, who was vexed at his blushes, and determined not to be abashed.

'Ah, what am I?' demanded Madame Clairin, swinging open her fan. 'I'm the dullest thing here. They've not had your success with my sister-in-law.'

'It would have been very easy to have it. Madame de Mauves is kindness itself.'

'To her own countrymen!'

Longmore remained silent; he hated the talk. Madame Clairin looked at him a moment, and then turned her head and surveyed Euphemia, to whom M. de Chalumeau was serving up another epigram, which she was receiving with a slight droop of the head and her eyes absently wandering through the window. 'Don't pretend to tell me,' she murmured suddenly, 'that you're not in love with that pretty woman.'

'*Allons donc!*' cried Longmore, in the best French he had ever uttered. He rose the next minute, and took a hasty farewell.

VI

He allowed several days to pass without going back; it seemed delicate not to appear to regard his friend's frankness during their last interview as a general invitation. This cost him a great effort, for hopeless passions are not the most deferential; and he had, moreover, a constant fear, that if, as he believed, the hour of supreme 'explanations' had come, the magic of her magnanimity might convert M. de Mauves. Vicious men, it was abundantly recorded, had been so converted as to be acceptable to God, and the something divine in Euphemia's temper would sanctify any means she should choose to employ. Her means, he kept repeating, were no business of his, and the essence of his admiration ought to be to respect her freedom; but he felt as if he should turn away into a world out of which most of the joy had departed, if her freedom, after all, should spare him only a murmured 'Thank you.'

When he called again he found to his vexation that he was to run the gauntlet of Madame Clairin's officious hospitality. It was one of the first mornings of perfect summer, and the drawing-room, through the open windows, was flooded with a sweet confusion of odors and bird-notes which filled him with the hope that Madame de Mauves would come out and spend half the day in the forest. But Madame Clairin, with her hair not yet dressed, emerged like a brassy discord in a maze of melody.

At the same moment the servant returned with Euphemia's regrets; she was indisposed and unable to see Mr Longmore. The young man knew that he looked disappointed, and that Madame Clairin was observing him, and this consciousness impelled him to give her a glance of almost aggressive frigidity. This was apparently what she desired. She wished to throw him off his balance, and, if he was not mistaken, she had the means.

'Put down your hat, Mr Longmore,' she said, 'and be polite for once. You were not at all polite the other day when I asked you that friendly question about the state of your heart.'

'I have no heart – to talk about,' said Longmore, uncompromisingly.

'As well say you've none at all. I advise you to cultivate a little eloquence; you may have use for it. That was not an idle question of mine; I don't ask idle questions. For a couple of months now that you've been coming and going among us, it seems to me that you have had very few to answer of any sort.'

'I have certainly been very well treated,' said Longmore.

Madame Clairin was silent a moment, and then – 'Have you never felt disposed to ask any?' she demanded.

Her look, her tone, were so charged with roundabout meanings that it seemed to Longmore as if even to understand her would savor of dishonest complicity. 'What is it you have to tell me?' he asked, frowning and blushing.

Madame Clairin flushed. It is rather hard, when you come bearing yourself very much as the sibyl when she came to the Roman king,[5] to be treated as something worse than a vulgar gossip. 'I might tell you, Mr Longmore,' she said, 'that you have

as bad a *ton* as any young man I ever met. Where have you lived,
– what are your ideas? I wish to call your attention to a fact which
it takes some delicacy to touch upon. You have noticed, I suppose,
that my sister-in-law is not the happiest woman in the world.'

Longmore assented with a gesture.

Madame Clairin looked slightly disappointed at his want of
enthusiasm. Nevertheless – 'You have formed, I suppose,' she
continued, 'your conjectures on the causes of her – dissatisfaction.'

'Conjecture has been superfluous. I have seen the causes – or at
least a specimen of them – with my own eyes.'

'I know perfectly what you mean. My brother, in a single word,
is in love with another woman. I don't judge him; I don't judge
my sister-in-law. I permit myself to say that in her position I would
have managed otherwise. I would have kept my husband's affection, or I would have frankly done without it, before this. But my
sister is an odd compound; I don't profess to understand her.
Therefore it is, in a measure, that I appeal to you, her fellow-
countryman. Of course you'll be surprised at my way of looking at
the matter, and I admit that it's a way in use only among people
whose family traditions compel them to take a superior view of
things.' Madame Clairin paused, and Longmore wondered where
her family traditions were going to lead her.

'Listen,' she went on.'There has never been a De Mauves who
has not given his wife the right to be jealous. We know our history
for ages back, and the fact is established. It's a shame if you like,
but it's something to have a shame with such a pedigree. The De
Mauves are real Frenchmen, and their wives – I may say it – have
been worthy of them. You may see all their portraits in our
Château de Mauves; every one of them an "injured" beauty, but
not one of them hanging her head. Not one of them had the bad
taste to be jealous, and yet not one in a dozen was guilty of an
escapade, – not one of them was talked about. There's good sense
for you! How they managed – go and look at the dusky, faded
canvases and pastels, and ask. They were femmes d'esprit. When
they had a headache, they put on a little rouge and came to supper
as usual; and when they had a heart-ache, they put a little rouge
on their hearts. These are fine traditions, and it doesn't seem to
me fair that a little American bourgeoise should come in and

interrupt them, and should hang her photograph, with her obstinate little *air penché*,[6] in the gallery of our shrewd fine ladies. A De
Mauves must be a De Mauves. When she married my brother, I
don't suppose she took him for a member of a *societé de bonnes
œuvres*. I don't say we're right; who is right? But we're as history
has made us, and if any one is to change, it had better be Madame
de Mauves herself.' Again Madame Clairin paused and opened and
closed her fan. 'Let her conform!' she said, with amazing audacity.

Longmore's reply was ambiguous; he simply said, 'Ah!'

Madame Clairin's pious retrospect had apparently imparted an
honest zeal to her indignation. 'For a long time,' she continued,
'my sister has been taking the attitude of an injured woman,
affecting a disgust with the world, and shutting herself up to read
the "Imitation."[7] I've never remarked on her conduct, but I've
quite lost patience with it. When a woman with her prettiness
lets her husband wander, she deserves her fate. I don't wish you
to agree with me – on the contrary; but I call such a woman a
goose. She must have bored him to death. What has passed
between them for many months needn't concern us; what provocation my sister has had – monstrous, if you wish – what ennui
my brother has suffered. It's enough that a week ago, just after
you had ostensibly gone to Brussels, something happened to
produce an explosion. She found a letter in his pocket – a
photograph – a trinket – *que sais-je?* At any rate, the scene was
terrible. I didn't listen at the keyhole, and I don't know what
was said; but I have reason to believe that my brother was called
to account as I fancy none of his ancestors have ever been, – even
by injured sweethearts.'

Longmore had leaned forward in silent attention with his elbows
on his knees, and instinctively he dropped his face into his hands.
'Ah, poor woman!' he groaned.

'Voilà!' said Madame Clairin. 'You pity her.'

'Pity her?' cried Longmore, looking up with ardent eyes and
forgetting the spirit of Madame Clairin's narrative in the miserable
facts. 'Don't you?'

'A little. But I'm not acting sentimentally; I'm acting politically.
I wish to arrange things, – to see my brother free to do as he
chooses, – to see Euphemia contented. Do you understand me?'

'Very well, I think. You're the most immoral person I've lately had the privilege of conversing with.'

Madame Clairin shrugged her shoulders. 'Possibly. When was there a great politician who was not immoral?'

'Nay,' said Longmore in the same tone. 'You're too superficial to be a great politician. You don't begin to know anything about Madame de Mauves.'

Madame Clairin inclined her head to one side, eyed Longmore sharply, mused a moment, and then smiled with an excellent imitation of intelligent compassion. 'It's not in my interest to contradict you.'

'It would be in your interest to learn, Madame Clairin,' the young man went on with unceremonious candor, 'what honest men most admire in a woman, – and to recognize it when you see it.'

Longmore certainly did injustice to her talents for diplomacy, for she covered her natural annoyance at this sally with a pretty piece of irony. 'So you *are* in love!' she quietly exclaimed.

Longmore was silent awhile. 'I wonder if you would understand me,' he said at last, 'if I were to tell you that I have for Madame de Mauves the most devoted friendship?'

'You underrate my intelligence. But in that case you ought to exert your influence to put an end to these painful domestic scenes.'

'Do you suppose,' cried Longmore, 'that she talks to me about her domestic scenes?'

Madame Clairin stared. 'Then your friendship isn't returned?' And as Longmore turned away, shaking his head, – 'Now, at least,' she added, 'she will have something to tell you. I happen to know the upshot of my brother's last interview with his wife.' Longmore rose to his feet as a sort of protest against the indelicacy of the position into which he was being forced; but all that made him tender made him curious, and she caught in his averted eyes an expression which prompted her to strike her blow. 'My brother is monstrously in love with a certain person in Paris; of course he ought not to be; but he wouldn't be a De Mauves if he were not. It was this unsanctified passion that spoke. "Listen madam," he cried at last: "let us live like people who understand life! It's

260

unpleasant to be forced to say such things outright, but you have a way of bringing one down to the rudiments. I'm faithless, I'm heartless, I'm brutal, I'm everything horrible, – it's understood. Take your revenge, console yourself; you're too pretty a woman to have anything to complain of. Here's a handsome young man sighing himself into a consumption for you. Listen to the poor fellow, and you'll find that virtue is none the less becoming for being good-natured. You'll see that it's not after all such a doleful world, and that there is even an advantage in having the most impudent of husbands."' Madame Clairin paused; Longmore had turned very pale. 'You may believe it,' she said; 'the speech took place in my presence; things were done in order. And now, Mr Longmore,' – this with a smile which he was too troubled at the moment to appreciate, but which he remembered later with a kind of awe, – 'we count upon you!'

'He said this to her, face to face, as you say it to me now?' Longmore asked slowly, after a silence.

'Word for word, and with the greatest politeness.'

'And Madame de Mauves – what did she say?'

Madame Clairin smiled again. 'To such a speech as that a woman says – nothing. She had been sitting with a piece of needlework, and I think she had not seen her husband since their quarrel the day before. He came in with the gravity of an ambassador, and I'm sure that when he made his *demande en mariage* his manner was not more respectful. He only wanted white gloves!' said Madame Clairin. 'Euphemia sat silent a few moments drawing her stitches, and then without a word, without a glance, she walked out of the room. It was just what she should have done!'

'Yes,' Longmore repeated, 'it was just what she should have done.'

'And I, left alone with my brother, do you know what I said?'

Longmore shook his head. '*Mauvais sujet!*' he suggested.

'"You've done me the honor," I said, "to take this step in my presence. I don't pretend to qualify it. You know what you're about, and it's your own affair. But you may confide in my discretion." Do you think he has had reason to complain of it?' She received no answer; Longmore was slowly turning away and passing his gloves mechanically round the band of his hat. 'I hope,' she cried, 'you're not going to start for Brussels!'

Plainly, Longmore was deeply disturbed, and Madame Clairin might flatter herself on the success of her plea for old-fashioned manners. And yet there was something that left her more puzzled than satisfied in the reflective tone with which he answered, 'No, I shall remain here for the present.' The processes of his mind seemed provokingly subterranean, and she would have fancied for a moment that he was linked with her sister in some monstrous conspiracy of asceticism.

'Come this evening,' she boldly resumed. 'The rest will take care of itself. Meanwhile I shall take the liberty of telling my sister-in-law that I have repeated – in short, that I have put you *au fait*.'

Longmore started and colored, and she hardly knew whether he was going to assent or demur. 'Tell her what you please. Nothing you can tell her will affect her conduct.'

'Voyons! Do you mean to tell me that a woman, young, pretty, sentimental, neglected – insulted, if you will – ? I see you don't believe it. Believe simply in your own opportunity! But for heaven's sake, if it's to lead anywhere, don't come back with that *visage de croquemort*.[8] You look as if you were going to bury your heart, – not to offer it to a pretty woman. You're much better when you smile. Come, do yourself justice.'

'Yes,' he said, 'I must do myself justice.' And abruptly, with a bow, he took his departure.

VII

He felt, when he found himself unobserved, in the open air, that he must plunge into violent action, walk fast and far, and defer the opportunity for thought. He strode away into the forest, swinging his cane, throwing back his head, gazing away into the verdurous vistas, and following the road without a purpose. He felt immensely excited, but he could hardly have said whether his emotion was a pain or a joy. It was joyous as all increase of freedom is joyous; something seemed to have been knocked down across his path; his destiny appeared to have rounded a cape and brought him into sight of an open sea. But his freedom resolved itself somehow into the need of despising all mankind, with a single exception; and the fact of Madame de Mauves inhabiting a planet contaminated by the presence of this baser multitude kept his elation from seeming a pledge of ideal bliss.

But she was there, and circumstance now forced them to be intimate. She had ceased to have what men call a secret for him, and this fact itself brought with it a sort of rapture. He had no prevision that he should 'profit,' in the vulgar sense, by the extraordinary position into which they had been thrown; it might be but a cruel trick of destiny to make hope a harsher mockery and renunciation a keener suffering. But above all this rose the conviction that she could do nothing that would not deepen his admiration.

It was this feeling that circumstance – unlovely as it was in itself – was to force the beauty of her character into more perfect relief, that made him stride along as if he were celebrating a kind of spiritual festival. He rambled at random for a couple of hours, and found at last that he had left the forest behind him and had wandered into an unfamiliar region. It was a perfectly rural scene, and the still summer day gave it a charm for which its meagre elements but half accounted.

Longmore thought he had never seen anything so characteristically French; all the French novels seemed to have described it, all the French landscapists to have painted it. The fields and trees were of a cool metallic green; the grass looked as if it might stain your trousers, and the foliage your hands. The clear light had a sort of mild grayness; the sunbeams were of silver rather than gold. A great red-roofed, high-stacked farm-house, with white-washed walls and a straggling yard, surveyed the high road, on one side, from behind a transparent curtain of poplars. A narrow stream, half choked with emerald rushes and edged with gray aspens, occupied the opposite quarter. The meadows rolled and sloped away gently to the low horizon, which was barely concealed by the continuous line of clipped and marshalled trees. The prospect was not rich, but it had a frank homeliness which touched the young man's fancy. It was full of light atmosphere and diffused sunshine, and if it was prosaic, it was soothing.

Longmore was disposed to walk further, and he advanced along the road beneath the poplars. In twenty minutes he came to a village which straggled away to the right, among orchards and *potagers*.[9] On the left, at a stone's throw from the road, stood a little pink-faced inn, which reminded him that he had not breakfasted, having left home with a prevision of hospitality from Madame de Mauves. In the inn he found a brick-tiled parlor and a hostess in sabots and a white cap, whom, over the omelette she speedily served him, – borrowing license from the bottle of sound red wine which accompanied it, – he assured that she was a true artist. To reward his compliment, she invited him to smoke his cigar in her little garden behind the house.

Here he found a *tonnelle*[10] and a view of ripening crops, stretching down to the stream. The tonnelle was rather close, and he preferred to lounge on a bench against the pink wall, in the sun, which was not too hot. Here, as he rested and gazed and mused, he fell into a train of thought which, in an indefinable fashion, was a soft influence from the scene about him. His heart, which had been beating fast for the past three hours, gradually checked its pulses and left him looking at life with a rather more level gaze. The homely tavern sounds coming out through the open windows, the sunny stillness of the fields and crops, which covered so much vigorous natural life, suggested very little that was transcendental, had very little to say about renunciation, – nothing at all about spiritual zeal. They seemed to utter a message from plain ripe nature, to express the unperverted reality of things, to say that the common lot is not brilliantly amusing, and that the part of wisdom is to grasp frankly at experience, lest you miss it altogether. What reason there was for his falling a-wondering after this whether a deeply wounded heart might be soothed and healed by such a scene, it would be difficult to explain; certain it is that, as he sat there, he had a waking dream of an unhappy woman strolling by the slow-flowing stream before him, and pulling down the blossoming boughs in the orchards. He mused and mused, and at last found himself feeling angry that he could not somehow think worse of Madame de Mauves, – or at any rate think otherwise. He could fairly claim that in a sentimental way he asked very little of life, – he made modest demands on passion; why then should his only passion be born to ill-fortune? why should his first

– his last – glimpse of positive happiness be so indissolubly linked with renunciation?

It is perhaps because, like many spirits of the same stock, he had in his composition a lurking principle of asceticism to whose authority he had ever paid an unquestioning respect, that he now felt all the vehemence of rebellion. To renounce – to renounce again – to renounce forever – was this all that youth and longing and resolve were meant for? Was experience to be muffled and mutilated, like an indecent picture? Was a man to sit and deliberately condemn his future to be the blank memory of a regret, rather than the long reverberation of a joy? Sacrifice? The word was a trap for minds muddled by fear, an ignoble refuge of weakness. To insist now seemed not to dare, but simply to be, to live on possible terms.

His hostess came out to hang a cloth to dry on the hedge, and, though her guest was sitting quietly enough, she seemed to see in his kindled eyes a flattering testimony to the quality of her wine.

As she turned back into the house, she was met by a young man whom Longmore observed in spite of his preoccupation. He was evidently a member of that jovial fraternity of artists whose very shabbiness has an affinity with the element of picturesqueness and unexpectedness in life which provokes a great deal of unformulated envy among people foredoomed to be respectable.

Longmore was struck first with his looking like a very clever man, and then with his looking like a very happy one. The combination, as it was expressed in his face, might have arrested the attention of even a less cynical philosopher. He had a slouched hat and a blond beard, a light easel under one arm, and an unfinished sketch in oils under the other.

He stopped and stood talking for some moments to the landlady with a peculiarly good-humored smile. They were discussing the possibilities of dinner; the hostess enumerated some very savory ones, and he nodded briskly, assenting to everything. It couldn't be, Longmore thought, that he found such soft contentment in the prospect of lamb chops and spinach and a *tarte à la crême*. When dinner had been ordered, he turned up his sketch, and the good woman fell a-wondering and looking off at the spot by the streamside where he had made it.

Was it his work, Longmore wondered, that made him so happy? Was a strong talent the best thing in the world? The landlady went back to her kitchen, and the young painter stood as if he were waiting for something, beside the gate which opened upon the path across the fields. Longmore sat brooding and asking himself whether it was better to cultivate an art than to cultivate a passion. Before he had answered the question the painter had grown tired of waiting. He picked up a pebble, tossed it lightly into an upper window, and called, 'Claudine!'

Claudine appeared; Longmore heard her at the window, bidding the young man to have patience. 'But I'm losing my light,' he said; 'I must have my shadows in the same place as yesterday.'

'Go without me, then,' Claudine answered; 'I will join you in ten minutes.' Her voice was fresh and young; it seemed to say to Longmore that she was as happy as her companion.

'Don't forget the Chénier,'[11]cried the young man; and turning away, he passed out of the gate and followed the path across the fields until he disappeared among the trees by the side of the stream. Who was Claudine? Longmore vaguely wondered; and was she as pretty as her voice? Before long he had a chance to satisfy himself; she came out of the house with her hat and parasol, prepared to follow her companion. She had on a pink muslin dress and a little white hat, and she was as pretty as a Frenchwoman needs to be to be pleasing. She had a clear brown skin and a bright dark eye, and a step which seemed to keep time to some slow music, heard only by herself. Her hands were encumbered with various articles which she seemed to intend to carry with her. In one arm she held her parasol and a large roll of needlework, and in the other a shawl and a heavy white umbrella, such as painters use for sketching. Meanwhile she was trying to thrust into her pocket a paper-covered volume which Longmore saw to be the Poems of André Chénier; but in the effort she dropped the large umbrella, and uttered a half-smiling exclamation of disgust. Longmore stepped forward with a bow and picked up the umbrella, and as she, protesting her gratitude, put out her hand to take it, it seemed to him that she was unbecomingly overburdened.

'You have too much to carry,' he said, 'you must let me help you.'

'You're very good, monsieur,' she answered. 'My husband always forgets something. He can do nothing without his umbrella. He is *d'une étourderie –* '

'You must allow me to carry the umbrella,' Longmore said. 'It's too heavy for a lady.'

She assented, after many compliments to his politeness; and he walked by her side into the meadow. She went lightly and rapidly, picking her steps and glancing forward to catch a glimpse of her husband. She was graceful, she was charming, she had an air of decision and yet of sweetness, and it seemed to Longmore that a young artist would work none the worse for having her seated at his side, reading Chénier's iambics. They were newly married, he supposed, and evidently their path of life had none of the mocking crookedness of some others. They asked little; but what need one ask more than such quiet summer days, with the creature one loves, by a shady stream, with art and books and a wide, unshadowed horizon? To spend such a morning, to stroll back to dinner in the red-tiled parlor of the inn, to ramble away again as the sun got low, – all this was a vision of bliss which floated before him, only to torture him with a sense of the impossible. All Frenchwomen are not coquettes, he remarked, as he kept pace with his companion. She uttered a word now and then, for politeness' sake, but she never looked at him, and seemed not in the least to care that he was a well-favored young man. She cared for nothing but the young artist in the shabby coat and the slouched hat, and for discovering where he had set up his easel.

This was soon done. He was encamped under the trees, close to the stream, and, in the diffused green shade of the little wood, seemed to be in no immediate need of his umbrella. He received a vivacious rebuke, however, for forgetting it, and was informed of what he owed to Longmore's complaisance. He was duly grateful; he thanked our hero warmly, and offered him a seat on the grass. But Longmore felt like a marplot, and lingered only long enough to glance at the young man's sketch, and to see it was a very clever rendering of the silvery stream and the vivid green rushes. The young wife had spread her shawl on the grass at the base of a tree, and meant to seat herself when Longmore had gone, and murmur Chénier's verses to the music of the gurgling river. Longmore looked awhile from one to the other, barely stifled a sigh, bade them good morning, and took his departure.

He knew neither where to go nor what to do; he seemed afloat on the sea of ineffectual longing. He strolled slowly back to the inn, and in the doorway met the landlady coming back from the butcher's with the lamb chops for the dinner of her lodgers.

'Monsieur has made the acquaintance of the *dame* of our young painter,' she said with a broad smile, – a smile too broad for malicious meanings. 'Monsieur has perhaps seen the young man's picture. It appears that he has a great deal of talent.'

'His picture was very pretty,' said Longmore, 'but his *dame* was prettier still.'

'She's a very nice little woman; but I pity her all the more.'

'I don't see why she's to be pitied,' said Longmore; 'they seem a very happy couple.'

The landlady gave a knowing nod.

'Don't trust to it, monsieur! Those artists, – *ça n'a pas de principes!* From one day to another he can plant her there! I know them, *allez*. I've had them here very often; one year with one, another year with another.'

Longmore was puzzled for a moment. Then, 'You mean she's not his wife?' he asked.

She shrugged her shoulders. 'What shall I tell you? They are not *des hommes sérieux*, those gentlemen! They don't engage themselves for an eternity. It's none of my business, and I've no wish to speak ill of madame. She's a very nice little woman, and she loves her *jeune homme* to distraction.'

'Who is she?' asked Longmore. 'What do you know about her?'

'Nothing for certain; but it's my belief that she's better than he. I've even gone so far as to believe that she's a lady, – a true lady, – and that she has given up a great many things for him. I do the best I can for them, but I don't believe she's been obliged all her life to content herself with a dinner of two courses.' And she turned over her lamb chops tenderly, as if to say that though a good cook could imagine better things, yet if you could have but one course, lamb chops had much in their favor. 'I shall cook them with bread crumbs. *Voilà les femmes, monsieur!*'

Longmore turned away with the feeling that women were indeed a measureless mystery, and that it was hard to say whether there was greater beauty in their strength or in their weakness. He walked back to Saint-Germain, more slowly than he had come, with less philosophic resignation to any event, and more of the urgent egotism of the passion which philosophers call the supremely selfish one. Every now and then the episode of the happy young painter and the charming woman who had given up a great many things for him rose vividly in his mind, and seemed to mock his moral unrest like some obtrusive vision of unattainable bliss.

The landlady's gossip cast no shadow on its brightness; her voice seemed that of the vulgar chorus of the uninitiated, which stands always ready with its gross prose rendering of the inspired passages in human action. Was it possible a man could take *that* from a woman, – take all that lent lightness to that other woman's footstep and intensity to her glance, – and not give her the absolute certainty of a devotion as unalterable as the process of the sun? Was it possible that such a rapturous union had the seeds of trouble, – that the charm of such a perfect accord could be broken by anything but death? Longmore felt an immense desire to cry out a thousand times 'No!' for it seemed to him at last that he was somehow spiritually the same as the young painter, and that the latter's companion had the soul of Euphemia de Mauves.

The heat of the sun, as he walked along, became oppressive and when he re-entered the forest he turned aside into the deepest shade he could find, and stretched himself on the mossy ground at the foot of a great beech. He lay for a while staring up into the verdurous dusk overhead, and trying to conceive Madame de Mauves hastening toward some quiet stream-side where he waited, as he had seen that trusting creature do an hour before. It would be hard to say how well he succeeded; but the effort soothed him rather than excited him, and as he had had a good deal both of moral and physical fatigue, he sank at last into a quiet sleep.

While he slept he had a strange, vivid dream. He seemed to be in a wood, very much like the one on which his eyes had lately closed; but the wood was divided by the murmuring stream he had left an hour before. He was walking up and down, he thought, restlessly and in intense expectation of some momentous event.

Suddenly, at a distance, through the trees, he saw the gleam of a woman's dress, and hurried forward to meet her. As he advanced he recognized her, but he saw at the same time that she was on the opposite bank of the river. She seemed at first not to notice him, but when they were opposite each other she stopped and looked at him very gravely and pityingly. She made him no motion that he should cross the stream, but he wished greatly to stand by her side. He knew the water was deep, and it seemed to him that he knew that he should have to plunge, and that he feared that when he rose to the surface she would have disappeared. Nevertheless, he was going to plunge, when a boat turned into the current from above and came swiftly toward them, guided by an oarsman, who was sitting so that they could not see his face. He brought the boat to the bank where Longmore stood; the latter stepped in, and with a few strokes they touched the opposite shore. Longmore got out, and, though he was sure he had crossed the stream, Madame de Mauves was not there. He turned with a kind of agony and saw that now she was on the other bank, – the one he had left. She gave him a grave, silent glance, and walked away up the stream. The boat and the boatman resumed their course, but after going a short distance they stopped, and the boatman turned back and looked at the still divided couple. Then Longmore recognized him, – just as he had recognized him a few days before at the café in the Bois de Boulogne.

VIII

He must have slept some time after he ceased dreaming, for he had no immediate memory of his dream. It came back to him later, after he had roused himself and had walked nearly home. No great ingenuity was needed to make it seem a rather striking allegory, and it haunted and oppressed him for the rest of the day. He took refuge, however, in his quickened conviction that the only sound policy in life is to grasp unsparingly at happiness; and it seemed no more than one of the vigorous measures dictated by such a policy, to return that evening to Madame de Mauves. And yet when he had decided to do so, and had carefully dressed himself, he felt an irresistible nervous tremor which made it easier to linger at his open window, wondering, with a strange mixture of dread and desire, whether Madame Clairin had told her sister-in-law that she had told him. . . His presence now might be simply a gratuitous cause of suffering; and yet his absence might seem to imply that it was in the power of circumstances to make them ashamed to meet each other's eyes. He sat a long time with his head in his hands, lost in a painful confusion of hopes and questionings. He felt at moments as if he could throttle Madame Clairin, and yet he could not help asking himself whether it was not possible that she might have done him a service. It was late when he left the hotel, and as he entered the gate of the other house his heart was beating so that he was sure his voice would show it.

The servant ushered him into the drawing-room, which was empty, with the lamp burning low. But the long windows were open, and their light curtains swaying in a soft, warm wind, and Longmore stepped out upon the terrace. There he found Madame de Mauves alone, slowly pacing up and down. She was dressed in white, very simply, and her hair was arranged, not as she usually wore it, but in a single loose coil, like that of a person unprepared for company.

She stopped when she saw Longmore, seemed slightly startled, uttered an exclamation, and stood waiting for him to speak. He looked at her, tried to say something, but found no words. He knew it was awkward, it was offensive, to stand silent, gazing, but he could not say what was suitable, and he dared not say what he wished.

Her face was indistinct in the dim light, but he could see that her eyes were fixed on him, and he wondered what they expressed. Did they warn him, did they plead or did they confess to a sense of provocation? For an instant his head swam; he felt as if it would make all things clear to stride forward and fold her in his arms. But a moment later he was still standing looking at her; he had not moved; he knew that she had spoken, but he had not understood her.

'You were here this morning,' she continued, and now, slowly, the meaning of her words came to him. 'I had a bad headache and had to shut myself up.' She spoke in her usual voice.

Longmore mastered his agitation and answered her without betraying himself: 'I hope you are better now.'

'Yes, thank you, I'm better – much better.'

He was silent a moment, and she moved away to a chair and seated herself. After a pause he followed her and stood before her, leaning against the balustrade of the terrace. 'I hoped you might have been able to come out for the morning into the forest. I went alone; it was a lovely day, and I took a long walk.'

'It was a lovely day,' she said absently, and sat with her eyes lowered, slowly opening and closing her fan. Longmore, as he watched her, felt more and more sure that her sister-in-law had seen her since her interview with him; that her attitude toward him was changed. It was this same something that chilled the ardor with which he had come, or at least converted the dozen passionate speeches which kept rising to his lips into a kind of reverential silence. No, certainly, he could not clasp her to his arms now, any more than some early worshipper could have clasped the marble statue in his temple. But Longmore's statue spoke at last, with a full human voice, and even with a shade of human hesitation. She looked up, and it seemed to him that her eyes shone through the dusk.

'I'm very glad you came this evening,' she said. 'I have a particular reason for being glad. I half expected you, and yet I thought it possible you might not come.'

'As I have been feeling all day,' Longmore answered, 'it was impossible I should not come. I have spent the day in thinking of you.'

She made no immediate reply, but continued to open and close her fan thoughtfully. At last, – 'I have something to say to you,' she said abruptly. 'I want you to know to a certainty that I have a very high opinion of you.' Longmore started and shifted his position. To what was she coming? But he said nothing, and she went on.

'I take a great interest in you; there's no reason why I should not say it, – I have a great friendship for you.'

He began to laugh; he hardly knew why, unless that this seemed the very mockery of coldness. But she continued without heeding him.

'You know, I suppose, that a great disappointment always implies a great confidence – a great hope?'

'I have hoped,' he said, 'hoped strongly; but doubtless never rationally enough to have a right to bemoan my disappointment.'

'You do yourself injustice. I have such confidence in your reason, that I should be greatly disappointed if I were to find it wanting.'

'I really almost believe that you are amusing yourself at my expense,' cried Longmore. 'My reason? Reason is a mere word! The only reality in the world is *feeling!*'

She rose to her feet and looked at him gravely. His eyes by this time were accustomed to the imperfect light, and he could see that her look was reproachful, and yet that it was beseechingly kind. She shook her head impatiently, and laid her fan upon his arm with a strong pressure.

'If that were so, it would be a weary world. I know your feeling, however, nearly enough. You needn't try to express it. It's enough that it gives me the right to ask a favor of you, – to make an urgent, a solemn request.'

'Make it; I listen.'

'*Don't disappoint me.* If you don't understand me now, you will to-morrow, or very soon. When I said just now that I had a very high opinion of you, I meant it very seriously. It was not a vain compliment. I believe that there is no appeal one may make to your generosity which can remain long unanswered. If this were to happen, – if I were to find you selfish where I thought you generous, narrow where I thought you large,' – and she spoke slowly, with her voice lingering with emphasis on each of these words, – 'vulgar where I thought you rare, – I should think worse of human nature. I should suffer, – I should suffer keenly. I should say to myself in the dull days of the future, "There was one man who might have done so and so; and he, too, failed." But this shall not be. You have made too good an impression on me not to make the very best. If you wish to please me forever, there's a way.'

She was standing close to him, with her dress touching him, her eyes fixed on his. As she went on her manner grew strangely intense, and she had the singular appearance of a woman preaching reason with a kind of passion. Longmore was confused, dazzled, almost bewildered. The intention of her words was all remonstrance, refusal, dismissal; but her presence there, so close, so urgent, so personal, seemed a distracting contradiction of it. She had never been so lovely. In her white dress, with her pale face and deeply lighted eyes, she seemed the very spirit of the summer night. When she had ceased speaking, she drew a long breath; Longmore felt it on his cheek, and it stirred in his whole being a sudden, rapturous conjecture. Were her words in their soft severity a mere delusive spell, meant to throw into relief her almost ghostly beauty, and was this the only truth, the only reality, the only law?

He closed his eyes and felt that she was watching him, not without pain and perplexity herself. He looked at her again, met her own eyes, and saw a tear in each of them. Then this last suggestion of his desire seemed to die away with a stifled murmur, and her beauty, more and more radiant in the darkness, rose before him as a symbol of something vague which was yet more beautiful than itself.

'I may understand you to-morrow,' he said, 'but I don't understand you now.'

'And yet I took counsel with myself to-day and asked myself how I had best speak to you. On one side, I might have refused to see you at all.' Longmore made a violent movement, and she added: 'In that case I should have written to you. I might see you, I thought, and simply say to you that there were excellent reasons why we should part, and that I begged this visit should be your last. This I inclined to do; what made me decide otherwise was – simply friendship! I said to myself that I should be glad to remember in future days, not that I had dismissed you, but that you had gone away out of the fulness of your own wisdom.'

'The fulness – the fulness!' cried Longmore.

'I'm prepared, if necessary,' Madame de Mauves continued after a pause, 'to fall back upon my strict right. But, as I said before, I shall be greatly disappointed, if I am obliged to.'

'When I hear you say that,' Longmore answered, 'I feel so angry, so horribly irritated, that I wonder it is not easy to leave you without more words.'

'If you should go away in anger, this idea of mine about our parting would be but half realized. No, I don't want to think of you as angry; I don't want even to think of you as making a serious sacrifice. I want to think of you as – '

'As a creature who never existed, – who never can exist! A creature who knew you without loving you, – who left you without regretting you!'

She turned impatiently away and walked to the other end of the terrace. When she came back, he saw that her impatience had become a cold sternness. She stood before him again, looking at him from head to foot, in deep reproachfulness, almost in scorn. Beneath her glance he felt a kind of shame. He colored; she observed it and withheld something she was about to say. She turned away again, walked to the other end of the terrace, and stood there looking away into the garden. It seemed to him that she had guessed he understood her, and slowly – slowly – half as the fruit of his vague self-reproach, – he did understand her. She was giving him a chance to do gallantly what it seemed unworthy of both of them he should do meanly.

She liked him, she must have liked him greatly, to wish so to spare him, to go to the trouble of conceiving an ideal of conduct for him. With this sense of her friendship, – her strong friendship she had just called it, – Longmore's soul rose with a new flight, and suddenly felt itself breathing a clearer air. The words ceased to seem a mere bribe to his ardor; they were charged with ardor themselves; they were a present happiness. He moved rapidly toward her with a feeling that this was something he might immediately enjoy.

They were separated by two thirds of the length of the terrace, and he had to pass the drawing-room window. As he did so he started with an exclamation. Madame Clairin stood posted there, watching him. Conscious, apparently, that she might be suspected of eavesdropping, she stepped forward with a smile and looked from Longmore to his hostess.

'Such a tête-à-tête as that,' she said, 'one owes no apology for interrupting. One ought to come in for good manners.'

Madame de Mauves turned round, but she answered nothing. She looked straight at Longmore. And her eyes had extraordinary eloquence. He was not exactly sure, indeed, what she meant them to say; but they seemed to say plainly something of this kind; 'Call it what you will, what you have to urge upon me is the thing which this woman can best conceive. What I ask of you is something she can't!' They seemed, somehow, to beg him to suffer her to be herself, and to intimate that that self was as little as possible like Madame Clairin. He felt an immense answering desire not to do anything which would seem natural to this lady. He had laid his hat and cane on the parapet of the terrace. He took them up, offered his hand to Madame de Mauves with a simple good night, bowed silently to Madame Clairin, and departed.

IX

He went home and without lighting his candle flung himself on his bed. But he got no sleep till morning; he lay hour after hour tossing, thinking, wondering; his mind had never been so active. It seemed to him that Euphemia had laid on him in those last moments an inspiring commission, and that she had expressed herself almost as largely as if she had listened assentingly to an assurance of his love. It was neither easy nor delightful thoroughly to understand her; but little by little her perfect meaning sank into his mind and soothed it with a sense of opportunity, which somehow stifled his sense of loss. For, to begin with, she meant that she could love him in no degree nor contingency, in no imaginable future. This was absolute; he felt that he could alter it no more than he could transpose the constellations he lay gazing at through his open window. He wondered what it was, in the background of her life, that she grasped so closely: a sense of duty, unquenchable to the end? a love that no offence could trample out? 'Good heavens!' he thought, 'is the world so rich in the purest pearls of passion, that such tenderness as that can be wasted forever, – poured away without a sigh into bottomless darkness?' Had she, in spite of the detestable present, some precious memory which contained the germ of a shrinking hope? Was she prepared to submit to everything and yet to believe? Was it strength, was it weakness, was it a vulgar fear, was it conviction, conscience, constancy?

Longmore sank back with a sigh and an oppressive feeling that it was vain to guess at such a woman's motives. He only felt that those of Madame de Mauves were buried deep in her soul, and that they must be of some fine temper, not of a base one. He had a dim, overwhelming sense of a sort of invulnerable constancy being the supreme law of her character, – a constancy which still found a foothold among crumbling ruins.'She has loved once,' he said to himself as he rose and wandered to his window; 'that's forever. Yes, yes, – if she loved again she would be *common*.' He stood for a long time looking out into the starlit silence of the town and the forest, and thinking of what life would have been if *his* constancy had met hers unpledged. But life was this, now, and he must live. It was living keenly to stand there with a petition from such a woman to revolve. He was not to disappoint her, he was to justify a conception which it had beguiled her weariness to shape. Longmore's imagination swelled; he threw back his head and seemed to be looking for Madame de Mauves's conception among the blinking, mocking stars. But it came to him rather on the mild night-wind, as it wandered in over the house-tops which covered the rest of so many heavy human hearts. What she asked he felt that she was asking, not for her own sake (she feared nothing, she needed nothing), but for that of his own happiness and his own character. He must assent to destiny. Why else was he young and strong, intelligent and resolute? He must not give it to her to reproach him with thinking that she had a moment's attention for his love, – to plead, to argue, to break off in bitterness; he must see everything from above, her indifference and his own ardor; he must prove his strength, he must do the handsome thing; he must decide that the handsome thing was to submit to the inevitable, to be supremely delicate, to spare her all pain, to stifle his passion, to ask no compensation, to depart without delay and try to believe that wisdom is its own reward. All this, neither more nor less, it was a matter of friendship with Madame de Mauves to expect of him. And what should he gain by it? He should have pleased her! . . . He flung himself on his bed again, fell asleep at last, and slept till morning.

Before noon the next day he had made up his mind that he would leave Saint-Germain at once. It seemed easier to leave without seeing her, and yet if he might ask a grain of 'compensation,' it would be five minutes face to face with her. He passed a restless day. Wherever he went he seemed to see her standing before him in the dusky halo of evening, and looking at him with an air of still negation more intoxicating than the most passionate self-surrender. He must certainly go, and yet it was hideously hard. He compromised and went to Paris to spend the rest of the day. He strolled along the boulevards and looked at the shops, sat awhile in the Tuileries gardens and looked at the shabby unfortunates for whom this only was nature and summer; but simply felt, as a result of it all, that it was a very dusty, dreary, lonely world into which Madame de Mauves was turning him away.

In a sombre mood he made his way back to the boulevards and sat down at a table on the great plain of hot asphalt, before a café. Night came on, the lamps were lighted, the tables near him found occupants, and Paris began to wear that peculiar evening look of hers which seems to say, in the flare of windows and theatre doors, and the muffled rumble of swift-rolling carriages, that this is no world for you unless you have your pockets lined and your scruples drugged. Longmore, however, had neither scruples nor desires; he looked at the swarming city for the first time with an easy sense of repaying its indifference. Before long a carriage drove up to the pavement directly in front of him, and remained standing for several minutes without its occupant getting out. It was one of those neat, plain coupés, drawn by a single powerful horse, in which one is apt to imagine a pale, handsome woman, buried among silk cushions, and yawning as she sees the gas-lamps glittering in the gutters. At last the door opened and out stepped M. de Mauves. He stopped and leaned on the window for some time, talking in an excited manner to a person within. At last he gave a nod and the carriage rolled away. He stood swinging his cane and looking up and down the boulevard, with the air of a man fumbling, as one may say, with the loose change of time. He turned toward the café and was apparently, for want of anything better worth his attention, about to seat himself at one of the tables, when he perceived Longmore. He wavered an instant, and then, without a change in his nonchalant gait, strolled toward him with a bow and a vague smile.

It was the first time they had met since their encounter in the forest after Longmore's false start for Brussels. Madame Clairin's revelations, as we may call them, had not made the Baron especially present to his mind; he had another office for his emotions than disgust. But as M. de Mauves came toward him he felt deep in his heart that he abhorred him. He noticed, however, for the first time, a shadow upon the Baron's cool placidity, and his delight at finding that somewhere at last the shoe pinched *him*, mingled with his impulse to be as exasperatingly impenetrable as possible, enabled him to return the other's greeting with all his own self-possession.

M. de Mauves sat down, and the two men looked at each other across the table, exchanging formal greetings which did little to make their mutual scrutiny seem gracious. Longmore had no reason to suppose that the Baron knew of his sister's revelations. He was sure that M. de Mauves cared very little about his opinions, and yet he had a sense that there was that in his eyes which would have made the Baron change color if keener suspicion had helped him to read it. M. de Mauves did not change color, but he looked at Longmore with a half defiant intentness, which betrayed at once an irritating memory of the episode in the Bois de Boulogne, and such vigilant curiosity as was natural to a gentleman who had intrusted his 'honor' to another gentleman's magnanimity, – or to his artlessness. It would appear that Longmore seemed to the Baron to possess these virtues in rather scantier measure than a few days before; for the cloud deepened on his face, and he turned away and frowned as he lighted a cigar.

The person in the coupé, Longmore thought, whether or no the same person as the heroine of the episode of the Bois de Boulogne, was not a source of unalloyed delight. Longmore had dark blue eyes, of admirable lucidity, – truth-telling eyes which had in his childhood always made his harshest taskmasters smile at his nursery fibs. An observer watching the two men, and knowing something of their relations, would certainly have said that what he saw in those eyes must not a little have puzzled and tormented M. de Mauves. They judged him, they mocked him, they eluded him, they threatened him, they triumphed over him, they treated him as no pair of eyes had ever treated him. The Baron's scheme had been to make no one happy but himself, and here was Longmore already, if looks were to be trusted, primed for an enterprise more inspiring than the finest of his own achievements. Was this candid young barbarian but a *faux bonhomme* after all? He had puzzled the Baron before, and this was once too often.

M. de Mauves hated to seem preoccupied, and he took up the evening paper to help himself to look indifferent. As he glanced over it he uttered some cold commonplace on the political situation, which gave Longmore an easy opportunity of replying by an ironical sally which made him seem for the moment aggressively at his ease. And yet our hero was far from being master of the situation. The Baron's ill-humor did him good, so far as it pointed to a want of harmony with the lady in the coupé; but it disturbed him sorely as he began to suspect that it possibly meant jealousy of himself. It passed through his mind that jealousy is a passion with a double face, and that in some of its moods it bears a plausible likeness to affection. It recurred to him painfully that the Baron might grow ashamed of his political compact with his wife, and he felt that it would be far more tolerable in the future to think of his continued turpitude than of his repentance. The two men sat for half an hour exchanging stinted small-talk, the Baron feeling a nervous need of playing the spy, and Longmore indulging a ferocious relish of his discomfort. These rigid courtesies were interrupted however by the arrival of a friend of M. de Mauves, – a tall, pale, consumptive-looking dandy, who filled the air with the odor of heliotrope. He looked up and down the boulevard wearily, examined the Baron's toilet from head to foot, then surveyed his own in the same fashion, and at last announced languidly that the Duchess was in town! M. de Mauves must come with him to call; she had abused him dreadfully a couple of evenings before, – a sure sign she wanted to see him.

'I depend upon you,' said M. de Mauves's friend with an infantine drawl, 'to put her *en train.*'

M. de Mauves resisted, and protested that he was *d'une humeur massacrante;* but at last he allowed himself to be drawn to his feet, and stood looking awkwardly – awkwardly for M. de Mauves – at Longmore. 'You'll excuse me,' he said dryly; 'you, too, probably, have occupation for the evening?'

'None but to catch my train,' Longmore answered, looking at his watch.

'Ah, you go back to Saint-Germain?'

'In half an hour.'

M. de Mauves seemed on the point of disengaging himself from his companion's arm, which was locked in his own; but on the latter uttering some persuasive murmur, he lifted his hat stiffly and turned away.

Longmore packed his trunk the next day with dogged heroism and wandered off to the terrace, to try and beguile the restlessness with which he waited for evening; for he wished to see Madame de Mauves for the last time at the hour of long shadows and pale pink-reflected lights, as he had almost always seen her. Destiny, however, took no account of this humble plea for poetic justice; it was his fortune to meet her on the terrace sitting under a tree, alone. It was an hour when the place was almost empty; the day was warm, but as he took his place beside her a light breeze stirred the leafy edges on the broad circle of shadow in which she sat. She looked at him with candid anxiety, and he immediately told her that he should leave Saint-Germain that evening, – that he must bid her farewell. Her eye expanded and brightened for a moment as he spoke; but she said nothing and turned her glance away toward distant Paris, as it lay twinkling and flashing through its hot exhalations. 'I have a request to make of you,' he added. 'That you think of me as a man who has felt much and claimed little.'

She drew a long breath, which almost suggested pain. 'I can't think of you as unhappy. It's impossible. You have a life to lead, you have duties, talents, and interests. I shall hear of your career. And then,' she continued after a pause and with the deepest seriousness, 'one can't be unhappy through having a better opinion of a friend, instead of a worse.'

For a moment he failed to understand her. 'Do you mean that there can be varying degrees in my opinion of you?'

She rose and pushed away her chair. 'I mean,' she said quickly, 'that it's better to have done nothing in bitterness, – nothing in passion.' And she began to walk.

Longmore followed her, without answering. But he took off his hat and with his pocket-handkerchief wiped his forehead. 'Where shall you go? what shall you do?' he asked at last, abruptly.

'Do? I shall do as I've always done, – except perhaps that I shall go for a while to Auvergne.'

'I shall go to America. I have done with Europe for the present.'

She glanced at him as he walked beside her after he had spoken these words, and then bent her eyes for a long time on the ground. At last, seeing that she was going far, she stopped and put out her hand. 'Good by,' she said; 'may you have all the happiness you deserve!'

He took her hand and looked at her, but something was passing in him that made it impossible to return her hand's light pressure. Something of infinite value was floating past him, and he had taken an oath not to raise a finger to stop it. It was borne by the strong current of the world's great life and not of his own small one. Madame de Mauves disengaged her hand, gathered her shawl, and smiled at him almost as you would do at a child you should wish to encourage. Several moments later he was still standing watching her receding figure. When it had disappeared, he shook himself, walked rapidly back to his hotel, and without waiting for the evening train paid his bill and departed.

Later in the day M. de Mauves came into his wife's drawing-room, where she sat waiting to be summoned to dinner. He was dressed with a scrupulous freshness which seemed to indicate an intention of dining out. He walked up and down for some moments in silence, then rang the bell for a servant, and went out into the hall to meet him. He ordered the carriage to take him to the station, paused a moment with his hand on the knob of the door, dismissed the servant angrily as the latter lingered observing him, re-entered the drawing-room, resumed his restless walk, and at last stepped abruptly before his wife, who had taken up a book. 'May I ask the favor,' he said with evident effort, in spite of a forced smile of easy courtesy, 'of having a question answered?'

'It's a favor I never refused,' Madame de Mauves replied.

'Very true. Do you expect this evening a visit from Mr Longmore?'

'Mr Longmore,' said his wife, 'has left Saint-Germain.' M. de

Mauves started and his smile expired. 'Mr Longmore,' his wife continued, 'has gone to America.'

M. de Mauves stared a moment, flushed deeply, and turned away. Then recovering himself, – 'Had anything happened?' he asked, 'Had he a sudden call?'

But his question received no answer. At the same moment the servant threw open the door and announced dinner; Madame Clairin rustled in, rubbing her white hands, Madame de Mauves passed silently into the dining-room, and he stood frowning and wondering. Before long he went out upon the terrace and continued his uneasy walk. At the end of a quarter of an hour the servant came to inform him that the carriage was at the door. 'Send it away,' he said curtly. 'I shall not use it.' When the ladies had half finished dinner he went in and joined them, with a formal apology to his wife for his tardiness.

The dishes were brought back, but he hardly tasted them; on the other hand, he drank a great deal of wine. There was little talk; what there was, was supplied by Madame Clairin. Twice she saw her brother's eyes fixed on her own, over his wineglass, with a piercing, questioning glance. She replied by an elevation of the eyebrows, which did the office of a shrug of the shoulders. M. de Mauves was left alone to finish his wine; he sat over it for more than an hour, and let the darkness gather about him. At last the servant came in with a letter and lighted a candle. The letter was a telegram, which M. de Mauves, when he had read it, burnt at the candle. After five minutes' meditation, he wrote a message on the back of a visiting-card and gave it to the servant to carry to the office. The man knew quite as much as his master suspected about the lady to whom the telegram was addressed; but its contents puzzled him; they consisted of the single word, '*Impossible*.' As the evening passed without her brother reappearing in the drawing-room, Madame Clairin came to him where he sat, by his solitary candle. He took no notice of her presence for some time; but he was the one person to whom she allowed this license. At last, speaking in a peremptory tone, 'The American has gone home at an hour's notice,' he said. 'What does it mean?'

Madame Clairin now gave free play to the shrug she had been

obliged to suppress at the table. 'It means that I have a sister-in-law whom I haven't the honor to understand.'

He said nothing more, and silently allowed her to depart, as if it had been her duty to provide him with an explanation and he was disgusted with her levity. When she had gone, he went into the garden and walked up and down, smoking. He saw his wife sitting alone on the terrace, but remained below strolling along the narrow paths. He remained a long time. It became late and Madame de Mauves disappeared. Toward midnight he dropped upon a bench, tired, with a kind of angry sigh. It was sinking into his mind that he, too, did not understand Madame Clairin's sister-in-law.

Longmore was obliged to wait a week in London for a ship. It was very hot, and he went out for a day to Richmond. In the garden of the hotel at which he dined he met his friend Mrs Draper, who was staying there. She made eager inquiry about Madame de Mauves, but Longmore at first, as they sat looking out at the famous view of the Thames, parried her questions and confined himself to small-talk. At last she said she was afraid he had something to conceal; whereupon, after a pause, he asked her if she remembered recommending him, in the letter she sent to him at Saint-Germain, to draw the sadness from her friend's smile. 'The last I saw of her was her smile,' said he, – 'when I bade her good by.'

'I remember urging you to "console" her,' Mrs Draper answered, 'and I wondered afterwards whether – a model of discretion as you are – I hadn't given you rather foolish advice.'

'She has her consolation in herself,' he said; 'she needs none that any one else can offer her. That's for troubles for which – be it more, be it less – our own folly has to answer. Madame de Mauves has not a grain of folly left.'

'Ah, don't say that!' murmured Mrs Draper. 'Just a little folly is very graceful.'

Longmore rose to go, with a quick nervous movement. 'Don't talk of grace,' he said, 'till you have measured her reason.'

For two years after his return to America he heard nothing of Madame de Mauves. That he thought of her intently, constantly, I need hardly say: most people wondered why such a clever young man should not 'devote' himself to something; but to himself he seemed absorbingly occupied. He never wrote to her; he believed that she preferred it. At last he heard that Mrs Draper, had come home, and he immediately called on her. 'Of course,' she said after the first greetings, 'you are dying for news of Madame de Mauves. Prepare yourself for something strange. I heard from her two or three times during the year after your return. She left Saint-Germain and went to live in the country, on some old property of her husband's. She wrote me very kind little notes, but I felt somehow that – in spite of what you said about "consolation" – they were the notes of a very sad woman. The only advice I could have given her was to leave her wretch of a husband and come back to her own land and her own people. But this I didn't feel free to do, and yet it made me so miserable not to be able to help her that I preferred to let our correspondence die a natural death. I had no news of her for a year. Last summer, however, I met at Vichy a clever young Frenchman whom I accidentally learned to be a friend of Euphemia's lovely sister-in-law, Madame Clairin. I lost no time in asking him what he knew about Madame de Mauves, – a countrywoman of mine and an old friend. "I congratulate you on possessing her friendship," he answered. "That's the charming little woman who killed her husband." You may imagine that I promptly asked for an explanation, and he proceeded to relate to me what he called the whole story. M. de Mauves had *fait quelques folies*, which his wife had taken absurdly to heart. He had repented and asked her forgiveness, which she had inexorably refused. She was very pretty, and severity, apparently, suited her style; for whether or no her husband had been in love with her before, he fell madly in love with her now. He was the proudest man in France, but he had begged her on his knees to be readmitted to favor. All in vain! She was stone, she was ice, she was outraged virtue. People noticed a great change in him: he gave up society, ceased to care for anything, looked shockingly. One fine day they learned that he had blown out his brains. My friend had the story of course from Madame Clairin.'

Longmore was strongly moved, and his first impulse after he had recovered his composure was to return immediately to Europe. But several years have passed, and he still lingers at home. The truth is, that in the midst of all the ardent tenderness of his memory of Madame de Mauves, he has become conscious of a singular feeling, – a feeling for which awe would be hardly too strong a name.

Professor Fargo

I

The little town of P— is off the railway, and reached by a coach drive of twenty-five miles, which the primitive conditions of the road makes a trial to the flesh, and the dulness of the landscape a weariness to the spirit. It was therefore not balm to my bruises, physical or intellectual, to find, on my arrival, that the gentleman for whose sake I had undertaken the journey had just posted off in a light buggy for a three days' holiday. After venting my disappointment in a variety of profitless expletives, I decided that the only course worthy of the elastic philosophy of a commercial traveller was to take a room at the local tavern and await his return. P— was obviously not an exhilarating place of residence, but I had out-weathered darker hours, and I reflected that having, as the phrase is, a bone to pick with my correspondent, a little accumulated irritation would arm me for the combat. Moreover, I had been rattling about for three months by rail; I was mortally tired, and the prospect of spending a few days beyond earshot of the steam whistle was not unwelcome. A certain audible, rural hush seemed to hang over the little town, and there was nothing apparently to prevent my giving it the whole of my attention. I lounged awhile in the tavern porch, but my presence seemed only to deepen the spell of silence on that customary group of jaundiced ruminants who were tilting their chairs hard by. I measured thrice, in its length, the dusty plank sidewalk of the main street, counted the hollyhocks in the front yards, and read the names on the little glass door plates; and finally, in despair, I visited the cemetery. Although we were at the end of September, the day was hot, and this youthful institution boasted but a scanty growth of funereal umbrage. No weeping willow, no dusky cypress offered a friendly

shelter to the meditative visitor. The yellow grass and the white
tombstones glared in the hot light, and though I felt very little
merrier than a graveyard ghost, I staid hardly longer than one who
should have mistaken his hour. But I am fond of reading country
epitaphs, and I promised myself to come back when the sun was
lower. On my way back to the inn I found myself, on a lately
opened cross street, face to face with the town hall, and pausing
approached its threshold with hopes of entertainment scarcely less
ardent than those which, during a journey abroad, had guided my
steps toward some old civic palace of France or Italy. There was,
of course, no liveried minion to check my advance, and I made my
way unchallenged into the large, bare room which occupied the
body of the edifice. It was the accustomed theatre of town
meetings, caucuses, and other solemn services, but it seemed just
now to have been claimed for profaner uses. An itinerant lecturer,
of a boisterous type, was unpacking his budget and preparing his
mise en scène. This seemed to consist simply of a small table and
three chairs in a row, and of a dingy specimen of our national
standard, to whose awkward festoons, suspended against the blank
wall at the rear of the platform, the orator in person was endeav-
oring to impart a more artistic grace. Another personage on the
floor was engaged in scrawling the date of the performance, in red
chalk, upon a number of printed handbills. He silently thrust one
of these documents at me as I passed, and I saw with some elation
that I had a resource for my evening. The latter half of the page
consisted of extracts from village newspapers, setting forth the
merits of the entertainments. The headings alone, as I remember
them, ran somewhat in this fashion:

A MESSAGE FROM THE SPIRIT WORLD

THE HIGHER MATHEMATICS MADE EASY TO LADIES
AND CHILDREN

A NEW REVELATION! A NEW SCIENCE!

GREAT MORAL AND SCIENTIFIC COMBINATION

PROFESSOR FARGO, THE INFALLIBLE WAKING MEDIUM AND
MAGICIAN, CLAIRVOYANT, PROPHET, AND SEER!

COLONEL GIFFORD, THE FAMOUS LIGHTNING CALCULATOR
AND MATHEMATICAL REFORMER!

This was the substance of the programme, but there were a great many incidental *fioriture* which I have forgotten. By the time I had mastered them, however, for the occasion, the individual who was repairing the tattered flag, turned round, perceived me, and showed me a countenance which could belong only to an 'infallible waking medium.' It was not, indeed, that Professor Fargo had the abstracted and emaciated aspect which tradition attributes to prophets and visionaries. On the contrary, the fleshly element in his composition seemed, superficially to enjoy a luxurious preponderance over the spiritual. He was tall and corpulent, and wore an air of aggressive robustness. A mass of reddish hair was tossed back from his forehead in a leonine fashion, and a lustrous auburn beard diffused itself complacently over an expansive but by no means immaculate shirt front. He was dressed in a black evening suit, of a tarnished elegance, and it was in keeping with the festal pattern of his garments, that on the right forefinger of a large, fat hand, he should wear an immense turquoise ring. His intimate connection with the conjuring class was stamped upon his whole person; but to a superficial glance he might have seemed a representative of its grosser accomplishments. You could have fancied him, in spangled fleshings, looking down the lion's mouth, or cracking the ring-master's whip at the circus, while Mlle Josephine jumped through the hoops. It was his eyes, when you fairly met them, that proved him an artist on a higher line. They were eyes which had peeped into stranger places than even lions' mouths. Their pretension, I know, was to pierce the veil of futurity; but if this was founded, I could only say that the vision of Ezekiel and Jeremiah was but another name for consummate Yankee shrewdness. They were, in a single word, the most impudent pair of eyes I ever beheld, and it was the especial sign of their impudence that they seemed somehow to undertake to persuade you of their disinterested benevolence. Being of a fine reddish brown color, it was probable that several young women that evening would pronounce them magnificent. Perceiving, apparently, that I had not the rustic physiognomy of a citizen of P—, Professor Fargo deemed my patronage worth securing. He advanced to the cope of the platform with his hands in his pockets, and gave me a familiar nod.

'Mind you come to-night, young man!' he said, jocosely imperious.

'Very likely I shall,' I answered. 'Anything in the world to help me through an evening at P—.'

'Oh, you won't want your money back,' the Professor rejoined. 'Mine is a first-class entertainment; none of your shuffling break-downs. We are perfect, my friends and I, in our respective parts. If you are fond of a good, stiff, intellectual problem, we'll give you something to think about.' The Professor spoke very slowly and benignantly, and his full, sonorous voice rolled away through the empty hall. He evidently liked to hear it himself; he balanced himself on his toes and surveyed the scene of his impending exploits. 'I don't blow my own trumpet,' he went on; 'I'm a modest man; you'll see for yourself what I can do. But I should like to direct your attention to my friend the Colonel. *He's* a rare old gentleman to find in a travelling show! The most remarkable old gentleman, perhaps, that ever addressed a promiscuous audience. You needn't be afraid of the higher mathematics; it's all made as pretty as a game of billiards. It's his own daughter does the sums. We don't put her down in the bills, for motives of delicacy; but I'll tell you for your private satisfaction that she is an exquisite young creature of seventeen.'

It was not every day that I found myself in familiar conversation with a prophet, and the opportunity for obtaining a glimpse of the inner mechanism of the profession was too precious to be neglected. I questioned the Professor about his travels, his expenses, his profits, and the mingled emotions of the itinerant showman's lot; and then, taking the bull by the horns, I asked him whether, between ourselves, an accomplished medium had not to be also a tolerable conjurer? He leaned his head on one side and stood stroking his beard, and looking at me between lids shrewdly half closed. Then he gave a little dry chuckle, which expressed, at my choice, compassion either for my disbelief in his miracles or for my faith in his urbanity.

'I confess frankly,' I said, 'that I'm a skeptic. I don't believe in messages from the spirit world. I don't believe that even the depressing prospect of immortality is capable of converting people who talked plain sense here on earth into the authors of the inflated platitudes which people of your profession pretend to transmit from them. I don't believe people who have expressed themselves for a lifetime in excellent English can ever be content with conversation by raps on the dinner table. I don't believe that you know anything more about the future world than you do about the penal code of China. My impression is that you don't believe so yourself. I can hardly expect you, of course, to take the wind out of your own sails. What I should vastly like you to do is, to tell me *viva voce*, in so many words, that your intentions are pure and your miracles genuine.'

The Professor remained silent, still caressing his prophetic beard. At last, in a benevolent drawl, 'Have you got any dear friend in the spirit land?' he asked.

'I don't know what you call the spirit land,' I answered. 'Several of my friends have died.'

'Would you like to see 'em?' the Professor promptly demanded.

'No, I confess I shouldn't!'

The Professor shook his head.

'You've not a rich nature,' he rejoined blandly.

'It depends on what you call rich. I possess on some points a wealth of curiosity. It would gratify me peculiarly to have you say outright, standing there on your own platform, that you're an honest man.'

It seemed to give him pleasure to trifle with my longing for this sensation. 'I'll give you leave,' he said, for all answer, 'to tie my hands into the tightest knot you can invent – and then I'll make your great-grandfather come in and stop the clock. You know I couldn't stop a clock, perched up on a mantel shelf five feet high, with my heels.'

'I don't know,' said I. 'I fancy you're very clever.'

'Cleverness has nothing to do with it. I've great magnetism.'

'You'd magnetize my great-grandfather down from heaven?'

'Yes, sir, if I could establish communication. You'll see to-night what I can do. I'll satisfy you. If I don't, I shall be happy to give you a private sitting. I'm also a healing medium. You don't happen to have a toothache? I'd set you down there and pull it right out, as I'd pull off your boot.'

In compliment to this possibility, I could only make him my

bow. His, at least, was a 'rich nature.' I bade him farewell, with the assurance that, skeptic as I was, I would applaud him impartially in the evening. I had reached the top of the hall, on my way out, when I heard him give a low, mellifluous whistle. I turned around, and he beckoned to me to return. I walked back, and he leaned forward from the platform, uplifting his stout forefinger. 'I simply desire to remark,' he said, 'that I'm an honest man!'

On my return to the hotel I found that my impatience for the Professor's further elucidation of his honesty made the interval look long. Fortune, however, assisted me to traverse it at an elastic pace. Rummaging idly on a bookshelf in the tavern parlor, I found, amid a pile of farmers' almanacs and Methodist tracts, a tattered volume of 'Don Quixote.'[1] I repaired to my room, tilted back my chair, and communed deliciously with the ingenious hidalgo. Here was 'magnetism' superior even to that of Professor Fargo. It proved so effective that I lost all note of time, and, at last on looking at my watch, perceived that dinner must have been over for an hour. Of 'service' at this unsophisticated hostelry there was but a rigidly democratic measure, and if I chose to cultivate a too elegant absence of eagerness for beefsteak pie and huckleberry pudding, the young lady in long, tight ringlets and short sleeves, who administered these delicacies in the dining-room, was altogether too haughty a spirit to urge them on my attention. So I sat alone and ate them cold. After dinner I returned for an hour to La Mancha, and then strolled forth, according to my morning's vow, to see the headstones in the cemetery cast longer shadows. I was disappointed on the epitaphs; they were posterior to the age of theological *naïveté*. The cemetery covered the two opposed sides of a hill, and on walking up to the ridge and looking over it, I discovered that I was not the only visitor. Two persons had chosen the spot for a quiet talk. One of them was a young girl, dressed in black, and seated on a headstone, with her face turned toward me. In spite of her attitude, however, she seemed not to perceive me, wrapt as she was in attention to her companion – a tall, stout fellow, standing before her, with his back to me. They were at too great a distance for me to hear their talk, and indeed in a few minutes I began to fancy they were not speaking. Nevertheless, the young girl's eyes remained fixed on the man's face; he was holding her spellbound by an influence best known to himself. She was very pretty. Her hat was off, and she was holding it in her lap; her lips were parted, and her eyes fixed intently on her companion's face. Suddenly she gave a bright, quick smile, made a rapid gesture in the air, and laid her forefinger to her lips. The movement, and the manner of it, told her story. She was deaf and dumb, and the man had been talking to her with his fingers. I would willingly have looked at her longer, but I turned away in delicacy, and walked in another direction. As I was leaving the cemetery, however, I saw her advancing with her companion to take the path which led to the gate. The man's face was now turned to me, and I straightway recognized it, in spite of the high peaked white hat which surmounted it. It was natural enough, I suppose, to find Professor Fargo in a graveyard; as the simplest expedient for ascertaining what goes on beyond the tomb might seem to be to get as close as possible to the hither cope of it. Besides, if he was to treat the townsfolk to messages from their buried relatives, it was not amiss to 'get up' a few names and dates by the perusal of the local epitaphs. As he passed me, however, and flourished his hand in the air by way of salutation, there was a fine absence in his glance of any admission that he had been caught cheating. This, too, was natural enough; what surprised me was that such a vulgar fellow should be mated with so charming a companion. She gave me as she passed the trustfully unshrinking glance of those poor mortals who are obliged to listen, as one may say, with their eyes. Her dress was scanty and simple, but there was delicacy in her mobile features. Who was she, and how had *he* got hold of her? After all, it was none of my business; but as they passed on, walking rather briskly, and I strolled after them, watching the Professor's ponderous tread and the gliding footfall of the young girl, I began to wonder whether he might not be right – might not, in truth, have that about him which would induce the most venerable of my ancestors to revert from eternity and stop the clock.

II

His handbills had done their office, and the Town Hall, when I entered it that evening, was filled with a solemnly expectant auditory. P— was evidently for the evening a cluster of empty houses. While my companions scanned the stage for the shadow of coming events, I found ample pastime in perusing the social physiognomy of the town. A shadow presently appeared in the person of a stout young countryman, armed with an accordion, from which he extracted an ingenious variety of lamentable sounds. Soon after this mysterious prelude, the Professor marshalled out his forces. They consisted, first and foremost, of himself, his leonine *chevelure*, his black dress suit, and his turquoise ring, and then of an old gentleman who walked in gravely and stiffly, without the Professor's portentous salaam to the audience, bearing on his arm a young girl in black. The Professor managed somehow, by pushing about the chairs, turning up the lamps, and giving a twist to the patriotic drapery in the background, to make his audience feel his presence very intimately. His assistants rested themselves tranquilly against the wall. It took me but a short time to discover that the young girl was none other than the companion of the Professor's tour of inspection in the cemetery, and then I remembered that he had spoken in the morning of the gentleman who performed the mathematical miracles being assisted by his daughter. The young girl's infirmity, and her pretty face, promised to impart a picturesque interest to this portion of the exhibition; but meanwhile I inferred from certain ill-suppressed murmurs, and a good deal of vigorous pantomime among the female spectators, that she was found wanting in the more immediate picturesqueness demanded of a young lady attached to a show. Her plain black dress found no favor; the admission fee had justified the expectation of a good deal of trimming and several bracelets. She, however, poor girl, sat indifferent in her place, leaning her head back rather wearily against the wall, and looking as if, were she disposed, she might count without trouble all the queer bonnets among her judges. Her father sat upright beside her, with a cane between his knees and his two hands crossed on the knob. He was a man of sixty-five – tall, lean, pale, and serious. The lamp hanging above his head deepened the shadows on his face, and transformed it into a sort of pictorial mask. He was very bald, and his forehead, which was high and handsome, wore in the lamplight the gleam of old ivory. The sockets of his eyes were in deep shadow, and out of them his pupils gazed straight before him, with the glow of smouldering fire. His high-arched nose cast a long shadow over his mouth and chin, and two intensified wrinkles, beside his moustache, made him look strangely tragic. With his tragic look, moreover, he seemed strangely familiar. His daughter and the Professor I regarded as old friends; but where had I met this striking specimen of antique melancholy? Though his gaze seemed fixed, I imagined it was covertly wandering over the audience. At last it appeared to me that it met mine, and that its sombre glow emitted a spark of recognition of my extra-provincial and inferentially more discriminating character. The next moment I identified him – he was Don Quixote in the flesh; Don Quixote, with his sallow Spanish coloring, his high-browed, gentlemanly visage, his wrinkles, his moustache, and his sadness.

Professor Fargo's lecture was very bad. I had expected he would talk a good deal of nonsense, but I had imagined it would be cleverer nonsense. Very possibly there was a deeper cleverness in it than I perceived, and that, in his extreme shrewdness, he was giving his audience exactly what they preferred. It is an ascertained fact, I believe, that rural assemblies have a relish for the respectably ponderous, and an honest pride in the fact that they cannot be bored. The Professor, I suppose, felt the pulse of his listeners, and detected treasures of latent sympathy in their solemn, irresponsive silence. I should have said the performance was falling dead, but the Professor probably would have claimed that this was the rapture of attention and awe. He certainly kept very meagrely the promise of his grandiloquent programme, and gave us a pound of precept to a grain of example. His miracles were exclusively miracles of rhetoric. He discoursed upon the earth life and the summer land, and related surprising anecdotes of his intimacy with the inhabitants of the latter region; but to my disappointment, the evening passed away without his really bringing us face to face with a ghost. A number of 'prominent citizens' were induced to step upon the platform and be magnetized, but the sturdy agricultural temperament of P— showed no great pliancy under the Professor's manual blandishments. The attempt was generally a failure – the only brilliant feature being the fine impudence with which the operator lodged the responsibility of the *fiasco* upon what he called his victim's low development. With three or four young girls the thing was a trifle better. One of them closed her eyes and shivered; another had a fearful access of nervous giggling; another burst into tears, and was restored to her companions with an admonitory wink. As every one knew every one else and every one else's family history, some sensation was probably produced by half a dozen happy guesses as to the Christian names and last maladies of certain defunct town worthies. Another deputation of the prominent citizens ascended the platform and wrote the names of departed friends on small bits of paper, which they threw into a hat. The Professor then folded his arms and clutched his beard, as if he were invoking inspiration. At last he approached the young girl, who sat in the background, took her hand, and led her forward. She picked the papers out of the hat and held them up one by one, for the Professor to look at. 'There is no possible collusion,' he said with a flourish, as he presented her to the audience. 'The young lady is a deaf mute!' On a gesture of her companion she passed the paper to one of the contemplative gray heads who represented the scientific curiosity of P—, and he verified the Professor's guess. The Professor risked an 'Abijah' or a 'Melinda,' and it turned out generally to be an Ezekiel or a Hepzibah. Three several times, however, the performer's genius triumphed; whereupon, the audience not being up to the mark, he gave himself a vigorous round of applause. He concluded with the admission that the spirits were shy before such a crowd, but that he would do much better for the ladies and gentlemen individually, if they would call on him at the hotel.

It was all terribly vulgar rubbish, and I was glad when it was over. While it lasted, the old gentleman behind continued to sit motionless, seeming neither to see, to hear, nor to understand. I wondered what he thought of it, and just what it cost his self-respect to give it the sanction of his presence. It seemed, indeed, as if mentally he were not present; as if by an intense effort he had succeeded in making consciousness a blank, and was awaiting his own turn in a kind of trance. Once only he moved – when the Professor came and took his daughter by the hand. He gave an imperceptible start, controlled himself, then, dropping his hand a little, closed his eyes and kept them closed until she returned to his side. There was an intermission, during which the Professor walked about the platform, shaking his mane and wiping his forehead, and surveying the audience with an air of lofty benevolence, as if, having sown the seed, he was expecting to see it germinate on the spot. At last he rapped on the table and introduced the old gentleman – Colonel Gifford, the Great Mathematical Magician and Lightning Calculator; after which he retreated in turn to the background – if a gentleman with tossing mane and flowing beard, that turquoise ring, and generally expansive and importunate presence, could be said to be, under any circumstances, in the background. The old gentleman came forward and made his bow, and the young girl placed herself beside him simply, unaffectedly, with her hands hanging and crossed in front of her – with all the childish grace and serenity of Mignon[2] in 'Wilhelm Meister,' as we see her grouped with the old harper. Colonel Gifford's performance gave me an exquisite pleasure, which I am bound to confess was quite independent of its intrinsic merits. These, I am afraid, were at once too numerous and too scanty to have made it a popular success. It was a very ingenious piece of scientific contrivance, but it was meagrely adapted to tickle the ears of the groundlings. If one had read it – the substance of it – in a handsomely printed pamphlet, under the lamp, of a wet evening when no one was likely to call, one would have been charmed at once with the quaint vivacity of the author's mode of statement, and with the unexpected agility of one's own intellect. But in spite of an obvious effort to commend himself to understandings more familiar with the rule of thumb than with the differential calculus, Colonel Gifford remained benignantly but formidably unintelligible. He had devised – so far as I understood it – an extension of the multiplication table to enormous factors, by which he expected to effect a revolution in the whole science of accounts. There was the theory, which rather lost itself, thanks to his discursive fervor, in the mists of the higher mathematics, and there was the practice, which, thanks to his daughter's coöperation, was much more gracefully concrete. The interesting thing to me was the speaker's personality, not his system. Although evidently a very positive old man, he had a singularly simple, unpretentious tone. His intensity of faith in the supreme importance of his doctrine gave his manner a sort of reverential hush. The echoes of Professor Fargo's windy verbiage increased the charms of his mild sincerity. He spoke in a feeble, tremulous voice, which every now and then quavered upward with excitement, and then subsided into a weary, plaintive cadence. He was an old gentleman of a single idea, but his one idea was a religion. It was impossible not to feel a kindness for him, and imagine that he excited among his auditors something of the vague good will – half pity and half reverence – that uncorrupted souls entertain for those neat, keen-eyed, elderly people who are rumored to have strange ways and say strange things – to be 'cracked,' in short, like a fine bit of porcelain which will hold together only so long as you don't push it about. But it was upon the young girl, when once she had given them a taste of her capacity, that they bestowed their frankest admiration. Now that she stood forward in the bright light, I could observe the character of her prettiness. It was no brilliant beauty, but a sort of meagre, attenuated, angular grace, the delicacy and fragility of the characteristic American type. Her chest was flat, her neck extremely thin, her visage narrow, and her forehead high and prominent. But her fair hair encircled her head in such fleecy tresses, her cheeks had such a pale pink flush, her eyes such an appealing innocence, her attitude such a quaint unconscious felicity, that one watched her with a kind of upstart belief that to such a stainless little spirit the working of miracles might be really possible. A couple of blackboards were hung against the wall, on one of which the old man rapidly chalked a problem – choosing one, of course, on the level of the brighter minds in the audience. The young girl glanced at it, and before we could count ten dashed off a great bold answer on the other tablet. The brighter minds were then invited to verify, and the young lady was invariably found to have hit the mark. She was in fact a little arithmetical fairy, and her father made her perform a series of gymnastics among numbers as brilliant in their way as the vocal flourishes and roulades of an accomplished singer. Communicating with her altogether by the blackboard, he drew from her a host of examples of the beauty of his system of transcendent multiplication. A person present was requested to furnish two enormous numbers, one to multiply the other. The old man wrote them out. After standing an instant meditative and just touching her forehead with her forefinger, she chalked down the prodigious result. Her father then performed rapidly, on the blackboard, the operation according to his own system (which she had employed mentally), and finally satisfied every one by repeating it in the roundabout fashion actually in use. This was all Colonel Gifford's witchcraft. It sounds very ponderous, but it was really very charming, and I had an agreeable sense of titillation in the finer parts of my intellectual mechanism. I felt more like a thinking creature. I had never supposed I was coming to P— to take a lesson in culture.

It seemed on the morrow as if, at any rate, I was to take a lesson in patience. It was a Sunday, and I awoke to hear the rain pattering against my window panes. A rainy Sunday at P— was a prospect to depress the most elastic mind. But as I stepped into my slippers, I bethought myself of my unfinished volume of 'Don Quixote,' and promised myself to borrow from Sancho Panza a philosophic proverb or so applicable to my situation. 'Don Quixote' consoled me, as it turned out, in an unexpected fashion. On descending to the dining-room of the inn, while I mentally balanced the contending claims of muddy coffee and sour green tea, I found that my last evening's friends were also enjoying the hospitality of the establishment. It was the only inn in the place, and it would already have occurred to a more investigating mind that we were fellow-lodgers. The Professor, happily, was absent; and it seemed only reasonable that a ghost-seer should lie in bed late of a morning. The melancholy old mathematician was seated at the breakfast table cutting his dry toast into geometrical figures. He gave me a formal bow as I entered, and proceeded to dip his sodden polygons into his tea. The young girl was at the window, leaning her forehead against the pane, and looking out into the sea of yellow mud in the village street. I had not been in the room a couple of minutes when, seeming in spite of her deafness to feel that I was near, she turned straight round and looked at me. She wore no trace of fatigue from her public labors, but was the same clear-eyed, noiseless little sprite as before. I observed that, by daylight, her black dress was very shabby, and her father's frock coat, buttoned with military precision up to his chin, had long since exchanged its original lustre for the melancholy brilliancy imparted by desperate brushing. I was afraid that Professor Fargo was either a niggardly *impresario*, or that the great 'moral and scientific combination' was not always as remunerative as it seemed to have been at P—. While I was making these reflections the Professor entered, with an exhilaration of manner which I conceived to be a tribute to unwonted success.

'Well, sir,' he cried, as his eyes fell upon me, 'what do you say to it now? I hope we did things handsomely, eh? I hope you call that a solid entertainment. This young man, you must know, is one of the scoffers,' he went on, turning to the Colonel. 'He came yesterday and bearded the lion in his den. He snaps his fingers at spirits, suspects me of foul play, and would like me to admit, in my private character, that you and I are a couple of sharpers. I hope we satisfied you!'

The Colonel went on dipping his toast into his tea, looking grave and saying nothing. 'Poor man!' I said to myself; 'he despises his colleague – and so do I. I beg your pardon,' I cried with warmth; 'I would like nothing of the kind. I was extremely interested in this gentleman's exhibition;' and I made the Colonel a bow. 'It seemed to me remarkable for its perfect good faith and truthfulness.'

'Many thanks for the compliment,' said the Professor. 'As much as to say the Colonel's an apostle, and I'm a rascal. Have it as you please; if so, I'm a hardened one!' he declared with a great slap on his pocket; 'and anyhow, you know, it's all one concern,' and the Professor betook himself to the window where Miss Gifford was standing. She had not looked round at him on his entrance, as she had done at me. The Colonel, in response to my compliment, looked across at me with mild benignity, and I assured him afresh of my admiration. He listened silently, stirring his tea; his face betrayed an odd mixture of confidence and deprecation; as if he thought it just possible that I might be laughing at him, but that if I was not, it was extremely delightful. I continued to insist on its being distinctively *his* half of the performance that had pleased me; so that, gradually convinced of my respectful sympathy, he seemed tacitly to intimate that, if we were only alone and he knew me a little better, it would do him a world of good to talk it over. I

determined to give him a chance at the earliest moment. The
Professor, meanwhile, waiting for his breakfast, remained at the
window experimenting in the deaf and dumb alphabet with the
young girl. It took him, as an amateur, a long time to form his
sentences, but he went on bravely, brandishing his large, plump
knuckles before her face. She seemed very patient of his slowness,
and stood watching his gestures with the same intense earnestness
I had caught a glimpse of in the cemetery. Most of my female
friends enjoy an unimpeded use of their tongues, and I was unable
from experience to appreciate his situation; but I could easily fancy
what a delightful sense of intimacy there must be in this noiseless
exchange of long looks with a pretty creature toward whom all
tendresse of attitude might be conveniently attributed to compassion. Before long the Colonel pushed away his cup, turned about,
folded his arms, and fixed his eyes with a frown on the Professor.
It seemed to me that I read in his glance a complete revelation of
moral torture. The stress of fortune had made them associates, but
the Colonel jealously guarded the limits of their private intimacy.
The Professor, with all his audacity, suffered himself to be
reminded of them. He suddenly pulled out his watch and clamored
for his coffee, and was soon seated at a repast which indicated that
the prophetic temperament requires a generous diet. The young
girl roamed about the room, looking idly at this and that, as if she
were used to doing nothing. When she met my eye, she smiled
brightly, after a moment's gravity, as if she were also used to
saying to people, mentally, 'Yes, I know I'm a strange little
creature, but you must not be afraid of me.' The Professor had
hardly got that array of innumerable little dishes, of the form and
dimensions of soap-trays, with which one is served in the rural
hostelries of New England, well under contribution, before a
young lady was introduced who had come to request him to raise a
ghost – a resolute young lady, with several ringlets and a huge
ancestral umbrella, whose matutinal appetite for the supernatural
had not been quenched by the raw autumnal storm. She produced
very frankly a 'tin-type' of a florid young man, actually deceased,
and demanded to be confronted with his ghost. The day was
beginning well for the Professor. He gallantly requested her to be
seated, and promised her every satisfaction. While he was hastily

despatching his breakfast, the Colonel's daughter made acquaintance with her bereaved sister. She drew the young man's portrait
gently out of her hand, examined it, and then shook her head with
a little grimace of displeasure. The young woman laughed good-
naturedly, and screamed into her ear that she didn't believe she
was a bit deaf and dumb. At the announcement the Colonel, who,
after eyeing her while she stated her credulous errand with solemn
compassion, had turned away to the window, as if to spare himself
the spectacle of his colleague's unblushing pretensions, turned
back again and eyed her coldly from head to foot. 'I recommend
you, madam,' he said sternly, 'to reserve your suspicions for an
occasion in which they may be more pertinent.'

Later in the morning I found him still in the dining-room with
his daughter. Professor Fargo, he said, was in the parlor, raising
ghosts by the dozen: and after a little pause he gave an angry
laugh, as if his suppressed irritation were causing him more than
usual discomfort. He was walking up and down, with slow, restless
steps, and smoking a frugal pipe. I took the liberty of offering him
a good cigar, and while he puffed it gratefully, the need to justify
himself for his odd partnership slowly gathered force. 'It would be
a satisfaction for me to tell you, sir,' he said at last, looking at me
with eyes that fairly glittered with the pleasure of hearing himself
speak the words, 'that my connection with Professor Fargo implies
no – no – ' and he paused for a moment – 'no intellectual approval
of his extraordinary pretensions. This, of course, is between
ourselves. You're a stranger to me, and it's doubtless the height of
indiscretion in me to take you into my confidence. My subsistence
depends on my not quarrelling with my companion. If you were to
repeat to him that I went about undermining the faith, the
extremely retributive faith, as you see' (and he nodded toward the
parlor door), 'of his audiences, he would of course dissolve our
partnership and I should be adrift again, trying to get my heavy
boat in tow. I should perhaps feel like an honest man again, but
meanwhile, probably, I should starve. Misfortune,' he added
bitterly, 'makes strange bedfellows; and I have been unfortunate!'

There was so much melancholy meaning in this declaration that
I asked him frankly who and what he was. He puffed his cigar
vigorously for some moments without replying, and at last turned

his fine old furrowed visage upon me through a cloud of smoke. 'I'm a fanatic. I feed on illusions and cherish ambitions which will never butter my bread. Don't be afraid; I won't buttonhole *you*; but I have a head full of schemes which I believe the world would be the happier for giving a little quiet attention to. I'm an inventor; and like all inventors whose devices are of value, I believe that my particular contrivance would be the salvation of a misguided world. I have looked a good deal into many things, but my latest hobby is the system of computation of which I tried to give a sketch last night. I'm afraid you didn't understand a word of it, but I assure you it's a very beautiful thing. If it could only get a fair hearing and be thoroughly propagated and adopted, it would save our toiling human race a prodigious deal of ungrateful labor. In America alone, I have calculated, it would save the business community about 23,000 hours in the course of ten years. If time is money, they are worth saving. But there I go! You oughtn't to ask me to talk about myself. Myself is my ideas!'

A little judicious questioning, however, drew from him a number of facts of a more immediately personal kind. His colonelship, he intimated, was held by the inglorious tenure of militia service, and was only put forward to help him to make a figure on Professor Fargo's platform. It was part of the general humbuggery of the attempt to *bribe* people to listen to wholesome truths – truths the neglect of which was its own chastisement. 'I have always had a passion for scientific research, and I have squandered my substance in experiments which the world called fruitless. They were curious, they were beautiful, they were divine! But they wouldn't turn any one's mill or grind any one's corn, and I was treated like a mediæval alchemist, astray in the modern world. Chemistry, physics, mathematics, philology, medicine – I've dug deep in them all. Each, in turn, has been a passion to which I've given my days and my nights. But apparently I haven't the art of finding favor for my ideas – of sweetening the draught so that people will drink it. So here I am, after all my vigils and ventures, an obscure old man, ruined in fortune, broken down in health and sadly diminished in hope, trying hard to keep afloat by rowing in the same boat as a gentleman who turns tables and raises ghosts. I'm a proud man, sir, and a devotee of the exact sciences. You may imagine what I suffer. I little fancied ten years ago that I was ever going to make capital, on a mountebank's booth, of the pathetic infirmity of my daughter.'

The young girl, while her father talked, sat gazing at him in wistful surprise. I inferred from it that this expansive mood was rare; she wondered what long story he was telling. As he mentioned her, I gave her a sudden glance. Perceiving it, she blushed slightly and turned away. The movement seemed at variance with what I had supposed to be her characteristic indifference to observation. 'I have a good reason,' he said, 'for treating her with more than the tenderness which such an infirmity usually commands. At the time of my marriage, and for some time after, I was performing a series of curious chemical researches. My wife was a wonderfully pretty little creature. She used to come tripping and rustling about my laboratory, asking questions of the most comical ignorance, peeping and rummaging everywhere, raising the lids of jars, and making faces at the bad smells. One day while she was in the room I stepped out on the balcony to examine something which I had placed to dry in the sun. Suddenly I heard a terrific explosion; it smashed the window-glass into atoms. Rushing in, I found my wife in a swoon on the floor. A compound which I had placed to heat on a furnace had been left too long; I had underestimated its activity. My wife was not visibly injured, but when she came to her senses again, she found she had lost her hearing. It never returned. Shortly afterwards my daughter was born – born the poor deaf creature you see. I lost my wife and I gave up chemistry. As I advanced in life, I became convinced that my ruling passion was mathematics. I've gone into them very deeply; I consider them the noblest acquisition of the human mind, and I don't hesitate to say that I have profound and original views on the subject. If you have a head for such things, I could open great vistas to you. But I'm afraid you haven't! Ay, it's a desperately weak-witted generation. The world has a horror of concentrated thought; it wants the pill to be sugared; it wants everything to be made easy; it prefers the brazen foolery that you and I sat through last night to the divine harmonies of the infinite science of numbers. That's why I'm a beggar, droning out my dreary petition and pushing forth my little girl to catch the coppers. That's why I've had to strike a partnership with a vulgar charlatan. I was a long time coming to it, but I'm well in for it now. I won't tell you how, from rebuff to rebuff, from failure to failure, through hope deferred and justice denied, I have finally come to this. It would overtax both your sympathy and your credulity. You wouldn't believe the stories I could relate of the impenetrable stupidity of mankind, of the leaden empire of Routine. I squandered my property, I confess it, but not in the vulgar way. It was a carnival of high research, a long debauch of experiment. When I had melted down my last cent in the consuming crucible, I thought the world might be willing to pay me something for my results. The world had better uses for its money than the purchase of sovereign truth! I became a solicitor; I went from door to door, offering people a choice of twenty superb formulated schemes, the paltriest of which contained the germs of a peaceful revolution. The poor unpatented visions are at this hour all in a bundle up stairs in my trunk. In the midst of my troubles I had the ineffable pleasure of finding that my little girl was a genius. I don't know why it should have been a pleasure; her poor father's genius stood there before me as a warning. But it was a delight to find that her little imprisoned soundless mind was not a blank. She had inherited my passion for numbers. My folly had taken a precious faculty from her; it was but just I should give her another. She was in good hands for becoming perfect. Her gift is a rare one among women, but she is not of the common feminine stuff. She's very simple – strangely simple in some ways. She has never been talked to by women about petticoats, nor by men about love. She doesn't reason; her skill at figures is a kind of intuition. One day it came into my head that I might lecture for a livelihood. I had listened to windy orators, in crowded halls, who had less to say than I. So I lectured, sometimes to twenty people, sometimes to five, once to no one at all. One morning, some six months ago, I was waited upon by my friend there. He told me frankly that he had a show which didn't draw as powerfully as it deserved, and proposed that, as I also seemed unable to catch the public ear, we should combine our forces and carry popularity by storm. His entertainment, alone, was rather thin; mine also seemed to lack the desirable consistency; but a mixture of the two might produce an effective compound. I had but five dollars in my pocket. I disliked the man, and I believe in spiritualism about as much as I believe that the sun goes round the earth. But we must live, and I made a bargain. It was a very poor bargain, but it keeps us alive. I took a few hints from the Professor, and brightened up my lucky formulas a little. Still, we had terribly thin houses. I couldn't play the mountebank; it's a faculty I lack. At last the Professor bethought himself that I possessed the golden goose. From the mountebank's point of view a pretty little deaf and dumb daughter, who could work miracles on the blackboard, was a treasure to a practical mind. The idea of dragging my poor child and her pathetic idiosyncrasies before the world was extremely repulsive to me; but the Professor laid the case before the little maid herself, and at the end of a fortnight she informed him that she was ready to make her curtsey on the platform as a "lightning calculator." I consented to let her try, and you see that she succeeded. She draws, not powerfully, but sufficiently, and we manage to keep afloat.'

Half an hour later the Professor returned from his morning's labors – flushed, dishevelled, rubbing his hands, evidently in high good humor. The Colonel immediately became silent and grave, asked no questions, and, when dinner was served shortly afterwards, refused everything and sat with a melancholy frown and his eyes fixed on his plate. His comrade was plainly a terrible thorn in his side. I was curious, on the other hand, to know how the Colonel affected the Professor, and I soon discovered that the latter was by no means his exuberant impudent self within the radius of his colleague's pregnant silence. If there was little love lost between them, the ranting charlatan was at least held in check by an indefinable respect for his companion's probity. He was a fool, doubtless, with his careful statements and his incapacity to take a humorous view of human credulity; but, somehow, he was a venerable fool, and the Professor, as a social personage, without the inspiration of a lecture-room more or less irritatingly interspaced, and with that pale, grave old mathematician sitting by like a marble monument to Veracity, lacked the courage to ventilate his peculiar pretensions. On this occasion, however, he swallowed the Colonel's tacit protest with a wry face. I don't know what he had brought to pass in the darkened parlor; whatever it was, it had agreeably stimulated his confidence in his resources. We had been joined, moreover, at dinner by half a dozen travellers of less oppressively skeptical mould than the Colonel, and under these circumstances it was peculiarly trying to have to veil one's brighter genius. There was undischarged thunder in the air.

The rain ceased in the afternoon, and the sun leaped out and set the thousand puddles of the village street a-flashing. I found the Colonel sitting under the tavern porch with a village urchin between his knees, to whom he seemed to be imparting the rudiments of mathematical science. The little boy had a bulging forehead, a prodigious number of freckles, and the general aspect of a juvenile Newton. Being present at the Colonel's lecture, he had been fired with a laudable curiosity to know more, and learning that Professor Fargo imparted information à domicile, had ventured to believe that his colleague did likewise. The child's father, a great, gaunt, brown-faced farmer, with a yellow tuft on his chin, stood by, blushing at the audacity of his son and heir, but grinning delightedly at his brightness. The poor Colonel, whose meed of recognition had as yet been so meagre, was vastly tickled by this expression of infantine sympathy, and discoursed to the little prodigy with the most condescending benevolence. Certainly, as the boy grows up, the most vivid of his childish memories will be that of the old man with glowing eyes and a softened voice coming from under his white moustache – the voice which held him stock-still for a whole half hour, and assured him afterwards that he was a little Trojan. When the lesson was over, I proposed a walk to the Colonel, and we wandered away out of the village. The afternoon, as it waned, became glorious; the heavy clouds, broken and dispersed, sailed through the glowing sky like high-prowed galleys, draped in purple and silver. I, on my side, shall never forget the Colonel's excited talk, nor how at last, as we sat on a rocky ridge looking off to the sunset, he fairly unburdened his conscience.

'Yes, sir!' he said; 'it's a base concession to the ignoble need of keeping body and soul together. Sometimes I feel as if I couldn't stand it another hour – as if it were better to break with the impudent rascal and sink or swim as fate decrees, than get a hearing for the truth at such a cost. It's all very well holding my tongue and insisting that I, at least, make no claims for the man's

vile frauds; my connection with him is itself a sanction, and my
presence at his damnable mummeries an outrage to the purity of
truth. You see I have the misfortune to believe in something, to
know something, and to think it makes a difference whether people
feed, intellectually, on poisoned garbage or on the ripe, sweet fruit
of true science! I shut my eyes every night, and lock my jaws, and
clench my teeth, but I can't help hearing the man's windy rubbish.
It's a tissue of scandalous lies, from beginning to end. I know
them all by heart by this time, and I verily believe I could stand
up and rattle them off myself. They ring in my ears all day, and I
have horrible dreams at night of crouching under a table with a
long cloth, and tapping on the top of it. The Professor stands
outside swearing to the audience that it's the ghost of Archimedes.
Then I begin to suffocate, and overturn the table, and appear
before a thousand people as the accomplice of the impostor. There
are times when the value of my own unheeded message to mankind
seems so vast, so immeasurable, that I am ready to believe that
any means are lawful which may enable me to utter it; that if one's
ship is to set sail for the golden islands, even a flaunting buccaneer
may tow it into the open sea. In such moods, when I sit there
against the wall, in the shade, closing my eyes and trying not to
hear – I really *don't* hear! My mind is a myriad miles away –
floating, soaring on the wings of invention. But all of a sudden the
odiousness of my position comes over me, and I can't believe my
senses that it's verily I who sit there – I to whom a grain of
scientific truth is more precious than a mountain of gold!'

He was silent a long time, and I myself hardly knew what
consolation to offer him. The most friendly part was simply to let
him expend his bitterness to the last drop. 'But that's not the
worst,' he resumed after a while. 'The worst is that I hate the
greasy rascal to come near my daughter, and that, living and
travelling together as we do, he's never far off. At first he used to
engage a small child beforehand to hold up his little folded papers
for him; but a few weeks ago it came into his head that it would
give the affair an even greater air of innocence, if he could make
use of my poor girl. It does, I believe, and it tells, and I've been
brought so low that I sit by night after night and endure it. She,
on her side, dreams of no harm, and takes the Professor for an

oracle and his lecture for a masterpiece. I have never undeceived her, for I have no desire to teach her that there are such things as falsity and impurity. Except that our perpetual railway journeys give her bad headaches, she supposes that we lead a life of pure felicity. But some fine day our enterprising friend will be wanting to put her into a pink dress and a garland of artificial flowers, and then, with God's help, we shall part company!'

My silence, in reply to this last burst of confidence, implied the most deferential assent; but I was privately wondering whether 'the little maid' was so perfectly ignorant of evil as the old man supposed. I remembered the episode at the cemetery the day before, and doubted greatly whether her father had countenanced it. With his sentiments touching the Professor, this was most unlikely. The young girl, then, had a secret, and it gave me real discomfort to think this coarse fellow should keep the key of it. I feared that the poor Colonel was yoked to his colleague more cruelly than he knew. On our return to the inn this impression was vividly confirmed. Dusk had fallen when we entered the public room, and in the gray light which pervaded it two figures at one of the windows escaped immediate recognition. But in a moment one of them advanced, and in the sonorous accents of Professor Fargo hoped that we had enjoyed our expedition. The Colonel started and stared, and left me to answer. He sat down heavily on the sofa; in a moment his daughter came over and sat beside him, placing her hand gently on his knee. But he let it lie, and remained motionless, resting his hot head on his cane. The Professor withdrew promptly, but with a swagger which suggested to my sense that he could now afford to treat his vanity to a dose of revenge for the old man's contempt.

Late in the evening I came down stairs again, and as I passed along the hall heard Professor Fargo perorating vigorously in the bar-room. Evidently he had an audience, and the scene was probably curious. Drawing near, I found this gifted man erect on the floor, addressing an assemblage of the convivial spirits of P—. In an extended hand he brandished a glass of smoking whiskey and water; with the other he caressed his rounded periods. He had evidently been drinking freely, and I perceived that even the prophetic vision was liable to obfuscation. It had been a brilliant day for him; fortune smiled, and he felt strong. A dozen rustic loafers, of various degrees of inveteracy, were listening to him with a speechless solemnity, which may have been partly faith, but was certainly partly rum. In a corner, out of the way, sat the Colonel, with an unfinished glass before him. The Professor waved his hand as I appeared, with magnificent hospitality, and resumed his discourse.

'Let me say, gentlemen,' he cried, 'that's it's not my peculiar influence with the departed that I chiefly value; for, after all, you know, a ghost is but a ghost. It can't do much any way. You can't touch it, half the time you can't see it. If it happens to be the spirit of a pretty girl, you know, this makes you kind of mad. The great thing now is to be able to exercise a mysterious influence over living organisms. You can do it with your eye, you can do it with your voice, you can do it with certain motions of your hand – as thus, you perceive; you can do it with nothing at all by just setting your mind on it. That is, of course, some people can do it; not very many – certain rich, powerful, sympathetic natures that you now and then come across. It's called magnetism. Various works have been written on the subject, and various explanations offered, but they don't amount to much. All you can say is that it's just magnetism, and that you've either got it or you haven't got it. Now the Lord has seen fit to bestow it on me. It's a great responsibility, but I try to make a noble use of it. I can do all sorts of things. I can find out things. I can make people confess. I can make 'em sick and I can make 'em well. I can make 'em in love – what do you say to that? I can take 'em out of love again, and make 'em swear they wouldn't marry the loved object, not if they were paid for it. How it is I do it I confess I can't tell you. I just say to myself, "Come now, Professor, we'll fix this one or that one." It's a free gift. It's magnetism, in short. Some folks call it animal magnetism, but I call it spiritual magnetism.'

There was a profound silence; the air seemed charged with that whimsical retention of speech which is such a common form of American sociability. I looked askance at the Colonel; it seemed to me that he was paler than usual, and that his eyes were really fierce. Professor Fargo turned about to the bar to replenish his glass, and the old man slowly rose and came out into the middle of the room. He looked round at the company; he evidently meant to say something. He stood silent for some moments, and I saw that he was in a tremor of excitement. 'You've listened to what this gentleman has been saying?' he began. 'I won't say, Have you understood it? It's not to be understood. Some of you, perhaps, saw me last night sitting on the platform while Professor Fargo said his say. You know that we are partners – that for convenience' sake we work together. I wish to say that you are not therefore to believe that I assent to the doctrines he has just promulgated. "Doctrines" is a flattering name for them. I speak in the name of science. Science recognizes no such thing as "spiritual magnetism"; no such thing as mysterious fascinations; no such thing as spirit-rappings and ghost-raisings. I owe it to my conscience to say so. I can't remain there and see you all sit mum when this gentleman concludes such a monstrous piece of talk. I have it on my conscience to assure you that no intelligent man, woman, or child need fear to be made to do anything against his own will by the supernatural operation of the will of Professor Fargo.'

If there had been silence on the conclusion of Professor Fargo's harangue, what shall I say to the audible absence of commentary which followed the Colonel's remarks? There was an intense curiosity – I felt it myself – to see what a clever fellow like the Professor would do. The Colonel stood there wiping his forehead, as if, having thrown down the gauntlet, he were prepared to defend it. The Professor looked at him with his head on one side, and a smile which was an excellent imitation of genial tolerance. 'My dear sir,' he cried, 'I'm glad you've eased your mind. I knew you wanted to; I hope you feel better. With your leave, we won't go into the philosophy of the dispute. It was George Washington, I believe, who said that people should wash their dirty linen at home. You don't endorse my views – you're welcome. If you weren't a very polite old gentleman, I know you'd like to say that, in a single word, they're the views of a quack. Now, in a single word, I deny it. You deny the existence of the magnetic power; I reply that I personally possess it, and that if you'll give me a little more time, I'll force you to say that there's something in it. I'll force you to say I can do something. These gentlemen here can't witness the consummation, but at least they can hear my promise.

I promise you evidence. You go by facts: I'll give you facts. I'd like just to have you remark before our friends here, that you'll take account of them!'

The Colonel stood still, wiping his forehead. He had even less prevision than I of the character of the Professor's projected facts, but of course he could make but one answer. He bowed gravely to the Professor and to the company. 'I shall never refuse,' he said, 'to examine serious evidence. Whatever,' he added, after a moment, 'it might cost my prejudices.'

III

The Colonel's incorruptible conservatism had done me good mentally, and his personal situation had deeply interested me. As I bade him farewell the next day – the 'Combination' had been heralded in a neighboring town – I wished him heartily that what was so painfully crooked in the latter might be straightened out in time. He shook his head sadly, and answered that his time was up.

He was often in my thoughts for the next six weeks, but I got no tidings of him. Meanwhile I too was leading an ambulant life, and travelling from town to town in a cause which demanded a good deal of ready-made eloquence. I didn't pretend that the regeneration of society depended on its acceptance of my wares, but I devoted a good deal of fellow feeling to the Colonel's experience as an uncredited solicitor. At the beginning of the winter I found myself in New York. One evening, as I wandered along a certain avenue, undedicated to gentility, I perceived, in the flare of a gas-lamp, on a placard beside a doorway, the name and attributes of Professor Fargo. I immediately stopped and read the manifesto. It was even more grandiloquent than the yellow hand-bill at P—; for to overtop concurrence in the metropolis one must mount upon very high stilts indeed. The 'Combination' still subsisted, and Colonel Gifford brought up the rear. I observed with interest that his daughter now figured in an independent and extremely ornamental paragraph. Above the door was a blue lamp, and beneath the lamp the inscription 'Excelsior Hall.' No one was going in, but as I stood there a young man in a white overcoat, with his hat on his nose, came out and planted himself viciously, with a tell-tale yawn, in the doorway. The poor Colonel had lost an auditor; I was determined he should have a substitute. Paying my fee and making my way into the room, I found that the situation was indeed one in which units rated high. There were not more than twenty people present, and the appearance of this meagre group was not in striking harmony with the statement on the placard without, that Professor Fargo's entertainment was thronged with the intellect and fashion of the metropolis. The Professor was on the platform, unfolding his budget of miracles; behind him, as at P—, sat the Colonel and his daughter. The Professor was evidently depressed by the preponderance of empty benches, and carried off his revelations with an indifferent grace. Disappointment made him brutal. He was heavy, vulgar, slipshod; he stumbled in his periods, and bungled more than once in his guesses when the folded papers with the names were put into the hat. His brow wore a vicious, sullen look, which seemed to deepen the expression of melancholy patience in his companions. I trembled for my friends. The Colonel had told me that his bargain with his impresario was a poor one, and I was sure that if, when the 'Combination' was in a run of luck, as it had been at P—, his dividend was scanty, he was paying a heavy share of the penalty for the present eclipse of fortune. I sat down near the door, where the hall was shrouded in a thrifty dimness, so that I had no fear of being recognized. The Professor evidently was reckless – a fact which rather puzzled me in so shrewd a man. When he had brought his own performance to an unapplauded close, instead of making his customary speech on behalf of his coadjutor, he dropped into a chair and gaped in the face of his audience. But the Colonel, after a pause, threw himself into the breach – or rather lowered himself into it with stately gravity – and addressed his humble listeners (half of whom were asleep) as if they had been the flower of the Intellect and Fashion. But if his manner was the old one, his discourse was new. He had too many ideas to repeat himself, and, although those which he now attempted to expound were still above the level of my frivolous apprehension, this unbargained abundance of inspiration half convinced me that his claim to original genius was just. If there had been something grotesquely sad in his appeal to the irresponsive intellect of P—, it was almost intolerably dismal to sit there and see him grappling with the dusky void of Excelsior Hall. The sleepers waked up, or turned over, at least, when Miss Gifford came forward. She wore, as yet, neither a pink dress nor an artificial garland, but it seemed to me that I detected here and there an embryonic hint of these ornaments – a ruffle round her neck, a colored sash over her black dress, a curl or two more in her hair. But her manner was as childish, as simple and serene as ever; the empty benches had no weary meaning for her.

I confess that in spite of my personal interest in my friend, the entertainment seemed wofully long; more than once I was on the point of departing, and awaiting the conclusion in the street. But I had not the heart to inflict upon the poor Colonel the sight of a retreating spectator. When at last my twenty companions had shuffled away, I made my way to the platform and renewed acquaintance with the trio. The Professor nodded with uncompromising familiarity, the Colonel seemed cordially glad to see me, and his daughter, as I made her my bow, gazed at me with even more than usual of her clear-eyed frankness. She seemed to wonder what my reappearance meant for them. It meant, to begin with, that I went the next day to see the Colonel at his lodging. It was a terribly modest little lodging, but he did me the honors with a grace which showed that he had an old habit of hospitality. He admitted frankly that the 'Combination' had lately been doing a very poor business, but he made the admission with a gloomy stoicism which showed me that he had been looking the event full in the face, and had assented to it helplessly. They had gone their round in the country, with varying success. They had the misfortune to have a circus keeping just in advance of them, and beside the gorgeous pictorial placards of this establishment, their own superior promises, even when swimming in a deluge of exclamation points, seemed pitifully vague. 'What are my daughter and I,' said the Colonel, 'after the educated elephant and the female trapezist? What even is the Professor, after the great American clown?' Their profits, however, had been kept fairly above the minimum, and victory would still have hovered about their banners if they had been content to invoke her in the smaller towns. The Professor, however, in spite of remonstrance, had suddenly steered for New

York, and what New York was doing for them I had seen the night before. The last half dozen performances had not paid for the room and the gas. The Colonel told me that he was bound by contract for five more lectures, but that when these were delivered he would dissolve the partnership. The Professor, in insisting on coming to the city, had shown a signal want of shrewdness; and when his shrewdness failed him, what had you left? What to attempt himself, the Colonel couldn't imagine. 'At the worst,' he said, 'my daughter can go into an asylum, and I can go into the poorhouse.' On my asking him whether his colleague had yet established, according to his vow, the verities of 'spiritual magnetism,' he stared in surprise and seemed quite to have forgotten the Professor's engagement to convert him. 'Oh, I've let him off,' he said, shaking his head. 'He was tipsy when he made the promise, and I expect to hear no more about it.'

I was very busy, and the pensive old man was gloomy company; but his character and his fortunes had such a melancholy interest that I found time to pay him several visits. He evidently was thankful to be diverted from his sombre self-consciousness and his paternal anxiety, and, when once he was aroused from the dogged resignation in which he seemed plunged, enjoyed vastly the chance to expatiate on his multitudinous and irrealizable theories. Most of the time his meaning was a cloud bank to me, but I listened, assented, applauded; I felt the charm of pure intellectual passion. I incline to believe that he had excogitated some extremely valuable ideas. We took long walks through the crowded streets. The Colonel was indefatigable, in spite of his leanness and pallor. He strode along with great steps, talking so loud, half the time, in his high, quavering voice, that even the eager pedestrians in the lower latitudes of Broadway slackened pace to glance back at him. He declared that the crowded streets gave him a strange exhilaration, and the mighty human hum of the great city quickened his heartbeats almost to pain. More than once he stopped short, on the edge of a curbstone or in the middle of a crossing, and laying his hand on my arm, with a deeper glow beneath his white eyebrows, broke into a kind of rhapsody of trancendental thought. 'It's for all these millions I would work, if they would let me!' he cried. 'It's to the life of great cities my schemes are addressed. It's to make millions wiser and better that I stand pleading my cause so long after I have earned my rest.' One day he seemed taciturn and preoccupied. He talked much less than usual, noticed nothing, and walked with his eyes on the pavement. I imagined that, in a phrase with which he had made me familiar, he had caught the tail of an idea and was holding it fast, in spite of its slippery contortions. As we neared his lodging at the end of our walk, he stopped abruptly in the middle of the street, and I had to give him a violent pull to rescue him from a rattling butcher's cart. When we reached the pavement he stopped again, grasped me by the hand, and fixed his eyes on me with a very extraordinary exaltation. We were at the top of the shabby cross-street in which he had found a shelter. A row of squalid tenements faced us, and half a dozen little Irish ragamuffins were sprawling beneath our feet, between their doorways and the gutter. 'Eureka! Eureka!' he cried. 'I've found it – I've found it!' And on my asking him what he had found, 'Something science has groped for, for ages – the solution of the incalculable! Perhaps, too, my fortune; certainly my immortality! Quick, quick! Before it vanishes I must get at my pen.' And he hurried me along to his dingy little dwelling. On the doorstep he paused. 'I can't tell you now,' he cried. 'I must fling it down in black and white. But for heaven's sake, come to-night to the lecture, and in the first flush of apprehension I think I can knock off a statement!' To the lecture I promised to come. At the same moment I raised my eyes and beheld in the window of the Colonel's apartment the ominous visage of Professor Fargo. I had been kindled by the Colonel's ardor, but somehow I was suddenly chilled by the presence of the Professor. I feared that, be the brilliancy of my friend's sudden illumination what it might, the shock of meeting his unloved *confrère* under his own roof would loosen his grasp of his idea. I found a pretext for keeping him standing a moment, and observed that the Professor disappeared. The next moment the door opened and he stepped forth. He had put on his hat, I suppose, hastily; it was cocked toward one side with a jauntiness which seemed the climax of his habitual swagger. He was evidently in better spirits than when I listened to him at Excelsior Hall; but neither the Professor's smiles nor his frowns were those of an honest man. He bestowed on my companion and me one of the most expansive of the former, gave his hat a cock in the opposite direction, and was about to pass on. But suddenly bethinking himself, he paused and drew from his pocket a small yellow ticket, which he presented to me. It was admission to Excelsior Hall.

'If you can use this to-night,' he said, 'I think you'll see something out of the common.' This intimation, accompanied with a wink of extreme suggestiveness, seemed to indicate that the Professor also, by a singular coincidence, had had a flash of artistic inspiration. But giving me no further clue, he rapidly went his way. As I shook hands in farewell with the Colonel, I saw that the light of the old man's new inspiration had gone out in angry wonderment over the Professor's errand with his daughter.

I can hardly define the vague apprehensiveness which led me to make that evening a peculiarly prompt appearance at Excelsior Hall. There was no one there when I arrived, and for half an hour the solitude remained unbroken. At last a shabby little man came in and sat down on the last bench, in the shade. We remained a while staring at the white wall behind the three empty chairs of the performers and listening to the gas-burners, which were hissing with an expressiveness which, under the circumstances, was most distressing. At last my companion left his place and strolled down the aisle. He stopped before the platform, turned about, surveyed the capacity of the room, and muttered something between a groan and an imprecation. Then he came back toward me and stopped. He had a dirty shirt-front, a scrubby beard, a small, wrathful black eye, and a nose unmistakably Judaic.

'If you don't want to sit and be lectured at all alone,' he said, 'I guess you'd better go.'

I expressed a hope that some one would turn up yet, and said that I preferred to remain, in any event, as I had a particular interest in the performance.

'A particular interest?' he cried; 'that's about what I've got. I've got the rent of my room to collect. This thing has been going on here for three weeks now, and I haven't seen the first dollar of *my* profits. It's been going down hill steady, and I think the Professor, and the Colonel, and the deaf and dumb young woman had better shut up shop. They ain't appreciated; they'd better try some other line. There's mighty little to this thing, anyway; it ain't what I call an attractive exhibition. I've got an offer for the premises for a month from the Canadian Giantess, and I mean to ask the present company to pay me down and vacate.'

It looked, certainly, as if the 'Combination' would have some difficulty in meeting its engagements. The Professor's head emerged inquiringly from a door behind the stage and disappeared, after a brief communion with the vacuity of the scene. In a few minutes, however, the customary trio came forth and seated itself gravely on the platform. The Professor thrust his thumbs into his waistcoat and drummed on the floor with his toes, as if it cost his shrewdness a painful effort to play any longer at expectation. The Colonel sat stiff and solemn, with his eyes on the ground. The young girl gazed forth upon the ungrateful void with her character-istically irresponsible tranquillity. For myself, after listening some ten minutes more for an advancing tread, I leaned my elbows on the back of the bench before me and buried my head; I couldn't bear any longer to look at the Colonel. At last I heard a scramble behind me, and looking round, saw my little Jew erecting himself on his feet on a bench.

'Gentlemen!' he cried out, 'I don't address the young woman; I'm told she can't hear. I suppose the man with the biggest audience has a right to speak. The amount of money in this hall to-night is just thirty cents – unless, indeed, my friend here is on the free list. Now it stands to reason that you can't pay your night's expenses out of thirty cents. I think we might as well turn down some of this gas; we can still see to settle our little account. To have it paid will gratify me considerably more than anything you can do there. I don't judge your entertainment; I've no doubt it's a very smart thing. But it's very evident it don't suit this city. It's too intellectual. I've got something else in view – I don't mind telling you it's the Canadian Giantess. It is going to open to-morrow with a matinée, and I want to put some props under that platform. So you'd better pay this young man his money back, and go home to supper. But before you leave, I'll trouble you for the sum of ninety-three dollars and eighty-seven cents.'

The Professor stroked his beard; the Colonel didn't move. The little Jew descended from his perch and approached the platform with his bill in his hand. In a moment I followed him.

'We're a failure,' said the Professor, at last. 'Very well! I'm not discouraged; I'm a practical man. I've got an idea in my head by which, six months hence, I expect to fill the Academy of Music.' Then, after a pause, turning to his companion, 'Colonel, do you happen to have ninety-three dollars and eighty-seven cents?'

The Colonel slowly raised his eyes and looked at him; I shall never forget the look.

'Seriously speaking,' the Professor went on, daunted but for an instant, 'you're liable for half the debt. But I'll assume your share on a certain condition. I have in my head the plan of another entertainment. Our friend here is right; we have been too intellectual. Very good!' and he nodded at the empty benches. 'I've learned the lesson. Henceforth I'm going to be sensational. My great sensation' – and he paused a moment to engage again the eye of the Colonel, who presently looked vaguely up at him – 'is this young lady!' and he thrust out a hand toward Miss Gifford. 'Allow me to exhibit your daughter for a month, in my own way and according to my own notions, and I assume your debt.'

The young girl dropped her eyes to the ground, but kept her place. She had evidently been schooled. The Colonel slowly got up, glaring and trembling with indignation. I wished to cut the knot, and I interrupted his answer. 'Your inducement is null,' I said to the Professor. 'I assume the Colonel's debt. It shall be paid this moment.'

Professor Fargo gave an honestly gleeful grin; this was better even than the Colonel's assent. 'You refuse your consent then,' he demanded of the old man, 'to your daughter's appearance under my exclusive management.'

'Utterly!' cried the Colonel.

'You are aware, I suppose, that she's of age?'

The Colonel stared at me with a groan. 'What under heaven is the fellow coming to?'

'To this!' responded the Professor; and he fixed his eye for a moment on the young girl. She immediately looked up at him, rose, advanced, and stood before him. Her face betrayed no painful consciousness of what she was doing, and I have often wondered how far, in her strangely simple mood and nature, her consciousness on this occasion was a guilty one. I never ascertained. This was the most unerring stroke I had seen the Professor perform. The poor child fixed her charming eyes on his gross, flushed face, and awaited his commands. She was fascinated; she had no will of her own. 'You'll be so good as to choose,' the Professor went on, addressing her in spite of her deafness, 'between your father and me. He says we're to part. I say you're to follow me. What do you say?'

For all answer, after caressing him a moment with her gentle gaze, she dropped before him on her knees. The Colonel sprang toward her with a sort of howl of rage and grief, but she jumped up, retreated, and tripped down the steps of the platform into the room. She rapidly made her way to the door. There she paused and looked back at us. Her father stood staring after her in helpless bewilderment. The Professor disappeared into the little ante-room behind the stage, and came back in a moment jamming his hat over his eyes and carrying the young girl's shawl. He reached the edge of the platform, and then, stopping, shook the forefinger with the turquoise ring at the Colonel.

'What do you say now?' he cried. 'Is spiritual magnetism a humbug?'

The little Jew rushed after him, shrieking and brandishing the unpaid bill; but the Professor cleared at half a dozen strides the interval which divided him from the door, caught the young girl round the waist, and made a triumphant escape. Half an hour later the Colonel and I left the little Jew staring distractedly at his unretributed gas-burners.

I walked home with the old man, and, having led him into his shabby refuge, suffered him to make his way alone, with groans, and tears, and imprecations, into his daughter's empty room. At last he came tottering out again; it seemed as if he were going mad. I brought him away by force, and he passed the night in my own quarters. He had spoken shortly before of the prospect of an asylum for his daughter, but it became evident that the asylum would have to be for him.

I sometimes go to see him. He spends his days covering little square sheets of paper with algebraic signs, but I am assured by his superintendent, who understands the matter, that they represent no coherent mathematical operation. I never treated myself to the 'sensation' of attending Professor Fargo's new entertainment.

Note on the Texts

Maqbool Aziz is producing what may be a full scholarly edition of *The Tales of Henry James*, Oxford, 1973– using what Aziz calls, in his discussion of the recension, the B texts, i.e. their 'first published' 'serial' versions. But in his *The Complete Tales of Henry James* (London, 1962–4) Leon Edel prints the 'original book form of the story where there was one' (which is the D text for Aziz). I have followed this astute practice, making only a few silent corrections, for it provides what is likely to be the most responsible and readable text. On this system where James revised, magazine necessities and crudities are dropped, corrected, and ironed out (sometimes the revisions are extensive as in 'A Light Man'); and, in the single case of 'Madame de Mauves', the very large-scale revisions of the New York Edition – 1907–9, and forty years on – are avoided. Late Henry James often had difficulty in reading early Henry James and tended to tinker locally and irresponsibly (almost as though he had a word processor – he *did* have an amanuensis at a typewriter). The results vary from sentence to sentence, as does opinion about the whole. Some readers love the effect – but then they are really loving late James and not the writer of this strong youthful collection. It certainly can be unhappy: as when the dry and haunting final phrase of 'Madame de Mauves', 'a feeling for which awe would be hardly too strong a name', is changed to the more obvious and explanatory 'a feeling of wonder, of uncertainty, of awe' – which attenuates and flattens one's response.

The spelling is in the American (honor) or English (honour) system according to where the book or magazine was printed. The details of publication are as follows:

1. *The Story of a Year*

a) *Atlantic Monthly*, XV, March 1865, 257–81.
b) [James's second tale and sixth printed work] Not revised.
c) Reprinted: 1947, 1950, 1962.

2. *A Landscape-Painter*

a) *Atlantic Monthly*, XVII, March 1866, 182–202.
b) Revised for *Stories Revived*, London, 1885. The 'Notice' says that the stories have been 'minutely revised and corrected – many passages being wholly rewritten' and that they 'have gained not lost freshness by the process of retouching'.
c) Reprinted: 1920 (title story), 1921–3, 1962.

3. *A Day of Days*

a) *Galaxy*, I, June 1866, 298–312.
b) Revised for *Stories Revived*, see 2 above.
c) Reprinted 1920, 1923, 1962; translated into Japanese 1926.

4. *A Light Man*

a) *Galaxy*, VIII, July 1869, 49–68.
b) Revised for: (i) *Stories by American Authors*, New York, 1884, where there are 'so many revisions as to amount almost to a rewriting of the story' (*A Bibliography of Henry James* by Leon Edel and Dan H. Laurence, London, 1957, 207) – see also HJL, 1, 357; (ii) *Stories Revived*, see 2 and 3 above.
c) Reprinted: 1920, 1921, 1962.

5. *Master Eustace*

a) *Galaxy*, XII, November 1871, 595–612.
b) Revised for *Stories Revived*, see 2, 3 and 5 above.
c) Reprinted: 1920 (title story), 1921–3, 1962.

6. *The Sweetheart of M. Briseux*

a) *Galaxy*, XV, June 1873, 760–79.
b) Not revised.
c) Reprinted: 1919, 1931, 1962.

7. *Madame de Mauves*

a) *Galaxy* XVII, February-March, 1874, 216–33, 354–74.
b) Reprinted with 'extensive revisions' in most of the tales (*Bibliography*, 26) but presumably few in this in: (i) *A Passionate Pilgrim*, New York, 1875; (ii) *The Madonna of the Future*, London, 1879; (iii) the 'Collective Edition', 1883; and in (iv) The New York Edition with more 'extensive' revision, 1907–9.

8. *Professor Fargo*

a) *Galaxy*, XVIII, August 1874, 233–53.
b) Not revised.
c) Reprinted: 1919, 1931, 1962.

Notes

James addressed his stories at first to a fairly wide audience – readers of the *Galaxy*, for example, would not be expected to be intellectuals – and I think it patronizing to modern readers to assume that they know much less or much differently from their forebears: 'Notes are often necessary, but they are necessary evils', says Dr Johnson in his *Preface to Shakespeare*. The real trouble with them when applied to the prose of art, as opposed to merely expository prose, is that they interrupt the flow and rhythm actually *more* than the absence of a piece of information – or even a translation – would do. They blunder in with more or less relevant matter, the essential point of which can in nearly every case be understood or gleaned from its context. An interruption is felt, whether the attention is diverted to the small print at the foot of the page or to the back of the book. The same is true of an editor's failure to resist the – considerable – temptation to intrude a petty critical commentary via the notes. I have in mind certain paperback editions of James's novels where interpretations of a ruthless mediocrity are forced upon one's conscientious but unwilling eyes.

The notes to this edition are, therefore, highly selective. What to include is a matter of tact in regard to the stories and guesswork as to a reader's ordinary fund of information. Everyone knows the whereabouts of Berlin or Boston; the identity of Leonardo; the meanings of *nous verrons*, *voilà*, *lieber Gott* and other common foreign expressions; and everyone can be trusted to work out that, for example, the revolution mentioned in the second paragraph of 'The Story of a Year' is the American and not the French or Roman. It is only when James's French does not translate itself or when I have thought the requisite knowledge to be recondite or specially local to place (in New England or Rome for example) or time (for example when Lord Tennyson was a popular poet) that I have disturbed James's prose with little numbers. And then often reluctantly.

For the same reason textual variants have not been included or discussed. For these, see Aziz op. cit.

I have been unable to discover the exact natures of *The Missing Bride* in 'A Landscape-Painter' and 'Thérésa' (despite consulting an expert on Offenbach) in 'Madame de Mauves'. But here, as so often, the context supplies a sufficient meaning.

The Story of a Year

1 (p. 21): *The Story of a Year*. Until 1953 this was thought to be James's first published piece of fiction. It still is the first good one; and its unrevised state makes it of special interest for those concerned with the earliness of early James, and thus for some readers of this selection.

Edel observes (*Life*, 183) that the year in which it is set in the war between the States, the Civil War, would be 1863 because that was when James's cousin Gus Barker was shot on the Rappahannock river. This date is useful. But the very consistent and specific chronology within the story ('On the second day after the party', 'On the fourth evening, at twilight . . .' etc.) suggests that James means his 'year' to be taken quite literally: so it should run from May 1862 to May 1863 – especially since General McClellan, whose portrait provides part of Lizzie's bedside furniture at first, was dismissed in November 1862. This sits comfortably with a composition 'two years' from the start of the action – in Spring 1864 when James wrote to T. S. Perry about just such a tale (March – HJL, 1, 50).

2 (p. 25): *stupid Yankee village*. Later we learn that the characters live in *Glenham*, an imaginary place in New England, which in spite of this description has the railway, a Water Cure, post office, Main Street and so on. It is contrasted (just below) with Boston and *Leatherborough*, another imaginary place on the imaginary River *Tan* which later (p. 38 onwards) seems to take on some of the metropolitan features of New York – though not its newspapers (p. 42). Another contributory possibility is Philadelphia.

3 (p. 23): épanchements. Outpourings, openings of the heart.

4 (p. 33): '*Scottish Chiefs*'. (*The*) – a widely read historical novel of 1810 by Jane Porter based on the heroic career of Sir William Wallace, and ending after his death with the victory of the Northern power under Robert Bruce at Bannockburn. As Edel remarks (*Life*, 183) many characters in this tale have Scottish names.

5 (p. 33): *General McClellan*. George Brinton McClellan (1826–85), 'the young Napoleon' and a former railway expert, was the white hope of the Union until his repeated failure to follow up initial advantages led Lincoln to dismiss him for 'the slows' after the Antietam campaign, on 7 November 1862. The President is supposed to have said that 'giving him reinforcements is like shovelling flies across a room'.

6 (p. 36): *stupid war-correspondence in the 'Times'*. Sir William Howard Russell (1820–1907), the great Irish journalist, is most famous for his *Despatches from the Crimea* which exposed the sufferings of the British troops at the hands of incompetence, forced the government to resign, and inspired Florence Nightingale. In 1862 he was hounded out of America by the Union press for 'writing too accurate a report of the Bull Run rout' (July) when raw Northern levies panicked and fled back over the Potomac bridges in front of the picnicking Washington gentry.

7 (p. 36): *General Halleck's despatches*. Henry Wager Hallck (1815–72) was General-in-Chief of the Union armies. Nicknamed 'old brains' because he had written a book on the Military Art, he proved 'so inept at field operations' that 'he took a month, though almost unopposed, to advance . . . twenty miles'; but subsequently became an invaluable liaison officer between Grant and Lincoln.

8 (p. 57): *nor uttered cry*. Tennyson, *The Princess*, 1847, vi, Introductory Song.

A Landscape-Painter

1 (p. 65): *Newport*. Rhode Island. Then the most fashionable, brilliant and bustling watering place in America.

2 (p. 66): *Venus Victrix*. The conquering Venus is associated with the Venus de Milo in an ecstatic passage by Paul de Saint-Victor almost certainly familiar to James (Edel, *Life*, 215–16).

3 (p. 66): Chowderville. An imaginary place obviously named to suggest the essence of New England (clam chowder etc.).

4 (p. 69): Vogue la galère!. Come what may (literally: row the galley).

5 (p. 70): *'Barkis is willing.'* (willin') – The refrain phrase used by the carrier Barkis in *David Copperfield* to convey his dogged devotion to (Clara) Peggotty.

6 (p. 81): arrière-pensée. Reserve; or here, perhaps, uncandid intention.

7 (p. 83): nil admirari. The attitude of being surprised at nothing, of nonchalance – a perennial ambition of the smart and achievement of the dull.

8 (p. 85): 'Hobbs, Nobbs, Stokes and Nokes'. Apparently a phrase meaning 'the lot of us together' related to 'hobnob' (itself derived from 'give and take' in duelling and drinking – see, for example, Twelfth Night, III, iv, 243).

9 (p. 86): Juno. In the myth – which James might have read in Tennyson's version in Oenone (1842) – Paris gives the prize for beauty to Venus as opposed to Juno and Minerva.

10 (p. 89): criarde. Obtrusive or daring.

11 (p. 90): the platters round. Not the metre of 'The Lord of Burleigh' – of which it has been argued (by Miriam Allott, Notes & Queries, N.S. 2 (1955), 220–21) that the whole story is a pastiche:

> He is but a landscape-painter,
> And a village maiden she.

– nor that of Locksley Hall. But rather like some parts of The Princess which James had quoted in 'The Story of a Year'. For example:

> Some to a low song oared a shallop by,
> Or under arches of the marble bridge
> Hung, shadow'd from the heat: some hid and sought
> In the orange thickets: others tost a ball
> Above the fountain jets, and back again
> With laughter: others lay about the lawns . . .

12 (p. 96): cockneys. 'A derisive appellation for a townsman' – not necessarily, and of course not here, a native of London.

A Day of Days

1 (p. 112): stone-pines of the Villa Borghese. The great park in Rome contains the Piazza de Sienna, a grassy hippodrome circled with stone-pines. This is probably what is referred to (in any case the reading 'stone-pipes' in Edel CT, 1, 154 is clearly a misprint).

2 (p. 113): Longfellow says so. The human value of natural sound – especially American natural sound – is so pervasive an idea in Longfellow's work that it is hard to localize this reference.

> At the door on Summer evenings
> Sat the little Hiawatha,
> Heard the whispering of the pine trees
> Sounds of music, sounds of wonder . . .
> (*Hiawatha*, III, 98–102)

But also, more pertinently perhaps, the reminiscences of 'My Lost Youth':

> I can see the breezy dome of groves,
> The shadows of Deering's woods . . .
>
> The song and silence in the heart,
> That in part are prophecies, and in part
> Are longings wild and vain . . .
>
> And the trees that o'ershadow each well-known street,
> As they balance up and down,
> Are singing the beautiful song,
> Are sighing and whispering still:
> A boy's will is the wind's will,
> And the thoughts of youth are long, long thoughts.

Dome, pines, prophecies . . .

A Light Man

1 (p. 122): *A Light Man*. In *The Book World of Henry James: Appropriating the Classics*, Ann Arbor and London, 1987, 208–11, Adeline R. Tintner argues with confidence that this tale is based, via Carlyle and Sainte-Beuve, on the situation of the aged Voltaire at Ferney with his two secretaries. This parallel is very well if we confine it to externals.

2 (p. 122): Men and Women. Browning's monologue poem (1855) ends:

> And, Robert Browning, you writer of plays,
> Here's a subject made to your hand.

This is an artistic consolation for the unhappy situation of a none the less jaunty narrator who in order to save his feeble friend from what he thinks the 'toils' and 'wanton eyes' of a predatory woman, has engaged her affections himself. He does not want her; she has every reason to reproach him; and his friend detests him as a traitor.

3 (p. 129): *Tübingen*. This had been the early nineteenth-century academic centre of a 'romantic' revival of Roman Catholic theology; but by 1857 was associated with the radical Hegelian Protestantism of F. C. Baur.

4 (p. 130): Ce que c'est de nous! This is what we can come to.

NOTES

5. (p. 130): Dans cette galère. In full, *'Que diable allait-il faire dans cette galère?'* (Molière, *Les Fourberies de Scapin*, 11.7) – 'What the devil is he doing in this galley?' – or 'in such a strange situation'. This was James's favourite humorous exclamation from the French.

6 (p. 134): Je l'ai bien soigné. I've taken good care of that.

7 (p. 137): brusquer. Treat roughly or with haste.

8 (p. 139): *Mrs Gamp*. The midwife with the chaotic umbrella in *Martin Chuzzlewit*.

9 (p. 147): il m'agace. He sets my teeth on edge, irritates me.

Master Eustace

1 (p. 158): en prince. As becomes explicit later (p. 172) this tale has *Hamlet* at the back of it. Or at least superficial aspects of the play, and chunks of half-submerged diction. This is easily noticed: but the parallels and variations are gone into in detail by Adeline R. Tintner, op. cit., 4–10 & seq. ubi plura.

2 (p. 163): *chibouque*. A long Turkish tobacco pipe.

3 (p. 164): *Parny*. Evariste de Parny (1743–1814). A light, melancholy, erotic poet.

The Sweetheart of M. Briseux

1 (p. 181): *M. La Harpe*. J-F de la Harpe, a journalist, editor, materialist and literary critic of the late eighteenth century.

2 (p. 187): *Egeria*. A goddess and nymph associated with Diana who was counsellor – and some think wife, though Plutarch denies this – to Numa Pompilius, the successor of Romulus, and King and law-giver to the Roman State. He is said to have sanctified his measures by invoking her inspiration and approval. She later became a fountain. James's curious use of 'lawful' may betray a confusion between her and the equally appropriate Aspasia, the wise and beautiful mistress of Pericles.

3 (p. 192): *the platform before the Lateran*. Probably that in front of the portico of St John Lateran from which in the nineteenth century celebrated views of the Campagna and the Sabine Hills could be enjoyed (they

are now obscured by modern suburbs). To the E.N-E. are the remains of arches for the entry of the Aqua Claudia, some of them incorporated into a modern aqueduct, some into the Porta Maggiore.

4 (p. 195): *Shelley . . . suggested it.* (1818)

> The sun is warm, the sky is clear,
> The waves are dancing fast and bright,
> Blue isles and snowy mountains wear
> The purple noon's transparent might . . .
> I see the Deep's untrampled floor
> With green and purple seaweeds strown;
> I see the waves upon the shore,
> Like light dissolved in star-showers, thrown:
> I sit upon the sands alone, –
> The lightning of the noontide ocean
> Is flashing round me, and a tone
> Arises from its measured motion,
> How sweet! did any heart now share in my emotion.

5 (p. 199): *'Corinne'.* The celebrated romantic novel, 1807, by Madame de Staël, intellectual hostess and political writer, enemy of Napoleon and friend of Benjamin Constant.

6 (p. 199): *beauty when unadorned.* The verse is probably:

> For loveliness
> Needs not the aid of ornament,
> But is when unadorned adorned the most.

– James Thomson, *The Seasons*, 'Autumn', 204 (1730–38), though Aphra Behn has the phrase 'beauty unadorned' in *The Rover*, Part ii, iv, 2 (1681).

7 (p. 200): coiffure de rapin. Art student's hair-style.

8 (p. 200): *not . . . the first comer.* Not just anybody (*pas le premier venu*).

9 (p. 201): Il faut que jeunesse se passe! Youth must run its course – with a strong sense of 'have its fling'.

10 (p. 201): Quel genre! What a style.

11 (p. 202): à sec. Exhausted and/or broke.

12 (p. 203): pour vous faire la cour. To pay court to you.

Madame de Mauves

1 (p. 218): *ultramontane works of fiction*. Ultramontane – over the mountains – in French history means very Catholic and pro-Papal. Obviously here (like comparable girlhood reading in *Madame Bovary*) these are the kind of novel allowed to young ladies by the nuns.

2 (p. 219): *Joinville and Commines*. Jean de Joinville (1224–1319), seneschal of Champagne, was the friend of Louis IX and wrote about him in the *Histoire de Saint Louis*. Philippe de Commines (1445–1509) was a Burgundian who transferred his allegiance to the French court and wrote celebrated accounts of the reigns of Louis XI and Charles VIII.

3 (p. 237): *Gérôme . . . and M. Gustave Flaubert*. Gérôme (1824–1904) is a painter known for his rather sensual exotic nudes, often of Turkish or Egyptian subjects. But by the 1870s he was fast becoming an 'official' artist.

At this time James thought Flaubert less important than he later judged him to be (his article of February 1876 is entitled 'Charles de Bernard and Gustave Flaubert: the Minor French Novelists'); and associated him primarily with a remorseless 'art for art' realism which only incidentally – 'the highly didactic nature of *Madame Bovary* is an accident' – conveyed any moral or spiritual vision.

4 (p. 243): jolie à croquer. Extremely pretty (good enough to eat).

5 (p. 257): *the sibyl when she came to the Roman king*. One of these inspired prophetesses approached Tarquin II with nine books which she offered to sell at a great price. He refused to buy, so she burnt three of them and offered the remaining six at the same price. Again he refused, so she burnt three more and offered the last three at the same price. These he bought, and they were installed in the temple of Jupiter on the Capitol to be consulted in times of national danger. (The temple burnt down in 82 BC and they were partially destroyed. However some sibylline writings were reassembled, reorganized and edited by Augustus, and were consulted in the ensuing centuries.)

6 (p. 259): air penché. Finical, over fastidious look.

7 (p. 259): *the 'Imitation'*. A translation of the famous book of devotion *De Imitatione Christi* by Thomas à Kempis (1380–1471).

8 (p. 262): visage de croquemort. Undertaker's look.

9 (p. 264): potagers. Kitchen gardens.

10 (p. 264): *tonnelle*. Arbour.

11 (p. 266): *Chénier*. André Chénier (1772–94), a fine early romantic poet whose sentimental reputation was perhaps enhanced, like that of Chatterton in England, by his premature death (on the guillotine).

Professor Fargo

1 (p. 292): *'Don Quixote'*. The pleasant parallels with this within the tale are pointed enough: they are elaborated and expanded in literal detail by Adeline R. Tintner, op. cit., 201–8. Incidentally (and see Note 1 to 'Master Eustace' above) 'Hamlet and Don Quixote' is the title of Turgenev's most famous essay, in which he proposes and contrasts two nineteenth-century types.

2 (p. 297): *Mignon*. In his review of Carlyle's translation of Goethe's great work James had (July 1865) picked on the episode of Mignon as the element in it appealing to the 'imagination' as opposed to the 'understanding'.

FOR THE BEST IN PAPERBACKS, LOOK FOR THE

In every corner of the world, on every subject under the sun, Penguin represents quality and variety – the very best in publishing today.

For complete information about books available from Penguin – including Pelicans, Puffins, Peregrines and Penguin Classics – and how to order them, write to us at the appropriate address below. Please note that for copyright reasons the selection of books varies from country to country.

In the United Kingdom: Please write to *Dept E.P., Penguin Books Ltd, Harmondsworth, Middlesex, UB7 0DA*

If you have any difficulty in obtaining a title, please send your order with the correct money, plus ten per cent for postage and packaging, to *PO Box No 11, West Drayton, Middlesex*

In the United States: Please write to *Dept BA, Penguin, 299 Murray Hill Parkway, East Rutherford, New Jersey 07073*

In Canada: Please write to *Penguin Books Canada Ltd, 2801 John Street, Markham, Ontario L3R 1B4*

In Australia: Please write to the *Marketing Department, Penguin Books Australia Ltd, P.O. Box 257, Ringwood, Victoria 3134*

In New Zealand: Please write to the *Marketing Department, Penguin Books (NZ) Ltd, Private Bag, Takapuna, Auckland 9*

In India: Please write to *Penguin Overseas Ltd, 706 Eros Apartments, 56 Nehru Place, New Delhi, 110019*

In Holland: Please write to *Penguin Books Nederland B.V., Postbus 195, NL–1380AD Weesp, Netherlands*

In Germany: Please write to *Penguin Books Ltd, Friedrichstrasse 10–12, D–6000 Frankfurt Main 1, Federal Republic of Germany*

In Spain: Please write to *Longman Penguin España, Calle San Nicolas 15, E–28013 Madrid, Spain*

In France: Please write to *Penguin Books Ltd, 39 Rue de Montmorency, F-75003, Paris, France*

In Japan: Please write to *Longman Penguin Japan Co Ltd, Yamaguchi Building, 2–12–9 Kanda Jimbocho, Chiyoda-Ku, Tokyo 101, Japan*

FOR THE BEST IN PAPERBACKS, LOOK FOR THE 🐧

PENGUIN CLASSICS

Matthew Arnold	**Selected Prose**
Jane Austen	**Emma**
	Lady Susan, The Watsons, Sanditon
	Mansfield Park
	Northanger Abbey
	Persuasion
	Pride and Prejudice
	Sense and Sensibility
Anne Brontë	**Agnes Grey**
	The Tenant of Wildfell Hall
Charlotte Brontë	**Jane Eyre**
	Shirley
	Villette
Emily Brontë	**Wuthering Heights**
Samuel Butler	**Erewhon**
	The Way of All Flesh
Thomas Carlyle	**Selected Writings**
Wilkie Collins	**The Moonstone**
	The Woman in White
Charles Darwin	**The Origin of Species**
	The Voyage of the Beagle
Benjamin Disraeli	**Sybil**
George Eliot	**Adam Bede**
	Daniel Deronda
	Felix Holt
	Middlemarch
	The Mill on the Floss
	Romola
	Scenes of Clerical Life
	Silas Marner
Elizabeth Gaskell	**Cranford and Cousin Phillis**
	The Life of Charlotte Brontë
	Mary Barton
	North and South
	Wives and Daughters